W9-CBX-987

DISCARD

WINTER PARK PUBLIC LIBRARY
460 E. NEW ENGLAND AVENUE
WINTER PARK, FL 32789

Books by Spider and Jeanne Robinson

STARSEED
STARDANCE

Books by Spider Robinson

TRUE MINDS
CALLAHAN'S LADY
TIME PRESSURE
CALLAHAN AND COMPANY
(omnibus)
CALLAHAN'S SECRET
MELANCHOLY ELEPHANTS
NIGHT OF POWER
MINDKILLER
THE BEST OF ALL POSSIBLE WORLDS
TIME TRAVELERS STRICTLY CASH
ANTINOMY
CALLAHAN'S CROSSTIME SALOON
TELEMPATH

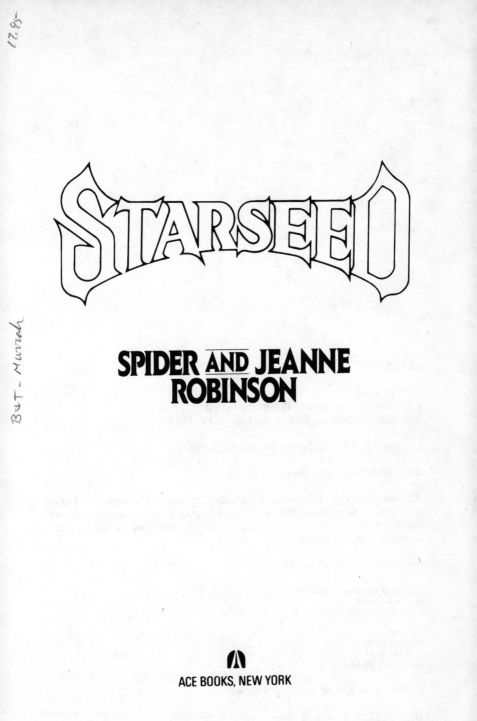

STARSEED

SPIDER AND JEANNE ROBINSON

ACE BOOKS, NEW YORK

STARSEED

An Ace Book
Published by The Berkley Publishing Group
200 Madison Avenue, New York, New York 10016

Copyright © 1991 by Spider and Jeanne Robinson

Book design by Caron Harris

All rights reserved. This book, or parts thereof, may not be reproduced in any form without permission. This is a work of fiction; all the characters and events portrayed in this book are fictional, and any resemblance to real people or incidents is purely coincidental.

First Edition: October 1991

Library of Congress Cataloging-in-Publication Data
Robinson, Spider.
  Starseed / Spider and Jeanne Robinson. — 1st ed.
    p. cm.
  I. Robinson, Jeanne. II. Title.
PS3568.O3156S74 1991
813'.54—dc20   90-23450
ISBN 0-441-78357-0

Printed in the United States of America

10 9 8 7 6 5 4 3 2 1

This one's for Charlie, Dorothy, Terri Luanna,
and Smokey

8/92

3876

ACKNOWLEDGMENTS

WE'D LIKE TO thank master roboticist Guy Immega for technical assistance in matters scientific, and Zoketsu Norman Fischer for technical assistance in matters of Zen. (Any mistakes, however, are ours, not theirs.) We also thank Dr. Oliver Robinow, Anya Coveney-Hughes, Herb Varley, David Myers, Evelyn Beheshti, Don H. DeBrandt, Greg McKinnon, Lynn Katay, all the members of Jeanne's women's group, and of course our patient and long-suffering agent, Eleanor Wood of the Spectrum Agency, for various kinds of aid and comfort without which we might never have finished this book. And we thank our editors, Susan Allison and Peter Heck.

In addition to the sources cited in the Acknowledgments of our original STARDANCE novel, we drew upon ZEN MIND, BEGINNER'S MIND by Shunryu Suzuki, EVERYDAY ZEN by Charlotte Joko Beck, WALKABOUT WOMAN by Michaela Roessner, HOW DO YOU GO TO THE BATHROOM IN SPACE? by William R. Pogue, CARRYING THE FIRE by Michael Collins, and ZEN TO GO by Jon Winokur, in completing this book. Further assistance was derived from Kenya AA and Kona Fancy coffee, Old Bushmill's whiskey, and the music of Johnny Winter (who was playing guitar 20 meters away while Jeanne wrote the Prologue), Ray Charles, Frank Zappa, Harry Connick, Jr., Benjamin Jonah Wolfe, Davey Graham, Michael Hedges, "Spider" John Koerner, and Mr. Amos Garrett, as well as Co-Op Radio and all the other jazz and blues FM stations received in Vancouver.

—*Vancouver, B.C.*
4 August 1990

PROLOGUE

> When Buddha transmitted our practice to
> Maha Kashyapa he just picked up a flower
> with a smile. Only Maha Kashyapa under-
> stood what he meant. No one else there
> understood.
> We do not know if this is a historical event
> or not—*but it means something* . . .
>
> —Shunryu Suzuki-roshi
>   ZEN MIND, BEGINNER'S MIND
>   (italics added)

I ALWAYS DANCED.

Like all babies I was born kicking; I just never stopped. All during my childhood it was that way. In the 1980s Gambier Island had a permanent population of about sixty, which no more than doubled in the summer—but it sure had a lot of theatres, with proscenium stages. The garden, the livingroom, a certain clearing in the woods near Aunt Anya's place . . . I danced in them all, and most of all in my room with the door closed. Sometimes there was thunderous applause; sometimes I danced for no one but myself; sometimes for intimate friends who vanished at a knock on the door. I remember clearly the moment I first understood that dancing was what I was going to do with my life.

Near sunset in late summer, 1985. Dinner and chores finished. My feet tickled. I told Dad where I was going, avoided Mom, and slipped out through the shed without banging the door. It was a kilometer and a half to the government wharf. The afternoon had been warm and wet— wet enough, I thought, to keep most of our neighbors indoors, and most boats at anchor. As I came over the last crest of the road and started down to the wharf, I saw I was right: I had the place to myself.

I began to run down the hill, kicking off my shoes and

1

tossing my jacket to the side of the road. At the far end of the
wharf I slowed and carefully descended the swaying gangway
to the big dock-float down at water level. I turned halfway
down and scanned the shoreline one more time to be sure. No
one in sight. I circled around the boathouse at the foot of the
gangway. The boathouse cut off sight of the land; there was
nothing but me and the sea and the islands in the distance,
grey-green mountains rising from the water. The water was
highlit with sparkles of colour from the sun setting behind me
over the forest. A warm mist came and went, invisibly. Even
dry clothes are a nuisance when you dance. My clothes went
under the rowboat that lay turtle-backed against the boathouse.
The float's surface was rough enough for safe footing when
wet, but soft enough for bare feet.

I turned my back to the land and faced the sea. There *are*
bigger theatres, but not on Earth. My parents were unrecon-
structed hippies, quasi-Buddhist; for their sake I bowed to the
sea . . . then waved to it for my own: the sober, dignified
wave a serious artist gives her expectant public when she is
eleven years old. A passing gull gave my cue. Ladies and
gentlemen, Rain McLeod! The music swelled . . .

I've become too sophisticated to remember the steps I
improvised. They must have been some mutant amalgamation
of what I thought ballet was, and all the Other Kinds of dance
I'd felt in my body but had no names for then. Nomenclature
doesn't matter to an eleven-year-old. I danced, and what was
in my heart came out my limbs and torso. I've wished since
that I could still dance like that, but I've lost the necessary
ignorance. I do remember that I was very happy. Complete.

Someone in the back row coughed—

Zalophus Californianus. A sea lion. Distinguished from
harbor seals, even at that distance, by the distinct ears. Passing
Gambier on his way back home from a day of raiding.
Fishermen hate sea lions, call them pirates of the sea. They'll
take one bite from each fish in your net, spoiling the whole
catch . . . then leave with the best one, waving it at you
mockingly as they go. I always secretly liked them. They
always danced: so it seemed to me. Drama and tragedy in the
water; slapstick comedy when they were on land. He was

perhaps fifty meters due east of the dock, treading water and staring at me. He coughed again, sounding very much like Grandfather.

I didn't let him interrupt me. I worked a friendly hello wave into what I was doing, and kept on dancing. I noticed him out of the corner of my eye from time to time, watching me in apparent puzzlement, but he was no more distraction than a cloud or gull would have been—

—until there were two of him.

For a moment I "treaded water" myself, planting my feet so I faced them and dancing only with torso and arms. They were identical, grey and wet, a few meters apart, their eyes and slick heads glistening with reflected sunset. The new one gave a cough of its own, softer and higher. Grandfather and Grandmother Meade. They watched me with no discernible expression at all, giving me their complete attention, perfect bobbing Buddhas.

So I danced for them.

Well, at them. I made no attempt to "translate" what I was feeling into Sea Lion dance, to mimic the body-language I'd seen them use, so they could understand better. Even at eleven I was arrogant enough to be more interested in teaching them *my* dance language, telling them who *I* was. When you're that young, expressing yourself is better than being understood. So I continued to dance in Human, and for the whole cycloramic world of sea and sunset—but began subtly aiming it at the sea lions, as though they were the two important critics in a packed theatre, or my actual grandparents come to see my solo debut.

What luck, to have spent my childhood so far from Vancouver's ballet classes that no one had yet told me how I was supposed to move. I was still able to move the way I needed to, to invent anything my heart required. It felt good, that's all this highly trained forty-six-year-old can remember. For a time machine and video gear, you can have anything I own.

The sea lions were twenty meters closer, and there were four of them now.

They were treading water in ragged formation, close enough for me to see whiskers. By logical extension of my original whimsy, the new arrivals were the paternal grandparents I'd never met, the McLeods. Ghosts in the audience. It gave an added layer of meaning to what I was doing, as much awareness of mortality and eternity as an eleven-year-old is capable of. I danced on.

The first breezes of evening found the sweat under my hair and on my chest and chilled them. I increased my energy output to compensate. I was grinning, spinning.

Seven sea lions. Twenty meters away, faces absolutely blank, staring.

Everything came together—sea, sky, purple clouds of sunset, sea lions—to generate that special magic always sought and so seldom found. I lost myself; the dance began dancing me. It burst out of me like laughter or tears, without thought or effort. My legs were strong, wind infinite, ideas came, every experiment worked and suggested the next. There's a special state of being, the backwards of a trance, where you transcend yourself and become a part of everything—where you seem to stand still, while the world dances around and through you. Many dancers never experience it. I'd been to that level a few times before, for fleeting moments. This time I knew I could stay as long as I wanted.

Time stopped; I went on.

Even an eleven-year-old body has limits; every dance has a natural, logical end. Eventually, with warm contentment and mild regret, I left Nirvana and returned to the world of illusion again. I was still, upright, arms upthrust toward the clouds, reaching for the unseen stars.

The float was ringed by more than a dozen sea lions, the farthest within five meters of me. I looked round at them all, half-expecting them to clap and bark like cartoon seals. They stared at me. Bobbing in silent syncopation, seeming to be thinking about what they'd just seen. My first applause . . .

I bowed, deeply.

And then waved, grandly.

Darkness was falling fast. Sweat dripped from me, my soles tingled, and many muscles announced their intention to wake up stiff tomorrow. I was perfectly happy.

This, I thought, *is what I'm supposed to do.* My Thing, as

Mom was always calling it: what I would do with my life. I understood now what I had always sensed, that Mom was going to hate it (though I didn't yet understand why) . . . but that didn't matter anymore.

Maybe that's when you become an adult. When your parents' opinions no longer control.

I kept silent when I returned home that night. But the next day I called Grandmother in Vancouver, and told her that she had won the tug of war with my mother. I moved into her huge house on the mainland, and let her enroll me in ballet class, and in normal school, like other kids. Within weeks I had been teased so much over the name "Rain M'Cloud" (which had never struck anyone on Gambier Island as odd) that I changed it to Morgan. It seemed to me a much more dignified name for a ballerina.

It was a long time before I saw Gambier Island again.

I always danced. But from the day of the sea lions, dancing was just about all I did, all I was. For thirty-two years. Until the day came when my body simply would not do it anymore. The day in April of 2017 when Doctor Thompson and Doctor Immega told me that even more surgery would not help, that I could never dance again. My lower back and knees were spent.

I tried the dancer's classic escape hatches for a few years. Choreography. Teaching. When they didn't work for me, I tried living without dance. I even tried relationships again. Nothing worked.

Including me. There were lots of trained, experienced professionals looking for work, as technological progress made more and more occupational specialties obsolete. There were few job openings for a forty-six-year-old who couldn't even type. Even the traditional unskilled-labour jobs were increasingly being done by robots. Sure, I could go back to school, and in only a few years of drudgery acquire a new profession—ideally, one which would not be obsolete by the time I graduated. But what for? Nothing interested me.

The salt of the earth had lost its savor.

I went back to Gambier Island. By now it was becoming a suburb of Vancouver; even in winter there were stores and cars and paved roads and burglaries. There was talk of a condominium complex. I sat for six months in the cabin where I had been born, waiting for some great answer to come from out of the sky. I visited my parents' graves frequently. Sat zazen in the woods. Split cords of wood. Read the first twenty pages of a dozen books. Walked the parts of the Island that were still wild, by day and night. Nature accepted my presence amiably enough, but offered no answers. Nothing.

I went down to the wharf and consulted the sea lions, as I had many times. They had nothing to say. They just looked at me, as if waiting for me to begin dancing.

After enough days of that, "nothing" started to look good to me. I filled out the Euthanasia application I had brought with me, putting down "earliest possible" for Date and leaving the space for Reason blank. I'd have a response within a week or two; by the end of the month, unless I changed my mind, my problems would be over.

In my bones, I was a dancer. And I couldn't dance anymore. Not anywhere on Earth . . .

That very night I was lying in the hammock behind the house, watching the stars, when my eye was caught by a large bright one. It moved relative to the other stars, so it was a satellite. It moved roughly north to south, and was quite large: it had to be Top Step. Funny I'd never thought of it before. The House the Stardance Built, as the media called it. Transplanted asteroid, parting gift of alien gods—the place where they made angels out of people. Hollow stone cigar, phallic womb in High Orbit. Gateway to immortality, to the stars, to freedom from every kind of human fear or need there was . . . and all it cost was everything you had, forever.

Dancers say, you go where the work is. Suddenly, at age forty-six, I had nowhere to go but up.

CHAPTER ONE

What shall it harm a man
If he loseth the whole world,
Yet gaineth his soul?

—Linda Parsons
*14th Epistle to the Corinthians
And Anyone Else Who Might Be Listening;*
transmission received 8 May 2005

HUNDREDS OF THOUGHTS ran through my head as the Valkyrie song of the engines began to rise in pitch. But most of them seemed to be variations on a single theme, and the name of the theme was this: Farewell—Forever—to Weight.

So many different *kinds* of weight!

Physical weight, of course. I had been hauling around more than fifty kilos of muscle and bone for the better part of four decades—and like all dancers, cursing every gram, even after I switched from ballet to modern. (That's 110 pounds, if you're an American. Any normal person would have considered me bone-thin . . . but the ghost of Balanchine, damn his eyes, has haunted dancers for over half a century.)

Soon I would have no weight, for the first time in my life, and for the rest of it—only my mass would remain to convince me I existed. A purist, they had told us at Suit Camp, will insist that there is no such thing as zero gravity, anywhere in the universe . . . only degrees of gravity, from micro to macro. But where I was going—any second now—I would experience microgravity too faint to be perceived without subtle instruments, so it would be zero as far as I was concerned.

It should have been a dancer's finest moment. To leap so high that you never come down again . . . wasn't that what all of us wanted? Why did I feel such a powerful impulse to bolt for the nearest exit while I still could?

7

Weight had always been my shame, and my secret friend, and my necessary enemy—the thing I became beautiful in the act of defying. In a sense, to an extent, weight had defined me.

In the end it had beaten me. I could try to kid myself that I was outmaneuvering it . . . but what I was doing was escaping it, leaving the field of battle in defeat, conceding victory.

But the physical weight was probably least in my thoughts as I sat there in my comfortable seat, on my way to a place where the concept of a comfortable seat had no meaning.

Do you have any idea how many kinds of weight each human carries? Even the most fortunate of us?

The weight of two million years of history and more . . .

Until this century, all the humans that had ever lived walked the earth, worked to stay erect, strove to eat and drink and to get food and drink for their children, sought shelter from the elements, yearned to acquire wealth, struggled to be understood. Everyone's every ancestor needed to eliminate their wastes and feared their deaths. Every one of us lived and died alone, locked in a bone cell, plagued by need and fear and hunger and thirst and loneliness and the certainty of pain and death. That long a heritage of sorrow is a weight, whose awful magnitude you can only begin to sense with the prospect of its ending.

And in a time measurable in months, all that weight was going to leave me, (if) when I entered Symbiosis. Allegedly forever, or some significant fraction thereof. I would never again need food or drink or shelter, never again be alone or afraid.

On the other hand, I could never again return to Earth. And some people maintained that I would no longer be a human being. . .

Now tell me: isn't that a kind of dying?

Not to mention the small but unforgettable possibility that joining a telepathic community might burn out my brain—no, more accurately and more horribly: burn out my *mind*.

Then there was the weight of my own personal emotional and spiritual baggage. Perhaps that should have been as nothing beside the weight of two million years, but it didn't feel that way. I was forty-six and my lifework was irrevocably finished, and I was the only person in all the world to whom that mattered. Why not go become a god? Or at least some kind of weird red angel . . .

Somewhere in there, among all my tumbling thoughts, was a little joke about the extremes some women will go to in order to lose weight, but no matter how many times that joke went through my head—and it was easily dozens—it refused to be funny, even once.

The Completist's Diet: you give up *everything*. That was another.

There were quite a few jokes in that cascade of last-minute thoughts, but none of them was funny, and I knew that none of my seventy-one fellow passengers wanted to hear them. There *was* a compulsive joker aboard, at the back of the cabin and to my right, loudly telling jokes, but no one was paying the slightest bit of attention to him. He didn't seem to mind. Even he didn't laugh at any of his witticisms.

The engine song which was the score for my thoughts reached a crescendo, and the joker shut up in mid-punchline. I vaguely recognized his voice; he'd been in my Section at Suit Camp; he was an American and his name was something Irish.

Just my luck. The wave of food poisoning that had run through Camp just days before graduation, cutting our Section down by over 30 percent, had spared this clown—and knocked out my roommate Phyllis, with whom I'd intended to keep on rooming at Top Step, and every other person I'd met whom I could imagine living with. Now I would probably end up paired off at random with some stranger who had the same problem. I hoped we'd be compatible. I'm not good at compatible.

I glanced around for the hundredth time for the nonexistent window . . . and my inner ear informed me that we were in motion.

Goodbye, world . . .

I felt a twinge of panic. *Not yet! I'm not ready* . . .

When I was a girl, travel to space *always* involved a rocket launch, with its familiar trappings of acceleration couches and countdowns and crushing gee forces on blastoff. I'd been vaguely aware of modern developments, but they hadn't really percolated through yet. So subconsciously I was expecting the irony of having my liberation from so many kinds of weight preceded by a whopping if temporary overdose of weight.

As usual, life served me up a subtler irony. The technology had improved. My last moments on Earth were spent sitting upright in something which differed from a commercial airliner mostly in its lack of windows and its considerably smaller dimensions—and the takeoff, when it came, yielded no more sense of acceleration than you get taking a methanol car from zero to sixty when you're first thinking of switching from fossil fuel.

I felt the spaceplane's wheels leave the ground, understood that my last connection with my mother planet was severed. Forever, unless I changed my mind in the next few months.

I fought down my growing sense of panic, flailing at it with big clumsy bladders full of logic. What had Earth ever done for me, that was worth sorrowing over its loss? What place on it was still fit for human habitation, and for how long? What did it have to offer, compared to greatly extended lifespan and freedom from every kind of suffering I knew—and *the chance that I might dance again?*

Like all babies leaving the womb, I felt the overwhelming impulse to burst into tears. Being mature enough to be self-conscious, I strove to suppress the urge. Apparently so did my fellow passengers; the engine song crescendoed without any harmonies from us. It began to diminish slightly as we passed the speed of sound and outran all but the vibrations that conduction carried through the hullplates.

It was then that my panic blossomed into full-grown terror.

It caught me by surprise. I had thought I'd already mastered this kind of fear, by preparing for it and educating it to death. All at once my gut did not care how confident I was of modern technology. It dimly understood that it was being taken to a place where any trivial mistake or malfunction could interrupt its all-important job, the production of feces and urine, and it reacted like a labor union, by convulsing with rage and threatening to shut down the whole system, right now. Other sister unions—heart, lungs, adrenals, sweat glands, autonomic nervous system—threatened to join the walkout, in the name of solidarity but on a wildcat basis. And management—my brain—had nothing to say except what management always says: I'm sorry, it's too late now, we're committed; let's pull together and try to salvage the situation.

Salvage the situation? said my body. *You're kidding. Remember Gambier Island in the winter, before you went to live in town with Grandmother? How silly it seemed to live someplace where all the heat could spill out through leaks, and if you couldn't make more fast enough you'd die? You're taking us to someplace where the* air *can leak out. And the heat. Any time some piece of machinery goes wrong. The definition of machine is, a thing that goes wrong the moment you start to depend on it. Get us out of this,* now!

To both this line of reasoning, and the specific sanctions my body threatened if it were thwarted, I could only reply like a long-suffering mother, *You should have thought of that before you left the house.* I could not even get the poor thing to a toilet for another hour, and I didn't care *how* good everybody said p-suit plumbing was these days. Like management every-when, I had to dig in and try to tough out the strike, even if it meant sending goon-squads to hold the sphincters by force.

I tried Zen breath control; I had none. I tried the mantra they'd given me at Suit Camp; it was only a meaningless series of syllables, and they kept speeding up in my head rather than slowing down. I tried all of what I call my Wings Things—the little rituals you perform in the wings to suppress stage fright, just before taking your stage—and none of them worked.

I was ignoring my two seatmates because I didn't know them and was too wound up to deal with small talk, and we hadn't been allowed carry-on luggage even as small as a book, and they don't put windows on spacecraft. That left only one source of diversion. I leaned forward and turned on the TV.

Because it looked just like a conventional airliner's flat-screen seatback TV, I was expecting the usual "choice" of six banal 2-D channels. There were only two—and I did not want the video feed from the bridge that mimicked a window; I switched it off hastily. But the other channel was carrying the one program—out of all the millions the human race has produced—that I would have wished for. I suppose I should have been expecting it.

The Stardance, of course.

That piece has always been a kind of personal visual mantra for me. For millions, yes, but especially for me. It turned my whole life upside down, once, triggered both my divorce and my switch from ballet to modern dance when I first saw it at twenty-two. It made me realize that my marriage was dead and that something had to be done about that, and it forced me to rethink dance and dancing completely. It consoled me at the end of a dozen ruined love affairs, got me through a thousand bad nights. I had seen it on flatscreen and in simulated holo, with and without Brindle's score; I'd once wasted three months trying to translate the entire piece into a modified Labanotation. I knew every frame, every step, every gesture.

It was midway through the prologue, when no one knows the Stardance is about to happen, and Armstead is just trying to study, with his four cameras, the aliens who've appeared without warning nearby in High Earth Orbit. Seen from different angles: a barely visible bubble containing half a hundred swarming red fireflies, glowing like hot coals, dancing like bees in a hive, like electrons in orbit around some nonexistent nucleus. Brindle's music is still soft and hypnotic, Glass-like; it will be a few more five-counts before Shara enters.

I glanced unobtrusively around. Most of the passengers I could see were looking at their own TVs, and several were swaying slightly in unison, like tall grass in a gentle breeze. The Stardance was important to all of us. We were following it into space.

Shara Drummond's p-suited image forms and grows larger on the screen. The music swells. The camera gives that involuntary jump as Armstead, horrorstruck, recognizes her. She was just on her way back to Earth on doctor's orders when the Fireflies arrived: any more exposure to zero gravity and her body will lose—forever—its ability to tolerate Earth-normal gravity. No one knows better than Armstead that his love is now a dead woman breathing. She has chosen to sacrifice herself, because of her Great Understanding (that the aliens communicate by dance) and her Great Misunderstanding (that they are hostile).

As always, the dialogue between her and the nearby Space Command battleship is edited down to her refusal to get out of the line of fire until she has tried to talk to the dancing Fireflies; the hour she spends in silent contemplation of them, trying to deduce their language of motion, is shrunk down to thirty seconds that always seem to take an hour to go by—

—and then it changed. At the point where she says, "Charlie . . . this is a take," and he says, "Break a leg, kid," and she begins to dance, the tape departed from the classic release version as edited by Armstead.

Charlie Armstead had four cameras in space that day, bracketing Shara and the aliens. But in cutting the Stardance, later, he used footage only from the three that were on Shara's side. This makes sense: from the other camera's vantage, the Fireflies are in the way. But the result is that the Stardance is seen only from a human perspective: we are either behind, or below Shara, watching as she (apparently) dances the aliens right out of the Solar System.

The version we were being shown now was from the fourth camera. I'd seen it before; years ago I had once gone to the trouble and expense of studying the raw, unedited footage from all four cameras. But I'd paid least attention to the fourth. Its footage was edited out for good artistic reasons: some of the best movements of the dance are obscured. The swarming aliens in the foreground spoil the view, glowing like embers, leaving ghost trails in their wake.

But in this context, it had a powerful impact. We saw Shara, for once, from the aliens' point of view.

She looked much smaller, more fragile. She was no longer the greatest choreographer of her century creating her master-piece. She was a little dog telling a big dog to get the hell out of her yard, *now*. You could almost sense the Fireflies' amusement and admiration. And pride: Shara was the end result of something they had set in motion many millions of years before, when they seeded Earth with life.

I saw things I had missed on my last viewing. From all three

other POVs Shara's helmet is opaque with reflected glare.
From this one you could see into it, see her face . . . and
now I saw that what I had taken on my previous viewing for
a proud, snarling, triumphant grin was in fact a rictus of terror.
For the first time it really came home to me that this woman
was dancing through a fear that should have petrified her.

I felt a powerful surge of empathy, and my own fear began
to ease a little. As I watched Shara's magnificent Stardance
from this new perspective, my breathing began to slow; my
heartbeat, which usually raced as the Stardance climaxed,
slowed too.

Peace came to me. It was the calm, the empty mind, that I
had sat zazen for countless hours to achieve for minutes. My
kinesthetic awareness faded; for once I was not acutely
conscious of the relative position of each muscle; my body
seemed to become lighter, to melt away . . .

Suddenly I smiled. It wasn't an illusion: my body *was*
growing lighter! We were already entering Low Earth Orbit.

It didn't diminish the feeling of tranquility; it enhanced it.
Space was going to be a good place to go. I no longer cared
how strange and dangerous this voyage was. I was where I was
supposed to be.

Onscreen, the Stardance reached its brilliant coda. The
Fireflies vanish, leaving only Shara, and far behind her the
twinkling carousel of the factory complex where she invented
zero gravity dance, where Armstead is watching her on his
monitors.

She poises in space for a long time, getting her breath, then
turns to the nearest camera and puffs out the famous line, "We
may be puny, Charlie . . . but by Jesus we're *tough.*" The
music overrides their audio then, but we know he is begging
her to come back inboard, and she is refusing. It's not just that
she is permanently adapted to free fall now and can never
return to Earth; nor that the only place she could live
indefinitely in space belongs to a man she despises with her
whole heart.

She is *done now*. She has accomplished everything she was
born to do. Or so she believes.

She waves at the camera, all four thrusters go off, and she

arcs down toward Earth, visible in frame now for the first time. Brindle's score swells for the last time, we follow her down toward the killing atmosphere—

—and again it changed. I'd never seen this footage before. It must have been shot by some distant Space Command satellite peace-camera, hastily tracking her as she fell through Low Orbit. The image was of inferior quality, had the grainy look of maximum enlargement and the jerkiness you get when a machine is doing the tracking. But it provided a closer look at those last moments than Armstead's cameras had from back up in a higher, slower orbit.

And so we saw now what everyone had missed then, what the world was not to know about for over three more years. Whoever examined that tape for the Space Command at the time must have just refused to believe either his eyes or his equipment, but there was no mistaking it. Shara Drummond simply disappeared. When her p-suit tumbled and burned in the upper atmosphere, it was limp, empty.

The next time any human would see her, years later, she would be a crimson-winged immortal orbiting one of the moons of Saturn, no more in need of a pressure suit than a Firefly. The first human ever to enter Symbiosis. The first and greatest Stardancer.

I felt awed and humble. As the credits rolled I reached out to shut off the set so I could savor the sensation—and knew at once that we were all the way into zero gravity. My arm did not fall when I told it it could; my center of mass pivoted loosely around my seatbelt.

The main engines had fallen silent, unnoticed, while I'd watched. We were more than halfway through our journey, officially in space. Now there would be a period of free fall before we began matching orbits with Top Step. I realized that my face felt flushed, and that my sinuses were filling up, just as I'd been told to expect. I was pleased to feel no stirrings of the dreaded dropsickness. Apparently the drugs they'd given us worked, for me at least.

Part of me wanted to unstrap and play, couldn't wait to explore this new environment, begin learning whether or not I could really dance in it. I hadn't danced in so long!

I saw other passengers experimenting with their limbs, grinning at each other. Why should it be surprising that in zero gee, one is lighthearted? No one seemed bothered by dropsickness. I turned and grinned at each of the seatmates I'd been ignoring.

To my left, in what would have been the window seat if spaceplanes had windows, was a black girl whose answering grin was spectacular; she had the whitest, most perfect teeth I'd ever seen. Zero gee made her already round cheeks cherubic. She was not a North American black but something more exotic; her hair was both wavy and curly, and her skin was the color of bitter chocolate. She looked startlingly young, no more than twenty-five, when I had understood the cutoff age was thirty; but for the instant our gazes met we communicated perfectly across cultural and generational distance.

The aisle seat to my right was occupied by a Chinese man in his late thirties. He was clean-shaven, and like everyone else's aboard, his hair was short. His face was impassive, and I couldn't tell whether his eyes were smiling or not. (In zero gee, *everyone* looks sort of Chinese: the puffy features caused by upward migration of body fluids mimic epicanthic folds at the eyes. If you *start out* Chinese, your eyes end up looking like paper-cuts.) But something in those eyes responded to me, I felt; we communicated too. A little more than I wanted to; I looked away abruptly. Wave of dizziness. Not a good idea to move head quickly in free fall.

There was a soft overall murmuring in the passenger cabin, audible even over the engine sound: the sum of everyone's grunts and sighs and exclamations. It was a sound of optimism, of hope, of pleased surprise. I think in another minute someone would have ignored instructions and unstrapped himself . . . and then we all would have, no matter what the flight attendants said.

But then there was a sound like a gunshot or the crack of a bat, and a banshee was among us, and I felt a draft—

In that year, 2020, the Space Command's traffic satellites were (as predicted since the 1980s) tracking over 20,000 known manmade objects larger than ten centimeters in diameter in the Low Earth Orbit band. Naturally no flight plan was accepted that could intersect any of them. But there were (also as predicted) countless *hundreds* of thousands, perhaps millions, of objects *smaller* then ten centimeters whizzing around in Low Orbit: too many to keep track of even if sensors had been able to see them. Screws, bolts, nuts, fittings, miscellaneous jettisoned trash, fragments of destroyed or damaged spacecraft, bits of dead spacemen burst by vacuum and freeze-dried by space, the assorted drifting trash of sixty years of spaceflight. Some of these little bits of cosmic shrapnel had relative velocities of more than fifteen kilometers a second. That's 5400 kilometers an hour—or a little more than 3200 miles per hour. At that speed, a beer-can ring is a deadly missile.

The chances of a collision depended on whose figures you accepted. The most optimistic estimate at that point in history was one chance in twenty; the most pessimistic, one in four. But even the pessimists conceded that the probability of a *life-threatening* collision was much lower than that.

Our number came up, that's all.

Whatever it was hulled us forward and from the left, just aft of the bulkhead that separated the passenger cabin from the cockpit.

Two months of training kicked in: nearly all of us got out p-suit hoods over our heads and sealed in a matter of seconds. The banshee wail was cut off, and the roar of air overridden by a softer hissing behind my head. Within moments I could feel my suit expanding. I could see now why they'd been so tight about carry-on items; even with the strict security, the air was filled with a skirling vortex of smuggled items: tissues, gum wrappers, a rabbit's foot, a pen and postcard dancing in lockstep, all converging on the source of the pressure leak. Small lighted panels in each seatback began blinking urgently in unison, as though the whole plane had acquired a visible pulse, doubtless telling us to fasten our seatbelts and return our seatbacks to the upright position. In my earphones grew the white noise of dozens of passengers talking at once in assorted languages and dialects. I tried to switch to Emergency channel . . . but for some reason this suit was not like the ones I had trained in: it had no channel selector switch.

I was not especially afraid. The warm glow of the Stardance was still on me, and we had rehearsed this dozens of times. There was nothing to worry about. Any second now, automatic machinery would begin dispensing globules of blue sticky stuff. The globs would be sucked onto the hole in the hull, and burst there. When enough of them had burst, the hole would be patched.

The hurricane went on, and there were no globs of blue sticky. I spotted one of the nozzles that should have been emitting them.

Okay, failsafes fail; that was why we had live flight attendants. Now they would converge on the leak with a pressure patch, and—

—where were the attendants?

I strained to see over the seats in front of me. Seconds ticked by and I could see no one moving. Finally I had to see what was going on: I unstrapped myself and tried to stand.

But my reflexes were obsolete. I rose with alarming speed, got my hands up too slowly, smacked my skull against the overhead hard enough to cross my eyes, ricocheted downward, hit the seat, bounced back upward, cracked my head again, and clutched desperately at the arms of my seat as I plumped back into it; the girl on my left grabbed my arm firmly to steady me. The seat to my right was empty; at the apex of my flight I had seen my other seatmate, the young Chinese, soaring forward down the aisle, graceful as a slow-motion acrobat.

I had also spotted the chief attendant, strapped into the front row aisle seat he had taken after giving us the standard preflight ritual. He was leaning to his left, arms waving lazily, like a dreaming conductor. His p-suit was slowly turning red from the hood down, and from the left side of the hood a fluid red rope issued. It rippled like a water snake, and ran with all the other airborne objects toward the hole in the hull, breaking up into red spheroids just before being sucked out into space. By great bad fortune the chief attendant's head had been in the path of whatever had hulled us . . .

Moving carefully, I managed to wedge myself into an equilibrium between the back of my seat and the overhead, and looked aft. I saw at once what was keeping the other attendant: Murphy's Law. She was struggling with her jammed seatbelt, weeping and shouting something I couldn't hear.

I looked forward again in time to see the young Chinese land feet first like a cat against the forward bulkhead, absorb the impact with his thighs so that he did not bounce from it, and instantly position all four limbs correctly to brace himself against the draft. Suddenly some other, powerful force pulled on him briefly, trying to yank him sideways and up, but he sensed it and corrected for it at at once. (The same force acted on me and the others; I could not figure out how to correct, and settled for clutching the seatback and overhead as tightly as I could until it passed.) A part of me wondered if he gave lessons. He had obviously been in free fall before.

But not in this vessel! The pressure patches could have been in any of four separate locker-sections—a total of more than two dozen small compartments, identified only by numbers.

I could see him pleading for silence, but no one could hear him above the general roar. I could see him gesturing for silence, but almost no one else could. The aft attendant could tell him which locker, but he could not hear her. He looked at me pleadingly.

I spun back to her, and wondered for a moment if she had gone mad with frustration: she had torn her hood back over her head and was waving furiously. Then I got it and pulled my own hood off. The babble of the earphones went away, and I could hear her shouting.

Just barely. The air was getting thin in here. But it was also coming my way: I could just make out a high distant Donald Duck voice, squawking the same word over and over again.

I should have been terrified that the word made absolutely no sense to me, but I did not seem to have time. Once I was sure I'd heard it right, I whirled and dutifully began braying it as loud as I could toward the Chinese.

"Before," I screamed, *"Before, before, before, before—"*

It felt good to scream: pressure change was trying to explode my lungs, and emptying them that way probably saved them serious damage. He already had his own hood off, he was quick; no, he was better than quick, because he instantly solved the puzzle that had baffled me; he yanked his hood back over his head, oriented himself and kicked off, and within seconds he was pulling the most beautiful pressure patch I'd ever seen out of Compartment B-4.

By then I was so dizzy from spinning my head back and forth I felt as though my eyeballs were about to pop out of their sockets—as indeed they probably were—and I had to pull my hood back on and let my seatmate haul me back down into my seat . . . where I spent some minutes concentrating on not soiling my p-suit. The internal suit pressure rose quickly, but at least as much of it came from my intestines as from my airtanks, and it got ripe enough in there to steam up my hood and make my eyes water for a few moments.

$$\triangle \quad \triangle \quad \triangle$$

I became aware that my seatmate was shaking my shoulder gently. I opened my eyes, and some of the dizziness went away.

She was pointing to her ears, then to her belt control panel, and shaking her head. I nodded, and fumbled until I found the shutoff switch for my suit radio. The babbling sound of dozens of frightened passengers went away. I noticed for the first time that all the blinking seatback signs were saying, not "FASTEN YOUR SEATBELTS," but "MAINTAIN RADIO SI-LENCE."

She touched her hood to mine. "Are ya right?" she called.

"Occasionally," I said lightheadedly, but I got it. Several weeks in Australia, even in the multilingual environments of Suit Camp, will give you a working familiarity with Aussie slang. She was an Aborigine. Now that I thought about it, I had noticed her once or twice in Camp, had wondered vaguely why, in the midst of one of the largest remaining Aboriginal reserves in Australia, she seemed to be the only Abo who was actually taking Suit Camp training. All the others I'd seen had been outside the Camp, in town and at the Cairns airport.

"You took an awful bloody chance," she said.

"It seemed like a good idea at the time," I called back.

"Too right! You saved us all, I reckon—you and the Chinese bloke. Fast as a scalded cat he was, eh? Hold on, here he comes."

The Chinese rejoined us. He was moving more slowly now that the emergency was past. The delicate grace with which he docked himself back in his chair, without a wasted motion or a bounce, pleased my dancer's eyes. I resolved to ask him at the first opportunity to tutor me in "jaunting," the spacer's term for moving about in zero gee.

He joined his hood to ours. "Thank you," he said to me.

As our eyes met I felt the old familiar tingle in the pit of the stomach that I had not felt in ages.

And suppressed it. I thanked him right back—but without putting any topspin on it. *I'm too old to climb these stairs again,* I told myself, *even in zero gee . . .*

"I thank you both," the Aborigine girl said. "Best put our ears on, but. I think they're getting it sorted out."

The seatbacks were now flashing, "MONITOR YOUR RADIO." We separated, and I switched my radio back on in time to hear the surviving attendant say, "—xt person that makes a sound, I am personally going to drag aft and cycle through the airlock, is that *fucking well understood?*"

She sounded sincere; the only sound in response was dozens of people breathing at different rates.

"Passenger in seat 1-E: is Mr. Henderson dead?"

"Uh . . . no. I've got my hand over the leak and the . . . the entry wound. His chest is still—"

"Jesus! Wait . . . uh . . . ten more seconds for cabin pressure to come back up and then get his hood off. Gently! Passenger 1-F, there's a first-aid kit in Compartment D-7 in front of you; get a pressure bandage and give it to 1-E; then try to get a pulse rate. Is anyone here a doctor or a paramedic?"

Breathing sounds. Someone grunting softly. A cough.

"Damn. Passenger in 6-B, answer yes or no, do you require medical assistance?"

Breathing sounds.

"Dammit, the woman who passed the word!—do you need help?"

Whoops—she meant me! I started to reply . . . and my

body picked that moment to finish restoring equilibrium, with prolonged and noisy eructations at both ends of my alimentary canal.

". . . no-o-o . . . " I finished, and everyone, myself included, began to howl with tension-breaking laughter—

—everyone except the attendant. "SILENCE!" she roared, loud enough to make my earphones distort, and the laughter fell apart. "It is past time you started acting like spacers. A real spacer is dying while you giggle. We all nearly died because none of you could read a flashing sign six inches from your face! You in 1-E—" That passenger was muttering *sotto voce* to someone who was helping him remove the injured attendant's hood. "—switch off your radios and chatter hood to hood if you must. Does anyone else need medical aid? No? Then listen up! I want all of you to keep your hoods on—even after you're certain the pressure has come back up. I'm going to switch to command channel now and report. You won't be able to hear it. I'll fill you all in the moment I am good and God damned ready . . . but not if I hear *one word* on this channel when I come back on. And if you switch off your radio, for Christ's sake *watch your seatback signs this time.*"

The moment she switched frequencies, several people began chattering. But they were loudly shushed; finally even the most determined—the loudmouth who'd been making jokes before takeoff—had been persuaded to shut up. The attendant's anger had sobered, humbled us. Despite weeks of training, we had screwed up, in our first crisis. Now we had to sit in silence like chastened children while the grown-ups straightened things out.

I switched my own mike off, and huddled with my seatmates until our three hoods were touching. There was an awkward silence. We all grinned at each other nervously.

"What happens now?" I said finally. "Losing all that air must have pushed us off course, right? Spoiled our vector, or whatever?"

"So we miss our bus," the Aborigine girl said. "Question is, how many go-rounds does it take to match up with it again—and how much air have we got to drink while we wait?"

"I think we'll be all right," the Chinese said. "The pilot maneuvered to correct, and I think she did a good job." His voice was a pleasant tenor. His English was utterly unaccented, newscaster's English.

"How do you reckon?" she asked.

"She didn't blast too quickly, and she didn't blast too slowly. And it was one short blast. I think she's good. We might make the original rendezvous, or something close to it."

His confidence was very reassuring. I thought again about asking him to teach me how to jaunt. And decided against it. There would be plenty of qualified instructors around . . . and I was here to simplify my life, not complicate it again.

The attendant came swimming down the aisle past us as he spoke. We sat up to watch. She checked the pressure patch first, popping a little round membrane of blue sticky between her fingers and watching to see if any of its droplets migrated toward the patch. Only when she was satisfied did she turn and check on Mr. Henderson, holding a brief hood-to-hood conference with the passenger who was taking care of him. Then she drifted aimlessly in a half crouch, talking to the pilot on the channel we couldn't hear. Finally she nodded and did something to her belt. The seatback signs began flashing "MONITOR YOUR RADIO" again. I switched mine on.

"Make sure your neighbor has his ears on," she said. "Is everybody listening? Okay, here's the word. Captain de Brandt is going to attempt to salvage our original rendezvous window. In about fifteen minutes the main engines will fire. You can expect about a half gee for about two minutes. There may be additional maneuvering after that, so remain strapped in and braced until I tell you otherwise. Expect acceleration warning in twelve minutes; until then I want you to take your hoods off to save your suit air. But be ready to seal up fast!"

"When will Channel One be coming back on TV?" someone asked. "I want to watch the docking." It was the compulsive joker, aft.

"We can't spare the bytes."

"Huh? That's not—"

"Shut up." She switched back to command frequency.

I took off my hood. The cabin pressure was lower now than

it had been before the blowout. Which was good: all the foul air gushed out of my suit as I unsealed it. I was briefly embarrassed, but in low pressure no one can smell anything very well; it passed without comment, as it were.

I wondered how much air I had left, if I should need it. These were cheap tourist p-suits we were wearing, with just enough air to survive a disaster like we'd just had, in four small cylinders fitted along our upper arms and shins. (In proper p-suits with full-size tanks at our backs, we'd have needed awfully complicated seats.)

There was a subdued murmur of conversation. Suddenly the attendant's strident voice overrode it; she must have pulled off her hood. "You! Nine-D, sit down and buckle up!"

"What the hell for? You said we've got twelve minutes—"

"Sit down!"

It was the joker again. "See here," he said, "we're not soldiers and we're not convicts. I've been looking forward to free fall for a long time, and I have a right to enjoy it. You have no authority—"

"Don't tell me: you're an American, right? This vessel is in a state of emergency; I have authority to break your spine! Sit or be restrained."

"Come, come, the emergency is passed, you said so yourself. Stop being hysterical and lighten up a little." He drifted experimentally out into the aisle. "We have a perfect right to *Jesus!*"

She had pushed off much too hard, I thought, with the full force of terrestrial muscles. She came up the aisle not in graceful slow motion, as my seatmate had earlier, but like a stone fired from a sling. Even I knew not to jump that hard in zero gee: you bash your head. But as she came she was tucking, rolling—

—she flashed past me quickly, but it's just about impossible to move too fast for a dancer to follow: I spun my head and tracked her. She ended her trajectory heels foremost, *smacked* those heels against the seats on either side of him, took all the kinetic energy of her hurtling body on her thighs, and came to a dead stop with her nose an inch from his, drifting just perceptibly to her left.

Try it yourself sometime: drop from a third-story window, and land in a sitting position without a grunt of impact, without a bruise.

I may had been the only one present equipped to fully appreciate what a feat she had just accomplished—but it made the loudmouthed American cross his eyes and shut up.

"You have the right to remain silent," she told him, loud enough to be heard all over the vessel; he flinched. "If you give up that right, I will break your arm. You have no right to counsel until such time as we match orbits with or land upon UN soil—which we don't plan to do." I don't think he was hearing her. He was busy with the tricky mechanics of getting back into his seat. "Does anyone else have any questions? No? You—strap him in there."

She kicked off backwards, repeated her feat by flipping in midair and braking herself against the first row of seats, came to rest with her back against the forward bulkhead, and glared around at us. Suddenly her expression softened.

"Look, people," she called, her voice harsh in the low air pressure, "I know how you feel. I remember my first time in free fall. But you'll have plenty of time to enjoy it later. Right now I want you strapped in. We're in a new orbit, one we didn't pick: there's no telling when the Captain may have to dodge some new piece of junk." She sighed. "I know you're not military personnel. But in space you take orders from anyone who has more experience than you, and ask questions later. A lot later. I've logged over six thousand hours in space, half of them in this very can, and I *will* space the next jerk who gives me any shit."

"Fair go," my Aborigine seatmate called. "We're with you!"

There was a rumble of agreement in which I joined.

"Look, Miss—" she added.

"Yes?"

"You asked for a doctor before. I ain't no whitefella doctor. My people reckon me a healer, but. Can I come see the bloke?"

The attendant started to answer, frowned and hesitated.

"I won't hurt him any."

"All right, come ahead. But be careful! Come *slow*. And headfirst—don't try to flip on the way, you're too green."

She unstrapped and clambered over me with some difficulty, clutching comically in all directions. A few people tittered. The Chinese steadied her and helped. Presently she was floating in the aisle like someone swimming in a dream . . . except that her swimming motions accomplished nothing. She looked over her shoulder to the Chinese. "Give us a hand then, will you, mate?"

He hesitated momentarily . . . then put his hand where he had to and gave her a gentle, measured push.

If a male dancer had done that in the studio, in a lift, I'd have thought nothing of it. But he wasn't a dancer, and this wasn't a studio. That's how I explained my sudden blush to myself.

"Ta," she called as she slowly sailed away. This time the titters were louder.

No, maybe I would not ask him for lessons in free fall movement.

He turned to me. "Excuse me," he said politely.

"No, no," I said, "I understand. If you'd pushed on her feet, she'd have pushed back and spoiled your aim. You're a spacer, aren't you?"

Even for a Chinese, his poker face was terrific. "Thank you for the compliment. But no, I'm not."

"Oh, but you handle yourself so well in free fall—"

"I have spent a little time in space, but I'm hardly a spacer."

Usually a set of features I can't read annoys me . . . but his were at least pleasant to look at while I was trying. Eyes set close, but not too close, together, their long lashes like the spread fins of some small fish, or the fletching of an arrow. Nose slightly, endearingly pugged; mouth almost too small, nearly too full, not quite feminine, chin just strong enough to support that mouth. I caught myself wondering what it would feel like to "Kissing cousin to one at the very least. My name is Morgan McLeod."

"I'm very pleased to meet you, Morgan. I'm Robert Chen."

We shook hands. His grip was warm and strong. The skin of his hand felt horny, calloused—the hand of a martial arts student. That meant that his body would be lean and muscular, his belly hard and "Flattery aside, Robert, you move beautifully. By any chance, have you ever been a dancer?" Definitely not going to ask this one for private movement lessons . . .

"Not really. I've studied some contact improv, but I've never performed. And if I'd spent my life at it, I wouldn't be in your league. I've seen you perform, several times. It's an honour to meet you."

Well. It is nice to be recognized. And, for a dancer, so rare.

"Thank you, Robert, but I'd say your own performance left little to be desired." Oh my God, I was speaking in double-entendres. Clumsy ones! "Uh . . . do you think you could teach me a little about how to move in zero gee?"

Well, hell. I was in space, and I was alive. Within the last hour I had been morbidly depressed, terrified, exalted, very nearly killed, and flattered. I was no longer afraid of anything at all. What harm could there be in a little extracurricular instruction?

$$\triangle \quad \triangle \quad \triangle$$

The Aborigine returned before Robert could reply, sailing over the seat tops, hands waving comically for balance. When she reached us she stopped herself against her seat, tried to do a one and a half gainer to end up seated, and botched it completely. She managed to kick both me and the man in front of her in the head. "Sorry. Sorry," she kept chirping. We all smiled. She was like a tumbling puppy. I found myself warming to her. She had the oddest way of carrying off clumsiness gracefully. Since I'd spent my life carrying off gracefulness clumsily, I found it appealing.

Finally she was strapped back in. She grinned infectiously. "I keep lookin' for the bloody fish," she said. "Like divin' the Barrier Reef, y'know? I'nt it marvelous? My name's Kirra; what's yours then?"

"Morgan McLeod, Kirra; I'm pleased to meet you. And this is Robert Chen."

"G'day, mate," she said to him, "that was good work you done before. You're fast as a jackrabbit."

"Thanks, Kirra," he said. "But I had the same inspiration rabbits do: mortal terror. How's Mr. Henderson?"

Her face smoothed over; for a moment she could have been her grandmother, or her own remotest ancestor. "Bloke's in a bad way," she said. "You could say he's gone and not be wrong. Oh, his motor's still turnin' over, and I reckon it might keep on. Nobody's at the wheel, but. His mind's changed forever." She fingered the thorax of her p-suit absently. I sensed she was looking for an amulet or necklace of some kind that usually hung there. "I tried to sing with him . . . ," she said softly, in a distant, sing-song voice. "We couldn't sing the same . . . was like a bag of notes was broken on the floor." She sighed, and squared her shoulders. "He needs a better healer than me, that's sure."

"They'll have good doctors at Top Step," Robert assured her.

She looked dubious, but politely agreed.

"I'm sorry, Morgan," he said to me. "You asked me a question before, whether I'd work with you on jaunting. I wanted to say—"

The pilot maneuvered without warning.

For a few instants there was a faint suggestion of an up and down to the world. A sixth of a gee or so. Coincidentally it was lined up roughly with our seatbacks in one axis, so the effect was to push us gently down into our seats. But if you considered the round bulkhead up front as a clock, "down" was at about 8:30: we all tilted to the right like bus passengers on a long curve. I found my face pressed gently against Robert's, my weight supported by his strong shoulder, with Kirra's head on my lap. A few complaints were raised, and one clear, happy, "Wheeee!" came from somewhere aft. His hair smelled good.

"Hang on, people," the attendant called. "Nothing to worry about."

In a matter of seconds the acceleration went away, and we drifted freely again. We all waited a few moments for a bang or bump to signal docking. Nothing happened.

As the three of us started to say embarrassment-melting things to each other, thrust returned again—in precisely the opposite direction. I suppose it made sense: first you turn the wheel, and then you straighten the wheel. But even Robert was caught by surprise. This time we were hanging upside down and sideways from our seats, Kirra and I with wrists locked like arm wrestlers and *Robert's* head in *my* lap. It felt dismayingly good there. Even through a cheap p-suit. Again the thrust went away.

"I wonder how long it'll be before we—" Kirra began, when an acceleration warning finally sounded, a mournful hooting noise. The attendant had time to call out, "All right, I want everybody to—" Then the big one hit.

Well, maybe a half gee, or a little more. But half a gee is a lot more than none, and it came on fast, and in an unexpected and disturbing direction. The pilot was blasting directly forward, along our axis, as though backing violently away from danger. The whole vessel shuddered. We all fell forward toward the seatbacks in front of us—"below" us now—and held a pushup together for perhaps thirty or forty seconds. There were loud complaints above the blast noise.

The acceleration faded slowly down to nothing again. There were two or three seconds of silence . . . and then there was a series of authoritative but gentle thumps on the hull, fore and aft, as though men with padded hammers were surreptitiously checking the welds. The seatbacks began flashing PLEASE REMAIN SEATED.

"We're here," Robert said. "A very nice docking. A little abrupt, but clean." I thought he was being ironic but wasn't sure.

"Keep your seatbelts buckled," the attendant called. "We'll disembark after Doctor Kolchar has cleared Mr. Henderson to be moved."

"That's it?" Kirra said.

I knew what she'd meant. On TV the docking of spacecraft is always seen from a convenient adjacent camera that gives the metal mating dance a stately Olympian perspective, an elephantine grace. A trip to space—especially one's first and last—should begin with trumpets, and end with the Blue Danube. This had been like riding a Greyhound bus through an endless tunnel . . . blowing a tire . . . riding on the rim for a while . . . and then running out of gas in the middle of the tunnel.

"That's it," Robert agreed. "Even if they'd had the video feed running, it wouldn't have looked like much up until the very end. To really appreciate a docking you've got to speak radar. But we're here, all right."

"We truly have reached the Top Step," I said wonderingly.

"That we have," Robert said. "Here comes the doctor." The red light was on over the airlock up front.

The hatch opened explosively, with a popping sound, and the airlock spat out a white-haired man in Bermuda shorts and a loud yellow Hawaiian shirt. His body orientation, fluttering hair and clothes, and the pack affixed somehow to his midsection made him look like a skydiver. The attendant caught him, began to warn him that this pressure was not secure, but he shushed her and began examining Mr. Henderson with various items taken from his belly pack. After a time I heard him say, "Okay, Shannon, let's move him. You help me with him. We're going to do it nice and slow."

"You!" the attendant called up the aisle. "The Chinese spacer in Row Six: you're in command." Robert blinked. "Come forward and take over, now. Breathing and digestion are permitted; limited thinking will be tolerated; everything else is forbidden, savvy?"

"Yes, Ma'am," he called forward.

Our eyes met briefly as he was unbuckling. For the first time I was able to see past that impassive expression, guess his thoughts. He was embarrassed, flattered . . . disappointed? At what?

"To be continued in our next," he murmured, and vaulted away.

At the interruption of our conversation?

"I hope so," I heard myself call after him.

Come to think of it, he still hadn't said whether or not he'd give me lessons in jaunting.

Oh God. What was I doing? What good could possibly come of this? Even for me, this was rotten timing.

"You want to mind that top step, they say," Kirra said softly, and when I turned to look at her she was grinning.

CHAPTER TWO

Two moves equals one fire.

—Mark Twain

WE DIDN'T HAVE long to wait. Less than a minute after the doctor and attendant left, the lock cycled open again and someone emerged.

The newcomer got our instant attention.

"Afternoon, folks," she said. "Welcome to Top Step. I'm a Guide, and my name is Chris."

No one said a word.

"Oh, excuse me." She courteously turned herself rightside up with respect to us.

It didn't help much. Even upside down in that confined space, her face had been far enough from the floor to be seen from the last row. And even rightside up she was startling.

Chris's p-suit had no legs, and neither did Chris.

I know I tried hard not to gape. I'm pretty sure I failed. One person actually gasped audibly. Chris ignored it and continued cheerfully, "I usually make a little speech at this point, but we want to get you out of suspect pressure as quickly as possible, so you've got a temporary reprieve. You are now about to do something you probably thought was impossible: leave a plane intelligently. By rows, remaining seated until it's your turn, and then leaving *at once*. You have no carryons or coats to fumble with, no reason to block the aisle—and good reason not to.

"See, if we cycle you through the airlocks a few at a time it'd take over an hour. But to keep the lock open at both ends and march you all out we have to equalize pressure between this can and Top Step—and there's no telling if or how long that patch there will take pressure. So we're going to do this with suits sealed, and we are not going to dawdle. I know

31

you're all free fall virgins; don't worry, we'll set up a bucket brigade and you'll be fine. One thing: if there's a blowout as you're passing through the lock, *get out of the doorway.* It doesn't matter which direction you pick, just don't be in the way. Okay? All right, Ev!"

That last was apparently directed to the Captain in the cockpit ahead. My ears began to hurt suddenly. The pressure was rising back toward Earth-normal. Like everybody, I swallowed hard, and watched that pressure patch as I sealed my hood.

"Okay, this side first. No chatter. First person to slow up the line gets assigned to the Reclamation Module for the next two months." A light over the lock blinked and the door opened. "First row: move!"

Getting up the aisle to the front was easy. Once there were no seatbacks to navigate with, it got trickier. But Chris fielded me like a shortstop and lobbed me to Robert at second, who pivoted and threw me to someone at first for the double play. That must have ended the inning; others tossed me around the infield to celebrate for a while.

I ended up turning slowly end over end in a large pale blue rectangular-box room. Several yellow ropes were strung across it from one biggest-wall to the opposite one. I caught a rope as I sailed past it.

Because I seemed to be drifting light as a feather, I badly underestimated how hard it would be to stop drifting. If that rope hadn't had some give to it, I might have pulled my arms out of their sockets. I had no weight, but I still had all my mass. I found the experience fascinating and mildly dismaying: in that first intentional vector change I made in space, I knew that some of the zero-gee dance moves I'd envisioned weren't going to work.

But I was too busy to think about kinesthetics just then. The room was half-full of my shipmates, with more coming at a steady pace. I saw that all of us were treating the biggest-walls as "floor" and "ceiling," and lining ourselves up parallel to the ropes between them—but there seemed to be considerable silent disagreement as to which way was up. Visual cues were all ambiguous. It was a comical sight.

Finally one side preponderated and the others gradually switched around to that "local vertical." I was one of the latter group, and as I reached the decision that I was upside down, I realized for the first time that I felt faintly nauseous. The feeling increased as I flipped myself over, diminished a little as the room seemed to snap back into proper perspective again.

The last of us came tumbling in, followed by the last member of the bucket brigade. The latter sealed the hatch, oriented himself upside down to us, let go of the hatch, and floated before it, hands thrust up into his pockets. He looked at us, and we craned our heads at him. A few of us cartwheeled round to his personal vertical again, and before long everyone had done so, with varying degrees of grace.

He seemed to be in his fifties. He wore a p-suit, opaque and deep purple. Compared to the clunky suits we wore, his looked like a second skin. His complexion was coal black, the kind that doesn't even gleam much under bright light. He was lean and fit, going bald and making no attempt to hide it, frowning and smiling at the same time. He looked relaxed and competent, avuncular. He reminded me a little of Murray, the business manager of one of the companies I'd worked with almost a decade before. Murray did the work of four men, yet *always* seemed perfectly relaxed, even during the week before a performance.

"You folks don't seem to know which way is up, do you?" he said pleasantly.

There were a very few polite giggles, and one groan.

He did something, and was suddenly upside down to us again. He was stable in the new position and had not touched anything. I didn't quite catch the move at the time—and still can't describe it; I'd have to show you—but I was fascinated. I wanted to ask him to do it again.

This time we all let him stay upside down.

"All right. My name is Phillipe Mgabi. I am your Chief Administrator for Student Affairs. On behalf of the Starseed Foundation, I'd like to welcome you all to Top Step, and wish you a fruitful stay. I'm sorry you had such an eventful journey here, and I assure you all that Top Step is considerably less

vulnerable than your shuttle was. You're as safe as any
terrestrial can be in space, now."

No one said thanks.

"I must remind you that you are no longer on United
Nations soil, in even a figurative sense. Top Step is an
autonomic pressure, like Skyfac or The Ark, recognized by the
UN but not eligible for membership, and wholly owned by the
Starseed Foundation. At the moment, you are technically
Landed Immigrants, although we prefer the term Postulants."

It was weirdly disorienting to be addressed by an upside
down person. It was almost impossible to decipher his facial
expressions.

"You were given the constitution and laws of Top Step back
at Suit Camp, and you'll find them in the memory banks—
along with maps, schedules, master directory, and for that
matter the entire Global Net. You have unrestricted and
unmetered access, Net-inclusive, free of charge for as long as
you're resident here."

There were murmurs. Unmetered access to the Net? For
everybody?

This whole operation struck me as being run like a dance
company financed by task-specific grants. In some areas they
were as cheap as a cut-rate holiday (Suit Camp had featured
outdoor privies, just like the ones I'd used as a little girl on
Gambier Island) . . . but when they spent, they spent like
sailors on leave. It seemed schizophrenic.

"The point is that you are responsible. You are presumed to
know your obligations and privileges as a Postulant. The
Agreements you have made are all in plain language, and you
are bound by them. They allow you a great deal of
slack . . . but where they bind, there is no give at all. I
recommend that you study them if you haven't already."

Out of the corner of my eye I saw the loudmouthed joker
start to say something, then change his mind.

"I hope all of you paid attention at Suit Camp. I said you
were as safe as any terrestrial in space. That compares
favorably with, say, New York . . . but not by much, and
space bites in different places and unexpected ways. As you
learned on your way up here." Ouch. "To survive long enough

to enter Symbiosis, you must all acquire and maintain a state of alert mindfulness—and there are few second chances. Space is not fair. Space is not merciful. I see you all nodding, and I know that at least three of you will be dead before your term is up. That is the smallest number of Postulants we have lost from a single class. I would like it very much if your class turns out to be the first exception to that rule."

Mgabi cocked his head, listening to something we couldn't hear. "And now I'm going to hand you over to your Orientation Coordinator. Any and all problems, questions, requests or complaints you may have during your stay in Top Step will go to her; I'm afraid I will not be seeing you on any regular basis myself. Dorothy?"

The hatch opened and admitted a red-haired woman in her seventies, frail and thin, dressed in Kelly green p-suit. One look at her face and I knew I was in good hands. She looked competent, compassionate and wise. She aligned herself to us rather than Mgabi.

"Hello, children," she said. "I'm Dorothy Gerstenfeld. I'm going to be your mother for the next two months. Daddy here—" She indicated Mgabi. "—will be away at the office most of the time, so I'll be the one who tucks you in and makes you do your chores and so on. I've got a squad of Guides to help me. My door is always unlocked and my phone is always on.

"Now I know you've all got a thousand questions—I know at least a few of you urgently want a refresher course in zero-gee plumbing!—but I've got a little set speech, and I find if I start with the questions I never get to it. So here goes:

"I've used the maternal metaphor for a reason . . . just as Doctor Mgabi entered this room upside down to you for a reason. He was trying to show you by plain example that you have come to a place where up and down have meaning only within your own skull. I am trying to suggest to you that for the next two months you are no longer adults, whatever your calendar age."

Mgabi drifted nearby in a gentle crouch. It was hard to read his inverted face, and he must have heard this dozens of times, but it seemed to me he paid careful attention, though he was

looking at us. He reminded me of an old black and white film
I saw once of Miles Davis listening to Charlie Parker take a
solo.

"It is said," she continued, "that space makes you childlike
again. Charles Armstead himself noted that in the historic
Titan Transmission. Free fall makes you want to play, to be a
child again. Look at you all, trying to be still, wanting to hop
around. Well you should . . . and shall! Look at me: I'm
considerably over thirty, and I've been six-wall-squash champion in this pressure for over five years now.

"Now, what are the three things a child hates the most?
Aside from bedtime, I mean. Going to school, doing chores,
and going to church, am I right?" People chuckled, including
me. "Well, you've all just spent several weeks in school. It
probably even felt like summer school, since all the Suit
Camps are in tropical locations. And now that school's out,
you're going to have to spend some time doing chores and
being in church." There were scattered mock-groans. "Not
only that, you're going to have to remember, every single time
without fail, to wear your rubbers when you go out!" That got
giggles.

"Don't worry," she went on, "before long you'll be going
out a lot, all you want—and there'll be plenty of time for play.
But church—or temple or zendo or synagogue or whatever
word you use for 'place where one prays'—is sort of what Top
Step is all about, what it's for. It's just a kind of church it's
okay to play in, that's all. It has only one sacrament, and only
you know—if you do—what it will take to become ready to
receive it. We know many ways to help you.

"If you use your time here wisely, then soon church will be
done, and school will be out forever, and you will become
more ideally childlike than you ever were as a child.

"I hope every one of you makes it."

A facile and pious cliché, surely—but when she said it, I
believed it. Your mother doesn't lie. This one didn't, at least.

"Remember: if you have any *practical* difficulties, I'm the
one you want to consult; don't bother Administrator Mgabi or
his staff without routing through me first. But few of your
problems are going to turn out to be practical—and some of

your practical problems will kill you before you have a chance to complain. When you do need help, it's more likely to be spiritual help. You'll find that Top Step has more *spiritual* advisers than any other kind. We have representatives of most of the major denominations inboard—you'll find a directory in your computer—but please don't feel compelled to stick with whatever faith you were raised in or presently practice. You'll find that personal rapport is a lot more important than brand name. All right, enough speeches—"

People with full bladders sighed, anticipating relief—but there was an interruption from the loudmouth. He wanted to report Shannon, our flight attendant, for what he called outrageous authoritarianism and psychological instability. "The woman is dangerous," he said. "I actually thought for a moment she was going to strike me! I want her relieved of duty and punished."

The rest of us made a collective growling sound. He ignored us.

"We'll discuss this in my office," Dorothy said, "as soon as I've—"

"Dammit, I want satisfaction, now."

Dorothy looked sad. "Eric," she said, "did you read your contracts with us?" It struck me, that she knew his name.

He didn't seem to notice. "I ran 'em past my legal software, sure. But she had no right—"

"She had every right. I saw all that happened, from my office. If Shannon had chosen to kill you, I would have been sad—but I would not have been cross with her."

He snorted. "She'd have had a busy time trying!"

Dorothy looked even sadder. "No, she wouldn't. Eric, *can't* we discuss this later, in my office?"

"I'm afraid not, ma'am. If the setup here actually requires me to take orders from every hired hand, let's get it straight right now so I can return to Earth at once."

Now she mastered her sorrow; her face smoothed over. "Very well. I'll take you back to your shuttle now. It will be departing almost immediately." She kicked off gently and jaunted toward him.

At once he was waffling. "Wait a minute! You can't just

throw me out without a hearing, after all the time I've invested—and you certainly can't make me go back in *that* crate, it's defective. And these p-suits are substandard, I want a real one, with a proper radio, and—"

She approached slowly, empty hands outstretched in a gesture of peace, maternal concern on her face. She killed most of her momentum on the empty rope just in front of his, setting it shivering, covered the last few meters very slowly, reached for his rope—

—and her hands slipped past it, touched Eric behind each ear with delicate precision. His eyes rolled up and he let go of the rope, slowly began to pivot around her hands. He snored gently.

Towing Eric, Dorothy jaunted slowly back to her original place by the hatch; it opened as she got there, and she aimed Eric out through it to someone out in the corridor. Then she turned to us.

All the sadness was gone from her face, now, replaced by resolution. She looked as strong, as powerful, as my own grandmother. "I'm sorry you've all had such an inauspicious trip so far." Small smile. "It can only get better from here. Now: Eric raised a good point. The p-suits you're all wearing *are* inadequate. They're tourist suits, designed only for emergency use by passengers in transit. They'll be going back to Earth on the shuttle, so please remove them now. You'll be issued your own personal suits—*real* suits, the best made—in just a little while." We all began removing our suits. "From here you'll go through Decontam, where there'll be wash-rooms for those who need one—and, I'm afraid, for those who don't think you do—and then you'll be guided to your rooms. You've got three hours before dinner; I recommend you spend them either at your terminals, learning your way around Top Step, or resting. There'll be plenty of time for physical exploring, believe me."

Again there was a bucket-brigade. We were warned not to attempt any maneuvers of our own along the way, but I intended to cheat just a little . . . until the line was held up by the first couple of jerks to do so, and people with full

bladders began to get surly. Sure, I knew more about kinesthetics than the two jerks. That gave me the opportunity to
make an even bigger jerk out of myself. I decided to be
patient.

There was plenty of time. We wouldn't be allowed to go
EVA for another four weeks, and we wouldn't be allowed to
enter Symbiosis until we'd had at least four weeks of EVA
practice . . . and we were entitled to hang around Top Step
making up our minds for another four weeks after *that,* if we
chose, before we had to either take the Symbiote, or go back
to Earth and start making payments on the air, food and water
we had used. I'd have lots of time to play with zero gee.

Having toured a lot of strange places with various dance
companies, I'd been through several sorts of stringent international decontamination rituals before, and thought I was
prepared for anything. You don't want to know about Top Step
Decontam, and I don't want to discuss it. Let's just say they
were thorough. Top Step is a controlled environment, and they
want it as sterile as possible.

When I got out the other end, naked, dry, and bright red, I
found myself drifting in a boardroom-sized cubic with five
other naked females. Kirra was among them, and I recognized
Glenn Christie, an acquaintance from Suit Camp. At the far
end of the space were what looked like several dozen drifting
footballs, tethered together. Kirra threw me a grin. "Am I still
black?" she called softly.

"On this side," I agreed.

She giggled, and . . . wriggled, somehow, so that she
spun end over end gracefully, like a ballerina pirouetting but in
three dimensions.

"Couple of pink places," I said, "but I think you had them
when you started. How did you *do* that?" It hadn't looked at
all like the maneuver Mgabi had used.

"Little pinker now, maybe. I dunno how I did it. You try
it."

When I try out a new move, I'm alone in the studio. I was
saved by the bell. An amplified voice came from nowhere in
particular. (I tried to locate the speaker grille, but it seemed to
be hidden.) It was female, a warm friendly contralto. After

what we'd just been through, it shouldn't have mattered much if she'd been a male with a leer in his voice . . . but I found myself liking her somehow, whoever she was. She sounded sort of like the best friend I never really had. "Welcome, all of you, to community pressure. One of the containers you see on the inboard side of the chamber will have your name on it. Please put on the contents and check them for fit: let me know if you have any problems." We all thanked her.

It occurred to me briefly to wonder why she wasn't present in the room. Surely we were as thoroughly decontaminated as we were ever going to be. But the tone of her voice said that whatever the reason was, it was unimportant, not anything scary, so I put it out of my mind.

Getting to the football-shaped containers got comical; we were like kids in some Disneyland ride, giggling and trying to help each other and getting tangled up and giggling some more. By the time I located the box with my name on it, we all had aching sides. The unseen woman did not chastise us for our antics; she seemed to understand that we were ready for some laughter.

The football opened along one seam. Inside it was a wad of something. As I stared at it in puzzlement, it swelled like bread-dough, like a backpacker's raincoat opening up.

"It's a p-suit!" Kirra said delightedly, shaking out hers.

Sure enough, we had all been issued our real p-suits. Expensive, state of the art, personally customized and form-fitting ones, as opposed to the cheap standardized movie-costumes we'd all worn aboard the Shuttle.

We'd practiced this in Suit Camp. Timing myself, I slid the bottom half on like greased pantyhose, pulled the rest up behind me and around my torso, put my arms in the sleeves, sealed the seam, and pulled the transparent hood down over my head. Elapsed time, twelve seconds. I thought that was pretty good. It went on easier than a body-stocking: while it was snug, the interior had been treated somehow to reduce friction. I didn't test the radio or any of the other gear, though I should have. Instead I pulled the hood back, and grinned at Kirra and Glenn and the other women. They grinned back.

Our suits were custom tailored to our bodies, and fit like

hugs. They were also, we discovered, customized for colour. They came out of the egg transparent, so we could inspect them for fit and flaws, and except for the barely visible tracery of microtubules that carried coolant and such around them, they looked like an extra layer of skin. But when we located the "polarization enabler controls" they'd taught us about in Suit Camp, and opaqued our suits, each of us was, from toes to collarbone, a different—and well chosen—colour. My own suit turned a light shade of burgundy that suited my complexion and hair colour, and Kirra's suit became a cobalt blue very close to the highlights that normal lighting raised on her dark black skin.

I liked the colours a lot. To me they were among the first signs that artists had had a part in the creative planning of this outfit.

"Any problems?" our unseen friend asked. "No? Then exit the chamber through the green-marked hatch in Wall Four. You'll be directed from there."

I looked around for the green-marked hatch. Where the hell was Wall Four? No walls were marked that I could see—at least not with numbers. One of them, to our right (we were all instinctively aligned to the same local vertical, without knowing how we'd selected it) was painted with a large broad red arrow, pointing in the direction we had come from, but that was little help. My companions were looking confused, too, but the unseen woman didn't cue us.

It took so long to find the hatch that in a few seconds I guessed where it must be. Sure enough, it was "up," over our heads. People hardly ever look up, for some reason. (Which seems to suggest that we haven't evolved significally since before we came down out of the trees, yes?) I nudged Kirra and pointed. She unsealed the hatch and went through. I followed on her heels, and we found ourselves at the bottom of a huge well-lit padded cavern.

I should have been expecting it; I'd seen pictures. But you just don't expect to step from someplace as clean and sterile and right-angled and high-tech and profoundly artificial as a

Decontam module into the Carlsbad Caverns. I nearly lost my
grip and fell up into it.

It was about the size of a concert hall and roughly
spherical—but the accent was on rough. Rough curves and
joins, the rough fractal topography of natural rock, overlaid
with some rough surface covering that looked like cheap
kitchen sponge stained dark grey. Tunnels departed from the
cavern in all directions; their gaping, irregularly sized and
shaped mouths were spaced asymmetrically around the chamber. Each tunnel had one or more pairs of slender elastic
bungee cords strung criss-cross across its mouth, obviously
used to either fling oneself into the tunnel, or catch oneself on
the way out; the larger the tunnel, the more cords.

This spheric pressure was half natural and half artificial. It
had happened, as much as it had been built. It was a sculpted
and padded cave. Perhaps a dozen people (none of them in
p-suits; one was naked) were drifting slowly across the vast
chamber in different directions. No two of them were using the
same local vertical, and none of them used ours. It was like
something out of Escher.

No, it *was* something out of Escher.

I remembered to move aside so others could use the hatch.
There were lots of handgrips nearby; I worked myself sideways like a crab and "lay on my back" a few inches "above"
the bulkhead I'd just come through. As Glenn and the other
three women emerged into the cave behind us, they too
grabbed handholds, stabilized themselves, and stared.

After a long few moments of silence, Glenn cleared her
throat. "Which way to the egress, do you suppose?"

The unseen woman spoke again. "Can all of you see the
tunnel that's blinking green over there, Inboard and One-ish?"

Again I failed to spot any speakers, and realized this time
that there were none; her voice was simply homing in on my
ears somehow. The last two terms she'd used were meaningless to me, but there was no mistaking the tunnel she meant.
Soft green lights around its mouth had suddenly started to flash
on and off. "We see it."

"That's where you're headed for, now."

"All the bloody way up there?" Kirra squeaked.

"Push off gently, Kirra," our companion said soothingly. I hadn't realized she knew our names. She must have a terrific memory. "Be prepared to take a long time getting there. You'll find that in jaunting long distances, aim is much more important than strength. And you're not in a hurry. Why don't you go first?"

"Well . . . I guess I—bloody hell!"

Kirra had absently let go of her handhold at some point, instinctively trusting to gravity to keep her in place. But there was none. In the twenty seconds or so we'd been here, she'd drifted far enough away from the floor (as I called that wall in my mind, since it had been under my feet when I started) to be unable to touch it again. Her attempts only put her into a tumble from which she couldn't figure out how to emerge. "Oh my," she groaned as she spun. "I think I'm gonna be a puke pinwheel in a minute . . ."

I tried to reach her, but I couldn't quite do it without letting go with my other hand myself. And the gap between us was slowly widening.

"Make a chain," our friend said, and one of the women I didn't know, who was nearest to me, reached and got one of my ankles in a one-handed deathgrip. I let go of my handhold, lunged, and got an equally firm grip on one of Kirra's ankles as it went by. Her mass tried to tug me sideways as I stabilized her spin, and partially succeeded. The woman holding me reeled us both in, a little too hard: Kirra and I *thumped* firmly together into what I thought of as the floor, and clutched it and each other.

Perhaps we shouldn't have used up our giggles earlier; we could have used some now.

"I'm right," Kirra said. "Ta, love . . . I feel a right idjit."

"It happens to everyone here, sooner or later," our unseen friend told her. "Proper etiquette is to lend assistance if needed and otherwise ignore it. Are you ready to jaunt now, Kirra?"

She was game. "Reckon so. Where's that blinkin' tunnel? Pun unintended." She spun round to face the cavern and got her feet under her . "Oh, there it is. See you on the other side, mates—"

She kicked off, gently, and began to rise into the air.

Now we giggled. We couldn't help it. Her lazy ascension looked *exactly* like a bad special effect. We heard her laughing too, with a child's delight. She mugged for us as she went, folded her arms and legs into tailor seat, opened out into a swan dive, then tucked and rolled and came out of it making exaggerated swimming motions—in our direction. Any embarrassment she might have felt a moment ago was gone. "I *dreamed* of this," she sang, her voice high and dreamy, "so many years ago, it's like a memory—"

I set my feet, let go of the wallbehindme/floorbeneathme bulkhead, took a deep breath, and jaunted after her.

△   △   △

If you've done it you know what I mean, and if you haven't I can't convey it. All I can say is, mortgage your condo, take the Thomas Cook Getaway Special, and jaunt in free fall once before you die. That way you'll know your way around Paradise when you get there.

△   △   △

We were all giggling like schoolgirls as we jaunted up through the vast chamber, drawing amused looks from the old hands. "I like it, Morgan," Kirra called down to me.

"Me, too," I called back. I was mildly disappointed that this big cave had no perceptible echo. But I suppose the fun of one would have worn off the first time you smacked your head on bare rock, or tried to make yourself understood to someone on the other side of the chamber.

Kirra had followed instructions, jaunted very gently and therefore slowly. My own jaunt had been a little more impulsive: I was gradually overtaking her. "Look out above— here I come!"

She glanced down, rotated on her axis, and opened her arms for me so that I slid up into a hug—one of the oddest, most pleasant experiences of my life! We grinned with delight and embraced.

Looking past her fanny I noticed four p-suited males emerging from a hatch near the one we'd just left. Robert wasn't among them. Well, what did I care?

At about the mid-point Kirra and I began to think about the other end of the journey, and plan our landing. As we did so, it suddenly dawned on us both that we were not floating *up*—we were upside down, falling. It was as if the whole cave had flipped end over end in an instant. We clutched each other even tighter . . . and then relaxed, trying to laugh at ourselves. But there was a queasy feeling in my stomach that hadn't been there before. This "thinking spherically" business they kept talking about at Suit Camp was going to take some work. And time . . .

I could see, now, why some people just can't ever get it. For the first time, I seriously wondered whether—dancer or no dancer—I might be one of them. I had automatically assumed that spherical perception would be a snap for any modern dancer, since we do our moving much farther from the vertical axis than ballet dancers . . . but when I thought about it, weren't even modern dancers *more* tied into gravity and perpendicularity than ordinary people? A civilian tries to not fall down; a modern dancer tries to move all over the place in odd and interesting ways, and not fall down: therefore she pays more attention, more of the time, to not falling down— pays more heed to gravity. Maybe I had *more* to unlearn than my companions . . .

But I thrust aside the thought, determined to keep enjoying this magic jaunt, and got Kirra to show me that reversing- your-vertical trick. It turned out to be something like trying to exaggerate a swan dive, if that helps you. I ordered my stomach to settle down. *Fine,* it said, *Define "down."* I told it "down" was toward my feet, and that seemed to help a little.

When I'd kicked off to follow Kirra, she'd been a near target, so I'd aimed well enough to jaunt right into her embrace. But the target she'd been aimed at was much farther away, and docking with me had probably further disturbed her course. We landed close to the tunnel mouth we wanted, but not very. About ten seconds later Glenn threaded it like a needle, spinning around the bungee cord like a high-bar gymnast, and those of us who could applauded. The others did no better than Kirra and I. We all met at the tunnel mouth.

"Not bad at all," our woman friend said. "And Glenn, that was excellent."

I understood that she was monitoring us from some remote location—but it seemed odd that she was still giving us her attention. Surely there were other women coming out of Decontam after us. Yes, there was one now: I could see her "up" there, emerging upside down from the hatch we'd left, gaping up at us . . .

The penny dropped.

Now how did one phrase this? "Uh . . . excuse me?"

"Yes, Morgan?" she said.

". . . are you organic?"

There was a smile in her voice now. "Elegantly put, dear. No, as you've guessed, I'm an AI program in Top Step's master computer."

"And a bloody clever one you are," Kirra said delightedly. "I never sussed. What's your name, love?"

"I'm generally known as Teena. If you think of a name you like better, tell me and I'll answer to that with you. At the moment I have one hundred and sixty-seven names. But if you want to refer to me, to another person, call me Teena."

I'd been crabwalking my way to the tunnel mouth with the others, but suddenly I paused. "Uh . . . Teena?" I began, pitching my voice too low for the others to hear. ". . . do you—I mean, is there any way to—"

"May I try to guess your questions, Morgan?" she murmured in my ear. "Yes, I will be monitoring you every minute you're in or near Top Step, while you're feeding the felcher or making love or just trying to be alone. No, there is no way to switch me off. But there's only a very limited sense in which I can even metaphorically be said to be *thinking about* what I perceive. In a very real sense, there is no me, save when I am invoked. My short-term memory is much less than a second, I don't save anything that is not relevant to health, safety or your direct commands, and even that can be accessed by only eight people in Top Step—to all of whom you gave that specific right when you sighed your contract. So please don't think of me as a Peeping Teena, all right?"

"I'll try," I said, resuming my journey to the tunnel mouth.

"It's just that . . . well, I've heard AIs before—but you're so good I'd swear you're sentient." Glenn heard that last and said, "Me too."

"Artificial sentience may be possible," Teena said, "but it won't be silicon-based."

One of the women I didn't know said something in Japanese.

"Why not?" Glenn translated.

"The map is not the territory," Teena said—and apparently the Japanese woman heard the answer in her own language. What a marvelous tool Teena was!

Glenn seemed disposed to argue, but Teena went on, "It's time we got you six to your quarters. Follow me—"

A group of little green LED lights along the tunnel wall began twinkling at us, then moved slowly away into the tunnel like Tinkerbell.

One at a time, we put our soles against the bungee cord and jaunted after them.

The tunnel itself was laser-straight, though its walls were roughly sculpted. There were numbered hatches let into the padded rock at odd intervals, and other, smaller tunnels intersected at odd intervals and angles. The main corridor was about eight or ten meters in cross section, with rungs spiraling along its length so that you could never be far from one. These came in handy as we progressed; we were to learn that a perfect tunnel-threading jaunt is almost impossible, even for free fall veterans. Old hands boast of their low CPH, or Contact-Per-Hectometer rate. (If you're a diehard American, a hectometer, a hundred meters, is the rest of humanity's name for about a hundred yards.) We soon began to pick up the trick of slinging ourselves along with minimal waste effort. No matter how fast or slow we progressed, the blinking lights that we followed stayed exactly five meters ahead of the foremost one of us, like one of those follow-from-in-front tails you see cops or spies do in the movies.

We overtook and passed a group of especially clumsy males. They were following pixies of a different colour, so there was minimal confusion between our two groups.

"Who you roomin' with, Morgan?" Kirra asked as we jaunted together.

"I don't know. The woman I planned to room with came down with the Foul Bowel three days ago—bad enough to get flown off to hospital. I guess I get pot luck."

"S'truth!" Kirra exclaimed. "Mine got right to the airlock this morning and decided what she really wanted to do was go back to her husband. Hey, you don't reckon . . . ? I mean, they sat us next to each other on the Shuttle, do you suppose that means— Hey Teena—"

"Yes, Kirra?" Teena said.

"Who's my bunkie gonna be?"

"You and Morgan will be· rooming together. That is why you were seated adjacent on the Shuttle."

"That's great!" Kirra said.

I was oddly touched by the genuine enthusiasm in her voice; it had been a long time since anyone had been especially eager for my company. I found that I was pleased myself; Kirra was as likeable as a puppy. "Thanks," I told her. "I think so too."

She grinned. "I ought to warn you . . . I sing. All the time, I mean. Puts some people off."

"Are you any good?"

"Yah. But I don't sing anything you know."

"I'll risk it. I dance, myself."

"So I hear; like to see it. That's settled, then. Thanks, Teena!"

It occurred to me that Teena hadn't answered Kirra's question until Kirra asked it. She'd heard us discussing it, presumably, but had not volunteered the information until asked. She'd told the truth, earlier: unless we called on her, she "paid attention" only to things like pulse, respiration, and location coordinates. (If everyone in Top Step ever called her at the same moment, would her system hang? Or did she have the RAM to handle it?) I found that reassurance comforting.

A woman who knew everything, needed nothing and was only there when you wanted her. I was willing to bet a man had written Teena. She was what my ex-husband had been looking for all his life.

Shortly Teena said, "We'll be pausing at that nexus ahead:

the one that's blinking now. Prepare to cancel your velocity."

The "nexus" was an intersection of several side tunnels, important enough to have bungee cords strung across the middle of the main tunnel to allow changes of vector. We all managed to grab one.

"We split up here," Teena said. "Soon Li, Yumiko, your quarters are this way—" Tinkerbell skittered off down one tunnel, then returned to hover at its entrance. "—Glenn, Nicole, Morgan and Kirra, yours are this way." Another tunnel developed green fairies.

We did each say level-taking politenesses appropriate to our culture, but even Yumiko didn't linger over it. We were all too eager to see our new home, our personal cave-within-a-cave. Have you ever approached a new dwelling for the first time . . . *after* the lease has been signed? Remember how your pulse raced as you got near the door? The schizoid cheap/lavish style of Top Step might just pinch here.

Our wing was P7; Teena pointed out the wing bathroom and kitchenette as we jaunted past them, stopped Kirra and me at a door marked P7-23. I'm not even sure I said goodbye to Glenn as she continued on past our door toward her own room and roommate. Teena had Kirra and me show the door-lock our thumbprints, whereupon it opened for us.

Home, sweet spherical home . . .

CHAPTER THREE

*When the 10,000 things are viewed in their oneness, we
return to the origin and remain where we
have always been.*
—Sen T'san

OUR NEW HOME didn't look *too* weird to us because we'd seen
pictures in Suit Camp. Still it was exotic; flat pictures don't do
justice to a spherical living space. We drifted around in it for
a while, staring at everything, trying out the various facilities,
lights and sound and video and climate control, teaching them
all to recognize our voices and so on, but the room somehow
kept refusing to become real for me. It was just too strange.

There was no "upper bunk" to fight over; one half of the
room was as good as the other. The hemisphere I arbitrarily
chose had, as a small concession to the ancient human patterns
of thought I was here to unlearn, a local vertical, a defined up
and down—the Velcro desk lined up with the computer
monitor and so on—but Kirra's half had a different one, at a
skewed angle to mine. Neither had any particular relationship
to the axis of the corridor outside. Looking from my side of the
room to Kirra's made me slightly dizzy. My eyes wanted to
ignore anything that disagreed with their personal notion of up
and down. Such things did not play by the rules, were
impolite, beneath notice.

Kirra and I each adapted to our own local orientation for a
moment, blinked at the items and documents attached to our
desks, the monitor screens that read WELCOME TO TOP
STEP, and so on. Then we turned back to look at each other.
Being out-of-phase was unsatisfactory; without discussion or
thought we both adapted to a compromise orientation halfway
between our two differing ones. We snapped into phase with
an almost audible click.

And we broke up.

We could not stop laughing. There was more than a bit of hysteria in it, on both sides. It was different by an order of magnitude from the giggling we had done earlier while scrambling for our new p-suits. Since breakfast I had been literally blown off the face of the Earth, nearly killed in orbit, told that I was a forty-six-year-old child, sexually—aroused? well, intrigued—for the first time in forever, molested most intimately and impersonally by Decontam devices, dumped into a weird Caveworld where falling off a log was not *possible,* guided through a bunch of absurdly Freudian tunnels by a woman who wasn't there . . . and now I was "home," in a place where my bed was a holster, and I could look up and see the soles of my roommate's feet. I can't speak for Kirra, but it wasn't until about halfway through that laugh that I realized just how lonely and scared and disoriented I was— which only made me laugh harder.

We laughed until the tears came, and then roared, because tears in free fall are so absurd, from both inside and outside. Kirra's eyes exuded little elongated saline worms, that waved and broke up into tiny crystal balls. I seemed to see her through a fish-eye lens that kept changing its focal length. Every time our laughter began to slow down, one of us would gasp out something like, "*Long* day," or, "Do you *believe* this?" and we'd dissolve again, as though something terribly funny had been said.

Our convulsions set us caroming gently around the room, and eventually we collided glancingly and climbed up each other into a hug. We squeezed each other's laughter into submission.

"Thanks, love," Kirra said finally. "I needed that belly-buster."

"Me too!" We sort of did a pushup on each other: pushed apart until we held each other by the biceps at arms' length. "Whoever decided you and I would be compatible roommates was either very good at their job or very lucky. I couldn't have laughed like that alone, or with somebody like Glenn."

We kept hold of each other's upper arms in order to maintain eye contact, to match our personal verticals. But nothing is still in free fall unless anchored. To keep our lower bodies

from drifting, we had instinctively invented a way of bracing
our shins against each other with ankles interlocked. I became
aware of it now, and admired it. Could there *be* such a thing
as an instinctive response to zero gravity? Or was it just that
bodies are a lot more adaptable than brains?

"All right," Kirra said, "let's get down to it. Who are you,
Morgan? Why are *you* here?"

I was more amused than offended by her forthrightness.
"You sure don't beat around the bush, do you?"

"Hell, I was born in the bush."

I pinched her.

"But I'll go first if you want," she continued.

"No, that's okay," I said. " 'Why am I here?' is easy.
I'm . . . I was a dancer. I was pretty famous, but more
important I was pretty good, but most important I was married
to it, it's all I ever did, and I can't do it anymore. I don't mean
I can't get hired. I mean I can't dance anymore. Not on Earth,
anyway. Not for a long time now. I looked around and found
out there's nothing else on Earth I care about. And my
problems are lower back and knees, and zero gee is supposed
to be great for both."

"I can see that," Kirra agreed.

"It's more than just the reduced stress. It's the calcium loss.
There's this doctor thinks it will actually help."

Human bones lose calcium rapidly in zero gravity—one of
many reasons why people who stay in space too long are stuck
there for life. The bones become too frail to return to terrestrial
gravity. Many of my fellow Postulants would be taking
calcium supplements, just in case they decided to change their
minds and return to Earth. But it happened that overcalcifica-
tion was a factor in both my back trouble and my knee
problems.

"So space is a place where one out of three doctors says
maybe I could dance again. For one chance in three of dancing
again, I would skin myself with a can opener. If I have to put
up with great longevity and freedom from all human suffering
and telepathic union with a bunch of saints and geniuses to get
that chance . . . well, I can live with that, I guess." I
grinned. "That sounds weird, huh?"

"Not to me. Well, what do you think? Can you dance here?"

"Well . . . I won't know until I've had time alone to experiment. I won't really know until I wake up the next morning. And I won't be sure for at least a week or two. But it feels good, Kirra. I don't know, it really does. I think it's going to work, maybe. Oh shit, I'm excited!"

She squeezed my arms and showed me every one of those perfect teeth. "That's great, love. I'm glad for you. Good luck, eh?"

The trite words sounded real in her mouth. "Thanks, hon. Okay, your turn now. What brings you to Top Step?"

"Well . . . do you know anything about Aborigines, Morgan?" she asked. "The Dreamtime? The Songlines?"

I admitted I did not.

"This is gonna take awhile . . . you sure you want to hear it?"

"Of course."

"Back before the world got started was the Dreamtime, my people reckon. All the Ancestors dreamed themselves alive, then, created themselves out of clay, created themselves as people and all the kinds of animals and birds and insects there are. And the first thing they did was go walkabout, singin'— makin' the world by singin' it into existence. Sing up a river here, sing a mountain there. Wherever they went, they left a Songline behind 'em, and the Song made the world around there, see? So there's Songlines criss-crossin' the world, and everyplace is on or near a Songline, with a Song of its own that makes it what it is. That's why we go Walkabout—to follow the Songlines and sing the Songs and keep recreating the world so's it doesn't melt away. Get it?"

"I think so. All Aboriginals believe this?"

"Most of us that's left. Our Dreamings ain't like whitefella religions. Our Songs were maps, trade routes, alliances, history: they held the whole country together, kept hundreds of tribes and clans living together in peace for generations. Even the whitefella couldn't completely change that. Those of us they didn't kill outright had trouble keepin' our faith, but.

Some of us went to the towns, tried on European ideas. Railroads were cuttin' across Songlines. Our beliefs didn't seem to account for the world we saw anymore, so we had to change 'em a bit. But we never got the Dreamtime out of our bones and teeth. Tribes that did . . . well, they're gone, see?

"So the last few generations, a mob of us left the reserves, left the cities and towns. We've gone back to the bush, gone back to bein' nomads, followin' the Songlines. There's not many of us left, see. We want to touch where we came from before we go from the world.

"If we're gonna try to keep our beliefs alive, we got to make 'em account for the world we see. And space is part of that world now. We've got to weave it into our world-picture somehow. Some o' the old stories speak of Sky-Heroes, spirit Ancestors departed into the sky. If that's so, they left Songlines, and Aborigines can follow them to space. That's my job: to try and find the Songlines of the Sky-Heroes."

I was fascinated. The bravery, the audacity of trying to make an ancient pagan religion fit the modern world was breathtaking. "Why you?"

"It's my Dreaming." She saw that I did not understand, and tried again: "Like you with dancin'. It's what I was born for. My mob, the Yirlandji, we're reckoned the best singers. And I'm the best o' the lot." There was neither boasting nor false modesty in her voice.

"Sing me something."

"I can sing you a *tabi*," she said. "A personal song. But you'll have to back off: I gotta slap me legs."

We let each other go, and drifted about a decimeter apart. She closed her eyes in thought for perhaps ten seconds, filling her lungs the whole time. Then she brought her thighs up and slapped them in slow rhythm as she sang:

> Mutjingga, kale neki
> Mingara, wija narani moroko
> Bodalla, Kalyan ungu le win
> Naguguri mina Kurria
> Jinkana kandari pirndiri
> Yirlandji, turlu palbarregu

Her voice was indeed eerily beautiful. It had the rich tone of an old acoustic saxophone, but it was not at all like a jazz singer's voice. It had the precision and the perfect vibrato of a MIDI-controlled synthesizer, but it was natural as riversong, human as a baby's cry, a million years older than the bone flute. It was warm, and alive, and magical.

The song she sang was made of nine tones that repeated, but with each repetition they changed so much in interval and intonation and delivery as to seem completely different phrases. Considering that I didn't understand a word, I found it oddly, powerfully, astonishingly moving; whatever she was saying, it was coming directly from her heart to my ears. As I listened, I was radically reevaluating my new roommate. This cute little puppy I'd been mentally patronizing was someone special, deserving of respect. She was at least as good at her art as I had ever been at mine.

When her song was over I said nothing for ten seconds or more. Her eyes fluttered open and found mine, and still I was silent. There was no need to flatter her. She knew how good she was, and knew that I knew it now.

Then I was speaking quickly: "Teena! Did you hear Kirra's song just now? I mean, do you still have it in memory?"

"Yes, Morgan."

"Would you save it for me, please? And download it to my personal memory?"

"Name this file," Teena requested.

" 'Kirra, Opus One.' "

"Saved." And that's why I can give you the words now—though I can't vouch for the spelling.

"Do you mind, Kirra? If I keep a copy of that—just for myself?"

"Shit no, mate. I sang it you, di'n I?" She looked thoughtful. "Hoy, Teena, would you put a copy in *my* spare brain as well? Label it 'Bodalla,' and put it in a folder named 'Tabi.' "

"Done."

She returned her attention to me. "I was singin' about—"

I interrupted her softly. "—about saying goodbye to Earth, about coming to space, something about it being scary, but such a wonderful thing to do that you just have to do it. Yes?"

She just nodded. Maybe people always understood her when she sang. I wouldn't be surprised.

I've since asked Teena for a translation of "Bodalla." She offered three, a literal transposition and two colloquial versions. The one I like goes:

> All-Mother, creator of us all
> Great spirit who controls the clouds, now I have come to the sky
> Farewell to the place-where-the-child-is-flung-into-the-air
> I journey now to see the Crocodile who lives in the Milky Way
> So I can send back a rope ladder
> to the Yirlandji, and to all the tribes

"But that's just a tabi," Kirra said. "Just a personal song of my own, like. That's not why I got sent here. See, what I'm special good at is feelin' the Songlines. Been that way since I was a little girl. Whenever my mob'd move to a new place, I always knew the Song of it before anybody taught me. Yarra, the . . . well, a woman that taught me, this priestess, like . . . she used to blindfold me and drive me to strange country, some place I'd never been. And when I'd been there a while, sometimes an hour, sometimes overnight, I could sing her the Song of that place, and I always got it right. I got famous for it. Tribes that had forgotten parts of their own Songs, or had pieces cut out of 'em by whitefella doin's, would send for me to come help 'em. So when the Men and Women of Power figured out this job here needed doing, there never was any question whose job it was."

"And you don't mind?" I asked. It was sounding to me a little as though she'd been drafted, and was too patriotic to complain.

"Mind?" she said. "Morgan, most of us do pretty good if we can get through life without screwin' anybody else up too bad. How many get even a chance to do somethin' *important,* for a whole people? I wouldn't miss it for the world. Oh Christ, I made a pun. That's just what I'm doin': not missin' it for the world."

"Where in Australia are you from?"

"Not far from Suit Camp," she said.

"You're saying double goodbyes today, then," I said without thinking.

"How d'ya mean?"

I felt like kicking myself, but I had to explain now. "A few months ago I said goodbye to Vancouver—to my home—in my heart. All of us here left home before we came to Suit Camp. Today all we're leaving is Earth. You're leaving home and Earth at the same time."

Implausibly, her grin broadened. "You're not wrong." Somehow at this aperture, the grin made her look even younger, no more than twenty. "This's the first time I been out of Oz in me life, and it feels dead strange. Probably be just as strange to go to Canada, but. Oz, Earth, all one to me. Hey, what do you say we get out of these suits and see if our new clothes fit?"

Each of us had been issued several sets of jumpsuits, in assorted colors. It wasn't especially surprising that they fit perfectly: after all, they'd been cut from the same set of careful measurements used to make our formfitting p-suits. We also got gloves and booties and belts, all made of material that did not feel sticky to the touch, but was sticky when placed against wall-material. Traction providers. Teena explained that although social nudity was acceptable here, it was customary for Postulants, First-Monthers like us, to wear jumpsuits if they wore anything; second-month Novices usually lived in their p-suits, for as long as it took them to make up their minds to Symbiosis. We admired ourselves in the mirror for a while, then I slid into my sleepsack and began learning how to adjust it for comfort, while Kirra got Teena to display three-dimensional maps.

"Teena," I said while Kirra was distracted, "where is Robert Chen billeted?" Absurdly, I tried to pitch my voice too low for Kirra to hear, without making it obvious to Teena that I was doing so. I have no idea whether Teena caught it, or if so whether it conveyed any meaning to her. How subtle was her "understanding" of humans?

All I know is that Kirra didn't seem to hear her reply, "P7-29."

Just down the corridor! "Thanks."

"You're welcome."

Okay, it's dopey to thank an electric-eye for opening the door for you. I wasn't thinking clearly; I was too busy kicking myself for asking the question. And for being elated by the answer. What did I care where he slept? I was *not* going to get that involved.

Certainly not for days yet.

△   △   △

When Kirra and I got bored with exploring our new home, we discovered we were hungry. We headed for the cafeteria, following some of Teena's pixies. And found ourselves outside in the corridor, at the end of a long line of hungry people, most hanging on to hand-rails provided for the purpose. Standing On Line is not much enhanced by zero gravity. Your feet hurt less, but there are more annoying ways for your neighbors to fidget. The line, like all lines, did not appear to be moving.

Kirra nudged me. From up ahead, someone was waving to us. Robert.

"You think we should join him?" she asked.

I hesitated. "Maybe he's just saying hello."

"Up to you," she said, and waved back.

He waved again. It was definitely an invitation for us both to join him.

My blood sugar decided for me. I think.

Cutting ahead on line in zero gee without actually putting my foot in anyone's face was tricky. In fact, I didn't manage it. Kirra and I were both cordially hated by the time we reached Robert. He ignored it and made room for us. "Morgan McLeod, Kirra—I'd like you to meet my roommate, Ben Buckley, from Sherman Oaks, California."

Ben was one of the strangest looking—and strangest—men I'd ever met. A big boney redhead with a conversational style reminiscent of a happy machine gun, he wore a permanent smile and huge sunglasses with very peculiar lenses. They stuck out for several centimeters on either side of his face, and flared. The temple shafts of the glasses were wide, and had small knobs and microswitches along their length. When we asked, he told us he had designed and made them himself . . . and his motivation just floored me.

Their purpose was to bring him 360° vision.

"Ever since I was a kid I loved messing with perception," he told us, his words tumbling all over one another. "Distortions, gestalt-shifts, changing paradigms, I couldn't get enough. New ways of seeing, hearing, grokking. My folks were die-hard hippies, I caught it from them."

"Mine, too," I said, and he gave me an incandescent smile.

"Then you know those funny faceted yellow specs they used to have, gave you bee's eyes? Most people keep them on for about ten seconds; a really spaced-out doper might leave 'em on for the duration of an acid trip; but I used to wear 'em for days, 'til my parents got nervous. And my dad had this colour organ, turned music into light patterns, and I spent time with that sucker until I could not only name the tune with the speakers disconnected, I could harmonize, and enjoy it." I'm putting periods at the ends of his sentences so you can follow them, but he never really paused longer than a comma's worth. "Learning to read spinning record labels, eyeglasses with inverting lenses, I loved all that stuff. When I was fourteen, I built a pair of headphones that played ambient sound to me backwards, a word at a time, so fast that once I learned to understand it the lip-synch lag was just barely noticeable. That's the kind of stuff that's fun to me. Then one day a year ago I thought, hey, what do I need a blind side for? so I built these glasses." Robert was looking very interested. "They're dual mode. I can get about 300° on straight optical—glasses like that were available back in the Nineties, although they didn't sell well—or I can kick on the fiber-optics in the earpieces and get full surround. I like to switch back and forth for fun. I like to put the front hemisphere into one eye, and the back half into the other—and switch *them* back and forth—but I can get something like full stereo parallax in both eyes at once with a heads-up-display like fighter pilots use."

Kirra managed to get in a word in edgewise. "Could I look through 'em, Ben?"

He smiled. "Sure. But if you're a normal person, it'd take

you about three months to learn to interpret the data. It'd look like a funhouse mirror."

"Oh. Turn round, okay?"

"Sure," he said again, and did so.

"Now: what am I doing?"

"Being somewhat rude," he reported accurately. "And that fingernail needs trimming."

Robert looked thoughtful . . . and tossed a pen at Ben's back. Ben reached around behind himself and caught it . . . then tumbled awkwardly from the effect of moving his arm. "See what I mean?" he said, stabilizing himself. "It has survival advantage: you can't sneak up on me. But I just enjoy it, you know?"

Kirra was getting excited. "I'll bet you're the only one in the class that really likes this zero-gee stuff, aren't you? It's what you enjoy best: bein' confused. Gosh, that must be a great thing to enjoy!"

He stared. "I like you," he said suddenly.

"Sure," she said.

They smiled at each other.

"Kirra's right," Robert said. "This 'thinking spherically' business that the rest of us are having so much trouble with must be the kind of thing you've been dreaming of all your life. Why did it take you so long to come to space?"

"I think I know," Kirra said.

Ben looked at her expectantly.

"You didn't want to use it up too quick," she said.

He smiled and nodded. "I held off as long as I could stand it," he agreed. His smile broadened. "God, it's great, too. Do you *believe* they gave us unlimited Net access?"

It was not sparks flying, not a mutual sexual awareness. It was a new friendship taking root. It was nice to watch. Yet as I watched them I felt vaguely melancholy. I wished I had a friend of the opposite sex. Robert and I might just be friends some day . . . but if so I could tell we were going to have to go through being lovers first, and I just didn't know if I had the energy.

A lover of mine used to have a quote on his bedroom wall,

from some old novel: *It's amazing how much mature wisdom resembles being too tired.*

My melancholy lasted right up until Kirra said, "Hey, the bloody queue's movin'!" Starving dancers are too busy for melancholy . . . the only reason their suicide rate isn't higher than it already is.

The cafeteria took some getting used to. But there was plenty of assistance; without any apparent formal structure to it, Second-Monthers (identifiable because they wore p-suits rather than our First-Monther's jumpsuits, but lacked the Spacer's Earring of EVA-qualified Third-Monthers) seemed to take it on themselves to be helpful to newcomers. They were extraordinarily patient about it, I thought. We must have been more nuisance than a flock of flying puppies. Maybe we were vastly entertaining.

Tables lined with docking rails jutted out from five of the six walls. The inner sides of the rails were lined with Velcro, like our belts, so you could back yourself up to one and be held in reasonable proximity to your food; there was a thin footrail on which to brace your feet—both "above" and "below" the table. *Both* sides of the tables were used. It provided an odd and interesting solution to the problem of sharing a table with strangers: you adopted the opposite veritcal to theirs, and your conversations never clashed. On the other hand, especially clumsy footwork in docking at table could kick your neighbor's dinner clear across the room. And you came to really appreciate the fact that in free fall, feet don't smell.

Eventually we got down to the real business of a meal: talking.

You hesitate to ask a new chum, so why did you come to Top Step? The answer may be that they're running away from some defeat on Earth. You're especially hesitant if you're there because you're running from some defeat on Earth yourself.

I didn't exactly question Robert over dinner, and he didn't exactly volunteer autobiography, but information transfer occurred by some mysterious kind of osmosis. In between the distractions of learning to eat in zero gravity, I learned that he had a fifteen-year-old son, who lived with his mother; she and Robert had divorced eight years before. I also found out how he had acquired his "spacer's legs." He was an architect; apparently he had already established himself as a successful traditional architect in San Francisco . . . when suddenly the new field of space architecture had opened up. The technical challenge had excited him; he had followed the challenge into orbit, found he had the knack for it, and prospered.

I'm not sure whether this next part is something he implied or I inferred, but the progression seemed logical. He found that he liked space—the more time he spent there, the more he liked it. In time he came to resent being forced to return to Earth regularly just to keep his body acclimated to gravity. The obvious question *Why not just stay in space, like a Stardancer?* had led naturally to *Why not* become *a Stardancer?* At this point in the history of human enterprise in space, a free-lance spacer's life is usually one of total insecurity . . . and a Stardancer's life is one of great and lasting security. And so, wanting to stay in space without having to scramble every moment to buy air, Robert found himself here in Top Step.

It seemed a rather shallow reason to come all this way. To abandon a whole planet and the whole human race, just to save on overhead while he pursued his art . . .

On the other hand, who was I to judge? He wasn't fleeing defeat, like me. Maybe architecture was as exciting an art as dance; maybe for him it was making elements dance. Maybe space was just an environment he liked.

Maybe there were no shallow reasons to become a Stardancer.

Maybe it didn't matter what your reasons were.

As all this was going through my mind, Robert went on: "But there's a little more to it than that. Another part of it is that when I started spending time in space, I found myself watching Earth a lot, thinking about what a mess it's in, how close it is to blowing itself up. I read somewhere once, Earth is just too fragile a basket for the human race to keep all its eggs in. We've got to get more established in space, soon.

"I know you can say Stardancers aren't part of the human race anymore, but I don't buy that. They all came from human eggs and sperm, and they've done more for Earth than the rest of the race put together. They fixed the holes in the ozone layer, they put the brakes on the greenhouse effect, they built the mirror farms and set up the Asteroid Pipeline, they made the Safe Lab so we can experiment with nanotechnology without being afraid the wrong little replicator will get loose and turn the world into grey goo—they can afford to be altruistic, because they don't *need* anything but each other. I think without the Starseed Foundation, there'd have been an all-out nuclear war years ago.

"So I guess I decided it was time I put some back in. From all I can learn, there aren't many architects in the Starmind, so I think I can be of help. I want to design and build things a little more useful to mankind than another damn factory or dormitory or luxury hotel."

"And the eternal life without want part doesn't hurt, does it?" Ben said, grinning, and Robert smiled back. It was the first real smile of his I'd seen. I tend to trust people or not trust them on the basis of their smiles; I decided I trusted Robert.

But I wished he'd smile more often.

CHAPTER FOUR

How is it possible that mystics 3,000 years ago have
plagiarized what we scientists are doing today?

—Karl Pribram

I COULD WRITE a whole chapter about my first free fall cafeteria
meal, my first free fall sleep, my first free fall pee . . . but
you can get that sort of thing from any traveler's account. The
next event of significance, the morning after our arrival at Top
Step, was my first class with Reb Hawkins-roshi.

The course was titled "Beginner's Mind"—a clue to me that
I would like it, since my mother's battered old copy of
Shunryu Suzuki-roshi's ZEN MIND, BEGINNER'S MIND
had been my own introduction to Buddhism. There are as
many different flavors of Buddhism—even just of Zen!—as
there are flavors of Christianity, and some of them give me
hives . . . but if this Hawkins's path was even tangent to
Suzuki's, I felt confident I could walk it without too much
discomfort.

You couldn't really have called me a Buddhist. I had no
teacher, didn't even really sit zazen on any regular basis. I'd
never so much as been on a retreat, let alone done a five-day
sesshin. My mother taught me how to sit, and a little of the
philosophy behind it, was all. By that point in my life I mostly
used Zen as a sort of nonprescription tranquilizer.

Robert, on the other hand, approached it with skepticism.
He was not, I'd learned the night before, a Buddhist—it's
silly, I know, but for some reason I keep expecting every
Asian I meet to be a Buddhist—but he had mentioned in
passing that if he *were* going to be one, he'd follow the Rinzai
school of Zen. (A rather harsh and overintellectual bunch, for
my taste.) Pretty personal conversation for two strangers, I
know; somehow we hadn't gotten around to less intimate

64

things, like how we liked to have sex. Nonetheless, I was proud of myself: I hadn't physically touched him even once.

Well, okay: once. But I *hadn't* kissed him goodnight before returning to my place! (Kirra kissed Ben . . .)

And I didn't look for him in the cafeteria crowd during breakfast—and didn't kiss him good morning when we met accidentally in the corridor on the way to class. I was too irritated: I'd had to stall around for over three minutes to bring about that accidental encounter, and I was mildly annoyed that he hadn't looked me up during breakfast. God, lust makes you infantile!

But he was adequately pleased to encounter me, so I let him take my arm and show me a couple of jaunting tricks I'd already figured out on the way to breakfast—with the net result that we were nearly late for class, and I arrived in exactly the wrong frame of mind: distracted. So a nice thing happened.

As the door of the classroom silently irised shut behind us, my pulse began to race. What could be more disorienting than being inside your headful of racing thoughts, toying with the tingles of distant horniness—and suddenly finding yourself face to face with a holy man?

He was in his fifties, shaven-headed and clean-shaven, slender and quite handsome, and utterly centered and composed. He was not dressed as a Zen abbot, he wore white shorts and singlet, but his face, body language and manner all quietly proclaimed his office. I think I experienced every nuance of embarrassment there is.

He met my eyes, and his face glowed briefly with the infectious Suzuki-roshi grin that told me he was a saint, and he murmured the single word, "Later," in a way that told me I was forgiven for being late and I had not given offense and we were going to be good friends as soon as we both had time; meanwhile, lighten up.

All of this in an instant; then his eyes swept past me to Robert, they exchanged an equally information-packed glance which I could not read, and he returned his attention to the group as a whole.

If I hadn't arrived for class in an inappropriate mental state, it might have taken me minutes to realize how special Reb was.

Most of the spiritual teachers I've known had a tendency to sit silently for a minute or two after the arrival of the last pupils, as if to convey the impression that their meditation was so profound it took them a moment to shift gears. But Reb was a genuinely mindful man: he was aware Robert and I were the last ones coming, and the moment we had ourselves securely anchored to one of the ubiquitous bungee cords, he bowed to the group—somehow without disturbing his position in space—and began to speak.

"Hello," he said in a husky baritone. "My name is Reb Hawkins, and I'll be your student for the next eight to twelve weeks."

Inevitably someone spoke up, a New Yorker by her accent. "'Student'? I thought you were supposed to be the teacher."

"I am supposed, by many, to be a teacher," he agreed pleasantly. "Sometimes they are correct. But I am *always* a student."

"Aaah," said the New Yorker, in the tones of one who has spotted the hook in a commercial.

Reb didn't seem to notice. "I *am* going to try to teach all of you . . . specifically, how to enter Titanian Symbiosis without suffering unnecessary pain. Along the way, I will teach you any other lessons I can that you request of me, and from time to time I will offer to teach you other things I think you need to know . . . but in this latter category you are always privileged to overrule me."

"If that's true," the New Yorker said, "I'm actually impressed."

I was becoming irritated with the heckling—but Reb was not. "In free fall," he said, "raising one's hand for attention does not work well. Would you help me select some other gesture we all can use, Jo?"

Jo, the New Yorker, was so surprised by the question that she thought about it. "How 'bout this?"

Is there a proper name for the four-fingered vee she made? My parents were Star Trek fans, so I think of it as the Spock Hello.

He smiled. "Excellent! Unambiguous . . . and just difficult enough to perform that one has a moment to reconsider
how necessary it really is to pre-empt the group's attention.
Thank you, Jo." He demonstrated it for those who could not
see Jo. "Is there anyone who can't make this gesture?"

Several of us found it awkward, but no one found it
impossible. I was less interested in my manual dexterity than
in his social dexterity. Hecklers heckle because they need
everyone in the room to know how clever they are. He had
given her a chance to make that point, reproved her so gently
that she probably never noticed, and I knew he would have no
further trouble from her that day. By persuading her not to be
his enemy, he had defeated her. I smiled . . . and saw him
notice me doing so. He did not smile back—but I seemed to
see an impish twinkle for a moment in his eye.

I like spiritual teachers with an impish twinkle. In fact, I
don't think I like any other kind.

"If any of you happen to be Buddhist, I am an Abbot in the
Soto sect. I trace my dharma lineage through Shunryu Suzuki,
and will be happy to do *dokusan* with any who wish it in the
evenings, after dinner."

I don't know how to convey the significance of Reb's
dharma lineage to a non–Soto-Buddhist. Perhaps the rough
equivalent might be a Christian monk who had been ordained
by one of the Twelve Apostles. Shunryu Suzuki-roshi was one
of the greatest Japanese Zen masters to come to America, way
back in the middle of the twentieth century—founder of the
San Francisco Zen Center and the famous Tassajara monastery
near Carmel.

"But this is not a class in Zen," he went on, "and you need
not have any interest in Buddha or his eightfold Path. What
we're going to attempt to do in this class is to discuss
spirituality without mentioning religion. The former can often
be discussed by reasonable people without anger; the latter
almost never can."

Glenn made the Spock Hello; he returned it, to mean she
had the floor. "What *is* 'spirituality without religion,' sir?"

"Please call me 'Reb,' Glenn. It is the thing people had,
before they invented religion, which caused them to gape at

sunsets, to sing while alone, or to smile at other people's babies. And other things which defy rational explanation, but are basic to humanity."

"I'm not sure what you mean," she said.

"By happy coincidence, practically the next thing in the syllabus is an example of what I mean," he said. "We're going to take a short field trip in just a few minutes, to see something which has nothing to do with religion, yet is profoundly spiritual. Can you wait, Glenn?"

"Of course, Reb."

"Good. Now: one of the main things we need to do is to begin dismantling the *patterns* in which you think. Some of you may think that you've never given much thought to spirituality—but in fact you've thought too much about it, in patterns and terms that were only locally useful. Space adds dimensions unavailable to any terrestrial. It's time you started getting used to the fact that you live in space now. So I'd like you all to unship all those bungee cords, and pass them to me."

I began to see what he was driving at. The cords, to which we were all loosely clinging, imposed a strictly arbitrary local vertical, the same one Reb had been using since I'd entered. But as we followed his instruction, "up" and "down" went away . . . and he began (without any visible muscular effort) to tumble slowly and gracefully in space. His face was always toward us, but seldom "upright," and as some of us unconsciously tried to match his spin—and failed—there was suddenly no consensus as to which way was up. We had to stop trying to decide. Soon we were all every which way, save that we all at least tried to face Reb. I found it oddly unsettling to pay attention to someone who was spinning like a Ferris wheel—which was his point.

I noticed something else. He had positioned himself roughly at the center of the wall behind him—and the majority of us, myself included, had unconsciously oriented ourselves, not only "vertical" with respect to him . . . but "below" him as well. He was the teacher, so most of us wanted to "look up to him." Several of the exceptions looked like people who'd pointedly if subconsciously fought that impulse. (Robert was

one of them.) Now the "upper" portion of the room was starting
to fill up, as we redistributed ourselves more . . . well, more
equally. Which again, I guess, was his point.

"That's more like it," he said approvingly as he stowed the
bungee cords in a locker. "When you've been in free fall a
while longer, you'll find the sight of a roomful of people
aligned like magnets amusing—because in this environment it
is."

An uneasy chuckle passed around the room.

"It's possible," he went on, continuing to rotate, "for a
normal terrestrial to enter Symbiosis without permanent psychic damage; it has happened. But *any* spacer will find it
enormously easier. Now for that field trip."

He reached behind himself without looking, caught the
hatch handle on the first try, pivoted on it while activating it,
and lobbed himself out of the room. His other hand beckoned
us to follow.

We left the room smoothly and graciously, with no jostling
for position or unnecessary speech. This man was having an
effect on us.

We proceeded as a group down winding, roughly contoured
corridors of Top Step. The image that came to my mind,
unbidden, was of a horde of corpuscles swimming single file
through some sinuous blood vessel. Whoever it belonged to
needed to cut down on her cholesterol.

I glanced back past my feet, saw that Robert had managed
to take up position immediately behind me. He smiled at me.
My mental image of our group changed, from corpuscles to
spermatazoa. I looked firmly forward again and tried to keep
my attention on spirituality—and on not jaunting my skull into
the foot of Kirra in front of me.

In a few minutes we had reached our destination. To enter,
we had to go through an airlock, big enough for ten people at
once—but it was open at both ends: there was pressure beyond
it. I wondered what the airlock was for, then. As I passed
through it, I heard a succession of gasps from those exiting
before me; despite this foreknowledge, as I cleared the inner
hatch, I gasped too. It was not the largest cubic in Top
Step—not even the largest I'd seen so far; you could have fit

maybe three of it in that big cavern where I'd met Teena the talking computer—but its largest wall was transparent, and on the other side of it was infinity.

We were at Top Step's very skin, gazing at naked space, at vacuum and stars. At the place where all of us hoped to live, one day soon . . .

From this close up, it did not look like terribly attractive real estate. Completely unfurnished. Drafty. No amenities. Ambiguous property lines, unclear title. *Big.* Scary . . .

How weird, that I was getting my first naked-eye view of space after more than twenty-four hours in space. Those stars were bright, sharp, merciless, horribly far away. It was hard to get my breath.

I wished Earth were in frame; it would have been less scary. This cubic seemed to be on the far side of Top Step. I wondered if there were a similar cubic on the other side, for folks who liked to look at the Old Home. Or did all of Top Step turn its collective back to Terra?

The last of us entered the room behind me and found a space to float in. We all gaped at the huge window together in silence.

Something drifted slowly into view, about ten meters beyond the window. A sculpture of a man, made of cherry Jell-O, waving a baton . . .

A Stardancer!

A real, live, breathing Stardancer. (No, unbreathing, of course . . . Stardancers must have some internal process analogous to breathing, but they do not need to work their lungs.) A *Homo caelestis,* a former human being in Titanian Symbiosis: covered, within and without, by the Symbiote, the crimson life-form that grows in the atmosphere of Saturn's moon Titan and is the perfect complement to the human metabolism. A native inhabitant of interplanetary space.

Except for the four-centimeter-thick coating of red Symbiote, he was naked. He would never need clothes again. Or, for that matter, air or food or water or a bathroom or shelter. Just sunshine and occasional trace elements. He was at home in space.

Of *course* we'd seen Stardancers before; we'd all come

here to *become* Stardancers. We'd seen them hundreds of times . . . on film, on video, on holo. But none of us had ever actually been this close to one before. Stardancer and Symbiote mate for life, and the Symbiote cannot survive normal terrestrial atmosphere, pressure, moisture or gravity. Stardancers sometimes lived on Luna for short periods, and it was said that one had once survived on Mars for a matter of days . . . but no Stardancer would ever walk the Earth.

The Symbiote obscured details like eyes and expression, but it was clear that, back when he'd been a human being, he'd been a big, powerful man, heavily muscled . . . and very well hung, I couldn't help but notice. He was cartwheeling in slow motion as he came into view, but when he reached the center of the vast window, he made a brief, complex gesture with his magic wand and came to a halt relative to us. From my perspective he was upside down; I tried to ignore it.

With a small thrill, I recognized him, even under all that red Jell-O. I'd seen his picture often enough, his and all the other members of The Six. He was Harry Stein!

The Harry Stein—designer/engineer of the first free fall dance studio—less than five meters away from me. Others began to recognize him too: a susurrant murmur of, "Stein-HarrySteinthat'sHarryStein," went round the room.

Reb spoke at normal volume, startling us all. "Hello, Harry."

What happened then startled me even more. I suppose I should have been expecting it: I knew that Teena could project audio directly to my ear, like an invisible earphone—and a voice on *two* earphones sounds like it's coming from inside your head. Nonetheless I twitched involuntarily when Harry Stein's voice said, "Hi, Reb. Hi, everybody. My name is Harry," right in my skull.

What made it even stranger was that I happened to have been looking at his face when he spoke, and even under that faintly shimmering symbiote I was sure his lips had not moved. His suit radio was linked directly to the speech-center of his brain: the speech impulses were intercepted on their way to his useless vocal cords and sent directly. I'd studied all this in Space Camp, but it was something else again to experience it directly.

"Hi, Harry," several voices chorused raggedly.

"Can't stay long," he said. "Got a big job in progress over to spinward. Just wanted to say hi. And so did I." With that last sentence, there was an odd, inexpressible change in his voice. Not in pitch or tone or timbre—it was still Harry Stein's voice—but it was not him speaking it. "Hello, everybody, this is Charlie Armstead speaking now." Armstead himself! "I'm sorry I can't be there to meet you all personally—as a matter of fact, I'm a few light-hours away as you hear this—but Harry's letting me use his brain to greet you. I *will* be meeting you all when you graduate, of course—but so will the rest of the gang, all of us at once, and I couldn't resist jumping the gun. Neither could I— Hi, everyone, Norrey Drummond, here." Jesus! "I'm out here with Charlie. I guess you're all a little confused right about now . . . but don't let it worry you, okay? Just take your time and listen to what Reb tells you, and everything will be fine. Now I'll hand you over to Raoul Brindle for a minute. Oh, before I go, I want to say a quick hello to Morgan McLeod—"

I gulped and must have turned almost as red as Harry Stein.

"—I've been a fan of yours for years. I loved your work with Monnaie Dance Group in Brussels, especially your solo in the premiere of Morris's *Dance for Changing Parts*. I hope we can work together some day."

"Thank you," I said automatically—but my voice came out a squeak. People were staring. Robert, Kirra and Ben were smiling.

"Here's Raoul, now. Howdy, gang! I'm on my way home from Titan with the Harvest Crew, riding herd on about a zillion tonnes of fresh Symbiote—but I wanted to pass on a personal greeting of my own, to Jacques LeClaire and to Kirra from Queensland; hi, guys! I hope you'll both make some music for me one day; I've heard tapes of your work, and I'd love to jam with both of you when I get back. Or maybe you'll graduate before then and come meet me halfway. I'll hand you back to Harry now. So long . . ."

I don't think an Aboriginal can blush: Kirra must have been

expressing her own embarrassment with body language. Fluently. And it was easy to pick out Jacques LeClaire in the crowd, too.

"Well, like I said," Harry went on, sounding like himself now—and don't ask me to explain that. "Work to do. Deadline's coming. I hope you'll all be in my family soon. See you later." He waved his thruster-baton negligently, and began drifting out of our field of view.

Not a word was spoken until he was gone. Then someone tried for irony. "What, Shara Drummond was too busy to say hello?" Some of us giggled.

"Yes," Harry's voice said, and the giggle trailed off. "Oh," the joker said, chastened.

There was another long silence. Then Kirra said softly, "Spirituality without religion—"

There was a subdued murmur of agreement.

"Lemme see if I've got this straight, Reb," she said. "If I needed to talk to one of that mob—"

"Just call them on the phone, like you would anyone else in space," Reb agreed. "If you really need an *instantaneous* response, you can ask for a telepathic relay through some other Stardancer whose brain happens to be near Top Step—but bear in mind that you will almost certainly be distracting their attention from something else. Don't do so frivolously. But if you don't mind waiting for both ends of the conversation to crawl at lightspeed, by radio, you can chat any time with any Stardancer who'll answer, anytime. Yes, Kirra?"

"What was that Raoul said about a harvest crew?"

"When Armstead and The Six originally came back from Titan after entering Symbiosis, they brought an enormous quantity of the Symbiote back with them, using the *Siegfried* to tow it. But that was about thirty years ago, and Top Step has graduated a lot of Stardancers since then. It's becoming necessary to restock . . . so an expedition was sent out three or four years ago to mine more from Titan's upper atmosphere. They're on their way back right now, with gigatonnes of fresh Symbiote. Some of you in this class will be partaking of it. Yes, Jo?"

Jo was using her Teacher-May-I gesture, I noticed. "Is there, like, a directory of their phone numbers, or what?"

"You just say, 'Teena, phone . . .' and the name of the Stardancer you want, just like calling anyone else in Top Step. If there are no Stardancers nearby with attention to spare to relay for you, she'll tell you, and ask if you want her to contact your party directly, by radio. Glenn, what's bothering you?"

Glenn did have a frown. "This business of telepathy being instantaneous. It just doesn't seem natural."

"Where you come from, it is not especially natural, occurs rarely and often requires decades of training and practice. Where you are going, it is far more natural than that discarded old habit, breathing."

"But everything else in the universe is limited to lightspeed. Why should telepathy be different?"

"Why should you ask that question?" Reb asked.

Glenn fell silent . . . but her frown deepened.

A thin professorial-looking man gestured for attention. "Yes, Vijay?" Reb said.

"I think I understand Glenn's dilemma. To be confronted with empirical proof that there is more to reality than the physical universe . . . how is one supposed to deal with that? It's—"

"—terrifying, yes. There might be a God lurking around out there, armed with thunderbolts, demanding insane proofs of love, inventing Purgatories and Hells. There are techniques for helping with that fear. You were taught some back at Suit Camp. Sitting correctly. Breathing correctly. I'll teach others to you, and they'll help a lot. But the only way to really beat that fear—or the other, perfectly reasonable fear many of you have, that you'll lose your ego when you join the Starmind—is to keep on confronting it. If you retreat from it, suppress it, try to put it out of your mind, you make it harder for yourself." He was looking at Glenn as he said that sentence, and she slowly nodded. Reb smiled. "All right, now we're going to learn the first technique of Kûkan Zen. Namely, how to sit zazen . . . in zero gee."

"I thought you said, 'without religion,'" Glenn complained.

He looked surprised. "But Zen isn't a religion—not in the usual sense, at least."

"It isn't? I thought it was a sect of Buddhism. Buddhism's a religion. It's got monks and temples and doctrines and all of that."

Reb nodded. "But it has no dogmas, no articles of faith, no God. It has nothing to do with telling other people how they ought to behave. There has never been a Buddhist holy war . . . except intellectual war between differing schools of thought. You can be a Catholic Buddhist, a Muslim Buddhist, an atheist Buddhist. So although it may be religious, in the sense that it's about what's deepest in us, it's not *a* religion."

"What is it, then?"

"It is simply an agreement to sit, and look into our actual nature."

The very first chapter of Suzuki-roshi's ZEN MIND, BEGINNER'S MIND concerns correct sitting posture: that should be a clue to how important he considered it.

On Earth the classic full lotus position is something a Soto Zen Buddhist may take or leave alone, as his joints and ligaments allow. But in Kûkan Zen (I learned later that Reb coined the term: *kûkan* is Japanese for "space"), the lotus posture becomes both more important and less difficult. It is fundamental in "sitting" kûkanzen, the space equivalent of sitting zazen.

In the absence of weight, if you *don't* tuck your feet securely under the opposite knees, any "sitting" posture you assume will require considerable muscular effort, impossible to maintain for any length of time. When you relax, you end up in the Free Fall Crouch, the body's natural rest position, halfway between sitting and standing.

What's wrong with that? you may ask. Well, the idea is that Sitting, in the Zen sense, is something you do with full and powerful awareness. It requires some effort to do properly. Sitting zazen on Earth is not like sitting in a chair or standing or lying down or squatting or anything else humans do as a matter of course. It is a special posture you assume for the purpose of meditation, and after enough self-conditioning, just assuming that posture will make you begin to enter a meditative state.

And terrestrial zazen posture involves total relaxation *in the midst of total attention.* If relaxation alone were the goal, you would meditate lying down. The attempt to maintain a specific, defined posture (spine straight, chin down, hands just so) involves just enough effort and attention to make you see that you are, in a way, accomplishing something although you're merely sitting. It's one of those paradoxes—like using your mind to become so mindful you can achieve no-thought—that lie at the heart of Zen.

Reb felt it necessary to maintain that paradox, even in an environment where it's more difficult to maintain anything but Free Fall Crouch. Full lotus position is stressful for most beginners, in gravity—but it becomes quite tolerable in zero gee. Even for someone a lot less limber than I am: over the next few days I saw senior citizens who hadn't touched their toes in decades spend time in lotus. The worst part is getting unfolded again.

Similarly, Reb was forced to modify hand arrangement. Suzuki's "cosmic mudra"—left hand on top of right, middle joints of middle fingers aligned, thumbtips touching—tends to come apart without gravity's help. Reb interlaced the fingers to compensate.

And of course the *zafu* (round pillow), and the slanted wooden meditation bench used by other Eastern religions, are useless in space. In their place Kûkan Zen uses one of the most ubiquitous items of space hardware, as humble and common-place as a pillow on Earth: the Velcro belt.

If you simply drift freely while meditating, you will naturally drift in the direction of airflow, and sooner or later end up bumping against the air-outgo grille. Distracting. But if you temporarily shut down the room's airflow to maintain your position, in a short time your exhalations will generate a sphere of carbon dioxide around your head and suppress your breathing reflex. Even more distracting.

So you leave the airflow running . . . and stick the back of your Velcro belt to the nearest convenient wall. People can tell you're meditating, rather than just hanging around, because your legs are tucked up in lotus and your hands are clasped.

When two or more people are sitting kûkanzen together, it's customary to all use the same wall, all face the same way, for the same reason that on Earth Suzuki's disciples sit facing the wall rather than the group. Humans are so gregarious it's hard for them to be in each other's visual field without paying attention to each other.

That's Kûkan Zen. Simple elegance, elegant simplicity.

The *second* chapter of Suzuki's book deals with breathing. We didn't get to that until the following day. Hawkins-roshi would put special emphasis on breathing (even for a Zen teacher), since once we graduated, we wouldn't be doing it anymore. . . .

At the close of our first lesson in Kûkan Zen 101, Reb said, "One thing before I let you all go. Does everyone understand why I brought you *here* to meet Harry Stein?"

Perhaps we did, but no one spoke.

"One of the reasons I brought you to this Solarium, when I could just as easily have had video piped into the classroom, is that here in this room you were as close to Harry as you could possibly get—you'd be little closer EVA, since a p-suit is a layer too—*and it made a difference.* You've all seen high-quality video and holo of Stardancers, dozens of hours of it in Suit Camp alone . . . but God, that was *the* Harry Stein himself, one of the original Six, right *there,* inches away, and it made a difference, didn't it?" There were nods and murmurs of agreement. Everyone in the room knew it made a difference. "Just what that difference *was* is one of those things— like the phenomenon of 'contact high'—that defy explanation unless you admit the existence of the thing I've labeled 'spirituality.' And your personal religion, whatever it may be, had nothing to do with it, did it?"

We left in a very quiet, thoughtful mood.

There was a food fight at lunch. A zero-gee food fight is amazing. Almost everybody misses, because they can't help aiming too high. Robert, having "space legs," did well—but his roommate Ben did almost as well, despite his klutziness. You couldn't sneak up on him. . . .

Glenn, I noticed, was infuriated at both the food fight, and how badly she lost. I could tell, just from her expression, that she believed handling oneself in free fall was something best conquered by intellect—and therefore, she ought to be one of the best at it. I'd seen the expression before, on the faces of beginner dance students who are also intellectuals. They see people they consider their inferiors picking up the essentials of movement quicker than they can, and it forces them to admit there are kinds of intelligence that do not live in the forebrain.

I didn't do very well in the food fight myself. I found that just as infuriating as Glenn did. But I covered it better.

Glenn's and my problem was addressed almost immediately. The schedule called for spending our afternoons in Jaunting class, learning how to move in zero gee.

Our instructor was Sulke Drager, a powerfully built woman whose primary job, I later learned, was rock-rat: one of the hardboiled types who blasted new tunnels and cubics into Top Step when needed. In between, she worked in the Garden and taught Jaunting, and worked two more jobs in other space habitats. She was not here for Symbiosis, like us: she was a spacer. A permanent transient, citizen of the biggest small town in human history. I think she privately thought we were all crazy.

I thought *she* was crazy. She had chosen a life with all the disadvantages of a Stardancer, and none of the advantages, it seemed to me. She could never go back to Earth; her body was long since permanently adapted to free fall. But she was not a telepathic immortal as we hoped to be. Just a human a long way from home, hustling for air money, hoping to bank enough to buy her retirement air. Talk about wage slaves! Sulke was as dependent as a goldfish.

Most of us were disappointed when she confirmed that it would be a good month before we got any EVA time. For about the first fifteen minutes, we were disappointed. That's how long it took us to convince ourselves that we weren't ready to go outdoors yet, Suit Camp or no Suit Camp. Theory is not practice.

(One thing I had never anticipated, for instance, in all the hours I'd spent trying to imagine movement in this environment: sweat that trickled *up*. Or refused to trickle at all, and just sort of pooled up in the small of your back until you flung or toweled it off. What a *weird* sensation!)

We were given wrist and ankle thruster-bracelets, but Sulke only allowed us to use them to correct mistakes: the first step was to learn to be as proficient as possible without external aids.

As I had been during the food fight—hell, since I'd arrived in space—I was dismayed to learn how clumsy I was in this environment. Like Glenn, I had assumed I had a secret weapon that would allow me to outstrip all the others. Instead, it seemed I had more to *unlearn* than most: inappropriate habits of movement were more deeply ingrained in me.

This infuriated me. So much that I probably worked twice as hard as anyone else in the class, using all the discipline and concentration I'd learned in thirty years of professional dance.

"No, no McLeod," Sulke said. "Stop trying to swim in air, you look like a drunken octopus." She jaunted to me and stopped my tumble, without putting herself into one. "Use your spine, not your limbs!"

It was a particularly galling admonition: in transitioning from ballet to modern dance, I had spent countless hours learning to use my spine. In one gee. "I thought I *was*." Someone giggled.

"Watch Chen, there, see how he does it? Chen, pitch forward half a rev, and yaw half." Robert performed the maneuver requested: in effect he stood on his head, spinning on his long axis so he was still facing her when he was done. His legs barely flexed, and his arms left his sides only at the end of the maneuver. "See what he did with his spine?"

"Yes, but I didn't understand it," I admitted.

"Put your hands on him, here, and here." She indicated her abdomen and the small of her back.

I refused myself permission to blush. I used my thrusters to jaunt to him, and was relieved to do a near-perfect job, canceling all my velocity just as I reached him, without tumbling myself again. He was upside down with reference to me; I couldn't read his expression. I put my hands where I'd been told.

"Keep a light contact as he begins, then pull your hands away," Sulke directed. "Reverse the maneuver, Chen."

So I didn't get my hands quite far enough out of the way, quite fast enough. As he spun backwards, his groin brushed down across the palm I'd had on his belly. Now I was blushing. When he finished—a little awkwardly this time—he wore that inscrutable-Asian face of his. But he was blushing a little too. The giggles from the rest of the class didn't help. "You're jumping ahead," Sulke called. "We don't get to mating for days, yet."

In free fall maneuvering, mating simply means interacting with another body. We'd all heard dozens of puns on the terms before we'd left Suit Camp, but this feeble one put the class in stitches. I thought wistfully about putting a few of them in traction. Then I did a quarter-yaw, to face Sulke, and copied Robert's maneuver, very nearly perfectly. The giggling became applause.

"Much better," Sulke said. "It must be a question of motivation. Buckley, you try it."

Robert and I exchanged a meaningful glance . . . and as I was trying to decide just what meaning to put into my half, something cracked me across the skull. It was one of Ben's elbows. Without cafeteria tables to hold on to and brace myself against, his enhanced visual perception was little help to him: he would be one of the klutziest in our class—that day, anyway. "Sorry, Morgan!"

I welcomed the distraction. "Forget it."

"Uh . . . could I . . . I mean, would you mind . . . ?"

For the next five or ten minutes, an orgy of belly-and-back-touching spread outwards from Robert and me, until everyone had mastered the forward half-pitch. (At least one other male was as careless with his hands as I had been with Robert. I pretended not to notice.) Then Sulke turned our collective attention to the roll and yaw techniques, which took up the rest of the class period.

After class there were a couple of free hours before dinner. I had Teena guide me back to Solarium One, where we'd seen Harry Stein—where Norrey Drummond had addressed me by name!—and sat kûkanzen for a timeless time, seeking some clarity, some balance. There were about a half dozen of us there, all doing the same thing. I don't know about the others; I left as confused and scattered as I'd arrived.

I sat by myself at dinner. A lot of us did, I think.

When I got back to my room Kirra was not there. I spent an hour or so at my desk, browsing through databanks, learning basic things about Top Step's layout. It is a huge, complex place, but interactive holographic maps help a lot in understanding it. I only had to bother Teena once. The important thing to remember from a navigational standpoint is that the arrow will always be painted on the wall farthest from Earth, and will point "outboard," toward the main docking area through which everyone enters Top Step. Eventually I sighed and collapsed the display back to the simple overview map I'd started with.

There was no sense putting it off any longer. I'd already stalled for almost a full day. I was as ready as I was ever going to be.

I described my requirements to Teena, and she found me a gym not presently in use, where I could try to dance.

$$\triangle \quad \triangle \quad \triangle$$

The space Teena directed me to was terrific—spacious, well padded, fully equipped, complete with top of the line sound and video gear. I could lock it from inside for up to an hour at a time. I locked it, selected music that did not dictate tempo, and—at last!—began trying my first dance "steps" in space.

The session was a disaster.

I spent a longer, slower time than usual warming up, and was careful not to overextend myself. But it was a fiasco. After an hour and a half of hard sweaty effort I had not put together five consecutive seconds I would want to show anyone. Not one single sequence I'd invented in my mind worked the way it was supposed to; not one combination I'd memorized from videos of Stardancers worked the way I'd thought it would. I was less graceful than a novice skater. Part of the problem was that the moves I'd envisioned always *stopped* when I was done with them . . . whereas every motion in free fall keeps going until something stops it. Every once in a while I accidentally created a moment of beauty . . . then could not reproduce it a second later. It was as though someone had randomly rewired a computer keyboard so there was no way to predict the effect of hitting any given key. And I kept poking my face through drifting mists of sweat globules that I'd spun off earlier, a truly disgusting experience.

I had not expected this to be easy. Well, okay, maybe I had. As I watched the video replay of my flounderings on the monitor, I was not sure it was possible.

It *had* to be possible. There was nothing back on Earth for me to return to. Shara Drummond had done this. Her sister Norrey had done it. Crippled defeated old Charlie Armstead had managed it. I had seen countless tapes of Stardancers who had had no dance training before coming to space, making shapes of almost unbearable beauty. Dammit, I was a good dancer, a great dancer.

Back on Earth, yeah, said the video monitor, *when you were younger* . . .

Finally I'd had all I could take for now. "That's it. Teena, wipe all tapes of this session."

"Yes, Morgan. There is a message for you, left after you told me to see that you were not disturbed. Will you accept it now?"

I sighed. "Why not?" Nothing happened, of course. I sighed again. "I mean, 'Yes, Teena, I'll take it now.'"

The monitor filled with Robert's face, wearing the vague smile everyone wears when leaving a phone message. "Hello, Morgan. You asked me if I'd tutor you in jaunting. I have time free this evening. Call me if you're still interested."

I thought about it while I got my breathing under control and toweled up sweat. I'd begun this evening confused and scattered. With diligent effort I had brought myself to miserable and depressed. It was time to cut my losses. "Record this message, Teena—" The screen turned into a mirror. "—Jesus, audio only!" It opaqued again. "Take one: 'Hello, Robert, this is Morgan. Thank you for your offer. Perhaps another time.' Cut. Too stiff. Take two: 'Hi, Robert, Morgan here. Maybe another night, okay? I just washed my spine and I can't do a thing with it.' Oh my God . . . take three: 'Robert, this is Morgan. Look, I don't know if it's a good idea if we—I don't think I—" I stopped and took a deep breath. "Teena, just send take one, to 'cut', okay? Then refuse all calls until I tell you otherwise."

"Yes, Morgan."

I used the gym's shower bag—God, I'll never get used to water that *slithers*, it's even weirder than sweat that won't trickle—and went back to my room. Halfway back, as an experiment, I had Teena stop guiding me, and tried to find my own way. I barked my shins a couple of times misjudging turns, I had to double back once, and my Contact-Per-Hectometer rate was humiliating . . . but I found my own damn home without help.

As the door irised open, song spilled out. Kirra was home. She was halfway into her sleepsack, her "swag," as she called it, and the lights were out in her hemisphere. My own lights were on low standby. She stopped singing to greet me. "Oh, don't stop," I protested, closing the door behind me.

"I haven't," she said. "You just can't hear it anymore. What you been up to, lovey?"

"Wasting time," I answered evasively. "Sing so I can hear, Kirra, really. If I fall asleep listening to music, I dream dances. At least I used to. I could use the inspiration."

So she went back to it. In this song her voice had about the range, pitch and tone of an alto recorder, if you know that sound. (I don't know why they were called that: they had no recording capacity at all.) It was soothing, hypnotic, resonated in my belly somewhere like a cat's purr.

I stripped and stuffed myself into my own sleepsack, told my room lights to slow-fade. *Today I talked with Charlie Armstead and Norrey Drummond,* I told myself. Kirra's warm sweet voice rose and fell in ways as unfamiliar to me as the words themselves. Just as I was drifting off to sleep I understood that they were unfamiliar to her too. She was singing about space, about zero gee. If there is no up or down, what's a melody to do? Her soothing voice washed away all turbulent emotion, set me adrift from my drifting body.

In my dreams there were sea lions. Highlit crimson by sunset, the colour of Stardancers. Floating all around me, all oriented to my personal vertical, treading air. Waiting patiently. For the first time, I wished I spoke Sea Lion.

CHAPTER FIVE

I humbly say to those who study the mystery,
Don't waste time.

—Sekito Kisen
Sandokai Sutra
(translated by Thomas Cleary)

KIRRA AND I both woke up with stiff necks. We hadn't learned yet that if you don't secure your head while you sleep in zero gee, you nod all night long, in time with your breathing. A terrestrial equivalent might be watching a tennis match for eight hours while lying on your side. We gave each other neck rubs before we got dressed. Kirra gave a first-rate neck rub. It's a rare skill, and blessed in a roommate. It was the first time I'd had friendly hands on me, and the first warm flesh I'd touched with my fingers, in I couldn't remember how many months.

I didn't see Robert at breakfast the next morning, and was just as glad. I wasn't sure what to say to him, how to act with him, how I felt about him. So far he had made no moves that were not ambiguous, that could not be read as simple friendliness. How would I respond if he did? Dammit, I didn't need this distraction now. I would tell him so . . . if the son of a bitch would only give me a clear opportunity!

When I realized I had spent all of breakfast thinking about not thinking about him, it occurred to me that it might be simplest to just get it over with. Have a quick intense affair, end it cleanly, and get on with preparing for Symbiosis.

Right. When had I ever had a quick intense affair that ended cleanly? Symbiosis would be hard enough without going out of my way to risk ego damage just beforehand.

He was in class when I got there, on the far side of the room. I took a vacant space near the door. In what would become a daily ritual, we all sat kûkanzen together for a half an hour; then we pushed off the wall and expanded to fill the room again. There were no bungee cords today; we were all in constant slight motion, forced into frequent touching, into learning the knack of stabilizing each other without setting up chain reactions of disturbance. It was interesting. When you're part of an unsecured group in free fall, you're *part of a group*. Like a driver watching cars far ahead for possible danger, you find yourself keeping track of movements three or four people away from you, because any motion anyone else makes will sooner or later affect you. You can't withdraw inward and ignore your fellows—because if you do, sooner or later you get an elbow in the eye.

Reb spoke that day of Leavetaking. It was his word for our primary task during our first month of Postulancy. Taking our leave, emotionally and psychologically, of all earthly things, of the kin and kindred we were leaving behind. "In effect you must do what a dying person does . . . with the advantages that you are not in pain or drugged or immobilized. You can take your leave with a clear mind and a clear heart. Most important, you have no need to be afraid. In your case, you *know* that the kind of dying you do will not mean the end of you, and your universe. In a sense, you'll get to have your afterlife now, while you're around to enjoy it." There were a few chuckles. "But I apologize, sincerely and humbly, if to any of you that sounds like blasphemy. I do not mean to imply that Symbiosis is the same as the afterlife or rebirth that terrestrial religions speak of. It is not. But it carries nearly the same price tag. You have to abandon everything to get there.

"You're a little like terminal patients with three months to live. You have one month to grieve, and one month to prepare, and then one month to decide. Don't waste a minute of it, is my advice. Life on earth is something to lose. Get your mourning done, so you can put it aside. Because life in space is something to look forward to."

Someone asked how you mourn your past.

"One of the best methods," Reb said, "is something of a cliché. Let your whole life pass before your eyes. Only you don't have to cram it into one final instant. Take a month. Remember. Re-member: become a member again. Remember your life, as much of it as you can; write your memoirs in your mind, or type them out or dictate them to Teena if it helps you. Every time you remember a good part, say goodbye to it. Every time you remember a bad part, say goodbye to that as well. If you come to a part that hurts to remember, sit kûkanzen with it until it doesn't hurt anymore. If you have a place you just can't get past, come to me for further help."

The rest of class was devoted to a long lecture/demonstration on how to breathe correctly—"You ought to get it right once before you give it up for good," he told us—but I won't record it here. Read Shunryu Suzuki-roshi if you're really interested, or Reb's book RUNNING JUMPING STANDING STILL. Before breaking for the day, Reb announced that anyone interested in formal kûkanzen sitting, with traditional Soto Buddhist forms, was welcome to come to his *zendo* any evening after dinner. He was also available for *dokusan*, private interviews. It seemed to me that his eyes brushed mine while he said this. After class I approached him and, when I had his attention, told him that I intended to join his evening meditation group, but that I had a private project of my own to complete first. He smiled and nodded. "You need to know if you can dance," he agreed. "Good luck." He gave his attention to the next person who wanted it.

I tottered off to lunch, more than a little surprised. Yes, he'd known every one of us by name on the first day. But to know so much about me as an individual implied either remarkable research for a teacher . . . or insight approaching telepathy.

On my way to lunch I missed a transition and spent a humiliating few minutes drifting free in the center of a corridor intersection until a Second-Monther came along and bailed me out. It caused me to work through a logic chain. If I was ever going to learn to remaster my body in this weird environment, and dance again, I was going to need all the help I could get. But help from Robert came with ambiguous strings attached. Therefore I needed someone else. A Second-Monther, like the one who'd just helped me? I'd seen few of them so far, they were billeted in a different section of Top Step, and the ones I'd passed in the corridors had all worn an air of quizzical distraction and seemed in a hurry. (I still hadn't seen any

Third-Monthers, but Kirra had; she said he'd looked "awful holy or awful high, or maybe both," in a sort of daze.) Still, there had been helpful Second-Monthers at meals; maybe I'd ask one of them for tutoring and see what they said.

But as I entered the cafeteria I changed my mind. Sulke Drager was eating by herself; I took my food over to her table and asked if I could join her. After a few conversational politenesses, I asked her if she'd be willing to tutor me after hours.

She laughed in my face. "How much are you offering per hour?"

Since Suit Camp, I'd gotten out of the habit of thinking about money. It was part of what I was leaving behind. But what money I owned was still mine until I entered Symbiosis and thereby donated it all to the Starseed Foundation. There wasn't much, mostly the carefully measured trickle of Grandmother's trust fund, but what did I need it for? Symbiosis or Euthanasia were my choices, and neither required capital. "How about two hundred dollars an hour? Uh, Canadian dollars."

She grimaced. "What do I know from dollars? How much is that in air-days or calories? Or even Deutschmarks? Never mind, you don't know and I don't care. Whatever it is, it isn't enough."

"Why not?"

She stopped eating and faced me. "I just got here from six hard sweaty hours in a p-suit over at the Mirror Farm. After I finish trying to teach you clowns here, I go put in another six hours as a glorified lab clerk over at the NanoTech Safe Lab—only six hours turns into eight because of what they put you through every time you enter and leave that place. Like what you got at Decontam, but worse. Then I can catch the shuttle home to Hooverville and catch a few hours of sleep. All this buys me just enough air and food to keep going. I haven't got an hour to spare. And if I did, the last thing in the System I'd spend it on is more of teaching one of you freebreathers how to swim."

"Sorry I asked."

"Look, you're a dancer, right? Do you enjoy teaching first position and pliés to beginners?"

I certainly couldn't argue with that. We finished our meals without further conversation.

I watched her during that afternoon's class. She worked hard and well with us, but she did it with a barely submerged air of resentment. I thought of her term for us. Freebreather. Analogous, no doubt, to freeloader. We did not sweat for the air we breathed. It was given to us by the Starseed Foundation. We loafed and probed our souls while Sulke scrambled to survive. She and the other hundreds of zero-gee-adapted spacers must all dislike us.

I noticed something else as I floundered with the others, trying instinctively and uselessly to swim in air. Robert's roommate Ben had become terrific at this . . . literally overnight. Yesterday he'd been as clumsy as the rest of us—and today he was as graceful and controlled in his movements as Robert. He learned new moves and tactics as fast as Sulke could show them to him; he even showed her one she didn't know. I don't think I could describe it; it seemed to involve having eyes in the back of your head.

Sulke called both Ben and me aside after class. Kirra and Robert both drifted a polite distance away to wait for us. "You still got a lot to learn—but you got damn good damn fast," she told him. "How?"

The trouble with asking Ben a question is, he's liable to answer. "Well, you know that psych experiment where they tape inverting lenses over your eyes, and for a while you're blind and then on the second day suddenly you can see again? Your brain tears down the whole visual system and rebuilds it upside down in two days; well I've been doing that kind of stuff for fun for almost thirty years, rewiring my brain for new paradigms; two days is what it usually takes me, I'm right on schedule. It's amazing what you can do with your own brain when you start messing around with the circuitry—do you know about the time The Great Woz rebuilt his own memory after an accident? He said he thought his brain from the zero to the one state. Sometimes I think I know what he meant—"

Sulke got a word in edgewise. "Whatever. McLeod here

needs some tutoring evenings. Why don't you help her out?"

He smiled at me sheepishly. "Gee, Morgan, I'd love to help you, but I'm kind of busy myself just now. I've got this little project I just started this morning; I'm working with Teena on memorizing Top Step: I want to get to the place where I can close my eyes and point to anyplace in the rock and get it right. And I want to spend some time with Kirra too. Uh, could I get back to you in two days?" While I was trying to cope with the enormity of his assumption that he could master the three-dimensional geography of this huge place in another two days, and wondering whether I could stand to study jaunting with this happy madman, he got a brainstorm. "No, you know what you should do? Robert! Hey, *Robert*—c'mere. You should ask Robert to help you, hey, that's a great idea, he's good at this stuff too, hey Robert, Morgan needs somebody to teach her jaunting and I'm booked: why don't you help her?"

Robert and I looked at each other. We both wanted to kick Ben, and neither wanted to show it. "I've offered," he said expressionlessly.

Sulke was studying us. "Well," she said, "I have to jet." She kicked away and left.

"Well, there you go, then," Ben said, hugely pleased with himself.

"Ben, love," Kirra said, "let's you and me go get some tucker and let them talk it over, eh?" You can't kick somebody in the shin surreptitiously in zero gee: you bounce away.

"Huh? Oh, sure. See you at supper, folks." He and Kirra left us alone.

I wanted to join them. But I suddenly realized I couldn't. I had carelessly let go of my handhold to let Sulke by, then failed to regain it in time. We'd all handed in our thruster units at the close of class. I was adrift; unless Robert helped me, it'd be at least a couple of minutes before I drifted near another wall. Damn!

He kept his position near the hatch and watched me. When the silence had stretched out for oh, half of forever, he said, "So what time tonight is good for you?"

"Robert," I said slowly, "we have to talk."

"Yes."

I was spinning very slowly; soon I'd be facing away from him. I knew the maneuver to correct for that. But if I screwed it up I'd put myself into a tumble from which he'd more or less have to rescue me. "Look . . . can we skip past a lot of bullshit?"

"Yes."

"What exactly do you want from me? I've been around, I know you're interested. But interested in what? I've got too much on my mind for high school guessing games: I'm busy. You want a quick roll in the hay, you want to go steady, you want my autograph, you want to have my baby, *what*?"

There are probably a thousand wrong answers to that question. The only right one I can think of is the one he came up with. "I want to get to know you better."

I sighed and studied his strange, beautiful face. I wanted to get to know him better. And I needed the distraction like a hole in the head.

I was having to crane my neck now to keep eye contact. So I tried to reverse my spin, and of course I bungled it and went into a slow tumble. They say you're not supposed to get dizzy in free fall, because your semicircular canals fill up completely and your sense of balance shuts down. But I'd only been in space a few days; the room whirled, I lost all reference points, I got dizzy.

"Stiffen up," Robert called, his voice coming closer. "Don't try to help me." I tensed all my limbs. He took me by the wrists, we pivoted around each other like trapeze artists and headed for the far wall together. He changed his grip and did something and we were in a loose embrace, feet toward our destination. "Ready? Landing . . . now." We let our legs soak up most of our momentum, ended up headed back toward the hatch, but moving slowly. We were touching at hands and knees. His eyes were a meter from mine.

"Look," I said, "the timing is lousy."

"Yeah," he agreed.

"See, I came here to dance. That's all, I came here to dance. Anything else comes second. I can't dance anymore on Earth. If I can't dance here either, I don't know if I'm going through with Symbiosis. And I don't know if I can dance here or not.

I thought I could, but I can't even seem to learn the equivalent
of crawling on all fours. Maybe I'm one of the ones who just
can't get it. I can't give you any kind of an answer until I
know. Does that make any sense?"

He thought about it as we reached the midpoint of the room
and he led us through our turnover. "It makes me want to teach
you everything I can, as fast as possible. What time is good
tonight?"

"Did you hear what I—"

"We Chinese are a notoriously patient people."

I sighed in exasperation.

"Let me help you, as a friend. No obligations. I've admired
your work for a long time; allow me this honour."

What the hell can you say to something like that? That
evening we spent two hours working out together in "my"
gym.

And it was a fiasco.

Early on we identified my major problem: an unconscious,
instinctive tendency to select one of the possible local verticals
and stubbornly declare it the "correct" one in my mind, so that
I became disoriented when out of phase with it. It is the most
common problem of a neophyte in free fall. Ten million years
of evolution insist on knowing which way "down" is, just in
case this weightlessness business should suddenly fail. Even a
false answer is preferable to no answer.

Identifying the problem didn't help solve it at all. Robert
was indeed patient, but I must have tried his patience. Finally
I thanked him, politely kicked him out, and spent another
couple of hours alone, trying to dance.

It wasn't a *total* disaster. But damn close. In the last ten
minutes I managed to put together one eight-second sequence
that didn't stink. The first time I did it was dumb luck, an
accident with serendipitous results. But I was able to reproduce it again . . . and again. About three times out of five.
If I didn't crash into something while I was trying. In
playback, it looked good from five of the six camera angles.

But I could not connect that eight seconds up with *anything*.
The third time I had to stop to towel away sweat from the

middle of my back I said the hell with it, got in and out of the shower bag, and went back to my room. Kirra was out. I climbed into my sleepsack, dimmed the lights, and studied holograms of some of my favorite Stardancer dance pieces, trying to understand how they made what they did look so effortless. I even went back as far as the oldest zero-gee dance there is, Shara Drummond's *Liberation*. She'd only been dancing in space for three weeks when Armstead recorded it. Until now, I'd never fully appreciated just how good it was.

After a while Kirra came in, humming softly to herself. "Hello, lovey. How'd it go?"

I collapsed the holo. "How'd it go with you? Ben show you any good moves?" She'd gone to his place to learn 3-D chess.

She came and docked with my sleepsack. Her grin was about to split her face. "Benjamin showed me his very best moves," she said in a dreamy singsong voice.

My eyes widened. "You're kidding!"

She shook her head, beaming. We squealed together and burst into giggles. "Tell me everything!" I demanded.

"Well, you know, I'd always wondered," she said, settling into a hug, "what'd it be like? I mean, what'd keep you squished together if not the weight?"

I'd always wondered too. "Right. So?"

"So it turns out it's as natural as breathin'. You hug with four arms is all, and then you . . . well, you dance. No- where near as hard as the stuff we do in class." She closed her eyes in reminiscence. "It was lots gentler than it is on Earth. And nicer. He didn't need to hold himself up, so he could keep on usin' his hands all the way through." She squealed and opened her eyes again. "Oh, it was awful nice! Benjamin says we'll get even better with time."

I nodded. "Wait'll you see how good he is in two days' time," I said, and made her laugh from deep inside.

She was my friend; I shared her joy. But a part of me was envious. I tried hard to hide it, to make the right noises as she chattered happily on, and thought I succeeded.

Maybe she smelled it. "So how'd you make out with your dancing, love?" she asked finally.

I found myself pouring out my frustrations to her. "And I

can't even *start* to figure out where I stand with him until I know whether or not I can dance in free fall," I finished, "and I can't even guess how long it's going to be before I know."

She looked thoughtful. "Tell me something."

"Sure."

"How's your back feel?"

"Why, not too—oh!"

"How 'bout those knees, then?"

My back did not hurt. My knees did not hurt.

"You worked out more in the last two days than you did in the last year, tell me I'm wrong," she said. "Have your legs buckled? Got crook back?"

No and no, by God. I was tired and ached in a dozen places, but they were no worse than one should expect when getting back into shape after a long layoff.

"You can do this. Matter of time, that's all."

I was thunderstruck. She was absolutely right. *My instrument was working again.* Hell, I had managed to transition from ballet to modern dance once: I could learn this. There was nothing stopping me! Nothing but time and courage. The sense of relief was overwhelming. I felt a surge of elation, and at the same time a delicious tiredness. Moments before I'd been suffering from fatigue; now I was just sleepy.

"Kirra, you're an angel," I cried, and hugged her harder, and kissed her. Then we smiled at each other, and she jaunted to her own bed and dimmed the lights. She undressed quickly and slid into the sack. "Night, lovey," she called softly.

"G'night, Kirra," I murmured. "I'm happy for you. Ben's sweet."

My last thought was *I'm going to sleep sounder tonight than I have in years,* and then almost at once I was deep under—

—and then I was wide awake, saying, "What the hell was that?" aloud, and Kirra said it too and we both listened and heard nothing but silence, total silence, and at last I thought *Silence? In a space dwelling?*

The air circulation system in Top Step is whisper quiet—but boy, do you miss that whisper when it stops!

Then a robot was speaking with Teena's voice, loudly, in my left ear.

In only the one ear, and very slowly, unmistakably Teena's voice but without any inflections of tone or pitch: she must have been talking to or with nearly every resident of Top Step at once, time-sharing like mad, no bytes to spare for vocal personality or stereo effect. "Attention! Attention! There has been a major system malfunction. There is no immediate cause for alarm, repeat, no cause for alarm. The circulation system is temporarily down. It is being repaired. All personnel are advised to remain in constant motion until further notice. Do not let yourself remain motionless for more than a few moments. If you can reach p-suit or other personal pressure, please do so, calmly." Not wanting to drain her resources any further, we asked no questions.

A moment later, her voice was superseded by that of Dorothy Gerstenfeld. She explained the nature of the problem, assured us it would be fixed long before it became serious, entreated us all not worry, and sounded so serene and confident herself that I did stop worrying. Her explanation was too technical for me to follow, but her tone of voice said I should be reassured by it, so I was.

The circulation system was only down for half an hour. Nothing to be afraid of: Top Step was immense and a lot of it was pressurized; there was more than enough air on hand to last us all much longer than half an hour in a pinch. The worst of it was nuisance: when the air stops flowing in a space habitat, you *must not* be motionless. If you are, exhaled CO_2 forms an invisible sphere around your head and slowly smothers you. There are many jobs aboard Top Step for which constant head motion is contraindicated, tracking a large-mass docking, for instance; such people had to find someone to fan their heads, or stop work for the duration. And everyone else had to keep moving. You can't imagine how annoying that can be until it's forced upon you. Not that being in motion takes any hard work, in zero gee—it's just that your natural tendency and subconscious desire is to *stop* moving as much as possible, to simulate the terrestrial environment you remember as natural, and overcoming that impulse gets wearing very quickly. Especially if you were tired to begin with.

But it was over soon enough. Kirra and I experimented with fanning each other's faces, and told each other campfire stories, and at last we heard the soft sound of the pumps coming back up to speed. Because I was alert for it, I became consciously aware for the first time of the movement of air on my skin as soon as it resumed.

"The emergency is over," Teena said, still in robot mode. "Repeat, the emergency is over. There have been zero casualties. Resume normal operations. Thank you."

"Thank you all for not panicking," Dorothy's voice added. "We have everything under control now. Resume your duties. Those of you on sleep shift, try to get back to sleep; you've a long day ahead."

I had surprisingly little difficulty feeling sleepy again, and Kirra was snoring—musically—before I was. As I was fading out again I had a thought. "Teena?" I whispered.

"Yes, Morgan?" Her reply was also whispered, but I could tell this was the old, fully human-sounding Teena again, so it was all right to bother her now.

"What caused the circulation system to go down?"

She almost seemed to hesitate. Silly, of course; computers don't hesitate. "A component was improperly installed through carelessness. It has been replaced."

"Oh. Glad it wasn't anything serious. A meteor or something. That reminds me: how is Mr. Henderson, the Chief Steward on my flight up here?"

"I'm sorry to say he died about four hours ago, without regaining consciousness."

"Oh." No one had needed to fan his head while the air was down.

"Good night, Morgan."

"G'night."

My last drifting thought was something about how lucky I'd been lately. Two life-threatening emergencies in forty-eight hours, and I'd lived through them both.

There weren't any more for *weeks*.

CHAPTER SIX

Tom Seaver: What time is it, Yogi?
Yogi Berra: You mean now?

A COMPANY MANAGER I toured Nova Scotia with once summed up that province as follows: "Too many churches; not enough bars." I'm afraid the same could be said of Top Step.

That overgrown cigar had churches and temples of almost every possible kind in its granite guts, over three dozen, including three different *zendos;* if I had wanted to do nothing but kûkanzen "sitting" or Rinzai chanting with my free time, I could have. But I'd never been all that committed a Buddhist—I'd never been fully committed to *anything* except the dance—and somehow it felt wrong to spend all of my last three months as a human being pursuing no-thought. I intended to do a *lot* of thinking, before I stepped outdoors and jaunted into a big glob of red goo and opened up my p-suit. I still wasn't absolutely sure I was going to go through with this.

I tended to spend my free time in one of four places: Solarium Three, Le Puis, my room, and the gym I came to think of as my studio.

Sol Three was a popular hangout for just about everyone in my class, and for some from the two classes ahead of us and some of the staff as well. Not Sol One, where I'd met Harry Stein and three others of The Six: this Solarium was, as its number indicates, all the way round the other side of Top Step. An accidental pun, for that's the side facing Earth: Sol Three overlooking Sol III. It was more commonly and informally known as the Café du Ciel—a reference I understood the first time I saw its spectacular view.

Have you ever been to New Orleans, to the old French Quarter? Do you know the Café du Monde? You sit outdoors and sip chicoried café au lait, and eat fresh hot beignets smothered with so much powdered sugar you mustn't inhale

while biting, and you watch the world go by. Look one way,
and there's the Mississippi, Old Man River himself, just
rolling along. Look another and you're seeing Jackson Square,
another and you're looking at the French Market. Street
buskers play alto sax, or vibes, or clarinet, very well. They say
if you sit in the Café du Monde long enough, sooner or later
you'll see everyone you know pass by.

The same is said of the Café du Ciel—and it's literal truth.

It tended to have a lot of people in it, and it tended to be
rather quiet, although there was no rule about noise. There were
no buskers there. There were no beignets available either—
powdered sugar isn't practical in free fall—but you could bring
a bulb of coffee from the cafeteria. What made the Solarium
reminiscent of the Café du Monde was the view.

The scenery was so majestic it was like being in some great
cathedral. When the Fireflies originally whisked Top Step
from the asteroid belt into High Earth Orbit as their final
parting gift to humanity, they picked a polar orbit concentric to
the day/night terminator, to keep the big stone cigar in
perpetual sunlight. So the Earth we saw from Solarium Three
was always half in sunlight and half in darkness, an immense
yin-yang symbol. Our orbit was high enough that you could
just see the entire globe at once. The slow grandeur of the
dance it did I cannot describe, spinning end-on when we were
passing over one of the Poles, then seeming to lurch crazily
sideways as our orbit flung us toward the Equator and the
opposite Pole. A whole planet endlessly executing the same
arabesque turn. If you haven't got graphic software that'll
simulate it, get an old-fashioned globe and see it for yourself;
it's the grandest roller coaster I know, endlessly absorbing. We
all felt its pull: there in the big window was everything we
were about to say goodbye to.

Second-month Postulants generally seemed to graduate into
being attracted more by Solariums One and Four, which faced
raw empty space: everything they were about to say hello to.
I visited those cubics a few times; they had even more of that
cathedral-hush feel. Too much for me, then.

(Only dedicated tanners spent much time in Sol Two—the
only true solarium, the one which always faced the Sun—and

for them I suppose it must have been Paradise. You could put a spin on yourself, go to sleep, and toast evenly on all sides without effort. But I never got the habit; skin cancer aside, a dancer with a tan is a dancer who's out of work.)

But sometimes looking at Earth made you want to make noise and have a little fun. So if I wasn't in Sol Three I could usually be found in Le Puis, our only tavern, where things were livelier.

To serve its several purposes, a tavern should have both places where one can be seen, and places where one cannot be seen. The designer of Le Puis had accomplished this splendidly. Being there was a little like being inside a stupendous honeycomb made of dozens of transparent globes, with a large spherical clearing at the center, in which danced two or three dozen small table-spheres, fuzzy with Velcro. The tables kept perfect station with each other; you could not move one more than a few inches before it maneuvered to correct, with little semivisible squirts of steering gas. (Odorless, I'm happy to report.) The pattern the tables made in space was not a simple grid, more of a starburst effect. You could hang around one of the tables (literally) until you met someone you liked, then adjourn for more private conversation to one of the dozens of surrounding sphericles—a word exactly analogous to "cubicle." By simply pulling the lips of the door closed, you soundproofed your sphericle. If you found that you wanted to get *really* private, the walls could be opaqued. It reminded me a little of the private chambers you sometimes find in really first-rate Japanese restaurants, with rice-paper-and-bamboo walls, soft cushions, and a door that sometimes slides open to admit attentive servers, fragrant food, and the chuckle of a nearby fountain.

I was with Kirra on my first visit to Le Puis; I guess it was our third or fourth day in Top Step. As we emerged from the igloo-tunnel that led from the main corridor into the heart of the honeycomb, we were approached by the largest and happiest human being I've ever seen, before or since.

"Crikey," Kirra said, watching him draw near. "Is that—?"

"God, I think it is," I said. "I should have guessed when I heard the name of this place."

"Hello, ladies," the apparition boomed as he came to a halt beside us. He wore an expression of barely contained glee. When he smiled, his cheeks looked like grapefruits. "Welcome to my joint. I got a nice little table for you. If you'll follow me . . ." He spun and jaunted gracefully away.

I've met a lot of celebrities in my time, but I felt a touch of awe. It was Fat Humphrey Pappadopolous, who used to own Le Maintenant, the Toronto restaurant in which Stardancers Incorporated was founded at the turn of the century. He was every bit as colourful and extraordinary as Charlie Armstead made him sound in the famous Titan Transmission of 1999.

Armstead says Humphrey was very fat when he was a groundhog. But I don't think he could have been as big then as he was the day I met him. I don't think you can be that fat in a one-gee field. In free fall, he was as graceful as any ballerina, and moved with stately elegance, like an extremely well-bred zeppelin.

He docked at a table with a good view of the room—even his bulk could not displace the table much—and we docked there too. "Let's see," he said to me, "you look to me like a nice dry white wine, maybe a Carrington 2004. And for you," he said to Kirra, "I got some Thomas Cooper, fresh from Oz. Peanuts and a little sharp cheese and some of those little oyster cracker things, right?" He drifted away, beaming.

He was one of those special people who so obviously love life, so much, that you feel like a jerk for not enjoying it as much as they are. And so you cheer up to about half their level, which is twice as cheerful as you were. And for the next little while, you notice that everyone you talk to seems to be smiling at you.

But how had he known Kirra was from Australia?

"Funny," I said, "he didn't *look* red. But that was exactly what I would have ordered, if he'd given me a chance. If I'd known he had a vintage that good in stock."

"Me too," she agreed. "Armstrong didn't lie about that bloke. He reads minds, all right. Without Symbiosis."

"Natural talent, I guess."

The airflow in this space was breezier than usual, with the temperature upped just a notch to compensate. I understood why when someone a few tables away lit up a pipe of marijuana. The smell was familiar, pleasant. I hadn't smoked in years myself, but it reminded me of good times past. Childhood on Gambier Island. The dorms at SFU, and the party on Legalization Day. Motel rooms after performances on the road. Perhaps it was time I took it up again. No, not until *after* I had mastered zero gee well enough to dance. If then.

Fat Humphrey returned with our drinks in free-fall drinking bulbs, docked on the next table while passing them to us. Kirra's was three times the size of mine. I'm not much of a drinker; it seemed she was. "How do you do that, Mr. Pappadopolous?" I asked. "Know what we want and how much?"

"Call me Fat. How do you know how much to breathe?"

I gave up. "This is my friend Kirra. I'm Morgan McLeod."

"Hello, Kirra." He held out his hand, and when she tried to shake it he took hers and kissed it. She dimpled. The same thing happened to me. "You wouldn't be the Morgan McLeod that danced *Indices of Refraction* with Morris, would you?"

I admitted it.

"Goddam. It's a pleasure to have you in my joint. You ever see her dance, Kirra?"

"No," she said.

"Then you one lucky person; you got a treat in store. Get Teena to dig some of her tapes and holos out of the Net for you."

"I will," she agreed.

I had never achieved the level of fame of a Baryshnikov or a Drummond, did not often get recognized by someone who was not in the dance world. It was dawning on me that Top Step was a nest of dance lovers.

"You wouldn't be Kirra from Queensland, wouldja?" he went on. "The singer?" Kirra dimpled and admitted it.

A nest of arts lovers.

"Both of you please be sure you sign my visitors' book on the way out. Look, I gotta tell this to ev'body comes here the first time: be careful with these." He produced from somewhere on his person a pair of small mesh bags, and tossed them to us. Peanuts and oyster crackers. A wedge of sharp cheese followed after them. "It ain't so bad if a little piece o' cheese gets away from you . . . but them peanuts and crackers got salt on 'em. Somebody gets one o' them in the eye, and maybe the bouncer has to go to work. And if you didn't guess from lookin' at me, I'm the bouncer." He shook with mirth at his own joke. We both promised we'd be careful. "Oh, Kirra, one more t'ing. You drinkin' that beer, an' you feel like you wanna burp, s'cuse me, but don't."

"Why not, Fat?"

"You back on Earth, your stomach got food on the bottom an' air on top, so you burp, no problem. But up here, the air an' the food is all mixed together, you see what I mean?"

She frowned. "Thanks, mate. Hey, how about the other direction?"

"No problem there. Lotsa people spend all their time up here fartin' around." He shuddered with mirth again. "I'll come back later and talk, okay? Meanwhile you both have a good time." He drifted majestically away.

We looked at each other and giggled together. Then we looked down at our drinks and snacks. Twice as many peanuts as oyster crackers. Kirra generally ate twice as much as I did at cafeteria meals. Fat Humphrey magic again.

"Something else, i'nt he?" Kirra said.

"He sure is. All right, out with it: tell me everything about Ben."

Her face glowed. "Oh, Morgan, i'nt he smashing? I don't usually fall for a bloke this quick—but oh my, he lights me up. He's so excited about everything, you know? The least little thing is special to him, and so it makes everything special for you to be around him. You know comin' here to space wasn't exactly my idea, I told you that: it just sort of landed on me plate and I took a bite—but Benjamin! He wants it so much, looks forward to it so much, I'm startin' to get kind of excited about it meself. He explains to me all about how marvelous it's gonna be, and I can understand it better. I was just thinkin' of all this as an extra long Walkabout—but he makes it sound like more fun than Christmas." She took a long swig of ale.

"He is fun to be around," I agreed. "He's sort of the backwards of my ex-husband. He had a way of making a good time dull."

She lowered her voice. "And he's a champion lover! He does a bit o' what Fat just did, knows what you want about a second before you know it yourself."

"Definitely the backwards of my ex."

"If I hadn't had to clear out so Robert could get some sleep, I might be there still. Hey, how are you and Robert gettin' along, then?"

"What the hell is that stuff floating in your beer?"

"What, this? It's yeast. Thomas Cooper leaves it in, for flavor. Kinda interestin' the way it swirls about like that: the zero gee saves you having' to shake up the bottle to get it off the bottom. Seriously, though, what about you and Robert? I had this lovely idea how handy it'd be if you two hit it off like Ben and me. We could swap roomies and—"

"Whoa!" I said. "Take your time." Change the subject again? No, deal with it. "I don't know how I feel about Robert . . . but I do know I'm not in any hurry. The most important thing on my mind right now is learning how to dance all over again, and that's all I want to think about until I get it done or it kills me. Robert will have to wait." *Now* change the subject. "I wonder how Fat Humphrey manages to decant wine properly in free fall? This is delicious."

Kirra started to answer, then took a sip of beer instead. "Look, Morgan, answer me this. Are we roommates, or are we friends?"

"Friends," I answered without hesitation. "I hope."

"Then listen'a me. There's some blokes you can hold at arm's length and after a while they go away. But I know you, and I've seen you with Robert. He's got a hook in you . . . just a little one, maybe, but a hook. And you got one in him. You try keepin' him at arm's length forever, your arms're gonna start gettin' shorter. He ain't gonna go away. You want to get on with your dancin', it might be less distraction to just go ahead an' get it over with, see where it goes an' get it integrated. Might help to have somethin' to dance *about,* eh?"

I don't remember exactly what mumbled evasion I made.

Just then a welcome distraction presented itself: the floorshow began.

Well, not exactly a floorshow. A single performer, a busker, doing an act I would have thought impossible in zero gee: juggling.

Free fall juggling is done barefoot. You do not make the balls or clubs or whatever go in a circle, because they won't. Instead you make them go in a rectangle. Hand to hand to foot to foot to hand. This particular juggler used orange balls of some resilient material, the size of real oranges. It seemed he was known and liked here; people broke off conversations to watch him and clap along. He had twinkling eyes and a goatee. Except for a G-string, he was barefoot to the eyebrows. He began in a slow motion that would simply not have been possible on Earth, then got faster and faster until the balls began to blur into an orange rectangle in the air before him. He started with four, but kept adding more from a pouch at his waist. I thought I counted as high as sixteen. Then suddenly he changed the pattern, so that they crossed over and back in front of him in an X pattern, and then went back to a rectangle again. There was applause. He brought his feet up and hands down until the rectangle was a square, then a horizontal rectangle, and returned to the basic position. More applause. Suddenly he had one hand high over his head and the rectangle was a triangle. With the suddenly freed left hand he took a joint from his pocket and struck it alight, took a deep puff. Loud applause. He seemed to pay no attention at all to the balls. He took another puff, tossed the joint to the nearest patron, and resumed work with all four limbs. The balls began to ever so gradually slow down, until they were individually distinguishable, and continued to slow. Within a minute he was back in the slow motion he'd started with—yes, there were sixteen balls—and still they kept decelerating. Without warning he flipped over, upside down to his original orientation, without disturbing the stately progress of the balls. Thunderous applause. Suddenly all the balls exploded outward from him, in a spherical distribution. I half-ducked, but none came near me, or anyone else. All sixteen bounced off something harmless and returned to him in almost-unison; he

caught them all in his pouch and folded at the waist in a free
fall bow. The house came down.

"Teena," I asked, "how do I tip that juggler five dollars?"

"It's done, Morgan," Teena said in my ear. "I've debited
your account. His name is Christopher Micah."

He began a new routine involving what seemed to be razor-
sharp knives. I didn't see how he could deal with knives with
his feet—and didn't get to find out that day, because just then
there was a small disturbance behind me. Kirra and I turned to
look. Micah kept on working, properly ignoring the distraction.

Fat Humphrey was drifting just outside one of the opaqued
bubble booths, talking softly to someone inside, who was
answering him in too loud a voice. It seemed to be the
second-oldest argument in history: the customer wanted more
booze and Fat was cutting her off, politely and firmly. I started
to turn back to catch Micah's knife act, when all at once I
recognized the voice. It was Sulke.

Everyone else had returned their attention to the show. Kirra
and I exchanged a glance and quietly slipped over to see if we
could be of help, taking our drinks and munchies with us.

We were. Fat was handicapped somewhat by being an old
friend of hers, but because Kirra and I were her students
we were able to cheerfully bully her into quieting down. We
swarmed into her booth with her, winked at Fat, and sealed the
door to keep the noise inside.

"S'not fair, gahdammit," she complained. "I'm not even
near drunk enough."

Kirra sent a peanut toward her in slow motion. "Catch
that."

She missed in three grabs, then tried to catch it in her mouth
and muffed that too. It went up her nose, and she blasted it
clear with a loud snort. "I didn't say I wasn't drunk. Said I
wasn't drunk *enough.*"

"For what?" I asked soothingly.

"To fall asleep, gahdammit. This is my one day off a week,
the day I catch up on all the sleep I missed, an' if I fuck up and
miss any I'll never get caught up."

"How come you gotta be drunker'n this to fall asleep?" Kirra asked.

"Because I'm scared." She heard the words come out and frowned. "No, I'm not, gahdammit, I'm pissed off is what I am! I'm not scared of anything. But I'm mad as hell."

"About what?"

She sneered. "Hmmph! How would you know? You ground-hogs. You freebreathers. Never paid for an hour's air in your life, either of you. Where'd you come from, McLeod, North America somewhere, right? Worst come to worst, you could always go on welfare. Kirr', you could always jungle up and live off the land. There's *no fuckin' land to live off up here*."

"Rough," Kirra agreed.

"You don't know the half of it! Nineteen friggin' outfits in space I can work for, and eighteen of 'em suck wind. The only place that doesn't treat you like shit is this one . . . and now crazy bastards are shootin' at it."

"Shooting at it!" I exclaimed. "What do you mean?"

"Aw fer chrissake, you really think the air plant went down last night by accident? You have any idea how many different systems have to fail in cascade before that can happen? You probably think it was space junk put a hole in your Elevator on the way up here, huh?"

I was shocked. "What makes you think it wasn't?"

"You were there. Did you see the object that hulled you?"

"Well, no. I think it ended up in the Steward's head."

She shook her head. "There was nothin' in Henderson's head but burned meat. It was a laser. They're keepin' it quiet, but a frenna mine saw the hull."

"But who the hell would want to hurt Top Step?"

She stared. "You serious? Religious fanatics, wanna pull down the false angels and their wicked cosmic orgy. Shiites, Catholics, Fundamentalists, take your pick. Then you got the Chinese, since old Chen Ten Li got tossed out on his ear. Then there's the other eighteen sonofabitch outfits I tol' you 'bout, and their parent corporations dirtside. Top Step could outcompete any one of them at what they do, and the only reason it doesn't is because the Starseed Foundation chooses not to. How could they not all hate this place?"

I thought of the epidemic of food poisoning that had run through Suit Camp just before takeoff. "Jesus."

She was frowning hugely. "Gahdammit. Not supposed to talk about this shit with you people. Prob'ly get shit for it. Bad for morale. Might get scared an' go home, kilobucks down'a tube. Forget I said anything, okay?"

"Sure," Kirra said soothingly.

"Thanks," Sulke said. "You're okay, for a freebreather." She reached out and snatched Kirra's beer, finished it in a single squeeze.

I placed my own drink unobtrusively behind me, and hoped it would stay there. "Sulke, tell me something. If being a free-lance spacer is really so bad—and I believe you—then why not opt out? Take that last step and become a Stardancer like us? Then you could tell Skyfac and Lunindustries and all the rest to go take a hike."

She boiled over. "You outa your gahdam mind? You people are all assholes. Worse than assholes, you're *cowards:* solving your problems by runnin' away from them. You won't catch me doin' that shit. Maybe I can't ever go home again, but at least I'm human! I've hung around Stardancers a long time, and by Jesus they ain't human, and I can't *understand* how in hell a human bein' could deliberately stop being a human bein'. I'll teach you fools how to swim, but I got nothing but contempt for ya. Nobody gets inside Sulke Drager's head but Sulke Drager, an' don' you forget it, see?"

Like all true spacers, she was a rugged individualist. She was certainly paying a high price to be one in space.

"Do you have to go EVA to get home, Sulke?"

"Crash here on my day off," she said, eyes beginning to cross. "And even if I did, I can navigate safely in free space when I'm *dree* times trunker than this. That's why it's not fair that fat bastard cut me off."

"Well, since he did," Kirra said reasonably, "what do we want to stay around here and class up his place for him, then?"

"Damn right," I agreed. "Sleep's too precious to miss on his account. Let's quit this program."

Sulke allowed herself to be taken home. Teena guided the three of us to the dormitory where employees crashed. It was basically a cube full of sleepsacks, with minimal amenities and few entertainment facilities. If Top Step was the best of nineteen employers in space, the others had to be pretty bad.

By the time we got back to Le Puis, Micah had finished for the night. But the tenor sax player who'd replaced him was very good, had a big full Ben Webster sound, so we stayed and drank and tipped him, and this time remembered to sign Fat Humphrey's guest book—in tipsy scrawls—before we left. As we were doing so, he came up beside us. "You handled Sulke real nice," he said, "and I like her. You two didn't spend no money in here tonight, you understand?" We thanked him.

Then Kirra went to keep her rendezvous with her bug-eyed lover, and I went off to my gym to work.

To my surprise, the wine helped. This time I managed to set sixteen beats I could stand to watch on replay, and repeat them more or less at will. I was going to beat this! It was even harder than transitioning from ballet to modern had been, and I was no longer in my twenties . . . but I was going to do it.

It helped me forget the uneasiness that Sulke's talk of sabotage had put in the back of my mind. I was pretty sure she was wrong, anyway.

△   △   △

Kirra was still out when I got back to our room. I sat kûkanzen for about an hour, watched dance holos for a while in bed, then put on a sleep mask and earphones that played soft music so she wouldn't wake me when she came in.

Nevertheless I woke an hour or so later. There are no bedsprings to creak in zero gee, and they were probably making an honest effort to be quiet, but Kirra was after all a singer.

I thumbed the sleep mask up onto my forehead.

I can't claim I was a voyeurism virgin. Dancers generally lead a lively life, and once or twice in my checkered past I had watched live humans go at it—often enough, it had seemed to me. It's the oldest dance there is, of course, but as a spectator art it palls quickly, once the excitement of taboo-breaking is past.

But I never watched anyone *make love,* which is different, even to a mere witness.

Let alone in zero gee, which changes things.

They were beautiful together, moving in slow joyous unison, singing a soft, wordless song in improvised harmony, flexing together inside their sleepsack like a single beating heart.

A host of emotions ran through my mind. Annoyance that they were being so impolite, followed by the thought that in a few months I would be "in the same room with" *thousands* of love-making people, that soon none of us would ever again make love in private, that dealing with this disturbing situation was the best possible rehearsal I could have for what was to come, that if I couldn't deal with two friends making love three meters away, I'd never be able to deal with forty-odd thousand strangers making love inside my skull . . .

. . . and I couldn't get around the fact that watching them was turning me distinctly on. I had to deal with that, and with the fact that I was staring as much at Kirra as at Ben, and with jealousy of Kirra, and with the way my own growing arousal wanted me to get up and go find Robert and fuck his brains out, and with how another part of me that I didn't understand wouldn't let me do that, and it was hard to think about any of this stuff when I was getting horny enough to bark, and finally my hand crept down to my clitoris and began to move in slow circles, and as they increased in speed I realized with shock that Ben, unlike most men, had not taken his glasses off to copulate—

—his 360° vision glasses!

I froze in embarrassment for a long moment . . . and then I told myself he was too busy to pay attention to what was going on behind his back—no, I told myself the hell with it—and finished what I had started.

Eventually so did they. And then I think all three of us fell asleep. I know I did, feeling more relaxed than I had since I'd left Earth.

The next day the three of us discussed it over breakfast— Kirra brought it up, asking if they'd awakened me—and after some talk we agreed to be the kind of friends who can be that intimate among one another. It was something new for me, and a bit of a stretch: I'd never allowed anyone to observe me in ecstasy before except the one who was causing it. But in the days that followed I came to find it quite pleasant and natural to read a book, or watch TV, while Kirra and Ben made love a few meters away . . . and more than once the sight inspired me to pleasure myself. Kirra and Ben were delighted with this state of affairs, as it gave them a convenient place to make love whenever they wished—it seemed Robert was more inhibited, and so it was less comfortable for them in Ben's room.

I think it's different for men, harder to watch and not participate, harder to let yourself be watched. For some of them masturbation seems to represent a kind of defeat in their minds. Sad.

△   △   △

Those first few days in Top Step pretty much set the pattern for the next four weeks . . . to the extent that there was a pattern. Meals and classes loosely defined the day, but we had great slabs of unstructured free time after both morning and afternoon class, and our evenings, to spend as we wished—piefaced in Le Puis if that was what we chose.

One thing we all did a lot was swap life stories. There'd been no time to do so back at Suit Camp, where every spare minute was spent studying or undergoing tests. I can't recall how many times I told my own story until everyone had heard it. One common theme that ran through the stories I heard in return was technological obsolescence. Just as the automobile had once ruined the buggy whip trade, the recent enormous strides in nanotechnology (made with much help from the Starseed Foundation) had made a lot of formerly lucrative occupations superfluous. Suddenly a lot of white-collar workers found themselves facing the same dilemma as a dancer or an athlete in her forties: should I start life over from square one, or opt out of the game altogether? Quite a few of them chose Symbiosis.

Another common topic of conversation was politics, but—and I know you'll find this hard to believe, for I did—political discussions somehow never once degenerated into arguments. Even in the first weeks, we were starting to find all political differences of Earthbound humans less and less relevant to anything in our own lives—and the tendency increased with time.

I'd expected to work harder than this. I said as much to Reb one day during class, sometime during the first week. "I guess I just pictured us all spending most of our time . . . working."

"At what, Morgan?"

"I don't know, studying concrete stuff we'll need when we're Stardancers. Solar system navigation, ballistics, solar sailing, astronomy, uh, zero-gee engineering and industry, nanotechnology, picotechnology—things like that." There was a murmur of agreement from the others in the class.

"You may study any of those, if you wish," he said. "Some of you are doing so, on your own initiative. But it's not necessary. Studying *data,* memorizing facts, is not necessary. You won't need those facts until you become a Stardancer and join the Starmind . . . and then you'll *have* them. That's the beauty of telepathy."

He was right, of course. The instant I entered Symbiosis, I'd be part of the group consciousness Reb called the Starmind. I'd have total access to the combined memories of all living Stardancers, something over forty thousand minds. Anything they knew, I would know, when and if I needed to know it.

As they would know everything I knew . . .

You can be told about something like that a thousand times, and remind yourself a million . . . and still you just can't get your mind around it, somehow.

"What you need to study," Reb continued, "is not facts . . . but attitude, a flexible mindset, so that encompassing that much scope doesn't destroy you. That's why meditation is the best work you can do."

"What exactly do you mean by 'destroy'?" a woman named Nicole asked. I thought: *what a dumb question.*

Reb brightened. "A good question."

"I think so," Nicole agreed. "I know the *odds* of failure—I passed the exam like everybody. One percent of those who enter Symbiosis suffer what they called 'catastrophic mental trauma.' But I don't know what that *means*. I mean, they explained it to me back dirtside—but I need somebody to explain the explanation. Can somebody's mind really . . . well, collapse, from having forty thousand other minds suddenly crash in on it?"

There was nervous laughter.

Reb did not smile. "Sometimes," he said.

The laughter died.

"Those forty thousand minds do *not* all come crashing in at once . . . but the significance of their existence does. Some minds find that intolerable."

"What happens to them?" Nicole asked.

"What happens when a star implodes?" Red replied.

"Depends on how massive it is," someone said.

Reb nodded. "It is much the same with a panicked ego. Whether it can survive telepathic union depends on how massive it is."

"How do you mean?"

"Think of a mind which has never loved," Reb said. "It *knows* that it is the center of the Universe, the only thing that is truly real, that matters. Then its body swallows some mysterious red gunk, and WHACK! suddenly it knows better. The walls of its skull drop away; for the first time ever, it is naked. Observed . . . no, more: *touched* . . . in its most intimate chinks and crannies by forty thousand strangers. Mind sees Starmind, and knows its own true smallness. By all accounts it is a terrifying realization."

This was exactly what I had been trying to imagine for weeks. Could I live with that much truth? Did I have the courage to be that naked? To let that big an audience come swarming over the stage?

"Now sometimes an ego is so entrenched in itself that it *refuses* to yield the floor, *will not* love nor be loved. It rejects what it perceives—incorrectly—as a threat to its identity. Mad with fear, it seeks escape, and there is nowhere to go but inward. It implodes like a collapsing star, literally an ego deflating. Most often it shrinks down to a small hard dense

core, like a neutron star. Invisible. Invulnerable. It must hurt
terribly. Such catatonics can sometimes be saved, healed.
With time. With skill. Many wise and compassionate minds
work nonstop to do so; so far they have a discouraging success
rate."

He had our total attention.

"But once in a long while, an imploding star is so massive,
it collapses past the point where it can exist. It leaves our
Universe, becomes a black hole. Similarly, if an ego is
massive enough, it may react to telepathic union by collapsing
past the point where it can sustain itself. It suicides rather than
surrender. It simply . . . goes away. The flame blows out.
You could say it dies. What is left is a very long-lived
humanoid with the mind of a plant or a starfish. These few are
placed in stable orbits, and they are . . ." He paused. "Uh,
'cherished' is closer than 'mourned,' I think. By the rest of the
Starmind."

"What's the ratio of deaths to comas?" Nicole asked.

"About one to a hundred. Roughly the same as the overall
ratio of failures to successes."

You could hear gears grinding as she tried to work out the
arithmetic. Several seconds passed. "So out of every thousand
people who eat red—"

"Out of every *ten* thousand who attempt Symbiosis, ninety-
nine will go into stasis, and one will die," he told her.
"Approximately. In fact there have been eight deaths, and five
hundred and eighty-seven catatonics, of whom fifty-three have
been healed so far . . . and an additional six have died."

There was a glutinous silence in the room.

Not that many of us, or even any of us, were surprised.
Nicole may have been the only person in the room to whom
these figures were news. I certainly knew them; it seemed to
me that anyone who had come this far without knowing them
was an idiot. But they were sobering statistics just the same.

And, it was just dawning on me for the first time that the
Starmind, as Reb called it, the telepathic community I was
proposing to join, did not discriminate against people I
considered idiots. I was dismayed by how dismayed that made
me. Me, an intellectual snob? Apparently.

"Look on the bright side," Reb said. "You are five hundred times *more* likely to die *during training,* before you ever get to Symbiosis. Die completely, soul *and* body, in some EVA accident. And you're two hundred times more likely to suffer serious mental breakdown and be sent dirtside."

Now, there were some grim figures. Out of every hypothetical standard class of one hundred, an average of five died before ever attempting Symbiosis . . . and two went seriously nuts from brooding about it. I'd read about one class, back in the early days of Top Step, where nearly half had died, most of them in a single ghastly accident.

Then there was the drop-out rate to be considered. An average of twelve in every class changed their minds and went home—often at the last minute. Another five balked: when three months were up, they decided not to decide. The Foundation would let you hang around Top Step as long as you wanted . . . *if* you were willing to work for your air, *and* had a job skill they needed at the time. After eleven more months—if you were still alive—your body was permanently, irrevocably adapted to zero gee: you had to either sign on with the Foundation permanently—if they would have you—or else become part of the permanent-transient population of spacers, like Sulke. Or, of course, get off the dime and eat Symbiote.

"But if you survive long enough to attempt Symbiosis," Reb went on, "your chances of success are much higher than those of, say a pregnant woman to birth successfully. The kind of mind that will collapse when exposed to telepathy tends not to come here to Top Step at all. Either it never applies, or we filter it out in the preselection stage, or it drops out during Suit Camp."

"So why go through two or three months of preparation?" Nicole asked. "I read that some people have become Stardancers without it."

"Because experience has shown it eases the transition," Reb said patiently. "At best, Symbiosis is painful . . . one Stardancer likened it to a turtle having its shell ripped away . . . but those who have had the training agree it helps enormously. If you can learn to live without the false distinctions of 'up' and 'down,' you probably can learn to live with the equally false distinctions between 'me' and 'not-me.' "

"So why so much free time, why aren't we working all the time?" Nicole wanted to know.

"Oh, for Christ's sake, Nicole!" Glenn blurted. By this time I was so annoyed with Nicole's broken-record questioning myself that I grunted in agreement.

Reb looked at me. "You cannot think Nicole's question is foolish, Morgan. You asked it yourself a minute ago."

You blush easier in free fall, and more spectacularly.

"But it is foolish, nonetheless," he went on gently. "You *are* working all the time, Nicole. Everyone is, everyone everywhere. You can't help but keep working. Didn't you know that?"

She looked confused.

"Nicole, I could have uncommon intuition and insight, and spend every minute of the next two months in your company, and *still* I would not know a tenth as much as you do about what you need to learn now, and what is the best way for you to learn it. Even Fat Humphrey's kind of 'telepathy' doesn't go that deep. That's why we try to make sure you'll have lots of so-called 'free' time here, to work on it without being distracted. There isn't a lot of time left before you will have to make a big decision, and we don't want your schooling to get in the way of your education."

"But what are we supposed to *do* with all this free time?"

"You will know," Reb told her. "You will know."

CHAPTER SEVEN

When the ordinary man attains knowledge
He is a sage;
When the sage attains understanding
He is an ordinary man.

—Zen koan

I CERTAINLY KNEW what to do with *my* time. Each night Robert tutored me for an hour, then I spent the rest of the evening dancing in private until I couldn't move anymore. I hadn't worked so hard in years. But my back and knees continued to hold up, thanks to free fall . . . and as the days turned into weeks, I began to get somewhere. By the end of the second week I could do a fair imitation of *Liberation,* and I could quote sections of *Mass Is a Verb.* More important, I was making some progress on a new piece of my own. Choreography had never been my strong suit—but there was something about zero gee that made it come easier. I still wasn't ready to show anything to an audience, but I was content to be making progress, however slow it might be. I had thought, for an endless time, that I was finished as a dancer. It was like a miracle, like being reborn, to get another chance; there was no hurry. I luxuriated in each painful minute.

Ben and Kirra knew what to do with their time too—and I don't just mean making love. Ben did *not* fully acquire all the fundamentals of jaunting in two days—much less the fine points—but he did become the star pupil in our shift, and under his tutelage Kirra too became something of prodigy. They progressed just as fast in morning class, learning less tangible skills like spherical thinking, spatial orientation and conscious control of their own metabolisms and mental states. By the third week Reb admitted that they were good enough to start EVA instruction right away . . . but the system wasn't set up to allow it, and they stayed behind with the rest of us dummies, serving as assistant instructors in Sulke's class. (And, at Reb's insistence, getting paid for doing so. They both donated their unwanted salaries to the Distressed Spacer's Fund, which made Sulke happy.)

Robert was almost as adept when he arrived as Ben became, but seemed disinterested in teaching the group. He spent most of his free time, according to Ben, designing free fall structures on his computer terminal in his room. I rarely saw him in Le Puis. Occasionally I ran across him in Sol Three. He was always by himself. We would chat quietly, then part. Part of me had hoped that he'd take me off the hook by becoming involved with some other woman. I certainly wouldn't have blamed him if he had; most of our fellow students seemed to be pairing up. He continued to tutor me every night, without pressing me for further intimacy. We remained aware of each other, slowly building a charge.

It had been a long time since a man had courted me with that kind of mixture of determination and patience. I liked it.

△   △   △

According to Teena, our class had one of the most painless, trouble-free Postulancies in the history of Top Step. Only three of us dropped out and went back to Earth during the first two weeks (all three for the most common of reasons: persistent inability to tolerate a nonlinear environment, to live without up and down). None of us got so crazy that we had to be sent home. None of us died, or sustained serious injuries. There were no incidents of violence, even on the level of a fistfight. Six of us got married—all at once, to each other. (Ben and Kirra were that kind of committed, but never bothered with any formal ceremony or celebration.) All of us formed friendships, which expanded in informal affinity groups, which somehow did not become exclusionary cliques. Dorothy Gerstenfeld logged an all-time record minimum of complaints and emergencies. As Reb said one day, smiling his Buddha smile, "Good fellowship seems to be metastasizing." People who wanted them gravitated to temple or *zendo* or shrink or encounter group or whatever it took to ease their pain or enhance their mindfulness, and Le Puis became the first bar

I'd ever seen that rarely seemed to have anything but happy drunks.

All this was in sorry contrast to the planet we orbited. From the great window in Sol Three, Earth *looked* peaceful, serene. But we all followed Earthside news, and knew just what an anthill in turmoil it really was. That was the month that China and Argentina were making war noises, and none of the other major players could figure out which side to back. For one three-day period we honestly thought they might start setting off Big Ones down there at any moment. Who really knew whether the UN-SDI net would actually work? One afternoon when I was meditating in Sol Three I mistook a sudden flare of reflected sunlight off Mar Chiquita, a huge Argentinian lake, for a nuke signature—just for an instant, but it was a scary instant.

I was surprised to find that political upheaval on Earth did not carry over to Top Step. We had several ethnic Chinese besides Robert in our class, and close to a hundred inboard altogether, as well as an equal number of Hispanophones and four actual Argentinians. (One of the three Suit Camps was located in Ecuador.) If there was ever so much as a harsh word exchanged among any of them, I didn't hear about it—and any space habitat has a grapevine that verges on telepathy.

I did some reading, guided by Teena, and learned that from the very beginnings of space exploration, spacers have always tended to feel themselves literally above the petty political squabbles of the groundhogs below. Immigrants to a new country can continue to cling to their ethnic or national or religious identity for a generation or two, but immigrants to space quite often seem to leave theirs on the launchpad. And Stardancer-candidates have even less reason to get agitated about the doings of nations than most spacers. In a matter of weeks, we'd all be surrendering our passports.

As for myself, I'd never felt especially patriotic about being a Canadian. But then, that was a notorious characteristic of most Canadians. The only thing we were proud of was not being Americans.

We all followed Earth news . . . but even as the drama below us began to get dangerously interesting, it became less and less relevant to us. We spent less and less time watching Earth in Sol Three. We retained concern for the suffering of human beings—but for humans *as a species:* the labels and abstractions they used to separate themselves seemed more and more absurd.

We weren't spacers yet. But we were no longer Terrans.

△   △   △

By the end of the third week, Reb and Sulke between them had brought us former groundhogs to the point where we could not only stand to be in the dark in zero gee, but could navigate reliably in darkness.

Do you have any idea how incredibly far that was?

One of the first humans ever to *live* in space, a member of the Skylab crew, woke one night to find that the light in his sleeping compartment had failed. That compartment compared with a coffin for roominess. He knew exactly where the switch for the emergency backup lighting was located. It took him nearly half an hour to find it, half an hour on the trembling verge of fullblown panic. And he was a hypertrained jock. The first time Reb doused the lights, for not more than a minute, the classroom rang with screams, and about a third of us ended up having to go change our clothes. In the total absence of either visual or kinesthetic cues, your hindbrain decides that the sensation of falling is literal truth, and you just come unstuck. All the rational thought in the world doesn't help. You clutch the first wall or structure or person you encounter like a panicking drowner, and hang on for dear life, heart hammering. Five of us dropped out that night.

But methodical disciplines of breath-control and muscle-control and self-hypnosis do help, and practice helps most of all. Once you get past the terror part, the disorientation diminishes quickly. We played orientation and navigation games. For instance: three of you crawl along the walls of the classroom in the dark, humming to each other, until your ears tell you that you're all roughly equidistant in the spherical room; then you jaunt for where you think the center of the room is, and try to meet your mates there . . . ideally without cracking your skull or putting someone's eye out. It was fun, once we all started getting good at it.

And it took us that last step toward sphericity, toward being comfortable without even an imaginary local vertical. We lost our tendency to line up with whomever we were talking to or working with, and started living three-dimensionally without having to make a mental effort.

And that started to affect us all in subtle psychological ways, broadening us, opening us up, undoing other sorts of equally rigid preconceptions about the universe. Up/down may be the first dichotomy a baby perceives (even before self/not-self), the beginning of duality, or either/or, yes/no logic. Hierarchy depends on the words "high" and "low" having meaning. Floating free of gravity is just as exhilarating in space as it is in dreams, and constant exhilaration can help solve a lot of human problems. The therapeutic value of skydiving has long been known, and we never had to snap out of the reverie and pull our ripcords.

One by one, we became more pleasant people to be with than we had been back on terra firma. Glenn, for instance, lost a great deal of her dogmatism, became more flexible, started making friendships with people she had considered airheads back in Suit Camp. Eventually she even lost the frown that had seemed her natural expression.

Yes, it was our time of Leavetaking, of saying goodbye to our earthly lives, and yes, some of it was spent in solemn meditation in Solarium or *zendo* or chapel or temple. But the solemnity was balanced by an equal and opposite quantum of gaiety.

Dorothy Gerstenfeld had been right, back on that first day: zero gee tended to make us childlike again in significant ways. We were doing some of the same sort of metaprogramming that a small child does—redoing it, really, with different assumptions—and do you remember how much *fun* it was being a small child?

We had the kind of late-night bull sessions I hadn't had with anyone since college, full of flat-out laughter and deep-down tears, like kids around an eternal campfire with all the grownups gone to bed.

There are so many games you can play in zero gee. Acrobatics; spherical handball, billiards, and tennis; monkey bars; tag . . . the list is endless. Even a moderately good frisbee thrower becomes a prodigy. You'd be astonished how many solid hours of entertainment you can get from a simple glass of water, coaxing it into loops and ropes and bubbles and lenses with the help of surface tension. A man named Jim Bullard devised a marvelous game involving a hollow ball within which a small quantity of mercury floated free, causing it to wobble unpredictably in flight; in gravity it would have just been a nuisance, but in zero gee it was an almost-alive antagonist. I used my Canadian background to invent one of my own: 3-D curling. The idea was to scale pucks so gently that air resistance caused them to come to rest in an imaginary sphere in the center of the room, while knocking away your opponent's pucks. Your teammate tried to help by altering the puck's trajectory inflight with a small compressed-air pen— with strictly limited air which had to last him the whole round. As in curling, it took forever to find out how good your shot was . . . and you all had to keep moving while you waited, since the room's air-circulation had to be shut off. Robert and I teamed up at it and soon were beating all comers. Ben invented a three-dimensional version of baseball—but it was so complicated that he never managed to teach it to enough people to get a game going. With assistance from Teena, Kirra actually managed to locate a piece of genuine wood some- where inboard (at a guess, I'd say there isn't enough real wood in all of space to build a decent barn; even the legendary Shizumi Hotel uses a superb fake), and borrowed tools to work it from one of the construction gangs who daily burrowed ever deeper into the rock heart of Top Step. When she was done, she got permission from Chief Administrator Mgabi, and took her creation down to the Great Hall. A small crowd went along to watch. She tested the breeze, locked her feet under a handrail to steady herself, and threw the thing with consider- able care and skill. That boomerang was still circling the Hall when she reached out and caught it three hours later. I wanted her to let it keep going, but she and I and the volunteers at the major tunnel mouths who kept passing pedestrians from jaunting out into the thing's flight path all had to get to class.

One of the best games of all could be played solo in your room without working up a sweat: browsing through the Net. We all had Total Access, like the most respected and funded scholars in the Solar System, and could research to exhaustion any subject that interested us, initiate datasearches on a whim which would have bankrupted us back on Earth, download music and literature and visual art to our heart's content. Ben in particular was heavily addicted to Netwalking, and it was a common occurrence for Kirra to have to drag him away from his terminal to go eat . . . whereupon he would begin babbling to her about what he'd just been doing or reading. Glenn too binged heavily, as did several others. As for myself, all I really used my access for was to watch hour after hour of Stardancer works, especially the ones that Shara Drummond and the Armsteads performed in. They were unquestionably the best dancers in space, and not just because they had been the first. By that point in history, all Stardancer dances were officially choreographed by the Starmind as a whole, in concert . . . and that must have been to a large extent true. But from time to time I was sure I recognized phrases or concepts that were pure Shara or pure Charlie/Norrey, even in works in which they didn't physically appear.

$$\triangle \quad \triangle \quad \triangle$$

On the last day of week three, Kirra sprang a surprise on us. Reb called her up beside him in class that morning, and told us that she had something special to share with all of us. Most of us knew by then about her background and reason for being here; for the benefit of those who didn't know all the details, she briefly sketched out the history of the Dreamtime, and the Songlines, and the importance of Song in the Aboriginal universe.

"My people want to start movin' out into space," she finished up, "and so my job is to start sussin' out the Songs for all this territory, so's we can come make Walkabout here without bein' afraid it'll all up and turn imaginary on us."

"How're you doing?" someone asked.

"Well, that's what I'm doin' here in front of you. It's been a lot slower goin' than I expected . . . I got the Song o' Top Step now, but. An' I want to sing it for all you bastards." (By now we had all learned that to an Australian, "bastard" held no negative connotations, meaning simply "person," usually but not always male. Similarly, "tart" merely meant "female person.")

A surprised and delighted murmur went through the room: most of us knew how much her responsibility weighed on her. I was thrilled.

"I just finished it this mornin' before brekkie, even Ben an' me roomie haven't heard it yet. You all been here as long as I have, you ought to hear it. This ain't just a tabi, a personal song, this is a proper corroboree Song, an' it calls for an audience. Anyway I wanted you all to hear it, an' Reb said it was all right with him if I did it here."

There were universal sounds of approval and encouragement.

"All right, then: here goes."

She took her boomerang from her pocket, slapped it rhythmically against her other palm for ten counts, and began to sing.

I cannot supply a translation of the words, and will not reproduce them as she sang them, because they were in Padhu-Padhu, a secret ritual language known only to Aboriginals, so secret (she explained to me later) that its very existence was unsuspected by Caucasian scholars until the late twentieth century.

And it doesn't matter, because there were very few words in what she sang. Very little of her song's information content was verbal. It was the melody itself that was important.

How can I describe that melody to you? I doubt that there is anything in your experience to compare it to. In fact, I doubt that there would have been much in another Aboriginal's experience to compare it to; I'd heard a number of their Songs from Kirra and this was unlike them in ways I'm not equipped to explain even if you were equipped to understand me. It did not behave like any other melody I'd ever heard, yet somehow without thereby becoming unpleasing to the ear.

It began at the very bottom of her alto register, and arced up in a smooth steady climb that suggested the shuttle flight from Earth. It opened out into a repeated five-tone motif whose majesty and regularity seemed to represent Top Step in its great slow orbit. Then the song changed, became busier. It behaved much like a jaunting Postulant, actually, gliding lazily, then putting itself into tumbles, then straightening out, bouncing off imaginary walls, coming to a halt and then kicking off again. Like a jaunter's progress, her melody never really stopped, for she had mastered the didgeridu player's trick of breathing in and out at the same time so that she never had to pause for breath. I closed my eyes as I listened, and the twists and turns her voice took evoked specific places in Top Step powerfully for me. The Great Hall, Solarium Three, a merry little flurry that was unmistakably Le Puis, a slow solemn ululation that was Harry Stein at the window of Solarium One. Somewhere in the middle was a frankly sensual movement that expressed zero gravity lovemaking, explicitly and movingly. Ben's humour was in it, and Kirra's mischievousness, and the richness of their love for each other. At the end, the five-tone theme returned, first with little trills of embellishment and then at last in its pure form, slower and slower until she drew out its last note into a drone, and fell silent.

I don't know how long we all drifted, silent, motionless, like so many sea lions. Reb was the first to shake off stasis and put his hands together, then Ben joined and then me and then the whole room exploded in applause and cheers that lasted for a long time. One of the loudest was Jacques LeClaire, the other musician in the room. She accepted our applause without smiling, as her due—or so I thought.

"It's called 'Taruru,'" she said when the noise had died down. "That means a lot o' things, really. 'Last glow of evening,' and 'dying embers,' and 'peace o' mind,' kinda rolled into one."

"Teena," Reb said, "save the Song Kirra just sang to her personal files as 'Taruru.'"

"Yes, Reb."

"Kirra," Reb went on, "I think you should send that recording, as is, to your tribe."

"You think? I can do it again any time, just like that: that's the point of a Songline Song."

"I understand. But send that copy. Please. I would be honoured." Ben and I and others made sounds of vigorous agreement. Jacques called, "*Oui!* That is a take."

She nodded. "Right, then. Teena, transmit 'Taruru' to my Earthside number, would you?"

"It's done. Receipt has . . . just been acknowledged by your phone."

"What time is it in Queensland now?"

"Five-fourteen PM."

"Bonzer. Yarra can play it for the Yirlandji Elders tonight after supper. Teena, everybody here can have a copy if they want."

There were more cheers. Kirra was well liked.

"You'll void your copyright," Glenn warned.

Kirra blinked at her. "What copyright? I didn't *make up* the bloody thing, mate, I just sang it. It's the Song of this place, see? It was here before I got here. You can't copyright the wind."

Now I understood why she'd heard our applause without smiling. She'd assumed we were applauding the Song, not her performance.

"One suggestion," Reb said.

"Yes, Reb?"

"Transmit a copy to Raoul Brindle."

There was a murmur. Brindle had been the most famous living composer for over thirty years. "*Oui,*" Jacques called again, and several others echoed him. "*Da!*" "*Sí!*" "*Hai!*"

Kirra looked thoughtful. "Be a bloody expensive phonecall, but. He an' the Harvest Crew aren't more than halfway back from Titan, it'd have to go by laser."

"If it did," Reb said, "Top Step would pay the cost; Raoul has left specific orders that he wants to hear anything you want to send him. But a laser is not necessary. Since you are willing to release the Song to the public domain, just phone any nearby Stardancer and sing it. Raoul will hear it instantly."

"Why, sure! I'll never get used to this telepathy business. Hey, Teena, send that Song to the nearest Stardancer that ain't busy, addressed to Raoul Brindle, would ya?"

"Transmission in progress," Teena said. "Routing through Harry Stein, in realtime. Transmission ends in a little over five minutes."

There was one more round of applause, and then Kirra joined the rest of us and Reb began regular class. But five minutes later, Reb paused in the middle of a sentence.

"Excuse me, friends. Teena has just informed me that there is a phonecall for Kirra from Raoul Brindle. Kirra?"

"Open line, Teena."

Raoul Brindle said, "Hello, Kirra."

"G'day, mate," she said, as though living legends phoned her up all the time.

"I don't want to interrupt your class. I just wanted to say that your Song has been heard by all members of the Starmind presently in circuit, from the orbit of Venus to that of Uranus. Our response condenses down to: *hurry, sister*. We await your Graduation. I'd be honoured if you'd sail on out here and meet me once you're Symbiotic. Oh, and there's a waiting list of one hundred and eighty-seven Stardancers who'd like to have a child with you if you're willing. Uh, I'm one of 'em."

Kirra blinked. "Well, if I'm gonna live forever I suppose I got to do somethin' with my time. I'm willin' to discuss it with the lot of you bastards—but the line forms behind me Benjamin here. I think he's got dibs on the first half dozen or so."

"No hurry," Raoul agreed. "I would like to score your Song for didgeridu, mirrimba and walbarra, if you don't mind."

"Oh please!" she said. "And send it me, will you? I hated havin' to leave me instruments behind. Have you really got 'em all out there with you?"

"In my head," he said. "Once you're Symbiotic, you'll find that's all you really need. But I can reprogram my simulator to make a recording you can hear now."

"That'd be smashin'. About this comin' out there to meet you, though . . . what's the point? I mean, I'll be just as near to you if my body's right here, won't I?"

"Even for telepaths, touch has special meaning," he said. "In one sense you're right . . . but I'd like to shake your hand sooner, rather than later. It shouldn't take you more than a few weeks."

"It would make a lovely honeymoon trip, love," Ben said. Under her influence he had lately been developing the ability to speak short sentences, and then stop. It was some of the strongest evidence I'd seen yet that Top Step could radically alter character.

She smiled suddenly. "Right, then. We'll do it—singin' all the way!"

The room rocked with cheers.

I could not completely suppress a twinge of envy. I wished I were coming along in my art as fast as she was in hers. But I was terribly happy for her.

△　△　△

The next day was Sunday. (I did mention that we used a six-day work week in Top Step, didn't I?) I spent the whole morning working out with Robert, the whole afternoon rehearsing in my studio, and the whole evening drinking Irish coffee in Le Puis with Robert and Kirra and Ben. Fat Humphrey had solved the zero-gee Irish coffee problem with a custom drinking bulb: a large chamber for coffee and booze, and a smaller one full of whipped cream; you sucked the former through the latter. Micah juggled, and Jacques Le-Claire put on a lovely impromptu performance on the house synth. To everyone's surprise, Glenn jumped in and sang two numbers, very well, in a pure, controlled alto. She was roundly cheered, and blushed deeply. Then Kirra had to sing the Song of Top Step for those who hadn't heard it. The applause was deafening. So many drinks were credited to her account that she never paid for another dram the whole time she was inboard. It was a memorable night.

Robert kissed me goodnight at my door, not pushing it. I sort of wished he had. But not enough to push it myself.

△　△　△

Monday we all came to class excited—some eager, some anxious. Today a new stage in our training began. We were all dressed in our p-suits, airtanks and all, and we certainly were a colourful bunch. As we entered the room, Reb gave each of us a quick, warm handclasp and a private smile. His p-suit was forest green. The room looked different: all Velcro had been stripped from the chamber; its spherical wall was smooth and shiny.

"As you know," he said when we were assembled, "today we begin a week of EVA simulation. We've discussed and prepared for it. Some of you may experience disorientation, fear, perhaps even panic. This is normal and nothing to be self-conscious about. If you feel it's becoming too much, say so and I'll turn the walls off at once. It may help to take a visual fix, now, on those nearest you."

I mapped myself in relation to Robert and Reb.

"Close your hoods, now."

We did so, and there was a soft sighing as my suit air kicked in. It was the only sound: these p-suits had radios that filtered out breathing sounds automatically, and there was no chatter.

"Remember," Reb's voice said in my ear then, "please do not use your thrusters until I tell you to. Try to remain still. This is going to be startling enough without having a train wreck. Are you all ready? Teena, begin simulation."

Top Step went away!

Suddenly we were all floating in raw, empty space. It didn't matter that we were all expecting it: the transition was as shocking as a roller-coaster plunge. A flurry of involuntary motion went through the room, and my earphones buzzed with the sum of dozens of grunts, gasps, and assorted exclamations—including my own "Dear Christ!" I swallowed hard and clung to my fix on Robert and Reb. If they were all right, I was too.

"Remember your breathing!" Reb called.

Oh yes. Inhale, *slowly,* hold it for the same interval, exhale *completely,* hold, *feel* the breath, follow it, become it . . . three weeks of training kicked in and I began to calm down, to try and appreciate the incredible sight.

The illusion provided by the spherical holo wall of the

classroom was terribly effective. Seeing space through the window of a Solarium is much different than actually being out *in* it, surrounded on all sides by infinity. Intellectually I knew it was an illusion, but it took my breath away just the same.

Earth was off to my left, turning lazily, Luna above my head, and the Sun was at my back. Top Step did not exist in this simulation, nor the Nanotech Safe Lab nor any of the other factories and modules that surrounded Top Step. All around me was eternal cold dark, and the ancient coals of a billion billion suns. For the first time in my life I began to get an emotional grasp of just how *far away* they were. In TV scifi the stars are just down the street. It suddenly came home to me just how preposterous was the notion that Man or Stardancer would ever reach them. Me, the whole human race, the whole Starmind: we were all brief, inconsequential flickers in this endless blackness—

The holo was so good that even the shadows were right. That is, the side of anyone that faced the Sun was brightly lit . . . and the other side seemed not to exist at all, unless it occulted some sunlit object behind it. In space there is no atmosphere to diffuse light and mitigate shadows. Of course there, in the room, there actually *was* air—we were breathing p-suit air only to maintain the simulation—but the holo corrected for that and fooled our eyes.

I had thought I was used to being in free fall. But I had never had this far to fall. In Top Step the longest you could possibly jaunt in a straight line before docking with something was about a hundred meters, in the Great Hall. But if someone were to give me a mischievous shove now, I would fall *for eternity* . . . or so my eyes tried to tell me, and my stomach believed them implicitly. I had no umbilical tether to catch me; in this simulation there was nothing closer than Terra to tether *to*.

Inhale, hold, exhale . . .

From Earth all you can see of the Milky Way is a streak in the sky like a washed-out rainbow. I could see the whole stupendous galactic lens edge on, bisecting the Universe. The starfield was so magnificent that for the first time in my life I understood how even some educated people could believe it ruled their destinies.

Reb said nothing further, let us soak in it. Someone was swearing, softly and steadily and devoutly, a female voice. Someone else was weeping, a male. Kirra was humming under her breath, quite unconsciously I think. All at once someone giggled, and then Jacques did too, and then others, and the very idea of giggling in space was so brave and silly that I had to laugh myself, and I think we might have gotten a group belly-laugh going if Nicole hadn't picked just then to scream. That first split second of it before the radio's automatic level control damped her volume went through my ears like a hot knife; involuntarily I started and went into a tumble. So did almost everyone else, and a train wreck began—

"Cut!" Reb told Teena calmly, and the illusion vanished at once.

We were back in our familiar classroom. The transition was just as wrenching as it had been in the other direction; we seemed to have been instantaneously teleported into the heart of Top Step. We floundered about like new chums, and gaped at each other. Reb flashed to Nicole's side and held her until she stopped screaming and began to cry softly against his chest. He summoned her roommate with his eyes, and had Nicole conducted from the room, sobbing feebly.

I found that Robert was by my side, and that I was glad he was there, and indeed was clutching tightly to his strong arm. Somehow he mentally integrated up our separate masses and vectors and used his wrist and ankle thrusters to bring us to a dead stop together, in a spot where no one else was on a collision course.

"Wow!" he said hoarsely.

"It still gets to you?" I asked.

"What do you mean, 'still'? I've been in space many times, yes—but that was my first time EVA. In simulation that good, I mean."

It surprised me a little, I'd sort of assumed a space architect would have to go outdoors to check on details of a job in progress. But it warmed me toward Robert to find him as moved and shaken as I was by the experience.

He was kind and sensitive and patient and attentive, and very attractive, and he wanted me. What was I waiting for? I couldn't explain it, even to myself. I just knew I wasn't ready.

"Are you ready?" Reb called, making me jump involuntarily. "All right, let's get back to the simulation."

Class went on.

Nicole showed up at lunch, looking wan and pale. But she wasn't at supper that night. She never came to classes again, and within two days she was back Earthside.

I visited her and said goodbye before she left. It was awkward.

We had EVA simulation in Sulke's class too for the rest of that week—only her simulations included holographic "objects" we had to match vectors with, and for the last two days she installed a real set of monkey bars which we learned to use like zero-gee monkeys. (Part of our training consisted of watching holos of real monkeys bred in free fall. God, they're fast! They make lousy pets, though: so far only cats and some dogs have ever learned to use a zero-gee litterbox reliably.)

Three more people had dropped out by the end of the week. Their egos were simply not strong enough to handle being dwarfed into insignificance by the sheer size of the Universe.

I asked Reb about that in class one day. "It just seems paradoxical. You need a strong ego to endure raw space—and we're all here to lose our egos in the Starmind."

"You are not here to lose your ego," he corrected firmly. "You're here to lose your irrational fear of *other* egos."

"Irrational?" Glenn said.

"On Earth it is perfectly rational," Reb agreed. "On Earth, there are finite resources, and so underneath everything is competition for food and breeding rights. All humans have occasional flashes of higher consciousness, in which they see that cooperation is preferable to competition—but as long as the game *is* zero sum, competition is the rational choice for the long run every time. Read Hofstadter's METAMAGICAL THEMAS, the chapter on the Prisoner's Dilemma game.

"But what the Symbiote has done is to change the rules, utterly. A human in Symbiosis has nothing to compete *for*.

Cooperation becomes more than rational and pleasant: it's inevitable."

"How long does it take to unlearn a lifetime's habit of competition?" Glenn asked.

"An average of about three-tenths of a second," Reb said. "It's what your heart has always yearned for: to stop fighting and love your neighbor. Once you become telepathic you *know*, in your bones, without question, that it's safe to do that now."

Robert spoke up—unusually; he seldom drew attention to himself in Reb's class. "Isn't competition good for a species? What pressure is there on Stardancers to evolve? Or have they evolved as far as they can already?"

"Oh, no," Reb said. "Charlie Armstead said once, 'We are infants, and we hunger for maturity.' Animals improve through natural selection only—the fit survive. Humans improve through natural selection, and because they want to. We did not *evolve* the science of medicine, we *built* it, painfully, over thousands of years, to preserve those natural selection would have culled. Stardancers improve because they want to, only. Their brave hope is that intelligence may just be able to do as good at evolution as random chance."

Robert nodded. "I think I see. It took *millions* of years for chance to produce human sentience . . . and then it took that sentience *thousands* of years to produce civilization. Telepathic sentience, that didn't have to fight for its living, might do comparable things in a lifetime."

I signaled for the floor. "I have trouble imagining how a telepathic society evolves."

Reb smiled. "So does the Starmind. Does it comfort you to know that our current knowledge suggests you'll have at least two hundred years to think about it?"

I grinned back. "It helps."

Robert signaled for attention again. "Reb, I've heard that a couple of Stardancers have died."

"Accidental deaths, yes. A total of four, actually."

"Well . . . how can a Stardancer die? I mean, each one's consciousness is spread through more than forty-thousand different minds. So for a Stardancer, isn't death really no more

than having your childhood home burn down? Your *self*
persists, doesn't it, even if it can't ever go home again?"

Reb looked sad. "I'm afraid not. It isn't consciousness that
diffuses through the Starmind, but the products of consciousness: thoughts and feelings. Consciousness itself is rooted in
the brain, and when a brain is destroyed, that consciousness
ends. Telepathy does not transcend death—the Starmind
knows no more about what lies beyond death than any human
does."

Robert frowned. "But all the thoughts that brain ever had,
remain on record, in the Starmind—and you've told us the
Starmind's memory is perfect. Wouldn't it be possible, given
every single thought a person's mind ever had, to reconstruct
it, and maintain it by time-sharing among forty-some thousand
other brains?"

"It has been tried. Twice. It is the consensus of the Starmind
that it never will be tried again."

"Why not?"

"What results is something like a very good artificial intelligence package. It has a personality, mannerisms, quirks . . .
but no *core*. It doesn't produce *new* thoughts, or feel new
feelings. Both such constructs asked to be terminated, and
were."

"Oh."

"On the other hand, no Stardancer has yet died of so-called
natural causes, and individuals as old as a hundred and ten are
as active and vigorous as you are. So I wouldn't lose any sleep
over it."

"I won't," Robert agreed. "I just wondered."

△   △   △

That Sunday there was a small celebration in the Café du
Ciel, acknowledging our transition from Postulant to Novice.
Phillipe Mgabi attended, the first time most of us had seen him
since our arrival, but it was mostly Dorothy's show. There
were no speeches, scant ceremony. Mostly it was tea and
conversation and good feelings. Some of us came forward and
told of things we had thought or felt since our arrival, difficulties we had overcome. A new marriage was announced,

and cheered. To my surprise, no gripes were aired. I think that had a lot to do with Phillipe Mgabi having been too busy to show his face for the past four weeks. I'd never seen such a smoothly running, well-organized *anything* before, and I knew how much hard work that kind of organization requires.

Under the influence of all this good fellowship, Robert and I reached a new plateau in our relationship, to wit, publicly. holding hands and necking. Nothing more serious than friendly cuddling; I think each of us was waiting for the other to make the first move. Well, I don't really know what he was waiting for.

Come to think of it, I don't know what I was waiting for either.

$\triangle$ $\triangle$ $\triangle$

And then came the day we'd anticipated for so long. I think it's safe to say we all woke up with a kids-on-Christmas-morning feeling. Today we would be allowed to leave the house!

Everyone showed up for breakfast, for once, and almost nothing was eaten. The buzz of conversation had its pitch and speed controls advanced one notch apiece past normal. A lot of teeth were showing. Then in the middle of the meal there was a subtle change. The feeling went from kids on Christmas morning to teenagers on the morning of the Chem Final. The laughter came more often, and more shrilly. A restless room in zero gravity is really restless; people bob around like corks in a high sea rather than undulating like seaweed. Smiles became fixed. A bulb of coffee got loose and people flinched away from it.

Kirra began to hum.

Under her breath at first, with a low buzzing tone to it. By the time I was aware of it, I found that I was humming along with her, and recognized the tune we were humming. The Song of Top Step. Ben joined softly in an octave below us. Kirra started to gently tap out the rhythm on the table. Someone two tables over picked up the melody, and that gave all of us the courage to increase our volume. Soon people were chiming in all over the cafeteria, even people from classes before or after ours. Not all of us knew the Song well enough to sing it, but most of us knew at least parts of it, and could join in for those. Those who couldn't carry a tune kept the rhythm with utensils. Those few who didn't know the Song at all stopped talking to listen. Even the spacers on the cafeteria staff stopped what they were doing.

We went through it three times together. The third was the best; by then almost everyone had it down. It was the kind of tune that's easy to learn quickly; even to ears raised on different musical conventions, it was *hummable*. Kirra held the final note, then let her voice tumble slowly down to the bottom of her range and die out. There was no applause. There was not a sound. Not a cough. Still bodies.

"Let's do it, then," Kirra said, and the stasis was ended. We went off to school together calmly, joyfully, quietly, as one.

CHAPTER EIGHT

Assuming Ascension, Assumption, assent
All of our nonsense is finally non-sent—
With honorable mention for whatever we meant
You are my content, and I am content.

—Teodor Vysotsky

REB AND SULKE were both waiting for us in Solarium Two. (For the rest of this week they would be teaching us together, twice a day; after that they'd teach separately again.) Although they knew us all by name and by sight, they marked us off on an actual checklist as we came through the open airlock chamber, and sealed both hatches carefully when we were all mustered. Reb was especially saintly, radiating calm and compassion, and Sulke was especially sour, nervous as a cat.

"If you haven't checked your air, do so now," she called. "We've got fresh tanks if you need them." We were all in our p-suits, and I would have bet all of us had been smart enough to check our air supply. I certainly had—six times. But little Yumiko had to come forward, shamefaced, to accept a pair of tanks and a withering glare from Sulke. "Check your thruster charges too. You're not gonna get much use out of them today, but start the habit of keeping them topped up." Three people had to disgrace themselves this time, coming forward to have their wristlets or anklets recharged. Ben was one of them.

"You've heard it a million times," Sulke told us in parade-ground voice. "I'll tell you one more time. Space does not forgive. If you take your mind off it for five seconds, it will kill you."

She took a breath to say more, and Reb gently cut her off. "Be mindful, as we have learned together, and all will be well."

She exhaled, and nodded slowly. "That's right. Okay, earthworms—" She caught herself again. "Sorry, I can't call

136

you that anymore, you've graduated." She grinned. "Okay,
*space*worms, attach your umbilicals. Make damn sure they're
hooked tight."

The term was outdated: they weren't real umbilicals like
the pioneers used, carrying air from the mothership; they were
only simple tethers. But they did fasten at the navel so the
imagery was apt. Each of us found a ring to anchor ours to on
the wall behind us. I checked carefully to make sure the
snaplock had latched snugly shut. The umbilical was about the
same diameter as spaghetti, guaranteed unbreakable, and was
a phosphorescent white so it would not be lost in the darkness.

"Radios on Channel Four," Sulke said. "Seal your hood
and hold on to your anchor. Is there anyone whose hood is not
sealed? Okay, here we go."

There was a dysharmonic whining sound as high-volume
pumps went into operation, draining the air from the Solarium.
As the air left, the noise diminished. The cubic was large, it
took awhile. We spent the time staring out the vast window.

Two was the only true solarium, the one that always faced
the Sun. Its window worked like modern sunglasses: you
could stare directly at the Sun, without everything else out
there turning dark as well. The p-suit hood added another layer
of polarization. The Sun looked like an old 60-watt bulb
head-on, but by its light you could see Top Step's own mirror
farm a few miles away, a miniature model of the three
immense ones that circle the globe, beaming down gigawatts
for the groundhogs to squabble over. It looked like God's
chandelier. I could also just make out two distant Stardancers,
their Symbiotes spun out into crimson discs, a little One-ish of
the mirror farm. (That's the side away from Earth in Top Step
parlance.) They looked like they were just basking in the sun,
rippling slightly like jellyfish, but for all I knew they could
have been directing construction out in the Asteroid Belt. Who
knows what a Stardancer is thinking? All other Stardancers,
that's who, and nobody else. There were no p-suited Third-
Monthers visible at the moment, though there were surely
some out there, too far to see or in other quadrants of space.

The sound of the pumps was gone now. The outside world
is miked in a p-suit, but the mike only functions in atmo-

sphere. There was no longer any air to support sound outside our suits, so we heard none.

"Hard vacuum," Sulke announced in my ear. "Maintain radio silence unless you have an emergency. And don't have an emergency. Here we go."

A crack appeared at the bottom of the great window. In eerie utter silence, it slid upward until it was gone. A great gaping hole opened out on empty space. Radio silence or no, there was a soft susurrant murmur. For a moment my mind tried to tell me that the Sun and empty space were *below* me, that the huge opening was a bomb bay and I was about to fall out. But I suppressed the fear easily. Reb had trained me well.

"All right," Sulke said, "starting over at this end, *one at a time,* move out when I tell you. Don't move until the person before you has reached the end of their leash, I don't want any tangles today. Try to fan out, so we end up making a big shaving brush. Rostropovitch, you're first."

Reb arranged himself like a skydiver, feet toward us, and gave a short blast on his ankle thrusters. "Follow me, Dmitri," he said softly, and jaunted slowly out into emptiness. Dmitri followed him, and then Yumiko, and the exodus began. When my turn came I was ready. A one-second blast, and I was in motion. As I passed through the open window there was a sensation as if I had pierced some invisible membrane . . . and then I was in free space, tether unreeling slightly behind me, concentrating on my aim.

The umbilical placed enough drag on me that I had to blast again halfway out. I did it for a hair too long, and reached the end of my rope with a jerk that put me into a slow-motion tumble. I stabilized it easily, and could have come to a stop—Sulke had trained me well, too—but I didn't. Like someone standing on a mountaintop and turning in circles, I rotated slowly. Now that I was no longer busy, I let myself take it all in.

And like my mates, I was dumbstruck.

It's like the psychedelic experience. It cannot be described, and only a fool will try. I know that even my clearest memories of the event are pale shadows.

In free space you seem to see better, in more detail than usual. Everything has an uncanny "realer than real" look, because there is no air to scatter the light that reaches your eyes. You see about 20 percent more stars than can be seen on the clearest night on Earth, just a little brighter and clearer than even the best simulation, and none of them twinkle. Venus, Mars and Jupiter are all visible, and visibly different from the other celestial objects.

For the first time I gained some real sense of the size of Top Step. It looked like a mountain that had decided to fly, a mountain the size of Mount Baker back where I came from. (Already I had stopped thinking, "back *home*.") Even though at that point in history something over a quarter of it had been tunneled out and put to assorted uses, the only externally prominent sign of human occupancy was the mammoth docking complex at the tip—and it had the relative dimensions of the hole in the tip of a fat cigar.

And at the same time all of Top Step was less than a dust mote. So vast is space that mighty Earth itself, off Three-ish, was a pebble, and the Sun was a coal floating in an eternal sea of ink. That made me some kind of subatomic particle. A pun awful enough to be worthy of Ben came to me: it had been too long since I'd been lepton. That made me think of Robert, and I recalled vaguely that the force that keeps leptons together is called the Weak Force. I was rummaging through my forebrain, looking for wordgames to anchor me to reality, cerebral pacifiers.

I looked around for Robert, spotted his turquoise p-suit coming into my field of vision perhaps twenty meters away — why, we were practically rubbing elbows. As in the classroom simulation holo, half of him was in darkness . . . but here in real space, there was enough backscatter of light from Top Step to make his dark side just barely visible. Other students floated beyond him; I picked out Kirra and Ben, holding hands. Jaunting as a couple is trickier than jaunting solo, but they had learned the knack.

Reb and Sulke let us all just be there in silence for a measureless time.

A forest of faint white umbilicals, like particle tracks from a cyclotron, led back to the Solarium we'd come from. Its huge window now seemed a pore in the skin of Top Step. All around us, stars burned without twinkling, infinitely far away. I became acutely aware of my breath whistling in and out, of the movement of my chest and belly as I breathed, of my pulse chugging in my ears, of the food making its way along my digestive tract and the sensation of air flowing across my skin. I felt a powerful spontaneous urge to try a dance step I'd been working on, something like an arabesque crossed with an Immelman roll. I squelched the urge firmly. Right place, wrong time.

I seemed to be at the center of the Universe, turning lazily end over end. My breathing slowed. Time stopped.

"I'm sorry, Reb," Yoji Kuramatso said sadly.

"It's all right, Yoji-san," Reb said at once. *"Daijôbu-da!"* He jetted toward Yoji, flipped over halfway there and decelerated, came to a stop beside him.

"I really thought I could handle it," Yoji said, his voice trembling slightly.

"Simpai suru-na, Yoji-san," Reb said soothingly. "Switch to Channel Six now."

They both switched their radios to a more private channel, and Reb began conducting Yoji back to Top Step, letting their umbilicals reel them slowly in rather than trying to use thrusters.

There was a murmur of embarrassment and sympathy. Yoji was liked.

"He did that great," Sulke said. "If you're going to panic, that's the way to do it. Quietly. Slowly. Is anyone else having trouble?"

No one spoke.

"Okay, we'll marinate until Reb gets back, and then we'll get to work."

Robert was passing through my visual field again. I didn't want to break radio silence, so I waited until he was facing my way and made a tentative come-here gesture. He worked himself into the right attitude, pointed his hands down at his feet and gave a short blast on both wrist thrusters. He glided toward me in ultraslow motion, stretching his hands out toward me as he came. I oriented myself to him. When he arrived, we locked hands like trapeze acrobats, only pressing instead of pulling, and I gave an identical blast in the opposite direction with my ankle-thrusters to kill his velocity. Maybe it was because we got it right that Sulke didn't chew us out for maneuvering without permission . . . or she may have had other reasons.

We drifted, facing each other, holding hands. The sun was at my back, so there was too much glare from his hood for me to see his face clearly. He must have seen mine well in the reflected light.

By mutual consent we moved to a new position, side to side, each with an arm around the other, facing infinity together. Part of me wanted to switch off my radio and talk with him hood-to-hood. But Sulke would have skinned me . . . and there really were no words, anyway.

If you are going to fall through endless darkness for timeless time, it is nice to have someone's arm around you.

After a while, Reb returned and we started doing simple maneuvers. Even classwork didn't break the mood, pop the bubble of our dreamlike state of awe and wonder. I don't mean we were in a trance—at all times we remained mindful, of our tethers and our thruster placement and our air supply—but at the same time we experienced something like rapture, a three-dimensional awareness. I had been in a similar mental/physical state before, often . . . but only onstage. I wondered which of the others had anything in their experience to liken this to.

I was going to like this. This had been a good idea. Way to go, Morgan.

We stayed out there until lunch time—and still it was over much too soon.

$$\triangle \qquad \triangle \qquad \triangle$$

I demolished twice as much food as usual at lunch; I'd have eaten more but they ran out. Most of the group was keyed up, happy, darting around like hummingbirds and chattering like magpies. Robert and I did not chatter. We touched hands, and legs, and ate together in silence, totally aware of each other.

That afternoon's class was with Reb only, in the cubic where he'd always held morning classes during the first month. For the first time, he allowed the gathering to devolve into a gabfest, encouraging us all to speak of what we had felt and thought that morning, to tell each other what it had meant to us. I was surprised at the diversity of things different people likened the experience to. Taking LSD, being in combat, falling in love, *kensho,* orgasm, electroshock, dying, being born, giving birth, writing when the Muse is flowing, doing math, an Irish coffee drunk . . . the variations were endless. For Robert it was the instant when a new design leaped into his head and began explaining itself.

One thing surprised me even more. Three of us reported that there was nothing in their previous lives to compare space to. They were the most profoundly affected of all of us, all three close to tears. This had been their first taste of transcendence. It seemed hard to believe, and terribly sad, to have lived so long without wonder.

Glenn confessed that she had several times come near giving up like Yoji and going back indoors. "I can take it as long as I'm perfectly still," she said. "I just tell myself I'm watching an Imax movie. But the minute I start to move the least little bit, and it all starts spinning around me, I just lose it. I lose my place. I lose my self. I can handle it okay indoors, even in the simulations, but out there is *different* . . ."

"But you didn't panic," Reb said.

"I came damned close!"

"So did I," Yumiko said softly.

"*Da.* Me too," Dmitri chimed in.

She stared at them. "You did?"

They nodded.

"Experienced spacers have been known to panic," Reb said. "Glenn, don't worry. You may simply not be ready yet to have a revelation of the scale you were given this morning. That is not a failure. You don't have to go back out tomorrow if you decide you're not ready. You may need to spend more time in meditation first. I'll be glad to spend private time with you if you like. Don't force yourself to continue if you feel it is harmful to you. Charlotte Joko Beck once said, 'A premature enlightenment experience is not necessarily good.' Looked at from a certain angle, enlightenment is a kind of annihilation—a radical self-emptying. There is time, plenty of time."

"All right," she said, "I'll sleep on it and let you know."

"You can do it, love," Kirra called out. "I know you can!"

"Goddam right," Ben seconded, and there were noises of agreement from others.

Glenn smiled, embarrassed but pleased. "Thanks."

$$\triangle \quad \triangle \quad \triangle$$

Reb dismissed class early, suggesting we all meditate privately when we felt ready.

Robert and I paused in the corridor outside the classroom, off to one side. As other Novices jaunted past us, we stared deep into each other's eyes, communicating wordlessly.

It seemed that almost everything I'd seen outside was there to be seen in those almond hazel eyes. Perhaps more—for space was indifferent to me, and utterly cold. Effortlessly I reached a decision which had eluded me for a month.

"A lot of things came clear out there today," I said. My voice was rusty.

"Yes." So was his.

"Teena, is my studio free for the afternoon?"

"Yes, Morgan."

I reached out and took Robert's left hand with my right. "Come with me."

He nodded, and we kicked off together.

Once inside the studio I dimmed the lights slightly, to about the level of dusk on Earth. I told Teena to hold all calls, and to see that we had privacy. I gently maneuvered Robert to a handhold near the camera I'd been calling Camera One and using for main POV.

"Stay here," I told him.

He nodded.

It took an effort to look away. I spun and jaunted to the far side of the room. I paused there. I unsealed my p-suit and took it off, making no attempt to strip erotically, simply skinning out of my clothes like an eleven-year-old on a shielded wharf.

I worked the thrusters from the suit and slid them over my bare wrists and ankles, seated the controls against my palms. I closed my eyes, and cleared my mind . . .

. . . and danced.

I had been working on a piece, but did not dance that. Nor did I quote existing works of others, although I was capable of it now. I had no choreographic plan; for the first time in over thirty-five years I simply let the dance come boiling out of me.

One of the reasons I had failed as a choreographer on Earth was that I had let them teach me too much, absorbed too many rules and conventions of dance to ever again be truly sponta-neous. But here I was a child again. Once again I could create.

And what came boiling up out of me first was much the same as what had come boiling out of the eleven-year-old Rain McLeod. I can't describe the dance to you: it was improvised, and the cameras were not rolling. But I can tell you what I was saying with it, when I began.

I was saying the same thing I had said with that first dance, back on Gambier Island. The same thing Shara Drummond had been saying in the Stardance.

Here I am, Universe! I'm here: look at me. I exist. I matter.

I was talking back to endless empty blackness spattered with shards of ancient starlight, to a universe cold and burning down forever, to all the awful immensity I had seen that morning.

At first I danced only with my muscles, maintaining my position in space while I spun and turned around my center, making shapes and changing them, stretching and contracting, hurling my spine about with the force of my limbs. Then I began to use my thrusters, first to alter attitude, and then to move me around the room. I borrowed some vocabulary from ice-skating, and adapted it to three-dimensionality, swooping in widening curves that came ever closer to the wall of the spherical gym, decorating them with axle-spins.

Robert watched, as expressionless as a sea lion, bobbing slowly in the air currents I was creating.

I made him the focal point of my dance, danced not just to him, but of him. As I did my dance began to change. I danced

Robert, as I saw him. I danced quiet competence, and ready courage, and strength and self-reliance and patience and mystery and grace.

There you are! You're there: I see you. You exist. You matter.

He understood. I saw him understand.

My dance changed again. I began to dance not of the awesome immensity of space, but of the exhilaration of being alive in it; to speak not of eternity but of now. I had proclaimed myself to the Universe; now I offered myself to him.

Here we are! We're here: look at us. "We" exists. We will matter.

He watched, so utterly relaxed that his head began to nod slowly with his breathing, as though he were asleep with his head unsecured. Or was he nodding agreement?

Finally I was done. I had said everything that was in my arms and legs and spine, everything in my heart. I floated facing him across the room, arms outstretched, waiting.

He sighed deeply, and let go of his handhold. Eyes locked with mine, he removed his p-suit, and released it to drift. And then he came to me, and then he came into me, and soon he came in me.

$\triangle$ $\quad$ $\triangle$ $\quad$ $\triangle$

We made love for hours, slow dreamy love in which orgasms were merely the punctuation in a long and unfolding statement. Zero gee changes everything about the oldest dance. Together we learned and invented, made shapes and figures impossible under gravity. Both of us kept the use of our hands; neither of us was on top. The room spun around us. We cried together, and giggled together, and planed sweat from each other's backs with our hands. We told each other stories of our failed marriages and past lovers. Even with the freedom of three dimensions, we were unable to find any embrace in which we did not fit together as naturally as spoons. We drifted in each other's arms between rounds of lovemaking, bumping occasionally into the wall, but never hard enough to cause us to separate.

△   △   △

By the time we remembered the existence of the so-called real world, it was too late to get supper at the cafeteria. Well, we might just have made it . . . but we had to shower first, and that turned into more lovemaking. But the grill at Le Puis is always open, so we headed there, arm in arm, aglow, kissing as we jaunted. People we passed smiled.

We stopped along the way to leave our p-suits in our rooms. We discussed dressing, but could not come up with any reasons for doing so, so we didn't bother. (I don't recall whether I've mentioned it before, but it should be obvious that Top Step had no nudity taboo. People who are uncomfortable with social nudity are not good candidates for Symbiosis.)

Fat Humphrey greeted us with a grin incredibly even bigger than usual, and a roar of delight. "So you finally got off the dime, eh? I t'ought I was gonna hafta be the one to tell you two you were in love. Hey, this makes me happy! Let's see, you gonna want a booth—right this way!"

He led us to a booth off in what would have been a corner if Le Puis had corners—far from any other patrons, I mean. We did not bother stating requests, indeed didn't even think about it. We gazed deep into each other's eyes in silent communication until Fat returned with food and drink. He opaqued the booth, and sealed it behind him as he left. I was mildly surprised by the amount of food, but Fat didn't make mistakes. Sure enough, when I next noticed, it was all gone. I don't remember what it was . . . but the drink was champagne.

As we were squeezing the last sips into each other's mouths, Fat scratched discreetly at the closure of our booth. Robert unsealed it; Fat passed in a pipe, then departed again, beaming. It turned out to contain just enough hashish for two tokes apiece. Robert took all four, and passed them to me in kisses; I drank intoxication from his mouth. We caressed each other, slowly, dreamily, not so much lustfully as affectionately. Music, selected by Fat Humphrey, began to play softly in the background. I hadn't heard it before then, but it fit the moment perfectly: Vysotsky's "Afterglow." I'm terrible with song lyrics, but one verse I retain verbatim:

> **Incandescent invention, and blessed event**
> **Tumescent distention, tumultuous descent**
> **Our bone of convention at last being spent**
> **I am your contents, and I am content**

Finally, I said, "Put that thing away so we can leave here without making a spectacle of ourselves."

"Oh, sure," he said. "Reb's taught me how to control my metabolism: I'll just wish it away."

"Right," I agreed, and struck the most erotic pose I could. Fifteen seconds later he conceded defeat by tickling me.

"Why leave?" he said. "It's private in here."

"True. But we'd jiggle it so much we might as well do it out in plain sight—and people are trying to eat. Besides, I want more room than this."

"Good thinking." He eased away from me and glanced down. "Well, if we wait for this to go away, we'll be here come Graduation. Let's brazen it out."

So we did. If anyone noticed, they kept it to themselves. Fat Humphrey waved as we left, clearly overjoyed at our happiness.

We ran into Glenn along the way, headed in the same direction we were. She didn't notice Robert's condition. She had left Le Puis just before us, and was a little squiffed. We said hello, and then regretted it, for she wanted to talk.

No, worse. If she'd just wanted to talk, we could have politely brushed her off when we reached our door. But she *needed* to talk. She was still trying to come to terms with all she'd seen outside that morning.

She had always been polite, taciturn, reticent to intrude on anyone's privacy with personal conversation; if she needed to unload now I felt an obligation to help. So when we reached my place I queried Robert with my eyes, got the answer I'd hoped for, and invited Glenn in.

"You know what it was?" she told us. "I was doing just fine

for the first while, I really was. And then I started thinking of the only other times I'd ever felt . . . I don't know, felt that close to God. Once when I birthed my daughter . . . and just about every time I ever walked in a forest. I started thinking that I could birth kids again for the next couple of centuries, if I go through with this—but that if I go through with this, I'll never go for a walk in the woods again. And I started to panic."

"Reb says once you're Symbiotic, you can reexperience any moment of your life, so vividly it's like living it again," I said. "Or anybody else's life who's in the Starmind."

"I know," she said. "But it won't be the same as being there. Even if it's close enough to fool me, it won't be the same."

"How real do you need reality to be?" Robert asked reasonably. "If it passes the Turing Test—if you can't tell it from a real experience—then what's the difference?"

"I *don't know*," she said, "but there's a difference. Look, you've walked in woods, haven't you?"

"Not in years," he admitted. "Woods are kind of hard to come by where I lived."

"But you know what I mean. When you walk in the woods, there are so many things going on at once, nobody could notice and remember them all. Leaves fluttering, birds chirping, wind in the branches, a hundred different smells of things growing and rotting—I could list things there are to notice in the woods for the next two hours and there'd still be a thousand things I left out, things I don't even consciously notice. So how am I going to remember them all clearly enough to recreate them in my mind? It just doesn't seem possible."

Robert frowned. "I don't know how to answer you."

I had an inspiration. "I know somebody who does. Teena—who's the nearest Stardancer who's got time to talk?"

"Greetings, Morgan McLeod," a feminine voice said. "I am Jinsei Kagami. May I do you a service?"

I was taken a little aback. I hadn't expected such snappy service; I'd been planning on time for second thoughts. It was like praying . . . and getting an answer! I was a little awed to find myself talking to a real live Stardancer.

Well, I told myself, *if you didn't want the djinn, you shouldn't have rubbed the lamp. At least don't waste her time . . .*

"My friends Glenn Christie and Robert Chen are here with me. Glenn would like to talk to you, if you're not too busy."

"There is time. Greetings, Glenn and Robert."

Robert said hello and made a low *gassho* bow to empty air. Glenn said, "Hello, Jinsei; Glenn here. I'm sorry to bother you."

Voices can smile. I know because hers did. "You do not, cousin. How may I help you?"

"Well, I . . . " Glenn frowned and gathered her thoughts. "I guess I'm having trouble believing that I won't miss Earth after Symbiosis. I've been trying to say goodbye to it since I got here—and today I went EVA for the first time, and all I could think of was the places on Earth that I have loved. Jinsei-*sama,* don't you ever miss . . . your old home?"

"Do you ever miss your mother's womb?" Jinsei asked.

Glenn blinked, and did not reply.

"Of course you do," Jinsei went on, "especially when you are very tired. And a fine sweet pain it is. I did too, when I was human. But I do not miss my mother's womb anymore. I can *be* there, whenever I want. I have access to *all* my memories, back to the moment my brain formed in the fifth month of my gestation. You cannot remember the events of one second ago as vividly as I remember every instant I have lived—I and all my brother and sister Stardancers. I can be anywhere any of us has ever been, do anything any of us has ever done. For the memories of fetal life alone, I would trade a dozen Earths."

Somehow even after meeting Harry Stein I had subconsciously expected that a Stardancer in conversation would be sort of dreamy and . . . well, spacey, like someone massively stoned. She sounded as alert and mindful as Reb.

" 'Every instant . . .' Even the painful ones?" Glenn asked.

"Oh, yes."

"Don't they hurt?"

"Oh, yes. Beautifully."

Glenn looked confused.

"I think what you are asking," Jinsei said gently, "is whether a Stardancer ever regrets Symbiosis."

"Uh . . . yes. Yes, that's just what I'm asking."

"No, Glenn. Not one. Not so far."

That extraordinary assertion hung there in the air for a moment. A life without regret? No, these Stardancers were not human.

Glenn was frowning. "What about the catatonics?" she asked.

"They're not Stardancers," Robert pointed out.

"They have not enough awareness to regret," Jinsei said. "When they are healed, they no longer regret . . . or perhaps it is the other way around. And the fraction who die renounce regret forever, along with all other possible experiences."

There was a short silence. Finally Glenn nodded slowly. "I think I see. Thank you, Jinsei. You have comforted me."

"I am glad, Glenn."

"Jinsei-*sama*?" Robert said.

"Yes, Robert?"

"Can a Stardancer lie?"

I thought the question rude, opened my mouth to say so . . . and found that I wanted to hear the answer. It was a question that had never occurred to me before.

Jinsei found it amusing. "Can you think of any answer I could make that would be meaningful?"

Robert blinked in surprise, and then chuckled ruefully. "No, I guess not. I don't even know why I asked that. I know the answer, or I wouldn't be here."

"Thank you," she said, and he looked relieved. "Forgive me: I find that I am needed; is there anything else I can do for you three?"

We said no and thanked her, and she was gone.

Glenn jaunted near and offered a hug. I accepted without hesitation. Her p-suit was cool on my bare flesh, but not unpleasantly so. "Thank you, Morgan, very much. I'd never have had the nerve to do that."

"Glad to. It seemed like it was called for. Are you okay now?"

"Yes, I think I am. I need to sit kûkanzen some more, but I think I'll be able to go back out there tomorrow—thanks to you and Robert. Good night."

To my mild surprise, she hugged Robert too. "Thank you for lending me some of your courage," she said, and left.

Robert and I looked at each other and smiled.

"Where were we?" I said.

"About to make some memories so good that we'll relive them every day for the next two hundred years," he said.

We certainly did our best. After a while reality turned all warm and runny, and when I was tracking again I noticed idly that Kirra and Ben were in the room now too. But there was no need to restart my brain: they were busy, just like we were. I don't think Robert even noticed. Good concentration, that man.

△   △   △

Yumiko died the next day.

For the second day in a row, she failed to check her air supply—and this time Sulke did not remind us before opening the Solarium window. An hour later Yumiko failed to respond to a direction. It's hard to see how one could run out of air without noticing something is wrong . . . but if Yumiko ever did realize she had a problem, she was too polite to bring it up. They say lifeguards in Japan have to be terribly alert, because most drowners there are too self-effacing to disturb everyone's *wa* by calling for help. When she was missed, it was too late.

(Reb flashed to her side, diagnosed her problem, threw her empty tanks into deep space and replaced them with his own, headed for home on what air he had in his suit, squeezing her chest energetically enough to crack ribs as he went—to no avail. When they got her out of the suit she was irretrievably brain dead.)

Sulke would not cancel the rest of the class, and insisted on taking us all out again in the afternoon. She was so clearly controlling anger that I knew she must be feeling horrid guilt—and she did not deserve it, in my opinion: there comes a time when the teacher must stop wiping the students' noses. She had *told* us yesterday, *space does not forgive*. But she could not forgive herself, either.

Reb conducted the funeral service that night. Little Yumiko had been a follower of *Ryobu Shinto,* or Two-aspect Shinto, an attempt to reconcile Shinto with Buddhism which had recently been revived in Japan after more than a thousand years of dormancy; apparently they used the Buddhist funeral rites. There were prayers offered in all the other holy places in Top Step as well; sadly, those pages were well thumbed in all the hymnals.

Robert and I attended none of these observances. We held one of our own, in my room, saying goodbye to Yumiko and consoling ourselves in the only real way there is, the oldest one of all. I'm pretty sure Kirra and Ben were doing the same thing down the hall . . . and doubtless others were too. Sudden death seems to call for the ultimate affirmation of life. Sharing it brought Robert and me closer together; all smallest reservations gone, I gave my heart to him, opened to him as though he were my Symbiote, and he flowed into me.

As I was trying to fall asleep, I kept thinking that I had barely known Yumiko. Sure, she had been shy—but if I had made the effort, gotten to know her, she could have lived forever as real as real in my brain once I became Symbiotic. I hoped her roommate Soon Li had made the effort.

CHAPTER NINE

This is merely a series of events. Their only
correlation is that they all occurred within
the same time-frame.

—Boeing official, after eleven passengers were
sucked out of an airliner, Boeing's eighth
public relations disaster within a year

THE NEXT MORNING'S EVA was also eventful. Nobody died,
but the near miss was spectacular.

We had progressed in proficiency to the point where Sulke
would have half a dozen of us at a time unsnap our umbilicals
and practice thruster use without constraint—six being the
most she and Reb were confident of being able to supervise at
one time. Learning precise thruster control was *not* easy, and
several times Reb and Sulke had to rescue someone who'd
blundered into something they couldn't figure out how to
undo. Sulke tended to hair-trigger reflexes; she was determined not to lose any more students. But Reb's gentle good
humor counterbalanced her and kept it being fun.

Raise your hands as if in surrender, palms forward. Your
thrusters are now pointing in the same direction you're facing.
Put your arms down at your sides with your thumbs against
your thighs, and the thrust is in the opposite direction. By
torquing your forearms you can aim in almost any direction or
combination of directions. Your ankle-thrusters, however,
face in only one direction, "down," and have only the one axis
of motion. From those postulates all the equations of free-
space jaunting are derived—and they're complicated and often
counterintuitive.

It took, believe me, a lot of courage to let go of that
umbilical and hang alone and unsupported in space. I managed
to do it, and to get through my short stint without disgracing
myself or alarming Sulke, but my heart was pounding when I

reconnected myself to my tether. Ben and Kirra were in the next group, and I watched with interest, knowing that they would do this well.

They did it beautifully, well enough to draw spontaneous applause. (Clapping your hands in a p-suit is a waste of energy. You applaud by making approving sounds. *Softly*, as dozens of people are sharing the same radio circuit.) What they did was more calisthenics than dance, but the consummate grace and skill with which they did it made it dance. Ben especially had pin-point control, using the tiniest bursts of gas to start himself moving and stop himself again when he was where he wanted to be. When they had run through the sequence of exercises, he and Kirra improvised a phrase similar to a square dance do-see-do, jetting toward each other and pivoting in slow motion around each other's crooked elbow. As they separated again, Ben suddenly went into a violent high-speed spin, spraying yellow gas like a Catherine Wheel. It was lovely, and we started to applaud . . . and then suddenly it was ugly, asymmetrical and uncontrolled. The applause died away and we could clearly hear him say, "Oh, shit."

"What's wrong?" Kirra cried, beating Sulke to it by a hair.

"Both left thrusters jammed full open." I could see now that he was beating his right fist into his left palm, trying to free up the jammed controls, but it wasn't working. He gave it up and flailed wildly for a moment, moving through space like a leaf in a storm.

"Here I come!" Kirra cried.

"No!" Sulke roared.

"No—stay clear!" Ben agreed. "I'm rogue, it's too dangerous. Besides, I think maybe I . . ." Suddenly he came out of his tumble and his attitude stabilized. His left wrist was cocked over his head, balancing the ankle thrust; he was vectoring slowly away from us, but at least he was no longer a pinwheel. "There."

Kirra had reached him by then, having ignored both warnings. "What should I do, love?" she asked him, decelerating to match his vector, doing it perfectly.

"Dock with me upside down." She did, locking her arms behind his knees, being careful not to kick him in the face. "Can you find the snap-release for that ankle-thruster?"

"Right."

"Okay, on the count of three, hit it—and be sure you're not in the way of it when it lets go! One, two, *three!*" He disengaged his fuming wrist thruster at the same instant she released the other one. She and Ben wobbled briefly as the two renegade thrusters blasted off for opposite ends of the galaxy; then they used their remaining six thrusters to recover. By then Sulke had arrived, swearing prodigiously in low German. The three of them jaunted back to us together hand in hand, and Sulke snapped their tethers back on herself.

It was over too quickly for me to have time to be terrified for them—no more than twenty seconds from start to finish.

Sulke finished cursing and paused for breath. "You two—" she began, and took another breath. Reb started to say something, but she overrode him. "—are EVA rated. As far as I'm concerned, you can graduate yourselves whenever you're ready."

Ben and Kirra looked at each other. "There's still a lot you can teach us," Kirra said.

"Maybe so," Sulke said, "and I'll be happy to if you want—but you've both got what it takes to survive EVA. Hell, I couldn't have recovered that fast."

"That's just my trick specs," Ben said. "It's easier getting out of a spin if you can see everything at once: you don't have those long gaps when no useful information is coming in."

"That makes sense. But Kirra was just as quick."

"I had a secret weapon too," Kirra said. "I'm in love with the bastard."

We all broke up. Tension release.

"What the hell went wrong, exactly?" Sulke asked. "Did the palm-switches physically freeze closed?"

"No," Ben said. "The controls worked fine . . . they just stopped controlling anything. If I had to guess—and I do, the damn things are halfway to Luna by now—I'd say a passing cosmic ray fried the chip."

"Possible," Sulke agreed reluctantly. "Or it could have been a passing piece of space junk, the odds are about the same. Damn bad luck. The rest of you spaceworms take heed. *Anything* can happen out here. Stay on your toes. Okay, next group—"

△   △   △

Ben and Kirra were even merrier than usual at lunch. But I noticed that they slipped away early, and got to afternoon class late.

"My best advice to you all," Reb said about five minutes after they arrived, flushed and smiling, "would be to make love as much as you conveniently can during the next three weeks."

The whole room *rippled*. There was a murmur made of giggles and gasps and exclamations and one clear, "I heard *that*," which provoked more giggles.

"I'm completely serious," Reb said. "I can think of no better rehearsal for telepathy than making love. If you're a strict monosexual, now would be an excellent time to try to conquer your prejudice. There *are no sexual taboos in Top Step, because there are none in the Starmind.* You are preparing to enter a telepathic community, and in a telepathic community, you are naked to *everyone*. Sexual taboos won't work there. Even more important, they're unnecessary there— humans need taboos precisely because humans are not telepathic."

The room was now in maximum turmoil, as physical touching took on sudden significance. "But what about disease?" someone called.

"If you weren't healthy when you got to Suit Camp, you are now," Reb said. "Confirmed at Decontam and guaranteed."

"What about pregnancy?"

"All methods of contraception are available at the Infirmary. But you have no reason to fear pregnancy. Where you are going, there is no possibility of any child ever wanting for anything, no such thing as an unhappy childhood or a bad parent. All children are raised by everyone."

That took some thinking about. Finally someone said, "Are you . . . are you trying to say that all Stardancers spend their time screwing? That this Starmind is some kind of ongoing orgy?"

"In a physical sense, no. Stardancers only physically join when conception is desired. But in a mental and spiritual sense, your description is close to the truth. Telepathic communion cannot be described in words, nor understood until it is experienced—but it is generally agreed that love-making is one of the closest analogies in human experience. The most essential parts of lovemaking—liberation from the self, joining with others, being loved and touched and needed and cherished, gaining perspective on the universe by sharing viewpoint—are all a constant part of every Stardancer's life. Regardless of whether he or she chooses to ejaculate or lubricate at any given moment. Leon, you have a question?"

"What's zero-gee childbirth like?" asked the man addressed. "Gravity can be kind of handy there."

"Not for the first nine months," Glenn called out, and was applauded.

Reb smiled. "In Symbiosis, childbirth is easy and painless. The symbiote assists the process, and so does the child itself."

Wow! In spite of myself, an idea came to me. I made the finger gesture for attention, and Reb recognized me with a nod. "Reb? How old is too old to birth in Symbiosis?"

"We don't know yet. No woman has ever reached menopause while in Symbiosis. Those women who've entered Symbiosis after menopause resumed ovulating, and Stardancers as old as ninety-two have conceived and birthed successfully. Ask again in fifty years and we may have an answer for you."

The class went on for quite some time, and a lot of people said a lot of things, but I don't remember much after that. I spent the rest of class trying to grapple with the fact that a door I had thought closed forever was opening up again, that all of a sudden it wasn't too late anymore to change my mind and have children. The thought was too enormous to grasp. I had known about this, intellectually, before I had ever left Earth— but somehow I had never let the implications sink in before.

Probably because I had not known anyone whose children I wanted to have . . . until now.

"Robert," I said that night in afterglow, "how do you feel about you and me having a child?"

He blinked. "Are we?"

"Not yet. I've still got my implant. But I could have it taken out at the Infirmary in five minutes, and be pregnant in ten. What do you think?"

He had sense enough not to hesitate. "I think I would love to make a baby with you. But I also think it would be prudent to wait until after Graduation."

"Huh. Maybe you're right."

"Are you absolutely a hundred percent sure you're going to go through with Symbiosis? I'm not. And I wouldn't want a decision either way to be forced on either one of us. If we both do Symbiosis, fine. If we both go back to Earth, fine. But wouldn't it be awful if we started a child, and then—"

"I guess." It would be least awful, perhaps, if I stayed in space and Robert went home: a husband/father must be much less essential in a telepathic family than in human society. But Robert had already had to walk away from one child in his life, and still felt grief over it.

And there was another horrid possibility. What if we conceived together—and then one of us was killed in training? It could happen. I didn't think I could have survived what had happened to Ben that morning, for instance.

"Another month or so, maybe less, and we'll know. Okay?"

"You're right." I was disappointed . . . but only a little. Morning sickness in a p-suit could be a serious disaster. There was plenty of time.

△   △   △

Without any actual discussion, Kirra started spending most of her time at Ben's place, leaving our room for Robert and me. They gave the two of us a week to focus on each other and our new love without distraction. Then one day they came by and invited us to join them for drinks at Le Puis, and the four of us reformed and reintegrated our friendship again. Soon it stopped making any difference which room we used, or whether it was already occupied when we got there. Robert was a little more reticent than I about making love with Ben and Kirra present, at first, but he got over it. I could sense that one day, whether before or after Graduation, we four were all going to make love with each other. But there didn't seem to be any hurry for that, either, and for the present I was just a little too greedy of Robert.

Even falling in love couldn't distract me completely from dance. After our first few days together, I resumed working for a few hours every evening. Sometimes Robert watched and helped; sometimes he stayed back in the room and designed support structures for asteroid mining colonies, or wrote letters to his son in Minneapolis. I slowly began to evolve a piece of choreography, which I took to calling *Do the Next Thing*.

Kirra too made progress in her art. In the middle of the week, while we were all outside in class, she sang her second song for us, the Song of Polar Orbit. I had to get my p-suit radio overhauled that night—the applause overloaded it—and so did others. Raoul Brindle phoned more congratulations and repeated his invitation to Kirra. Within a few days, Teena reported that the recording had been downloaded by over eighty percent of the spacer community, and that audience response was one hundred percent positive. Kirra told me privately that she was tickled to death; she had never before received so much approval from non-Aboriginals and white-fellas for her singing. And according to her Earthside mentor Yarra, the Yirlandji people were equally pleased. Ben, for his part, was fiercely proud of her.

On Sunday afternoon the four of us took a field trip together, to watch a Third-Monther enter Symbiosis. I cleared it with Reb; he had no objection. "As long as Ben and Kirra and Robert are along, you can't get into too much trouble. They're pretty much spacers already. But you be sure to stay close to them," he cautioned with a smile. I smiled back and agreed that we could probably manage that.

We left, not via the Solarium, but by a smaller personnel airlock closer to the docking end of Top Step. It was about big enough to hold three comfortably, but we left in pairs, as couples, holding hands.

The Symbiote mass floated in a slightly higher orbit than Top Step, because Top Step routinely exhausted gases that, over a long period of time, could have damaged or killed it. I can't explain the maneuvering we had to do to get there without using graphics prefaced by a boring lecture on orbital ballistics; just take my word for it that, counterintuitive as it might seem, to reach something ahead of you and in a higher orbit, you *decelerate*. Never mind: with Ben astrogating, we got there. It took a long lazy time, since we didn't have a whole lot of thruster pressure to waste on a hurried trip.

My parents used to have an antique lava lamp, which they loved to leave on for hours at a time. The Symbiote mass looked remarkably like a single globule of its contents: a liquid blob of softly glowing red stuff, that flexed and flowed like an amoeba. Years ago there had been so much of it that you could see it with the naked eye from Top Step. So many Stardancers had graduated since then that the remaining mass was not much bigger than an oil tanker. (That was why the Harvest Crew was fetching more from Titan.) But it was hard to tell size by eye, without other nearby objects of known size to give perspective—a common problem in space.

As we got nearer, we picked out such objects: half a dozen Stardancers, their solar sails retracted. We came to a stop relative to the Symbiote mass, and saw perhaps a dozen p-suited humans approaching it from a slightly different angle than us. One of them had to be Bronwyn Small, the prospective graduate, and the rest her friends come to wish her well. By prior agreement, we maintained radio silence on the channel they were using, so as not to intrude. We had secured Bronwyn's permission to be present, through Teena, but there can be few moments in anyone's life as personal as Symbiosis.

The p-suited figures made rendezvous with the six Stardancers. We approached, but stopped about a kilometer or so distant.

I guess I had been expecting some sort of ceremony, the speechmaking with which humans customarily mark important events. There was none. Bronwyn said short goodbyes to her friends, hugged each of them, and then turned toward the nearest of the Stardancers and said, "I'm ready."

"Yes, you are," the Stardancer agreed, and I recognized the voice: it was Jinsei Kagami. She did nothing that I could see—but all at once the Symbiote extended a pseudopod that separated from the main mass, exactly the way the blob in a lava lamp will calve little globular chunks of itself. The shimmering crimson fragment homed in on Bronwyn somehow, stopped next to her, and expanded into a bubble about four meters in radius, becoming translucent, almost transparent.

Without another word, Bronwyn jaunted straight into the bubble and entered it bodily. Within it, she could be seen to unseal her p-suit and remove it. She removed its communications gear, hung it around her neck, and then pushed the suit gently against the wall of the bubble that contained her. The Symbiote allowed the suit to emerge, sealed again behind it, and at once began to contract.

We were too far away to see clearly, but I knew that the red stuff was enfolding her and entering her at every orifice, meeting itself within her, becoming part of her.

She cried out, a wordless shout of unbearable astonishment that made the cosmos ring, and then was silent. She seemed to shudder and stiffen, back arched, arms and legs trembling as if she were having a seizure. She began turning slowly end over end.

There was silence for perhaps a full minute.

Then Jinsei said to Bronwyn's friends, "You may leave whenever you choose. Your friend will not be aware of her immediate surroundings again for at least another day . . . and it might be as much as one more day before you will be able to converse with her. She has a great deal to integrate."

"Is she all right?" one of them asked, sounding dubious.

" 'All right' is inadequate," Jinsei said, with that smile in her voice. " 'Ecstatic' is literally correct—and even that does not do it justice. Yes, she has achieved successful Symbiosis."

Bronwyn's friends expressed joy and relief at the news, and left as a group, talking quietly amongst themselves.

Ben gestured for our attention and pointed at his ear. We

four all switched to a channel on which we could chatter privately.

"Not much of a show," he said.

"I dunno," Kirra said dreamily. "I thought it was lovely."

"Me too," I said. "I could almost feel it happening to her. That moment of merging."

"So did I," Ben said. "I don't know, I guess I expected there to be more to it."

"More what?"

"Ceremony. Speeches. Hollywood special effects. Fanfares of trumpets. Moving last words."

"You men and your speechmaking," I said. "All those things ought to happen too every time a sperm meets an egg . . . but they don't."

"And I thought those *were* moving last words," Kirra said. "She said, 'I'm ready.' Can't get much more movin' than that."

"You're pretty quiet, darling," I said to Robert. "What did you think?"

He was slow in answering. "I think I feel a little like Bronwyn: it's going to take me at least a week to integrate everything well enough to talk about it."

"Too right," Kirra agreed. "I've had enough o' words for a while. But I *could* use a little nonverbal communication. Come on, Benjamin, let's go on home an' root until sparrow-fart."

(If you ever spend time in Oz, don't speak of rooting for your favorite team; "root" is their slang term for "fuck." Whether this is a corruption of "rut," or an indication that Aussies are fond of oral sex, I couldn't say. And "sparrowfart" is slang for "dawn.")

"That sounds like exactly what I'd like to do right now," he said.

"Me too," I agreed. " 'Ecstatic,' she said. I could use some of that. How about you, darling?"

" 'I'm ready,' " he quoted simply.

The trip back to Top Step was as long as the trip out, but there was no further conversation along the way. When we got there we found that four could fit into that airlock at once if they didn't mind squeezing. The route back to our quarters was one we had taken only once before, on the day of our arrival at Top Step—save that we bypassed Decontam. As we jaunted across the Great Hall, I felt again many of the same confused and confusing feelings I'd experienced on that first day, and hugged Robert tightly. He squeezed back.

Without any discussion, we all headed for my and Kirra's room, and entered together. Pausing only to store our p-suits and dim the lights, we went to bed.

Actually, the euphemism is misleading: we didn't use our sleepsacks. I did not want to be confined, needed to feel as free as a Stardancer, and it seemed Kirra did as well.

For over an hour I was almost completely unaware of Ben and Kirra, or anything else but Robert. We caromed off walls or furniture from time to time, but barely noticed that either. Then at some point the two drifting couples bumped into each other in the middle of the room, at a perpendicular so that we formed a cross. The small of my back was against Kirra's; our sweat mingled. I sensed her flexing her legs and tightening her shoulders, and knew kinesthetically what she was going to do and matched it without thinking: we spun and flowed and traded places. Ben blinked and smiled and kissed me, and I kissed him back. The dance went on. Ben was sweet, bonier and hairier than Robert but just as tenderly attentive. Perhaps a half an hour later, we all met again at the center of the universe and made a beast with four backs; awhile later I was back in Robert's arms, and slept there until Teena told us it was time for dinner.

We ate together without awkwardness, talking little but making each other smile often. After the meal, Ben kissed me, Robert kissed Kirra, and Robert and I went off to my studio together, while Kirra and Ben headed for Le Puis. They were asleep in Kirra's sleepsack when we got back; we slid into mine and were asleep almost at once.

$$\triangle \quad \triangle \quad \triangle$$

Glenn was murdered the next day.

We had all been weaned from our umbilicals by that point, and were spending that class touring the exterior of Top Step.

Most of the interesting stuff was down by the docking area. We were able to watch the docking of a Lunar robot freighter, carrying precious water from the ice mines. We should not have been able to: that freighter was not scheduled to arrive for another four hours, or Sulke would not have had us down there. Vessels are almost always punctual in space—the moment the initial acceleration shuts down, ETA can be predicted to the second. But while this can was on its way, the Lunar traffic control computer apparently detected a small pressure leak from the hold, and applied additional acceleration and deceleration to minimize transit time. Sulke was angry when the word came over the ops channel.

Oh, we were safe enough: we were at least half a kilometer from the docks. Sulke's gripe was that the event constituted an unplanned distraction from our curriculum—but we were all so eager to watch the docking that, after consultation with Reb, she reluctantly conceded that it would be instructive, and suspended lessons until it was over. I was pleased, since events had prevented me from watching my own docking five weeks earlier.

Long before we could see the freighter itself, we saw the tongue of fire it stuck out at us as it decelerated. Then the torch shut off, and we could see a spherical-looking object the size of a pea held at arm's length. It grew slowly to baseball size, then soccer ball, and by then it was recognizable as a cylinder seen end-on. It grew still larger, and began to visibly move relative to the stars behind it as it approached Top Step. Now it could be seen to be as large as the Symbiote mass I'd seen the day before, tiny in comparison to Top Step but huge in comparison with a human. From one side a thin plume of steam came spraying out of the hull to boil and fume in vacuum; on the opposite side you could just make out the less visible trail of the maneuvering jet that was balancing the pressure leak, keeping it from deforming the freighter's course to one side.

The ship was coming in about twice as fast as normal. But that's not very fast; dockings are usually glacial. Sulke had run out of educational things to point out long before the ship had approached close enough for final maneuvers. Since our first day EVA she'd generally kept us too busy to stargaze or chatter, but now we had time to rubberneck at the cosmos and ask questions.

"What's that, Sulke?" Soon Li asked, pointing to a far distant object in a higher orbit than our own.

Sulke followed her pointing arm. "Oh. That's Mir."

"Oh." Silence. Then: "I think someone ought to . . . I don't know, tear it down or blow it up or something."

"Would you want *your* grave disturbed?" Dmitri asked.

More silence.

"What are those people doing?" Dmitri wanted to know.

We looked where he was pointing, at the docking area itself. At first I saw nothing: those docks are *huge,* designed to accommodate earth-to-orbit vehicles, orbit-to-orbit barges or taxis, and Lunar shuttles like the one we were watching—as many as two of each at one time. But then I saw the two p-suited figures Dmitri meant, just emerging from a personnel lock between the two biggest docking collars.

"Those are wranglers," Sulke said. "As soon as that bucket docks, they'll hook up power feeds and refueling hoses and so on. If there's a nesting problem, they've got enough thruster mass to do some shoehorning too."

"What's wrong with that star?" Glenn asked, pointing in the direction of the slowly approaching freighter. She happened to be closest of us to it.

"Which one?" Sulke replied.

"That big one, a little Three-ish of the ship."

I spotted the one she meant. Indeed, there were three things odd about it. It was just slightly bigger than a star ought to be, and it was the only one in the Universe that was twinkling, the way stars appear to on Earth, and it had a little round black dot right smack in the center of it. That certainly was odd. It grew perceptibly as I watched; could it be a supernova? What luck, to happen to see one with the naked eye . . .

"Jesus Christ!" Sulke cried out. "Reb—"

"I see it," he said calmly. "Everyone, listen carefully: I want you to follow me at maximum acceleration, right now." He spun and blasted directly away from the docking freighter, all four thrusters flaring.

We wasted precious seconds reacting, and Sulke roared, *"Run for your fucking lives!"* That did it: we all took to our heels, slowly but with growing speed. I cannoned into someone and nearly tumbled, but managed to save myself and continue; so did the other.

"Operations—Mayday, Mayday!" Reb was saying. "Incoming ASAT, ETA five seconds. Wranglers—" He broke off. There was nothing to be said to the wranglers.

The antique antisatellite hunter-killer slammed into the freighter at that instant. There was no sound or concussion, of course. I caught reflected glare from the flash off Top Step in my peripheral vision, and tried to crane my neck around to look behind me, but I couldn't do it and stay on course, so I gave up. I'm almost sorry about that; it must have been something to see.

The water-ship was torn apart by the blast, transformed instantly into an expanding sphere of incandescent plasma, shrapnel and boiling water. It killed Ronald Frayn and Sirikit Pibulsonggram, the two wranglers, instantly. A half-second later it killed a Third-Monther named Arthur Von Brandenstein who had been meditating around the other side of Top Step, and had come to watch the docking like us, but had approached closer than Sulke would let us.

And a second later it caught up to our hindmost straggler, Glenn.

I'll remember the sound of her death until my dying day, because there was so little to it. It was a sound that would mean nothing to a groundhog, meant nothing to me then, and that every spacer dreads to hear: a short high whistle, with an undertone of crashing surf, lasting for no more than a second and ending with a curious croaking. It is the sound of a p-suit losing its integrity, and its inhabitant's final exhalation blowing past the radio microphone.

Later examination of tapes showed that the first thing to hit her was a hunk of shrapnel with sharp edges; it took both legs off above the knees, and that might well have sufficed to kill her, emptying her suit of air instantly. But you can live longer in a vacuum than most groundhogs would suspect, and it is just barely possible that we might have been able to get her inboard alive. But a split second later a mass of superheated steam struck her around the head and shoulders. P-suits were never designed to take that kind of punishment: the hood and most of the shoulders simply vanished, and the steam washed across her bare face—just as she was trying desperately to inhale air that was no longer there. When Sulke had us decelerate and regroup, she kept on going, spinning like a top. A couple of people started off after her, but Sulke called them back.

No one else died, but there were more than a dozen minor injuries. The most seriously injured was Soon Li, who lost two fingers from her left hand; she would have died, but while she was gawking at her fountaining glove, Sulke slapped sealant over it and dragged her to the nearest airlock. She suffered some tissue damage from exposure to vacuum, but not enough to cost her the rest of the hand. Antonio Gonella managed to crash into Top Step in his panicked flight, acquiring a spectacular bruise on his shoulder and a mild concussion. Two people collided more decisively than I had, and broke unimportant bones.

But the casualty that meant the most to *me* was Robert.

CHAPTER TEN

Once is happenstance;
twice is coincidence;
three times is enemy action.

—Ian Fleming

A SMALL PIECE of shrapnel, the size and shape of a stylus, was blown right through his left foot from bottom to top. It was a clean wound, and his p-suit was able to self-seal around the two pinhole punctures. If he cried out, it was drowned out by the white noise of dozens of others shouting at once, and when Sulke called for casualty reports, he kept silent. I didn't know he'd been hurt until we were approaching the airlock, several minutes after the explosion, and I saw that the left foot of his p-suit had turned red. My first crazy thought was that some Symbiote had gotten into his p-suit somehow; when I realized it was blood I came damned near to fainting.

Cameras caught the entire incident—there are always cameras rolling around the docks—and replay established conclusively that Robert was following me, keeping me in his blast shadow, when he was hit. Or else that shrapnel might have hit me.

The explosion had shocked me, and Glenn's ghastly death had stunned me, but learning of Robert's comparatively minor injury just about unhinged me. I think if Reb had not been present I would have thrown a screaming fit . . . but his simple presence, rather than anything he said, kept me from losing control. He got us all inside, kept us organized and quiet, did triage on the wounded and had them all prioritized by the time the medics arrived. Sulke was the last one in, but when she did emerge from the airlock she paused only long enough to inventory us all by eye, and then went sailing off to goddammit get some answers.

Robert was pale, and his jaw trembled slightly, but he

168

seemed otherwise okay. The sight of his torn foot, oozing balls of blood, made me feel dizzy, but I forced myself to hold it between my palms to cut off the bleeding. It felt icy cold, and I remembered that was a classic sign of shock. But his breathing was neither shallow nor rapid, and his eyes were not dull. He seemed lucid, responded reassuringly to questioning; I relaxed a little.

The medical team was headed by Doctor Kolchar, the doctor I'd seen briefly during my first minutes at Top Step. He was a dark-skinned Hindu with the white hair, moustache and glowering eyebrows of Mark Twain, dressed as I remembered him in loud Hawaiian shirt and Bermuda shorts. He handed off Nicole to Doctor Thompson, the resident specialist in vacuum exposure, and came over to look at Robert. He checked pulse, blood pressure and pupils before turning his attention to the damaged foot.

"You're a lucky young man," he said at last. "You couldn't have picked a better place to drill a hole through a human foot. No arterial or major muscle damage, the small bone destroyed isn't crucial, most of what you lost was meat and cartilage. Even for a terrestrial this would not be a serious injury. Do you want nerve block?"

"Yes," Robert said quietly but emphatically. Doctor Kolchar touched an instrument to Robert's ankle, accepted its advice on placement, and thumbed the injector. Robert's face relaxed at once; he took a great deep breath and let it out in a sigh. "Thank you, Doctor."

"Don't mention it. That block is good for twelve hours; when it wears off, come see me for another. Don't bother to set your watch, you'll know when it's time. Meanwhile, drink plenty of fluids—and try to stay off your feet as much as possible." He started to jaunt away to his next patient.

I was in no mood for bad jokes. "Wait a minute! Are you *crazy?* You haven't even dressed his foot. What about infection?"

He decelerated to a stop and turned back to me. "Madam, whatever punctured his foot was the size and shape of a pen. There's nothing like that in a cargo hold, and that's the only place I can imagine a bug harmful to humans living on a spacecraft. And you know, or should know, that Top Step is a sterile environment. His bleeding has stopped, and there was a little coagulant in what I gave him. If it makes you happy to dress his foot, here." He tossed me a roll of bandage. "But I'm a little busy just now." He turned his back again and moved away. I looked down at the bandage and opened my mouth to start yelling.

"It's all right, Morgan," Robert said. "Believe me, I won't bang it into anything." He smiled weakly in an attempt to cheer me up.

My rage vanished. "Oh, darling, I'm so sorry. Are you all right?"

"Nerve block is a wonderful thing. That hurt like fury!"

I pulled his head against my chest and hugged him fiercely. "Oh, Robert, my God—poor Glenn! What a horrible thing."

He stiffened in my arms. "Yes. Horrible."

A thought struck me. "Her body! Somebody's got to go and retrieve it! Teena, is anyone retrieving Glenn's body?"

"No, Morgan." Her voice was in robot mode; she must have been conducting many conversations at once.

"But someone has to!" Why? "Uh, her family might want her remains sent home. They can still track her, can't they?"

"Her suit transponder is still active," Teena said. "But in her contract with the Foundation she specified the 'cremation in atmosphere' option for disposition in the event of her death."

"Oh. Wait a minute—her last vector was a deceleration with respect to Top Step. She was slowing down in orbit—so she'll go into a *higher* orbit, right? I did the same thing myself yesterday. The atmosphere won't get her, she'll just . . . go on forever . . ." Oh God, without her legs, boiled and burst and dessicated! Much better to burn cleanly from air friction in the upper atmosphere, and fall as ashes to Earth—

"Your conclusion is erroneous, Morgan," Teena said. "She is presently in a higher orbit, yes—but she does not have the mass to sustain it, as Top Step does. In a short time her orbit will decay, and she will have her final wish."

"Oh." I felt inexpressible sadness. "Robert, let's go home.

You need rest. And I don't care what the doctor says, I'm going to bandage your foot."

"I'm not going anywhere until I get some answers," he said grimly. "I want to know who shot at us!"

Somehow I had not given that question a conscious thought—but as he said the words I felt a surge of anger. No, more than anger—bloodlust. "Look, there's Dorothy. Let's ask her, maybe she'll know something."

Dorothy Gerstenfeld had arrived just after the medics, and now she was the center of a buzzing swarm of people. She wore the impervious expression Mother wears when the children are throwing a tantrum, and spoke in firm but soothing tones. We jaunted in that direction, with me making sure no one jostled Robert's foot.

"—no hard information," she was saying. "We simply must wait until the investigation is complete. An announcement will be—"

"How do we know there aren't more missiles on the way right now?" Dmitri called out, and the crowd-buzz became more fearful than angry. I felt my stomach lurch; it had not occurred to me that we might still be in danger.

"At the moment we do not," she said. "But a UN Space Command cruiser is warping this way right now, and will be here in minutes. It has much more sophisticated detectors than we do. But if our assailants were planning any further attacks, I can't see why they would wait and give us time to regroup."

"How come our own anticollision gear didn't pick up that missile?" Jo demanded.

"Because it's designed to cope with meteors and debris, not high-speed ASATs at full acceleration," Dorothy said.

"Why the hell not?" Jo said shrilly. "You mean to tell me this place is a sitting duck?"

"Any civilian space habitat is a sitting duck," she said patiently. "Not one of them is defended against military attack."

"That's what the United Nations is for," Ben said.

Robert chimed in. "An effective defensive system for this rock would cost millions, maybe billions. It's not too hard to swat rocks and garbage—but if you want to stop ASATs *and* lasers, *and* particle beams, *and*—"

"I don't care *how* much it costs," Jo said angrily. "It's fucking crazy to have something this big and expensive undefended."

"Robert's right," Ben said. "There's just no way to do it effectively. What I don't understand is why we even have a system as good as we do. I mean, why did the Foundation burrow into Top Step from the front end instead of the back? If the docks were around behind, in shadow, there'd be a lot fewer collisions to defend against."

I recognized what Ben was trying to do by presenting an intriguing digression. Unfortunately someone knew the answer. "They figure it's more important to keep the Nanotech Safe Lab back there."

"You mean the Foundation thinks microscopic robots are more important than people?" Jo squawked.

"Jo, you know that's not fair," Dorothy said. "Nanoreplicators are important precisely because they could conceivably threaten people—all the people in the biosphere, not just the handful in this pressure."

"The hell with that," Jo said. "We're naked here . . . and you've got a responsibility to us." A handful of others buzzed agreement.

"Teena," Dorothy said calmly, "have the UN vessels arrived yet?" We could not hear the reply, but Dorothy relaxed visibly and said, "Repeat generally."

Teena's robot voice said, "*S.C. Champion* and *S.C. Defender* have matched our orbit and report 'situation stable.' "

There was a murmur of general relief.

"Teena," Dmitri called suddenly, "who fired that missile at us?"

"I do not know," Teena said.

There was a bark of laughter behind me. "Nicely done."

I spun and saw that Sulke had returned. She was smiling, but she looked angry enough to chew rock.

"What Teena means," she said to all of us, "is that she doesn't know the name of the individual who pushed the button."

"Sulke—" Dorothy began, with a hint of steel in her voice.

"You can't sit on it," Sulke said. "It's already on the Net, for Christ's sake. And they're entitled to know."

Dorothy took a deep breath and let it out with a sigh. "Go ahead."

Sulke's smile was gone now. "Credit for the attack has been formally claimed by the terrorist group known as the Gabriel Jihad."

Another incoming missile could not have caused more shock and consternation. "The fucking Caliphate!" Jo cried.

Dorothy's voice cut through the noise of the crowd. "The Umayyad Caliphate does not officially support the Gabriel Jihad."

"Oh, no," Jo shouted back. "The best police state since Stalin just can't seem to stamp out those nasty renegades somehow!"

"The Caliphate has publicly disassociated itself from the attack and denounced the Jihad," Dorothy insisted. "They maintain that the terrorists stole control of one of their hunter-killer satellites and launched one of its missiles."

"Yeah, sure! What is it, fifteen minutes since the fucking thing went off? That's plenty of time for a government to react to a total surprise!" That provoked a collective growl of anger. "The goddam Shiites have always hated Stardancers, everybody knows that."

"The Jihad are claiming that they've destroyed us," Sulke said. "The exact words were, 'the phallus of the Great Satan has been ruined.' They think they finished us."

"What, by blowing up a water-ship?" Ben said.

"*Bojemoi*," Dmitri burst out. "They did not know the ship would be there—it was not supposed to be for hours. They were trying to destroy the docking complex!"

"Jesus!" Robert exclaimed. "If the docks were destroyed, we . . . my God, we'd have to evacuate Top Step! We'd have to—there'd be no way to reprovision."

There was a stunned silence as we absorbed his words.

"There is nothing further we can accomplish here," Dorothy said. "Please return to your rooms and try to calm yourselves. We are safe for the present—and Administrator

Mgabi and the Foundation Board of Directors are pursuing every possible avenue to ensure that nothing like this ever happens again."

"What avenues?" Jo said. "Diplomacy? Fuck that! My friend Glenn is dead, they hard-boiled her head—I say we all go see Mgabi and—"

"Jo?" Reb interrupted.

"—demand that . . . what, Reb? I'm talking for Chrissake—"

"Dorothy said 'please.'"

Jo stared at him, and opened her mouth to say something, and stared some more. It was the closest thing to anger I'd ever heard in Reb's voice.

"She did," Ben agreed, iron in his own voice.

"That's right," Robert said. "I heard her clearly."

"Fair go, Joey," Kirra urged. "Mgabi needs us like a barbed wire canoe right now. Let the poor bastard do 'is bleedin' job, eh?"

Jo closed her mouth, looked around for support without finding any, and then shut her eyes tight and grimaced like a pouting child. "All right, God dammit," she said. "But I—"

"Thank you, Jo," Reb said. "Our sister Glenn was Episcopalian; funeral services will be held by Reverend Schiller in the chapel this evening at the usual time, and as usual there will be observances in all other holy places. I will be free from after lunch until then if any of you need to speak with me."

He spun and jaunted away, and the group dispersed.

I carried Robert back to our room like a package of priceless crystal, determined to bury my confusion and heartache in bandaging and nursing my wounded mate. Ben and Kirra discreetly left us alone and went on down the hall. And in less than five minutes, Robert and I were having our first and last quarrel.

$$\triangle \quad \triangle \quad \triangle$$

I hate to try and recreate the dialogue of that argument. It was bad enough to live through once.

It came down to this: Robert wanted to go back to Earth. As soon as possible.

No, I must recall some of the words. Because what he said first was *not* "I think we ought to go back to Earth as soon as possible." It wasn't even, "I want to go back to Earth; what do you think?" Or even, "I plan to go back to Earth, how do you feel?"

What he said, as soon as the door sealed behind us, was, "Can I use your terminal? I want to book a seat on the next ship Earthbound. Shall I book one for you too?"

Any of the other three would have been shock enough. God knows I had already had shock enough that day. But the way he phrased it added a whole additional layer of subtext that was just too overwhelming to absorb. He was saying, I want to go back to Earth so badly that I do not care whether you want to or not. He was saying, I can want something so much that I don't care what you want. It took me days to get it through my head, to convince my brain—I *refused* to know it, for just as long as I was able—but an instant after he said that, the pit of my stomach knew that Robert did not love me.

My brain reverted to the intelligence level of a be-your-own-shrink program. "You want to book a seat on the next ship to Earth."

"If it's not already too late. But it should take the others awhile to work it out. Hours, maybe days. None of them is exactly a theoretical relativist. Glenn probably would have caught on fast."

"And you want to know if I want you to book a seat for me."

"Come on, Morgan, I *know* you're bright enough to figure it out."

"I'm bright enough to figure it out."

"Marsport Control to Morgan: come in. You know exactly what I mean. We have to get off this rock."

He was right—I did know what he meant. And he was wrong—because that was only half of what he meant, and the least important half. But that was the half I chose to pursue. "Leave Top Step? *Why?*" I said, already knowing the answer.

"Why? Because *they're shooting at us!* This pressure is not safe anymore."

Perhaps I should have taken a long time to absorb that too.

It made me remember Phillipe Mgabi's words to us, our first day inboard: *You are as safe as any terrestrial can be in space, now.* It should have been a shock to realize how unsafe that really was, that even in vast Top Step I was terribly vulnerable. But I come from the generation that grew up being told that rain is poison and sex can kill. Part of me wasn't even surprised.

Argue it anyway. This argument is better than the next one will be.

"Just because some religious fanatics stole a missile?"

"Remember the mysterious something that hulled us on the way up here? You know that was a laser—hell, you and Kirra told *me*. And the failure in the circulation system that first week—do you have any idea how many failsafes there are on an air plant? That was only the fifth failure there's ever been, in fifty years of spaceflight! And now this. You know what they say: 'Three times is enemy action.'"

"But they're just a bunch of terrorists in burnooses, for Christ's sake—nobody can even prove they've got the Caliphate behind them."

He drifted close, stopped himself with a gentle touch at my breast. "Morgan, listen to me. If the People's Republic of China were to declare open war on the Starseed Foundation, I would not be unduly worried. But terrorists are *weak*—that's what makes them so terribly dangerous."

"They fired one lousy missile. If they could hack their way into a hunter-killer satellite, they could just as well have fired a dozen if they wanted to."

"What they did was scarier. They used precisely the minimum amount of force that would achieve their objective. That tells me they are *not* fanatics in burnooses. They've studied their Sun Tzu. One missile, all by itself, should have done the job. That it didn't is a miracle so unlikely I'm still shaking. If that water-ship hadn't sprung a leak at *just* the right time on its way here, we'd all be trying to figure out how to walk back to Earth right now. Without the docks, this place can't support life."

Oh God, he was right. I wanted badly to be hugged. He was close enough to hug. "Jesus Christ, Robert—they've been trying to kill us for two months, and the total body count is five. We ought to have time to finish out our course and Graduate."

"You just said yourself, they could send more missiles any time they want. There could be more on the way now."

"There are two goddam UN heavy cruisers out there!"

"Right now, yeah. They may even stay awhile. But have you considered the fact that *the Starseed Foundation is not a member of the United Nations, and the Caliphate is?*"

"But—that's ridiculous!"

"Sure, there's a friendly relationship of long standing—the member nations all know perfectly well there wouldn't still *be* a UN if it weren't for the Stardancers, whether they'll admit it or not—even the Caliphate knows that, that's just what's driving them crazy. But you tell me: if it comes to it, is the UN going to go to war to defend a corporation from one of its member nations? When, as you pointed out, it can't even prove the Caliphate is involved? You wait and see: within two or three days, India will have lodged a protest over the diversion of UN resources to protect a Canadian corporation, and then Turkey will chime in, and finally China . . . and one day those two ships will quietly warp orbit."

"They wouldn't."

"They might have no choice. Suppose there were a plausible diversion somewhere else. Say, somebody bombed the Shimizu Hotel? At any given time there's upwards of seven trillion yen on the hoof jaunting around inside that pressure, some of the most influential humans there are. The Space Command *hasn't* got a lot of military strength in space to spare: most of their real muscle is the Star Wars net, and that's aimed one way, straight down. I don't know how soon the next ship leaves here for Earth, but I do know I'm going to be on it."

Whether I'm beside you or not.

"You're just going to run away?"

Think well before saying that to your man, even if it's true—maybe especially if it's true; I might just as well have stuck a knife in his belly. Even his unexpressive face showed it. For an instant I remembered his torn foot, injured in trying to shield me, and almost said something to at least try to recall my words. But I was too angry.

He didn't let the pain reach his voice; it came out flat, firm, controlled. "You bet your life."

"You mean, just go home and waste all this? All this time, all this work, forget Symbiosis and run away?"

"It will not be wasted. We can always come back, sometime when it is safe again. Even if we never *do* come back, it hasn't been a waste: we've learned a lot and acquired a lot of very useful skills, and we found each other—" *You're a good three or four minutes late in mentioning that, buster.* "—but surely you see that all of that *will* be wasted if we die?"

"But—but we don't have to *quit*. We could . . . look, we could go to Reb and tell him we want to Graduate early! Right away. We could make him buy it—hell, you're spaceworthy already, and I know enough to survive long enough to reach the Symbiote mass, I've proved that, what more do I really need to know? Whatever it is, I'll *know* it as soon as I enter the Starmind! We could pull it off—"

He looked me square in the eye. "Are you ready to take Symbiote? Right now?"

I looked away. "Soon, I mean. A week, say."

He took my face in his hands and made me look back at him. "Morgan—I am not one hundred percent certain I want to go through with Symbiosis. It scares me silly. But I am one hundred percent sure I do not want to be pressured into it. If it's a choice between do it within a week and don't do it, make up your mind, the clock's ticking . . . I pass." He let go of me. "I don't know about you, but I could *use* another six months or so to think about it. And besides, I have no way to know we *have* a week."

"You think the UN will sell us out that fast?"

"No—but how would you like to go EVA tomorrow and find out you've got tanks full of pure nitrogen? The Jihad got to the circulation system: they could get to the tank-charging facilities. Or the Garden. There could be an unfortunate outbreak of botulism, or plague, or rogue replicators from the Safe Lab—all my instincts tell me to get out of here, fast. You mark my words: in twenty-four hours every scheduled seat Earthside will be booked, and they'll be screaming for special extra flights to handle the overflow. And a lot of people will be suddenly making plans to Graduate ahead of schedule, like you said. But I won't be one of them. I don't want to die. I don't want to risk dying, just at the very verge of life eternal. I'm going home, as fast as I can."

Damn him for being so intelligent! With anyone else I might have kept that first argument going for hours yet—but he had gone and won the fucking thing. What now? Refuse to concede that, and have us both repeat our lines with minor variations in word choice two or three more times?

No. God damn it. It was time to have the second argument . . .

"And you don't care if I come along or not?"

His mouth tightened and his nostrils flared. Again I had stung him. Good.

And again the son of a bitch controlled it and answered reasonably. "Of course I care, Morgan. You must know how much I care. But you're a free adult: I can't make your choice for you."

"The hell you can't! That's what you're trying to do!"

"I am not. I am trying very hard not to. Look, it's very simple, Morgan. There are two choices: Graduate too early, for the wrong reasons, under the gun, gamble with our lives and our sanity—or fall back and try again later. There's only one *sensible* choice. I hope with all my heart that you'll be sensible. But I can't *make* you be."

"You do, huh? Why do you hope that, Robert?"

He did not answer.

"Why do you hope that, Robert? Say the words. You've never said the words."

"Neither have you."

"Because I didn't think we needed to!"

"I didn't either!" he snapped back, letting anger show in his voice for the first time.

"Well, maybe we were wrong! *God damn you, I love you!*"

That silly statement hung in the air between us. As if any more irony were needed, the violence of our combined shouting had caused us to start drifting ever so slowly apart. I waved air with my cupped hands to try and cancel it, but he didn't follow suit, so I stopped.

He seemed to consider several responses. What he finally settled on was, "Do I correctly hear you say that if I loved you, I would be trying to tell you what to do with your life?"

"Of course not!"

"Don't you see that if you and I hadn't talked Glenn into staying here, she'd be alive now?"

That *hurt*. I counterattacked hastily. "And I don't mean anything more to you than Glenn did?"

"Morgan, for heaven's sake, be reasonable! I've spent thirty years trying to unlearn the idea that women are property, and if you want someone to go twentieth century and start giving you orders like a Muslim or a Fundamentalist . . . well, I'm afraid you'll have to get somebody else; it's just too late for me to start all over again. I don't want to be any grown-up's father."

Is there anything more infuriating than an argument-opponent with impeccable logic? The correct answer was: *I don't want you to give me orders—I want you to be so crazy in love with me that you can't cut your own marching orders until you know my plans*—but I just could not say that out loud . . . or even to myself.

"Damn you," I cried, "you leave my father out of this!"

Yes, there is something more infuriating than a logical opponent. A man who is impervious to illogic. He turned and found a handhold, pushed himself over to my terminal. He belted himself in so he could punch keys without ricocheting away, and looked back to me. "May I? I could just go through Teena, but I think you can guess why I'd rather not do that."

Days ago we had given each other the booting code to our personal terminal . . . as lovers will, and mere sexers will not. It's a step more intimate than swapping housekeys, much more intimate than sharing bodily fluids. Someone who can access your personal memory node can drain your financial accounts, read your mail, read your diary if you keep one, send messages in your name. Hands on your keyboard touch you more deeply than hands on your vagina. "Use your own terminal," I said.

"Certainly," he said calmly, and unstrapped again. "How many seats shall I reserve?"

"One!" I shouted.

"Morgan—" he began.

"Dammit, you don't want to be pressured to Graduate, but you're trying to pressure me into giving it up! Maybe forever—suppose *two* months from now they blow this place up, and the chance is gone for our lifetime?"

"Then we'll have a lifetime. That's the most they promise you when you get born. And we could have it together."

"But I could never *dance* again!"

"Then you have to decide whether it's me you want, or dance. If you stay here, and it happens just as you say . . . you and I will never see each other again."

"Not if you don't run out on me!"

At last I got to him. "I won't *be* running out on you if you do the smart thing and leave with me!" he said, raising his voice for the first time.

I had to press the advantage. "Go on, get out of here— you've got a plane to catch!"

He drew in breath . . . and let it out. And took another deep breath, and let that out, a little more slowly. "I'll reserve two seats. You can always cancel if you choose to."

I was still in my p-suit; I unsnapped an air bottle and threw it at him. Stupid: he was the only one of our class who had ever beaten Dorothy Gerstenfeld in 3-D handball. He side-stepped like a bullfighter and the tank shattered the monitor screen above my terminal, rebounded with less than half of its original force but spinning crazily. I was spinning myself from having thrown it, and whacked my head on something. The tank *swack*ed into Kirra's sleepsack and was stopped by it. When I looked around, Robert was gone.

Good riddance, I thought, and doubled over and wept in great racking sobs. My eyes grew tendrils of silvery tears; I smashed them into globular fragments that danced and eddied in the air like little transparent Fireflies before breaking apart and whirling away.

God damn him to hell, turning it around like that and dumping it back on me! Now if we break up it'll be my *choice, because I choose to cancel my seat home—and it's his fierce respect for my free womanhood that keeps him from saying*

*anything more than 'he hopes I'll be sensible.' He wouldn't
say the fucking words, even after I did!*

*So close to having it all! Another lousy two or three weeks and
I would have had* dance *and* Symbiosis *and* Robert. *How could I
have been so stupid, thinking they'd let me have it all?*

A part of my mind tried to argue. *You can still have Symbiosis.
The whole Starmind, all these people, will enfold you and—*

—and love me, right? When nobody else ever has.

A thought forced its way into my head. Robert had gone down
the hall to use his own terminal. Kirra and Ben were presumably
there. They would see what he was typing. Or he'd shield the
monitor, which would make them curious. At any moment Kirra
might come jaunting in here, grimly determined to have me cry
on her shoulder. I don't cry on anybody's shoulder. When I cry,
I cry alone. I forced my sobs to subside. I could not achieve
control of my breath, but I made the tears dry up. I jaunted to the
vanity, got tissues, and honked and wiped and snuffled and
wiped. I checked my face in the mirror, made myself wash it.
"Teena, is my studio free?"

"Repeat, please, Morgan," Teena said in her mechanical
voice.

I took a shuddering deep breath, got my voice under control,
and repeated the question. Yes, she said, it was available. I told
her I wanted it for the rest of the day, and she said that was
acceptable. I told her I wanted it for the rest of month, and she
said I would have to clear that with Dorothy Gerstenfeld or
Phillipe Mgabi. I started to tell her I wanted it for the rest of my
life . . . and thanked her and left for the studio. I actually got
within fifty meters of it before collapsing into tears again. What
triggered it was the sudden realization that I had not given a
single thought to Glenn since I'd gotten back to my room. And
now I was going to miss her funeral. The tears flew from my eyes
like bullets. No one was around to see, and I sealed the hatch
behind me before anyone came along.

If you're ever going to have a day like that, try to have it
later in the day. It took me *hours* to cry myself to sleep.

In similar situations back on Earth I used to lie on the studio
floor and cry, let the floor drink my tears as it so often drank
my blood. Here there was no floor. I missed it bitterly.

CHAPTER ELEVEN

A fallen blossom
Come back to its branch?
No, a butterfly!

—Moritake (1452–1549)

I GOT HOME a few hours before breakfast. Kirra was alone in the room, and woke as I came in. "Are you right, love?"

I knew that was Aussie for, *are you* all *right?*, but I couldn't help hearing the words as they sounded too. "Ask me again next year," I said to both questions. "You heard, huh?"

"We heard." She slipped out of her sleepsack. "Robert's found himself another room until the ship leaves."

"Where's Ben?"

"I told him I'd wait here for you alone 'til brekkie, then we were gonna hunt you down together."

By then she had reached me, and was hugging me. It helped a little, as much as anything could help. She did not say a single one of the clichés I'd been dreading, only held me. After a time she began singing softly, in Yirlandji, and that helped me a little too.

Awhile later she said, "Tucker?" and I said, "No. You go," and she nodded. "Bring you back somethin'?" she asked, and I said, "No." She left, and I slid into my sleepsack and went fetal.

She let me have the rest of the day, and then at around suppertime she showed up with what might just have been the only thing in human space that could have made me feel like eating. "You're not serious," I said when she took it out of its thermos bag and tossed it to me. "How could you possibly—"

"Sulke knows a bloke at the Shimizu."

"But it must have cost—"

"The bloke liked me Song o' Polar Orbit a lot; it's his shout."

183

Even in my misery it reached me. A full litre of fine Chilean chocolate chip ice cream. Back in Vancouver it would have been an expensive luxury; here it was a pearl without price. She had heard me speak longingly of it several times; she'd even remembered my favorite flavour. I had no idea what her favorite flavour was. "Pull up a spoon," I said, and we dug in together.

As we ate she filled me in on the news.

It was going just as Robert had predicted. Third-Monthers were Graduating en masse. Some of the rest of us, mostly Novices, had decided they were ready for early Graduation—from one to five weeks early!—and some, mostly Postulants, had suddenly remembered pressing business dirtside. Already there were no more seats available on the next regularly scheduled transport (two days hence), and the special charter that had been announced was filling up fast. Robert and I were not the only couple who had split up.

There were some students who took neither course. Some lacked the imagination to realize how comprehensive a disaster it would have been if that missile had destroyed the docks—and some were just the kind of people who insist on building their home on the slopes of Mount Vesuvius or in San Francisco. (Come to think of it, Robert was going home to San Francisco. What kind of logic was that?)

And of course there were the spacers on staff. Going dirtside was not an option for them. Those who could were trying to change jobs, or rather, eliminate Top Step from their job rotations. Those who could not were trying to get work deep inboard, on the theory that they'd be safer from attack. It was a shaky theory.

I was unsurprised to learn Kirra and Ben's choice.

"We're doin' it, love. Ben and me, this Sunday. I reckon you guessed we would."

"Good for you," I said. My eyes were stinging. "Pushing ahead the wedding. That makes me really happy."

"You want to join us?"

"Thanks for asking. But no. I'm not ready. Reb would never let me do it in this state. You two go on—I'll catch you up as soon as I can."

Privately I wondered if I meant that. I still was not utterly certain that I wanted to go through with Symbiosis. The idea of lowering all my defenses, forever, was seeming less and less attractive. Wouldn't it be just perfect if I finally decided to chicken out . . . *after* cutting my ties with Robert? If I played my cards right, I could come out of this with nothing at all.

△   △   △

The next couple of days were sheerest hell. I kept going over and over it in my mind. A thousand times I asked myself, why not just go back to Earth and Robert? So he didn't love me the way I loved him: he cared, and that could well become love in time. A thousand times I answered, because he had made it an ultimatum, and because he would not admit he had done so, and because I just couldn't risk losing dance forever, even for him.

And because he hadn't asked me to—just assumed I'd "be sensible."

A thousand times I concluded I had made the right decision. But I didn't call Teena and tell her to cancel the reservation Robert had made in my name.

He called me once, about twenty-four hours after the quarrel. I had instructed Teena not to put through any calls from him, so he recorded a long message. When she told me, I had her wipe it, unplayed. A mistake: I spent hours wondering what he had said.

Twice I forced myself to go to the cafeteria, using Teena to make sure he was not there at the time. The food tasted like hell. Once I let Ben and Kirra (almost literally) drag me to Le Puis. Even Fat Humphrey didn't cheer me up, nor the Hurricanes he prescribed for me. With Kirra right there listening, Ben made the politest pass I'd ever received; I almost smiled as I thanked him and turned him down.

That night Reb came to visit me in my room. He expressed sympathy, and offered to help in any way he could. He did not, as I'd half expected, try to persuade me to stop grieving. Instead he encouraged me to grieve, the faster to use it up. But I noticed something subtle about his word choice. He never said he was sorry Robert and I were breaking up. He only said he was sorry I was suffering over it.

A friend of my parents, back on Gambier Island, once responded to his wife's leaving him by taking their beloved dog back up into the woods and shooting him. I'd never understood how anyone could do something so simultaneously selfish and self-destructive until I found myself on the verge of making a pass at Reb. Hurt people do crazy things, that's all. I was luckier than my parents' friend had been: I caught myself in time, and Reb failed to notice, the nicest thing he could have done.

Later that night I started to record a message for Robert . . . then gave up and erased it unsent.

The next day the shuttle left for Earth.

I found myself in the corridor outside the Departure Lock, in an alcove where I could watch the queue forming. I avoided the gazes of those who lined up, and they avoided mine. Robert was one of the last to arrive, coming to a stop right outside my alcove. I saw him before he saw me. It had an almost physical impact. Then he saw me, and that was even worse. We looked at each other, treading air. He glanced at the others, then back to me.

He waved Earthward. "Come with me."

I waved starward. "Come with me."

He made no reply. After a time I left the alcove, grabbed a handhold and flung myself away into the bowels of the rock, not stopping until I reached hardhat territory. I joined a handful of gawkers and watched a new tunnel being cut. They struck ice, and that was good, because soon there were so many warm water droplets in the ambient air that a few tears more or less went unnoticed.

I cut classes that day, as I had the previous two, and spent some time in the studio in the afternoon, trying to dance. It was a fiasco. I sought out Reb's after-classes sitting group, and sat kûkanzen for a couple of hours, or tried to. It was my first time with the group. I had done a fair amount of sitting outside class, but never with the group. But that night I needed them to keep me anchored, to keep me from bursting into tears. Sitting, and the chanting after, helped, a little. Not enough.

I went to Le Puis, where Fat Humphrey allowed me to get drunk. He did so with skill and delicacy, so that I woke the next day without a hangover despite my best efforts.

But I was dumb enough to decide to go to morning class, and logy enough to sleepwalk through suit inspection, and so I came damned close to dying when a thruster I should have replaced went rogue on me at just the wrong moment. I was not able to recover as Ben had from a similar problem, and had to be rescued. By Ben, since Robert was no longer there to take care of it.

It straightened me up. I did not want to die—not even subconsciously, I think. Or if I did, I wanted it to be at a time and place, and by a method, of my own choosing; not in some stupid accident, not over a man. I won't say I started to feel better . . . but I did start to take better care of myself again. That's a beginning.

Sulke didn't chew me out for my stupidity. She was the one I'd gotten drunk with the night before, the one who'd gotten me to bed, as I had once done for her.

$$\triangle \qquad \triangle \qquad \triangle$$

I don't know, maybe it's easier to turn your back on Earth if there's someone down there you never want to see again. Perhaps it's easier to attain Zen no-thought if your thoughts are all painful ones anyway. I started to make real progress in my studies, both practical and spiritual.

When I arrived at Top Step, free fall had seemed an awkward, clumsy environment; the graceful Second- and Third-Monthers had seemed magical creatures. I didn't feel particularly magical now, but free fall seemed a natural way to live, and the new crop of Postulants seemed incredibly awkward and clumsy. My p-suit had once seemed exotic, romantic; now it was clothing. Sitting kûkanzen had once been unbearable boredom and discomfort: now it was natural and blissful. I told myself that I had learned a brutal lesson in nonattachment, which would actually help me in the transition to Symbiosis. All my bridges were burnt behind me. All I had left to lose were dance and my life itself. All I had to do was to go forward, or die trying.

One thing never changed. Space itself was always and forever a place of heart-stopping majesty and terrible beauty.

I even learned to stop resenting Kirra and Ben's happiness in time to preserve our friendship. I'm ashamed to admit how hard a learning that was. Other happy couples, triads and group marriages in Top Step somehow did not grate on me—but at first it seemed disloyal for my friends to be joyous when I was not. And Ben certainly had more than enough quirks for which one could work up a dislike. But Reb caught me at it, diagnosed my problem, and talked it over with me until I could be rational again. In my heart of hearts, I loved them both, and wished them well.

They both made an effort to bring me out of myself, to invite me for drinks and include me in their games and discussions. We three had been friends like this before I'd become Robert's lover; now we were again, that was all.

Only one thing was really keeping me from Symbiosis, now. I wanted to make one last dance before I went, to choreograph my farewell to human life while I was still human. I knew I would make other dances in concert with my Stardancer brothers and sisters, and perform in theirs, for centuries to come—but this last one would be mine alone, the last such there could ever be. In a way, it was almost good that Robert was gone, for now the dance could be all my own personal farewell, rather than ours.

I stopped calling the piece *Do the Next Thing*. Although those words are a pretty fair approximation of the meaning of life—they'll get you through when life itself has lost its meaning—they were a little too flip for the title of my last work as a human. Instead I began thinking of it simply as *Coda*.

There is a pun in there that perhaps only a choreographer would get. In music, a coda is the natural end of a movement, the passage that brings it to a formal close. In dance, it is the end of a *pas de deux*.

I worked on it for hours at a time, throwing out ideas like a Roman candle, ruthlessly pruning every one that wasn't just

right, then trying them in different combinations and juxtapo-
sitions, like someone trying to solve a Rubik's Cube by
intuition alone. I had the constant awareness that something
might kill me at any minute, but I tried not to let it hurry me.
Better to die with it incomplete than do a sloppy job of it.

It ate up a lot of time. Or kept the time from eating me up.
One of those.

"When are we gonna see this bleedin' dance, then?" Kirra
asked me that Friday. "Ben and me are gone day after
tomorrow."

"I'm sorry, love," I told her. "It's just not ready to show
yet."

"Why don't you do a bit of it just before we swallow the
stuff? It don't have to be finished—just a little bit to send us off
in style, like."

"Yeah," Ben chimed in. "We'd love to have you dance at
our GraduWedding, Morgan."

"And I'd love to," I said, "but it just won't be ready in time.
I'm sorry, I wish it could be."

"Ah, don't be stingy with it, Morgan," Kirra said. "I sung
for you, ain't I? An' Benjy taught you free fall handball an'
all. It's your shout."

I started to get irritated. Tact had never been the strong suit
of either of them . . . but this was a little excessive. Suddenly I understood something. Underneath their excitement
and anticipation, Kirra and Ben were both scared silly.

"I'll dance it at my own Graduation," I said, softer than I
might have. "You can both see it then."

"We'll be halfway to Titan by then," she protested.

"So what? As long as one Stardancer is in the neighbor-
hood, you'll have a front-row seat."

"Huh. Right enough, I guess."

"Have you two recorded your Last Words for your families,
yet?"

They let me change the subject. But I kept thinking about
their request, wishing I had something to give them for a
wedding gift, and a little while later I had a very bright idea.
I excused myself, went off and made a phone call. It worked

even better than I had hoped. I had to work hard to conceal my excitement when I rejoined them.

We three slept together that night, for the last time. It was a memorable night; people who are scared silly make incredible lovers. We spent the next day together, visiting all their favorite places. Solariums One and Three, Le Puis, the Great Hall, the games rooms and all the places where we'd shared so much fun and laughter. After dinner I slipped away while they weren't looking and let them have their last evening to themselves. They didn't come back to the room, and I fell asleep with a smile on my face.

The next day was Sunday. I didn't see them until dinner time; according to Teena they never left Ben's room until then. We talked awhile, and they gave some attention to their last meal. Then the two of them instigated one last food fight. It was glorious. You could tell how close a person was to Graduation by how little food they wore when the fight was over. Ben and Kirra were the only ones who ended up completely unmarked—somewhat unfairly, as they had started it. Either of them could dodge anything they saw coming, and Ben had no blind spot, and had enough attention to spare to guard Kirra's back and warn her of sneak attacks. I only got hit a couple of times myself, each time from behind.

I showered and was done in time to catch them coming out of Reb's room. "Hey, you guys. Hello, Reb."

"Hi, Morgan," Kirra said. "Guess it's time to get it done, eh?"

"Yeah. Listen, I know this is kind of last-minute, but . . . would you mind a bit of dance at your Graduation after all?"

They both brightened. "That'd be great, love," Kirra said. "Gee, I'm glad you changed your mind."

"Yeah," Ben agreed. "I'm dying to see *Coda*."

"Oh, it won't be *Coda*," I said. "I came up with something special for the occasion. I think you'll like it. Are you coming, Reb?"

"I wouldn't miss it," he said. He took Kirra's arm and I took Ben's, and the four of us jaunted away like a chorus line on skates.

A fair-sized group was waiting at the airlock. Kirra and Ben had invited anyone who wanted to come, and they were well liked; all of our class that were still around were present, and even some people I didn't know. There were hugs and handshakes and goodbyes, and then everybody put their hoods on. It took awhile to cycle everybody through the lock. While we were waiting outside, Kirra asked me, "Don't you need to warm up or somethin', love?"

"Not this time," I said.

She made a sound of puzzlement, but let it go.

When everyone was assembled outside, we set off as a group, led by Reb. Newer chums who drifted out of formation did their best to recover without drawing attention to themselves. We ascended like a slightly tipsy celestial choir; Top Step slowly fell away below us, and when it had dwindled into a distant cigar, the Symbiote Mass was visible above us. "Above" in an absolute sense, relative to Earth: by that time we had flipped ourselves so that it seemed to be below our feet. "I don't see any Stardancers waitin' to meet us," Kirra said as we closed in on the red cloud.

"Don't worry," I said. "They'll be along."

"Bloody well better. *I* don't know how to make that big glob squeeze off a piece my size."

"Relax, Kirra," Reb said. "Be your breath."

"Right. No worries, mate."

Our formation became most ragged as we came to rest near the Mass, but Reb issued quiet instructions and got us all together again with minimal confusion. Kirra and Ben floated a little apart from the rest of us. Ben's p-suit was a pale yellow that suited him and his red hair as well as cobalt blue suited Kirra. Between the two of them and the glowing red Symbiote Mass beside them, they had the rainbow covered. There was a moment of silence.

"Well, here we are," Kirra said finally. "I'd like to thank you all for comin'—"

"—or however you're reacting," Ben interjected, and she aimed a mock blow at him that he dodged easily. We all chuckled, and some of the solemnity went out of the occasion.

"We got no speeches to make or anythin'," she went on.

"But before we get down to it, our good friend Morgan McLeod is going to dance for us all." An approving murmur began.

"Me?" I said. "Oh, no!"

"What do you mean, 'no'? You promised."

"I asked if you'd mind a bit of dance. I didn't say I'd be dancing. Curtain!"

"I don't get you, love."

"Wait a second, spice," Ben said. "Here comes our stuff, I think." (Ben and Kirra called each other "spice," a term of endearment I find distinctly superior to "honey" or other sticky sweetness.)

She precessed to face the way he seemed to be looking. "Where?"

"No, no, there," he said, and pointed behind him and to his right.

"You and your trick eyes," she said, and faced the way he was pointing. "Right you are, here it comes. Still don't see any Stardancers, though." A red blob was slowly growing larger in the distance.

"You're looking at six of them," I said, enjoying myself hugely.

"Where?"

"Twelve, actually, but they're squeezed into six bodies at the moment. Kirra and Benjamin Buckley, allow me to present Jinsei Kagami, Yuan Zhongshan, Consuela Paixio, Sven Bjornssen, Ludmilla Vorkuta, and Walerij Pietkow."

The red blob was much closer now. Music swelled out of nowhere, a soft warm A chord with little liquid trills chasing in and out of it. It couldn't seem to make up its mind whether it was major or minor.

"They are all trained dancers themselves, but they have all agreed to lend remote-control of their bodies to six of their more distant siblings, who will now dance in your honour. These are Shara Drummond, Sascha Yakovskaya, Norrey Drummond, Charles Armstead, Linda Parsons, and Tom McGillicuddy. Choreography is by all six, around a frame by Shara. Music prerecorded by Raoul Brindle; playback, set design and holographic recording by Harry Stein. The piece is called *Kiss the Sky*."

By now the jumbled murmuring of our group was as loud as the soft music. Shara Drummond . . . and *all* of the original Six . . . *and* Yakovskaya, the first truly great dancer to join them in space, the man who had choreographed the *Propaedeutics* in his first week as a Stardancer . . . all dancing together, if only by proxy, for the first time in over a decade—with Brindle on synth! "Pull the other one," Kirra said. "I don't see a bloody soul. Just that great hunk of—oh!"

She and everyone fell silent. The approaching blob of Symbiote had suddenly flexed, and stretched in six directions at once to become a kind of six-pointed red snowflake, swirling gently as it approached, like a pinwheel in a gentle breeze, its axis of rotation pointed right at us.

It took a moment for the eye to get it into correct perspective: it was *not* just enough Symbiote for two people, but enough and more than enough for six, therefore somewhat farther from us than it had seemed to be. Six Stardancers had mingled their Symbiotes and were joined at the feet, held together by their linked hands, a hundred meters from us. The snowflake shifted and flowed, as the six dancers who comprised it changed their position in unison from one pattern to another by flexing elbows and knees, contracting and releasing.

The music acquired a slow, steady pulse in the bass. The pattern of the spinning snowflake changed with each beat, as if it were some great red heart clenching rhythmically. Percussion instruments and a Michael Hedges–like guitar began adding counterpoint accents to the rhythm. The total mass of Symbiote began to swell away from the dancers it contained, until it was a translucent crimson disc with six people at its heart, perhaps twenty meters in diameter. The disc swelled from the center and became a convex lens, nearly transparent; pink stars swam behind it, rippling. Lights came up. The lamps themselves were invisible to us, since they were tiny and dull black and pointing away from us, but we saw their blue and yellow reflections come up as highlights on the crimson lens, highlights that bled all the other colours there are at their edges.

The six children of the lens separated like a bud opening into a flower, fanned out in six directions and wedged themselves into the narrow parts of the lens wall. One of them doubled and jaunted back to the center of the lens, came to rest there . . . and then began to move. Even at a hundred meters, even behind that carmine film of Symbiote, even wearing a different body, there was no mistaking her. The familiar motif that emerged in brass in the underlying music only confirmed it. Jinsei's body it may have been, but it was Shara Drummond, the greatest dancer of our time, who took the first solo.

She wore thrusters at wrists and ankles, but could not have used them inside that lens, I think. She danced only with body and muscles, moving three-dimensionally in place, with her unmistakable fluidity and precision of line. It reminded me of a piece I'd seen years ago by a colleague recovering from a leg injury called *Dancing in Place:* confining himself to one spot on stage, standing on one leg, he had explored more ways of dancing and looking at dance than most performers can do using an entire stage. Shara/Jensei did the same now, tumbling, arching, turning, while her center stayed anchored to the center of the lens. She could have been a butterfly gifted with limbs, or a leaf in flight, or a protozoan swimming in the primordial soup. The brass stopped hinting at Shara's Theme and made a new statement, underlined by strings. Soon, inevitably, she drifted far enough from the center of the lens to touch its inner surface, and used it to jaunt back to her original place at the periphery.

This time two figures moved to the center and met there. Linda Parsons and Tom McGillicuddy, the hippie and the businessman who had met in space, fallen in love, and become the fourth and fifth founding members of Stardancers Incorporated (after Charlie, Norrey and Raoul). McGillicuddy at least was easy for me to identify: he had always been the least trained of the original company; even after decades of practice, and even wearing a better-trained body than his own, there were minor limitations to his technique. But Linda compensated for them so perfectly after thirty-four years of dancing with him that I don't think anyone else noticed. They did a *pas de deux* at the heart of the lens, like mating hummingbirds, and now the brass and strings made different but complementary statements to accompany them.

When they returned to their places at the rim, three figures replaced them. Charlie and Norrey and Sascha, legendary partners and friends, did a trio piece loosely derived from their famous *Why Can't We?*, as woodwinds brought in a third theme that fit the brass and string motifs like an interlocking puzzle; all three resolved into a major chord as the trio broke up and returned to the rim again.

Next a quartet of both Drummond sisters and Armstead and Yakovskaya, faster and more vigorous, interacting with the kind of precision and intuition that nontelepaths would have needed weeks of rehearsal to achieve; a great pipe organ added its voice to the music, which rose in tempo and resolved into a four-note diminished chord at the quartet's end.

Then everyone but Shara met at the center for a flashing quicksilver quintet, tumbling over one another like kittens in a basket; the music was all tumbling five-note ninth chords.

Finally all six danced together as a single organism, making strange, indescribable geometrical figures in three dimensions. As they danced, the lens filled out, became a sphere, which slowly contracted in on them, thickening and darkening as it came. Before long there was only a nearly opaque glowing red ball of Symbiote, flexing and shifting in time to the racing music. It quivered, trembled—

—then burst apart, becoming six separate Stardancers flying in different directions like a firework detonation. Their thrusters protruded through their individual coatings of Symbiote now, and they used them to put themselves into graceful wide loops, so that they returned to their starting point, missed colliding by inches, and then arced out again. Each had a different-coloured thruster exhaust; comet-tails of red, yellow, blue, orange, green, and purple attended them as they flew, leaving the afterimage of a multicoloured Christmas ribbon against the star-spangled blackness. The music swelled and soared with them as they danced, spilling trills in all directions to match their thruster spray. Eventually they all came together again in a tight formation like exhibition aircraft, and took turns passing each other back and forth from hand to hand.

There was joy in their dance, and hope, and endless energy, and manifest love for one another; from time to time one or another of them would laugh for sheer pleasure. I found that I was smiling unconsciously as I watched their dance unfold. I sneaked a look at Kirra and Ben; they were smiling too.

There was a short movement in which they were performing a kind of kinesthetic pun, moving mentally as well as physically, passing their *selves* from one host body to another. I don't know how many others caught it, but I clearly saw Shara Drummond's essence change bodies several times. Once or twice I spotted Yakovskaya or McGillicuddy transmigrating too. I think that for a time, the bodies' original owners were present and dancing as well.

Then Shara was stationary, spinning slowly around her vertical axis, apart from the other five as they continued to interact, watching how their dance changed in her absence; then in a reversed reprise of their solo-to-group progression, Tom dropped out, then Linda, then Charlie, then Norrey. Quintet, quartet, trio, pair, finally Yakovskaya was soloing within a pentagon of stationary spinning companions, and then he too stopped dancing and went into a spin. The music had decayed too, to a single voice, a cello, and the theme it was quoting was not Shara's signature motif this time, but Kirra's Song of Polar Orbit.

By some means I didn't and don't understand, all six of them began to move relative to one another, around their common center, as though they were jointly orbiting some invisible mini black hole. The orbits tightened inexorably, until they darted like the Firefly aliens themselves, like electrons dancing in mad attendance on some invisible nucleus. Hands met and joined just as the Song of Polar Orbit reached its coda; again they were a six-personed snowflake. Thrusters sprayed coloured fire and smoke, and they became a living, madly spinning Catherine Wheel.

The thrusters went dark, and they were a scarlet pinwheel.

Their Symbiotes merged, and they were a disc again.

A hole appeared in the center, making the disc look for all the world like an old-fashioned phonograph record (all right, I'm dating myself) spinning on a turntable, seen from above. My parents used to own an album like that, red and translucent, a novelty gimmick. The hole enlarged, so that the disc looked like a 45 RPM single; paradoxically its spin slowed rather than speeded up.

Suddenly the disc exuded some of its mass into the hole in the center, where a globe of red Symbiote grew like a pearl forming within an oyster. It moved away from the disc, coming toward us with infinite slowness. Toward Kirra and Ben. As it did so, the disc broke up into six Stardancers again, and they all braked violently to an instant stop, sudden total motionlessness. The music broke like a wave on a shore and faded to silence, the lights went out.

After several seconds of silence, there was wild applause.

Oh, I know I haven't conveyed it; dance can't be described. Look it up for yourself, it's on the Net. Not a major work by any means, but a moving and lyrical piece, just right for a wedding feast and Graduation. I was terribly pleased on Kirra and Ben's account.

They thanked me lavishly for the gift, and thanked all twelve of the dancers individually. "That was bloody marvelous," Kirra said. "Morgan, really, it was special!" She was grinning, but her p-suit hood was full of tear-tendrils.

"Just my version of chocolate chip ice cream from Chile," I said, grinning back at her. *Though it marks a much happier occasion than your gift did*. Dammit, I was leaking saline worms too.

"We're deeply honoured," Ben said. "Our GraduWedding has become part of dance history. Or almost. Get ready, spice, here it comes!"

Their blob of Symbiote was nearly upon them, a bead of God's blood.

"I'll sing at your Graduation, Morgan," Kirra promised me hastily. "Wait an' see if I don't! Goodbye—see you soon—cheerio, all! Let's go meet it, Benjy: one, two, three . . ."

They jaunted forward together, hit the Symbiote dead

center, passed inside it. They stripped quickly, took the communications gear from their p-suits and hung it around their necks, pushed the suits clear of the Symbiote and joined hands. It contracted in upon them and around and through them, and they were two Stardancers, convulsing with their first shock of telepathic onslaught but still holding hands. Their combined shout of exaltation was picked up by their throat mikes and hurled to the stars.

Then they were silent and adrift, marinating in Symbiosis.

The dancers had already begun tiptoeing away on scarlet butterfly wings of lightsail. The show was over.

Reb took my arm, and we all headed back to Top Step.

$$\triangle \qquad \triangle \qquad \triangle$$

They phoned me up five or six days later. They were well on their way out to meet the Harvest Crew returning with new Symbiote from Titan, about a day from rendezvous. It was an odd conversation. They both sounded as though they were very drunk or very stoned. Ben commented giddily that space now looked to him just like a newspaper. Black and white and red all over. They both assured me that Symbiosis was glorious, wonderful, not to be missed, but were quite unable to describe it in any more detail than that, at least in words. They did say they had two new senses, as expected, but could not describe or explain them any better than the instructors back at Suit Camp had. Kirra sang me part of a work in progress, *The Song of Symbiosis,* and made me promise to send a copy of it to Yarra and the Yirlandji people for her. It was terribly beautiful but very strange, haunting and confounding, hinting at things that even music can't carry. She said she was collaborating on a Song with Raoul (whom she would be physically meeting in only a few more hours), but did not sing any of it for me. I told them my dance was about two-thirds finished, and they both exhorted me to hurry up and complete it so I could come join them. I assured them I was going as fast as I could, especially since I no longer had any close friends inboard to take up my free time. Kirra, pausing to consult some mathematician I didn't know, worked out that they would in all likelihood be back with the fresh Symbiote just in time for my Graduation. We agreed to meet then, and I was very pleased to know they would be present for my own last breath.

I was hard at work on the piece the next day, had just solved a tricky and hard-to-describe esthetic problem in the third movement, when Teena said, "Morgan, Reb Hawkins needs to speak to you as soon as possible."

"Put him on," I said, brushing sweat from my back, and she did. I can't reproduce the dialogue and won't try. He told me the news, and I'm sure he did it as compassionately as it could have been done.

Shortly after Ben and Kirra had made rendezvous with the returning Harvest Crew, there had been an unexplained catastrophic explosion, cataclysmic enough to disrupt the entire mass of new Symbiote and kill the entire Crew. Raoul Brindle, Ben, Kirra, more than a dozen others, all were dead.

Black and white and red all over.

CHAPTER TWELVE

We die, and we do not die.

—Shunryu Suzuki-roshi,
ZEN MIND, BEGINNER'S MIND

THE NEWS ROCKED the Solar System, stunned humans and Stardancers alike.

Credit for the explosion was formally claimed, not by the Gabriel Jihad, but by a much older terrorist group, Jamaat al-Muslimeen. They too were rumored to have ties to the Umayyad Caliphate, though they were based in Trinidad rather than Medina, black Muslims rather than brown. It didn't seem to make much difference. There was so much outcry and mutual vituperation at the UN that they were forced to suspend all operations of the General Assembly for a week. That didn't seem to make much difference, either, at least not to those humans in space.

Just how the Jamaat had managed to pull off the bombing, they did not say. Of all the questions the incident raised, that one seemed to me to matter least of all.

But it seemed to fascinate Sulke. "It just couldn't possibly have been a missile," she insisted angrily.

We were drinking together in Le Puis, heavily, a few days after the tragedy; I was still in something like a protracted state of shock, and cared not at all for the question, but found myself arguing automatically. "Why not?"

"It's obvious. Peace missiles only aim down. ASATs only aim sideways, nothing shoots *away* from Earth except lasers and particle beams, and the biggest one there is would have to have been focused on the Symbiote for nearly an hour to burst it. But it was an instantaneous *blam.*"

"Anything with a power plant could be a big slow bomb."

"Self-propelling hardware in space is *very* carefully monitored, for pretty obvious reasons. There just isn't anything missing. And besides, if something had left its usual orbit and headed out of cislunar space, it would have been tracked by the Space Command. The screens prove no artifact ever approached the new Symbiote. The Chinese have got some scientific stuff vectoring around out in that general direction, but not within a hundred thousand klicks of the spot where the explosion took place, and they couldn't have fired off anything big enough to make that big a bang without being seen."

Janani Luwum, a huge First-Monther truckdriver from Uganda, was at the next table, near enough to eavesdrop, and wedged himself into the conversation. "I don't understand the ambiguity. Wasn't the new Symbiote itself being tracked?"

"Yes," Sulke agreed, "but not very closely or carefully. It wasn't *doing* anything interesting. They would have started paying more attention in a few days when deceleration began, but as things stand we have nothing better than automatic radar tracking at poor resolution."

"Then you don't *know* that there was no incoming missile: you only infer it."

"From goddam good evidence," she insisted. "Anything on a closing course would have triggered alarms. That aside, the Stardancers present would have noticed it coming, with that weird radar sense of theirs, and tapes of radio transmissions and reports from Stardancers who were in rapport at the time show no one was expecting trouble right up to the second it went off."

"Christ," Janani said, "I wonder what that must be like: being in telepathic rapport with someone while they're blown to pieces."

"I don't know," Sulke said with a shudder, "but I hear they have more than fifty new catatonics to try and heal."

"Those were not the first Stardancers ever to die," Janani's lover Henning Fragerhøi pointed out.

"No, there've been more than a dozen accidental deaths since the first Symbiosis," Sulke said. "But never before have so many died, so suddenly, so savagely. No Stardancer was ever murdered before."

"But how can you be sure it was murder?" Janani said. "You just finished proving there was no shot fired."

"That's right—but there was nothing along with them that could possibly have blown up like that. Nothing but Stardancers and Symbiote."

"Well, then," I said, tired of all the chattering, "it didn't happen. That's a relief. Thanks, Sulke. Can we get back to some serious drinking, now? Hey, Fat! Oh shit, I mean 'Pål.' Hey, Pål, we need more balls over here." We were able to get shitfaced in Le Puis because Fat Humphrey was not on duty; it was said that he'd been locked in his own quarters, drinking himself into a coma, since the disaster had happened. He had loved Kirra almost as much as I had. And he had been a personal friend of Raoul—had been there the day Raoul joined the newly formed Stardancers Incorporated, twenty years before. His relief bartender Pål Bøgeberg didn't seem to much care if the customers got drunk enough to riot; he brought the balls of booze I ordered without protest.

"It fucking well happened, all right," Sulke said. "But there's only one fucking way in the System it could have happened."

"Spontaneous combustion," I said sourly, and sucked a great gulp of gin.

"Stalking horse," she said, and squeezed a stream of gin at her own mouth, catching it with the panache of a longtime free fall lush.

"I don't understand," said Henning, for whom English was a second language. " 'Stocking hose'?"

"Stalking horse. A living mine. One of those Stardancers was boobytrapped. And since they were all telepathic, it had to have been done without their knowledge. Just how it was done, I can't imagine. My best guess is some kind of very tiny dart carrying seed nanoreplicators. It penetrated somebody's Symbiote without them noticing, somehow, and then the sneaky little nanoreps used that body's own materials to construct a bomb. As soon as it was big enough, *blooey!*"

"More likely the Symbiote itself was injected somehow," Janani said. "Enough matter there for a really big bomb, without the risk its host would notice it growing. Stardancers monitor their own bodies pretty closely, control even the unconscious systems and so forth: you'd think they'd notice a tumor large enough to explode with so much force."

"Either could be true," Sulke said. "There was a helluva lot of Symbiote, but it's made up of the wrong chemicals to make a really powerful bomb easily, and you'd see discoloration as it formed. But I've read in spy thrillers that nanoreplicators could synthesize a very powerful explosive from the materials in an ordinary human body, without disturbing any essential function. It could be hidden in the one large part of the body a Stardancer never pays any attention to."

"Where's that?"

"The lungs. Plenty of room, and all the nerves to that area are switched off permanently at Symbiosis, to keep you from panicking when you stop breathing for good."

"Shut *up*, for Christ's sake," I cried, horrified by the mental picture of death coalescing around someone's living heart while they jaunted along oblivious.

"The only thing I don't get is why whoever it was didn't notice the injection. The seed would have to have mass enough to be perceptible, be at least as big as a pinhead—and Stardancers notice collisions with objects that big. They have to, they live in a world of micrometeorites."

"If the subject is not changed in the next sentence spoken, I am going to squirt the rest of this gin in your eye," I said, and held it up threateningly. Sulke was not an easy drunk to intimidate, but maybe there was something in my voice. Her next sentence was a *non sequitur* that started a different argument, about who was *really* behind the bombing. It wasn't a true change of subject, but I let it go.

I don't remember much of the rest of that night, and what I remember of the next day doesn't bear repeating. I spent most of it in my sleepsack, moaning, with an icepack at the back of my neck—or rather, shuttling back and forth between there and the john. After an endless time of misery I decided I needed to sweat the pain out of me, and went to my studio.

There I found that my thoughts danced and whirled more than my body ever could.

Sick of this goddam piece. Sick of everything I can think of.

Not one close friend left anywhere in the Solar System. More than forty-three thousand new lovers waiting to marry me, but not one goddam friend. Reb'll be on my back any time now; I've cut classes for three days straight. Probably not the only one. Fuck it, there's nothing more they can teach me now that I need to know. Only thing holding me back is this goddam dance, and I wish I'd never started the frigging thing. Hadn't been so busy and distracted with it, self-involved, I might have put together a stronger thing with Robert. Jesus, my back hurts. Been hurting quite a bit lately; snuck up on me. Old injury trying to make a comeback. Repair it myself once I eat the Big Red Jell-O. Unless somebody injects me with a teeny little bomb factory. Or already has. No, I'd have noticed. Or would I? Apparently somebody *failed to notice it being done to them. How the hell could that be? How do you introduce something the size of a pinhead into someone's body without them noticing? Slip it in their soup? Awful chancey—might leave the wrong few drops in the container. Aerosol spray? No, the victim might choke on the thing. Damn, that knee's starting to twinge a bit too. Or am I imagining it? Oh, God damn it all. Everything, everything, everything falling apart at once. Friends gone, lover gone, never again the joyous invasion of my—*

I cried out.

"Are you all right, Morgan?" Teena asked with concern.

"Absolutely wonderful," I snarled.

She was sharp enough to detect pain in a human voice, but not subtle enough for sarcasm. "Sorry I disturbed you."

"Privacy, Teena. Switch off. Butt out!"

"Yes, Morgan," she said, and was gone, her monitors on me shut off until I called her again.

I tried to vomit, but there was nothing left in my system to expel. The new thought in my brain was so monstrous, so unthinkable, I wanted to spew it out of me like poison food, but I could find no way to do so even symbolically. I was suffused with horror. I curled up into a fetal ball, trembling violently.

—it can't be (it could be) it can't be (it could be) there must be some other way (name one) it can't be—

All at once I knew a way you could invade someone's body without them noticing. By concealing the invader in another, larger invasion they were joyfully accepting.

By fucking them.

Literally or figuratively, by sperm in one set of mucous membranes or by saliva in another at the other end, what difference did it make? The pinhead-sized object need not be hard or metallic like a real pinhead, might have been soft and malleable, easily mistaken for a morsel of food politely ignored in a passionate kiss—or unnoticed altogether amid ten ccs of ejaculate.

It made no sense for Ben to have infected Kirra, or the other way around: they had died together.

But Robert had made love with both of them.

(And left for Earth the very next day. Without inviting me to accompany him.)

And I was the only living person who knew that . . .

—it can't be, he couldn't (he could) he wouldn't (how the hell do you know) why would he, why would he, WHY WOULD HE DO SUCH A THING? (he's Chinese, they hate Stardancers) He's Chinese-American, not from China (who says so, and so what) no, I just can't believe it (oh you can believe it, all right, you just don't know for sure) I don't want to believe it, I don't want to know, it isn't true (there's only one good way to find out) it can't be—

In my blind drifting, I contacted the studio wall. And screamed.

△   △   △

Perhaps—no, certainly—I should have gone right to Reb with what I had figured out. Or to Dorothy Gerstenfeld, or Phillipe Mgabi . . . or all three. I had an urgent need to share my terrible hypothesis with *someone*. For all I knew, I was carrying a bomb inside *me*.

But I did not go to Reb, or anyone else. In fact, I stayed there in my studio, fetal and moaning, until I had recovered sufficiently that I thought I could keep the sick horror out of my face—at least well enough to fool shipboard acquaintances.

Part of it might have been reticence to share a sexual secret of my friends, whose permission I could no longer seek. But I don't think so. No sexual behaviour was scandalous in Top Step, and I did not think either Kirra or Ben would have considered it a secret.

No, what stopped me was simply that my theory was just that. A theory. I just could not make an accusation of such ghastly magnitude against a man I had loved, without the slightest shred of proof. The accusation alone would be so utterly damning—and how could a man possibly defend himself against such a charge if he were innocent? If I opened my mouth, and were wrong, and Robert were torn to pieces down on Earth by an angry mob of Stardancer-lovers . . .

But when I thought back, I realized that I could not recall any time Reb had expressed an opinion of Robert as a person—or of our relationship. And when we broke up, he'd said only that he was sorry I was sad. Had that hyperintuitive man sensed something about Robert that I had missed? I could not bring myself to ask him.

I had to know. For myself, for sure. And as soon as physically possible. No shilly-shallying around, like I'd been doing about Symbiosis; it was time to get off the dime and make a move, *now*. I might be carrying a second bomb, and who knew when it might go off?

It took me an hour or so to get my lines together and rehearse them until I could make them sound truthful. At first I wasn't sure I could do it. But I've always been a trouper. When I had it right, I called Reb and told him I was quitting.

He wanted to talk about it, of course, but I cut it as short as I could. In essence I claimed that Kirra's and Ben's deaths had soured space for me; it was no longer a place I wanted to go. There was enough truth in it for me to sound plausible, I guess: he bought it, reluctantly. He sounded sad, but made no real effort to argue, simply making sure my mind was made up.

Half an hour later Dorothy Gerstenfeld called and told me that I had a reserved seat on the next ship to Earth, leaving in a little under twenty-four hours. I thanked her and switched off. She didn't call back.

△   △   △

I spent the time wrestling with myself. What I hypothesized was grotesque, impossible. Logical, yes; theoretically and intuitively reasonable, yes, but simply not possible. Not my Robert! Inscrutable Oriental be damned, I just could not have known him so intimately and known him so little. Could I? What was the point of sabotaging my own Symbiosis, the only thing life had left to offer me, to chase down such a wild and ugly idea?

I had to, that was all.

As Robert himself had pointed out when he left, I could always come back again. I would see Robert, and question him closely, and look into his eyes as I did . . . and then I would apologize, and call Reb, and he would pull strings to let me come back up to Top Step and Graduate. One last quick visit to Earth, to lay two ghosts to rest, that was all.

I spent so much time convincing myself that I had to be mistaken that I gave no conscious thought at all to what I would do if it turned out I was not mistaken.

△   △   △

I was surprised by how hard it was to leave my p-suit behind. I had been essentially living in it for nearly a month now, and it had become home. But it did not belong to me anymore. I rode to Earth wearing a cheap tourist suit just like the one I'd worn on the trip up, a hundred thousand years ago.

No one came to see me off. Not even Reb. I'd been half-expecting him, but was grateful to be spared the task of trying to maintain a lie before so intuitive a man. Four other students left on the same shuttle, for the same reason I had claimed, and there were a handful of other passengers, mostly staff members traveling to Earth on business.

The trip itself was utterly without incident, or at least none that forced itself into my attention. I could have had a simulated window-view on my seatback TV this time, but did not want one. Emotionally it was my trip up, run backwards. The closer I got to Earth the heavier I felt, in body and mind,

the further my spirit sank, and I landed in a state of maximum
confusion and upset, heart pounding wildly under the unac-
customed load.

To my great relief, the spaceplane did not land at the same
spaceport from which I had left Earth. I didn't think I could
have borne seeing Queensland again, Kirra's home, and
thinking of her sweet smile blown into particles, expanding
slowly to fill the universe. Instead we grounded outside Quito,
Ecuador.

That was good in another way, too. Closer to San Francisco.

△   △   △

I felt like an elephant. Gone the dancer. My work had kept
me in good shape, so I didn't have as much trouble bearing my
returned weight as some others have. But I still felt like an
elephant. A pregnant elephant, pregnant with a son (they take
several months longer to bake than girl elephants, I've read)
and in my last month. Most disturbing to my dancer's mind,
my balance was no longer a matter of intuition. I had
unlearned a lot of habits in two and a half months of zero gee.
I had to keep reminding myself that it *mattered* whether I kept
a perpendicular relationship to the wall called "floor" or not,
and I tended to totter like an elderly drunken mammoth. Hair
felt weird lying against the back of my neck and against my
forehead. I kept letting go of things and then being startled
when they raced away to one of the six walls. Everything
had a cartoon, fun-house mirror look. The air smelled funny,
and didn't move enough; unconsciously I tended to keep
moving my head around so I couldn't smother in my exhalations. It seemed weird never to see anyone moving around
below my feet or above my head, to be stuck to the surface of
a planet, like a fly caught in the kind of flypaper my parents
used to hang from the ceiling on Gambier Island when I was
a child.

Customs was no problem, as I arrived with no possessions
whatsoever, not so much as a pair of socks. Credit was only a
thumbprint away. And getting outfitted with clothes and
necessaries took only an hour in the spaceport Traveler's Shop;

it would have been half that but I insisted on styles that would not be out of place in San Francisco and that took more time and more money.

But going through Immigration, first Ecuadorian (horrid) and then U.S. (three times as bad) took up the next day and a half; I finally emerged into the smoggy air of San Francisco with my nerves shot and my teeth aching from long clenching. I weighed a thousand kilos and felt a million years old and the air tasted like burnt flannel. I decided to get a hotel room and sleep for a week before taking further action. The driver of the cab I haled was fascinated by an airplane passenger from Quito with no luggage of any kind. I ignored him.

When I checked in, I signed the register, and then tried to *push* the pen back to the clerk. It bounced high from the countertop, and he looked at me with a knowing air. "Just down, eh? We have waterbeds available for those guests who suffer from gravity fatigue." I thanked him and accepted the service. As the bellhop was showing me into my room he made a discreet suggestion concerning other services he could arrange for guests, and I laughed in his face. A full month ago I had sworn never again to have sex in a gravity field, and I was in no mood to change my mind. That dreaded old friend, lower back pain, was already back in full force, for the first time in months.

I didn't leave that waterbed for three days, and didn't leave my room for a week.

If you want to know what that week was like, go to hell.

That's a kind of pun, I guess. By going to hell, you could certainly simulate that week.

Because now it was time to confront that burning question: *what if it turns out you're right?*

This had bearing on both strategy and tactics.

Suppose Robert were innocent. In that case, there was no problem. I could call him up, arrange to meet somewhere, watch his eyes very carefully while I outlined my suspicions, learn that I was wrong, and apologize if I decided I wanted to bother. In any case, my biggest problem would be coming up with a good exit line; I could be back in Top Step in a matter of days.

But suppose he were guilty? I call him up . . . and a little while later there is an unfortunate incident, a failed Stardancer candidate commits suicide in her hotel room in San Francisco; very sad but no next of kin to push it. Or perhaps, if there really is a little nanotechnological horror hidden somewhere in my body, the whole hotel vanishes in a large mysterious explosion.

No, wait. Just because I called him wouldn't mean the jig was up. I might well have thought things over up in Top Step and decided to follow Robert back to Earth for love. A nuisance, if he really was a high-tech assassin who cared nothing for me, but not a serious one. In that case, meeting with me somewhere for a fast brushoff would be the simplest way to get me off his back. So he agrees to meet me in a restaurant, and *then* he finds out the jig is up . . . and maybe I suffer a sudden heart attack over lunch, fall face down into the salad.

Dammit, if he *was* a hatchetman, it was for a large and wealthy and well-organized conspiracy. Half-assed terrorist groups don't have access to nanotechnological weapons; if they did they wouldn't be half-assed terrorists. If Robert was guilty, he was hotter than the fire that killed Kirra. In that case he was probably not even at his nominal address in San Francisco, but hiding in Beijing or someplace even harder to crack. Just leaving a message on his answering machine might be enough to get me snuffed by Triad hitmen.

Of course, that kind of paranoia only made sense if I assumed he was guilty. But if I didn't at least partly believe he was guilty, what was I doing here, fighting for breath and cursing the glue of gravity?

I had never thought along these kinds of lines in my life, had never known anyone who did except characters in holothrillers and spy novels. I had to work my plans out slowly, laboriously, all the while wanting desperately to believe I was making a fool of myself.

And I kept coming to a jerk at the end of the thought-chain.

If Robert is guilty, and if you work out some clever and safe scheme to get close enough to prove that to yourself— —then what will you do?

Kill him?

Was I capable of it?

Was I physically capable, first? The part of me that remembered his physical speed, grace and coordination raised a few questions as to how a laywoman suffering from gee fatigue went about killing a trained assassin in a public restaurant . . . but was willing to concede in theory that it might be done, with the element of surprise, if I didn't care about being arrested afterward, and if I struck the instant I was sure, without any hesitation at all.

That led to: was I psychologically and emotionally capable of murder? Of anyone, or of Robert? The part of me that liked to watch old Stallone movies wanted to think so. *Yo—lover or no lover, he killed my friends, he dies, end of story.* The part of me that had thought of him as my last forlorn chance at human love wanted to think so too. *He used me as a wartime convenience; no man does that to me and lives.* The part of me that was loyal to the Starmind wanted the deaths of so many Stardancers and the ruin of so much sacred Symbiote avenged. *His action was an act of war; a sneak attack must be repaid.*

But the part of me that thought of itself as an ethical person questioned my right to execute a sentence of death on another human being, however monstrous his crimes . . . and doubted I had the guts.

But what other option did I have? Denounce him to Stardancers Incorporated and the United Nations, betray him to Interpol, charge him before the High Court and the state courts of Queensland and California? With nothing but circumstantial evidence and lover's intuition to support the charges? I couldn't so much as nail him for breach of promise; the son of a bitch had never promised me anything.

Nagging additional minor thought: our brief four-way sexual liaison was not scandalous in Top Step, nor in many circles on Earth nowadays—but it might seem so to Kirra's or Ben's surviving kin.

That put those people in my mind. So the first thing I did upon leaving that grim hotel room was to make two short side trips. Well, one short, to Sherman Oaks . . . and the other rather longer, to north Queensland; I decided I had to face that land again after all.

Before I left, I put the best detective agency I could find onto tracing and locating Robert, with specific warning that he might just be clever enough to spot someone checking him out, and dangerous to kill them. It didn't faze them in the least. They didn't bother asking why, just told me when and where I could go for a report—so that it need not be sent to me at any address—and how much it would cost. I was spending life savings like water, but I didn't give a jaunting damn.

The visit to Ben's father was too sad to recount. The old man was utterly shattered by this latest in a series of crushing disappointments; Ben had been his last surviving blood kin, and now he was alone in the world. I knew all too well how he felt. I told him what a good man his son had been, and something of what Ben had meant to me, and what I could of his last few months of life. It seemed to comfort Mr. Buckley some, but not enough. We were both crying when I left.

With a last-minute attack of the cutes, I had introduced myself to him as Glenn Christie. I'd even gotten cash before leaving San Francisco so I wouldn't leave a digital credit trail, taken cabs so I wouldn't have to use my credit to rent a car.

I couldn't get to Australia that way, but I did take time to alter my appearance, by changing wardrobe, having my hair cut close to my skull and permed within an inch of its life, and darkening my complexion several shades. I paid cash for a standby seat, but had to give my right name; to compensate I made sure I was one of the last to board and sat in the wrong seat; on arrival I got in the wrong line at Customs & Immigration, with people from a different flight, and while I stood on line wedged my way into a voluble discussion in German despite knowing almost none of that language; mostly I nodded and listened alertly to whoever was speaking. Maybe it all helped; no one followed me from the airport. Or maybe I made a jerk of myself to no point—how could I tell?

Only by fucking up and being killed. I bought a minijeep from a used car lot in cash under a false name and headed north.

From Cairns International Airport to Yirlandji country is a long day's drive, about 800 kilometers as the crow flies—and stoned are any crows who ever flew like that. The road up the coast, looking out toward the Great Barrier Reef, is exquisitely beautiful, one of the greatest scenic drives left on Earth—and consequently winds and bucks like a snake caught in an accordion. Driving on the left side of the road for the first time in decades, I did well to average 60 kph. Even ignoring the scenery and banging straight along it would have been a thirteen-hour drive. But it was winter in Queensland, which means, just cool enough to stand it, and that beach constantly beckoning from the right got irresistibly inviting, even to a monomaniacal apprentice secret agent. The water had "cooled" to a temperature Canadian surf will never reach, maybe 26°C, which meant, the nice Beach Club lifeguard explained to me, that the box jellyfish (or sea-wasps, the deadliest things afloat) had all gone away for the season. It was the most glorious swim I'd ever had in my life, and the buoyancy of the water was so near to and yet far from zero gee that I wept salty tears into the sea, and gave serious thought to seeing if I could swim the forty or fifty kilometers out to the Reef. Finally I literally crawled ashore like some primordial ancestor, and baked for an hour before trying to walk again.

I stopped for directions in the Aboriginal Reserve north of Cooktown, and again the next day at the one north of Coen, where I left the main road and struck west toward the Gulf of Carpentaria. In mid-afternoon I met an Aboriginal at a gas station, Thomas Tjarndai, who agreed to guide me to Yirlandji country. I followed his ancient yammering motorbike through an hour of bad road, then followed him on foot through the bush for another hour, wondering darkly whether Yirlandji ever ate whitefella tourists. My back had been aching for days now. At least the knee was not acting up. When we reached the Yirlandji encampment, Thomas brought me to an elder named Billy Huroo, no more than five hundred years old and sharp as a Chinese pawnbroker. I gave him my right name in spite of myself, and told him a little of why I had come. In the distance, a child sang. To my shock I recognized a passage from the Song of Top Step. My eyes stung. At dusk Billy Huroo led me to the campfire of the witch woman Yarra and left me there.

She was ancient and thin, her skin like wrinkled black leather. Like Kirra's, her teeth were gleaming white. She wore only shorts and a knife. Her eyes made me think of Reb, decades older and female. She bade me welcome, gave me tea from a billy. I can't describe the taste, but it was very good. I told her my real name, started to tell her why I was there, and she cut me off. "You knew my *badundjari,*" she told me. "My beloved dream spirit. Kirra, the Singer, who makes Walkabout among the stars. You were her friend."

I nodded, and started to say that I was here to tell her of Kirra's last days. She cut me off again.

"You are here to ask me if you should kill her killer."

I dropped my jaw.

The fire crackled, the sparks flew upward. At last I sighed and said, "How can you know that?"

"From the way you sit. From your voice. I do not hear your words so much as the song of your voice. It is a song of blood rage."

"Yes." There was nothing else to say.

"You know who killed my *badundjari*?"

"I think so. I may know for sure in a day or two. If I am right . . . it was the blackest of betrayals." I explained as carefully as I could my suspicions.

"You believe he gave her a poison that became a bomb, this Symbiote to destroy. And he gave her this poison in the act of love?"

"I hope to know for sure in a day or two," I repeated, then blurted, "Oh, but *what will I do if it's true?*"

She grimaced at me, and slowly shook her head. "No one can tell you that. Not I. Not Emu, or Goanna Lizard, or Kangaroo, not a Rainbow Serpent nor a Sky-God nor any of the Ancestors who were here in the Dreamtime. Not even Menura, the lyrebird of the gullies, who was Kirra's totem. *You* must decide."

I closed my eyes and sighed again. A didgeridu was playing in the far distance, like a mournful dragon. "Yes. You're right."

"But tell me his full name and where he lives," she said. "When you have done whatever you decide to do . . . if he still lives . . . perhaps I will decide *I* need to do something about him."

"I'll tell you the moment I'm sure," I countered, knowing that I might be dead seconds after the moment I was sure. "If you have not heard from me within a week, then I was right and he has overcome me. In that case, and only then, call Top Step and ask Reb Hawkins who my lover was there. You can get access to a phone?"

She took one from a bag at her side. Of course. She'd probably first heard Kirra's space Songs on it. I recalled suddenly, with sharp pain, that I had never carried out my final promise to Kirra, to send her last song-fragments home to that very telephone. "You have my number?" she asked.

Yes I did. In my personal memory node in Teena, up in Top Step. I had not yet downloaded it, and didn't want to access it now for fear of leaving a trail to where I was on Earth. Yarra gave me the number again, and I memorized it rather than write it down. I gave her my personal security code, so that she could get at that last Song of Kirra's if I failed to live through what I was planning.

I slept beside her campfire that night. Nothing bit me.

CHAPTER THIRTEEN

Canst thou draw out Leviathan with an hook?
—Job, xli. 1

FORTY-EIGHT HOURS LATER I was back in my hotel room in San Francisco and my skin was its normal colour again. If anyone was following me, they were too good to be spotted. I was getting close to broke, but treated myself to the finest dinner the hotel could provide. I gave them fresh roasted coffee beans I had bought the day before from an unlikely madman named Gebhardt Kaiserlingck, who ran a wonderful screwball coffee plantation outside of Daintree, and insisted that the kitchen drip-brew them for me. I drank four cups with dessert and wanted more. It was the finest coffee I had ever tasted. A good omen, I felt.

The next morning I had three more cups with breakfast, and adjourned to the ladies' room. There I changed into male drag, using much the same makeup I had used for drag roles on stage in years past, and left without causing any apparent notice (well, it was San Francisco). I spent some time re-learning how to walk like a male, and knew I was remembering it correctly when a stewardess gave me the eye as I was passing through the lobby. An hour later I identified myself to a taco vendor as a client of the Bay City Detective Agency; he insisted on a thumbprint, did something with it under the counter, squinted at it and then at me, and passed me an envelope containing a report on one Chen, Robert. I read it on the city's last remaining cable car, holding it close so the passengers on either side could not have read it even with Ben's trick glasses.

The top sheet mostly recapitulated what little I already knew about Robert from the things he had told me; most of the new information was irrelevant, except that he had in fact been

observed to be living at the address I had for him. For the first
time since I'd left Top Step I began to seriously wonder if the
whole thing wasn't only a grotesque figment of my overheated
imagination, a psychosis manufactured by my mind to distract
me from a series of traumas.

But then there was the second page.

". . . first-order identity check seemed to establish that
subject's stated identity and background were genuine; all
expected records were in fact on file and no inconsistencies or
alterations were noted. But since you had expressed doubt
concerning subject's bona fides, further and more stringent
inquiries were instituted, as per attached statement. Second-
order ID check also proved out. Third-order check however
revealed that subject's given ID is bogus.

"Subject's true name is Chen Po Chang. He is the bastard
son of Chen Hsi-Feng, who is the son of the late Premier of the
People's Republic, Chen Ten Li. His last official place of
residence is Shanghai; he disappeared there four years ago in
March of 2016, concurrent with his father's disappearance
during the political upheaval which followed the death of Chen
Ten Li. He is not presently wanted in any jurisdiction for any
crime or malfeasance. Additional information may be accessed from any public database. Please inform us if you wish
any of this information communicated to relevant authorities,
or if you require any further action from us. See attachments."

The third sheet was an itemized statement that said I was a
pauper. It didn't know how right it was.

△ △ △

I had the evidence I had sought, right there in my hands.
Not proof that Robert had murdered Kirra and Ben—but
enough to throw strong suspicion on him. With that as a
start, further information might possibly be found by Interpol,
maybe even enough to tie him to the nanotechnological bomb.
The People's Republic had more nanotechnologists than any
other nation. (Not too surprising. They had more *anythings*
than most other nations.)

And so what?

Suppose I could tie him to the killing, with monofilament

strands of evidence. Who had jurisdiction over raw space, outside the cislunar band?

Was it even against the law—any nation's law or the UN's—to murder a Stardancer? The subject had never come up before. Nearly all motives for a murder were irrelevant in the case of Stardancers. They had nothing to steal, no territory to conquer, made love only with other Stardancers, and were damn near impossible to find if they didn't want to be found. The one thing generally agreed was that they were not human beings in the legal sense.

If I blew Robert's cover skyhigh, spread it across human space via UPI or Reuters, all I'd accomplish might be merely to annoy him and his secret masters, perhaps cause them to alter slightly whatever their plans were. At most Robert himself might suffer a tragic accident, walk out into traffic, say, and then no one would ever know what those plans were.

I composed an in-the-event-of-my-death letter, and used the last of my credit to send it up to Top Step, to my own personal memory node where Interpol itself couldn't get at it, programmed to start announcing itself to Reb, Dorothy and Phillipe Mgabi if I didn't personally disable it within twenty-four hours.

Then I called Robert's home.

"Morgan, is that really you? I can't see you—where are you?"

I told him I was in a phone booth at the airport and the phone's eye had been vandalized. He sounded so genuinely glad to hear my voice, to learn that I was really on Earth and in his city, that I was happy he could not see my face. I put great effort into controlling my voice. He offered to buy me dinner, named a restaurant. I demurred, insisting that I wanted to dine in a place I remembered from an old tour, picking the name out of the Yellow Pages as I spoke. I did vaguely remember it; mostly it was a place he had not chosen and could not have staked out already. And it was large enough and public enough to make violence awkward.

On the way I used the last of my cash to buy a Gyro model dart gun from a wirehead in a back alley off Haight Street. He claimed that the rocket-darts were tipped with lethal nerve poison, and used a passing rat the size of a raccoon to prove that at least the first one was. There were four left in the gun. He backed away from me very carefully after we'd made the exchange.

I was stone broke now. Maybe I should let Robert pick up the check for dinner before I killed him. If I was going to. I still did not honestly know whether I could.

Or even for sure that I intended to.

△   △   △

I deliberately got to the restaurant almost half an hour early. As the maître d'hôtel greeted me, I realized for the first time that the gravity had stopped bothering me. Even my lower back no longer ached unless I put stress on it. A little under two weeks to recover from over two months in free fall. Remarkable. I was an earthling again.

But on sudden impulse I decided to simulate gee fatigue for Robert, as though I had just landed within the past few days. He might underestimate me if he thought I was weak and logy, and I needed any edge I could get. As the maître d' led me to my table I tried to walk as though I were strapped with heavy weights, and sank into my chair with a great sigh.

The body language part was no trouble for me; most dancers are half actor. It was actually an interesting technical challenge: instead of doing what dancers almost always did, making difficult movements look easy, I had to make easy ones look difficult. The tricky part was the intellectual details. When had the most recent shuttle landed, and at which of the three Stardancer spaceports? I could fake small talk about either Queensland or Ecuador, but I knew nothing at all of Uganda. What day of the week was this, and what was the date? Damn, this melodrama stuff was more complicated than it looked. It seemed to me that the most recent shuttle had grounded three days before, in Australia. Excellent. I had a fund of fresh trivia about that part of the world.

An adorable waiter took my order for Irish coffee with no Irish whiskey in it. "*I* get it," he said archly as he set it before me, "you want him to think you're drinking. Good luck, honey." I winked at him, and he giggled. I sipped coffee with exaggeratedly weary gestures and looked around the restaurant, trying to spot a stakeout. There was a high percentage of tables with two or more males and no females, but perhaps not abnormally high for this town. And there was no reason why a stakeout team could not include female agents. Everyone looked normal and authentic and undangerous. Normal urban dinner crowd, Pacific Rim version. Every one of them could have been in the pay of the People's Republic for all I knew. Half of them were Asian. The roof seemed to hover over me oppressively, a potentially destructive mass held away by four flimsy walls. A pianist with a shaky left hand was mangling "We Are in Love" in the far corner of the room. Waiters glided to and fro as smoothly as if they were jaunting. The lights had a tendency to strobe if I looked at them. I wanted Fat Humphrey to float up and tell me what I wanted to eat. I wanted Reb to come and tell me what to do.

Thinking of Reb, I straightened my spine, joined my hands in *mudra* on my lap, and began measuring my breath. It helped.

I spotted Robert before he saw me.

Suddenly I remembered my ex-husband telling me once that I could lie very well with my body, but not with my face. Well, a lot had happened since then.

Robert spoke with the maître d', who pointed me out, and looked my way. Our eyes met. I concentrated on my breathing. I kept my face impassive, tried to relax every facial muscle completely. *I am suffering from high-gee lethargy.* He crossed the room to my table, with the graceful loping walk of a jungle cat, as I had imagined he would. No limp: his injured foot was healed. He stopped beside me, took my right hand in both of his, bent over it and kissed it. His lips lingered just an instant. He released it, sat across from me.

His expression was neutral, his eyes open and seemingly guileless. His face was different than I remembered, longer and leaner, the eyes less squinty, the wrinkles slightly more pronounced. His head appeared smaller, the hair lying close to the skull instead of fanning out. This was how he looked under gravity. I decided it made him even more attractive.

"It's good to see you," he said.

I said, "I'm glad to see you too. You look different in a gravity field."

He nodded. "Yes. So do you. I like what you've done with your hair."

There now, just what I needed: a nice sample lie to calibrate my bullshit detector. I knew perfectly well that my hair looked awful. "Thank you for the gallantry," I said. "It was ungodly hot in Queensland. The hair was always wet, and it kept crawling down my neck, so I had them hack it all off. I think I'm going to end up regretting it."

"No, really, it suits you well."

Okay, now see if you can get him to make some true *statements for comparison, and we'll get this polygraph interrogation started.* "I just hit dirt a few days ago. I can't get used to this up and down nonsense. It seems so arbitrary, like making all music be in the same key. And I can't believe how much my feet hurt!"

He nodded. "My first couple of days dirtside I couldn't imagine how humans had ever put up with gravity. It was just barely tolerable back when we didn't know any better— but now, something's simply got to be done about it. You must be exhausted."

"Irish coffee helps," I said. "It's great for reconciling you to gravity: it's got up and down built into it. The booze calms you down and then the coffee wakes you up." *Small talk, small talk—*

"Small talk," he said.

I nodded. "What do you say—stick to small talk until we've eaten?"

He nodded back. "Sounds sensible." The waiter arrived, and Robert ordered Irish coffee, "like the lady." The waiter nodded gravely, turned away—then stopped outside Robert's field of vision, pointed at him, and gave me an exaggerated thumbs up. *Keep this one.* When he returned a few moments later with the coffee, he stopped behind Robert again, pointed at the coffee and fanned himself: *this* glass had whiskey in it, in good measure. I slipped him another wink when Robert wasn't looking. I hoped Robert was going to tip him well, since I couldn't. Robert ordered something to eat and I said I'd have the same and he twinkled away, delighted at his role in my little intrigue.

"So you just got into town? Where are you staying?"

I'd anticipated the question, and had decided there was no reason to lie. I told him the correct name of my hotel. It didn't seem to matter; I need never go back there again. He nodded and said it was a good place, and I agreed.

Whatever it was we had ordered arrived. As we ate we kept jousting with our eyes, making contact and then finding reasons to look away, busying ourselves with the food. I felt like I was drowning in quicksand. No, in slowsand. But there was no hurrying things. I didn't want him to have any busy little distractions available when I started asking pointed questions.

Which led to: *what* pointed questions? I had been thinking about this moment for something like two weeks now, and I still did not know how to play it. Should I go right for the jugular, tell him everything I knew and all I had guessed, and demand a response? Or keep what I knew to myself, give him to understand that I wanted to resume our relationship, and see what he said about that? That could lead in short order to a bedroom, and what would I do then?

Or should I indicate ambiguous feelings, which would allow me to prolong our contact without having to go to bed with him? The problem with that one was, it made it easy for him to get rid of me if he didn't want to be under close scrutiny. No, the smart thing to do was feign passion and try to get as far inside his guard as I could. Feigning passion is natural for a performer. I could always plead gee-fatigue when things got intense.

But as I watched him eat, watched his slender fingers move, I knew I just could not go through with it. Perhaps it was exactly what he had been doing to me, all those passionate days and nights back in Top Step. But I could not do it to him.

The plates were empty. The second round of Irish coffees arrived. Mine was again denatured. The waiter winked at me for a change.

Well, then? Charge right in or dance around it as long as possible? Cowardice and caution both said to stall. *Crazy to risk everything on one roll of the dice. Lots of misdirection first, then slip it in under his guard while he's trying to figure out how to get into your pants.*

"Chen Po Chang?" I said suddenly.

"Yes, Morgan?"

And there it was.

"It was on your tongue, wasn't it?" *That's it, baffle him with misdirection.*

"Yes."

"Which one got it? Ben, or Kirra?"

"Kirra."

I nodded. "I just wondered. You knew they'd both be meeting the Harvest Crew." Under the table, I slid my hand into my handbag. Just the one question left, now. "Why?"

He seemed to think about it, as if for the first time. He started to answer twice, and changed his mind each time. Finally he said, "For my species."

"For your species." I seemed to be having trouble with my voice. "And what species would that be? Insect, or reptile?"

"*Homo sapiens,*" he said calmly. "It's us or them. Us or *Homo caelestis.* The universe isn't big enough for both of us."

"Why *not?* What could the two species possibly compete for?"

"Nothing at all. And everything. That's the point. Here below we scurry about like blind rats in a two-dimensional maze, hungry and thirsty and horny and terrified and alone, fighting like rats for food and power and breeding room and a chance to live before we die. And right over our heads, at the literal top of the hierarchy, there fly the angels, free of everything that plagues us, needing nothing, fearing nothing, looking down with fond amusement at our ape antics. Of course I hate them. Who would not?"

"For God's sake, this planet would have gone to pieces years ago if it weren't for—"

"And that too is the point. It would be bad enough if they kept themselves aloof, ignored us in our misery—but how can we not resent their monstrous charity? How long can the human race stand playing the role of the idiot nephew who must be cared for by his betters, the welfare client who has nothing conceivable to offer his benefactors in return? The racial psychic damage which that awareness causes is half the reason the world is so close to hysteria, so angry and self-destructive."

"So you want to exterminate the hand that feeds you."

"It may come to that," he agreed. "Sometimes I think that it might be enough to drive them from human space, to force them far above or below the ecliptic or out beyond Mars where we don't have to keep seeing them and interacting with them, take their damned Promised Land off somewhere where we don't have to look at it every day, right overhead, just out of reach."

"But it's *not* out of reach—"

"Oh shit, it is too! If all the Chinese in the world lined up at Suit Camps, how long would it take the last one to pass Top Step? Assuming a sufficient mass of Symbiote could be brought to orbit without pulling Luna out of its track."

"If the world wanted to, it could build more Suit Camps."

"And it doesn't. Most of us know in our guts that Stardancers are just plain inhuman. They're *alien*. They're like ants. They're a hive-mind. They're our enemy, and they'll be a damned hard one to beat."

"But why do they have to be *enemies*?"

"Morgan, *think*, won't you? Think about that hive-mind. That 'Starmind.' I know they breed like hamsters up there, but even after twenty years of it, well over half the minds that make up what they call the Starmind started out as human beings, on Earth, yes?"

"Exactly. They're our brothers and sisters, or at least our cousins."

"And how many million years old would you say is the human lust for power? For control? For dominance?"

"But there's none of that in the Starmind."

"Exactly. What can 'power' mean to a member of a telepathic commune? What is there to control? By what means can dominance be asserted? Mental machinery that has served men for countless generations is useless." He leaned forward and locked eyes with me. "But I ask you to consider this: that a telepathic group consciousness implies a group *subconscious* too. Submerged in that Starmind are the instincts of thousands of killer apes, the genetic heritage of the most successful predator ever evolved. Maybe competition and aggression aren't inherited, maybe they're not instinct but learned behaviour transmitted to each new generation—maybe the Stardancers born in space, who've never known want or fear or envy, are gentle creatures, without the Mark of Cain. But the majority of the Starmind comes from a long line of cutthroats. Human beings weren't built for Utopia, no matter what weird things may happen to their metabolisms. They know the only thing they could possibly need to fear, must fear, is us, is the rage and envy of the irrational human beings they have to share the Solar System with. They know a clash is inevitable one day, and they're doing their best to see that they'll win it. By creating a planet full of helpless welfare dependents. By showering us with gifts that lead us to a place where we need their gifts to survive. They've read their Sun Tzu. Don't you see, they're killing us with kindness!"

I closed my eyes briefly. I remembered one of my old dance-circle acquaintances, an intellectual snob, a sort of Alexander Woolcott/H.L. Mencken/Oscar Wilde wanna-be, saying, when he heard I was about to go to Top Step, "Stardancers? A society with no corruption, no hypocrisy, no neurosis and total respect for art—and worst of all, they're willing to let me join? How could I *not* despise them?" And I had laughed with the others, but privately thought he was a cripple, seeking approval of his deformity.

I felt a sense of unreality, a through-the-Looking-Glass feeling. In my wildest fantasies of this moment, it had gone much like this, with Robert calmly, rationally explaining why he had blown our friends to plasma. *Why is he telling me all this? Surely to God he does not expect that I will nod and say, Damn, you're right, I hadn't thought it through, Kirra and Ben just got in the line of fire, guess you can't make an interplanetary omelet without breaking some eggs, what can I do to help fight the menace of gods who have the nerve to be benevolent?*

I met his eyes again. "So you acted selflessly. For the good of humanity."

He didn't even shrug. "Of course not. Am I a Stardancer? I acted out of intelligent self-interest, like any sane human." He leaned forward, lowered his voice. "If our plans bear fruit, the *least* of the prizes to be won will be my father's return from exile to unchallenged power over China."

"So you put death in Kirra's sweet mouth." I slid the Gyrojet from the handbag. My thumb caressed the safety catch. Four darts. One for him, one for me, two surplus.

"Morgan, listen to me: for the first time in human history, total planetary domination is a genuine possibility—and it's only the first step in the forging of a System-wide empire. The tools are nearly at hand! How many lives, how many betrayals is that worth?"

His eyes were boring into mine. "I have a gun aimed at your belly, Chen Po Chang," I said softly. I hadn't meant to warn him.

"I know," he said just as quietly. "But you're not ready to use it yet."

"No. No, I'm not. First I want to know why you're telling me such weighty secrets. Do you think you can persuade me to join you?"

He hesitated before answering. "No. I wish I could. But you're a romantic. Because Stardancers look like angels, they must be angels. There's not enough greed in you for your own good." He looked bleak. "Oh, but I wish I could!"

"Why?" I said, a little too loudly. A woman at an adjacent table looked round; I lowered my voice again. "What the hell do you care? One day you'll be Emperor of the Galaxy and you can have the hottest concubines your precious race can produce. I'm a broken down forty-six-year-old has-been dancer you screwed for a few weeks once on assignment."

This was why I wasn't ready to shoot him yet. Or at least part of it. I needed to know what, if anything, I had been to him.

For the first time his iron control cracked. Pain showed in his eyes. He looked down at the table. "Screwing you was good cover. You were my target's roommate. Falling in love with you was stupid. So I was stupid." He finished his Irish coffee in a single gulp. "I was horrified at how hard it was to leave you. That terrorist bombing was the perfect excuse to cut out, just when I needed it . . . and it took me half an hour to make up my mind to take advantage of it. I knew there was no way I could take you with me—but it killed me to leave you behind. When I heard your voice on the phone, realized you were here on Earth again, there was a whole five or ten seconds there when I . . . when I . . ."

"When you got a hard on, wondering how I am in a gravity field. But now you know I know you for what you are, and how I feel about your cause. So I repeat: why are you admitting everything and telling me your secrets? You have a gun on me too, is that it?"

He shook his head. "I'm unarmed. And no one else will try to kill you. That much influence I have." He ran a hand nervously through his hair, brushing it back from his eyes, a gesture he'd never had in free fall. "I guess I'm telling you . . . because I have to. Because I wanted you to know."

"Pardon me," a kindly voice said.

A large heavily bearded stranger in a charcoal grey suit was standing at my side, hearty and jovial and avuncular. If they ever remade *Miracle on 34th Street* with an all-Asian cast, he'd be a finalist for the role of Kris Kringle. "I hope you'll forgive me for disturbing you . . . but are you Morgan McLeod, the dancer?"

I had danced in San Francisco hundreds of times, had actually achieved more fame here than in Vancouver, where I was "only a local." "Yes, but I'm afraid this isn't a good—"

"I won't disturb you. But please—would you?" He held out a scrap of paper and a pen. "Your work with Morris meant a lot to me."

The quickest way to get rid of him was to indulge him. I left the Gyrojet on my lap, concealed by the handbag, and signed the stupid autograph. As I handed it back, he took my hand, bent to kiss it—and just as he did so, he turned my hand over, so that instead of kissing the back of it, his full warm moist lips pressed my palm. I felt his tongue flicker momentarily between them. It was an odd, vaguely erotic thing for a man his age to do, with an escort sitting right there across from me.

I retrieved my hand hastily. "Thank you very much; you're very kind. Please excuse us."

"Of course, Ms. McLeod. Thank you. I have always loved your work." He turned away.

I turned back to Robert. No, to Po Chang. "All right," I tried to say to him, "Now I know. Now what?"

It came out, "All eyes down the put go, legs. Blower?"

I blinked and tried again. "Didn't dog core stable imagine? Both pressure."

A zipper appeared under his Adam's apple. It peeled down to his diaphragm, splitting his sternum and spreading his ribs, exposing his pink wet chest cavity. A tiny Negro in a clown suit was clinging desperately to the top of his heart, fighting to stay aboard as it beat and surged beneath him. As I watched, fascinated, he managed to get to his feet and wedge himself into equilibrium between the lungs. He opened a door in the left lung and showed me something awful inside. I turned away in shame. The stranger was still standing there, but he stood ten meters tall now on rippling rainbow legs. His beard was made of worms. I knew he wanted to see me dance, but there wasn't enough room on the table and the damned local vertical kept changing and there weren't enough pens.

A little corner of my mind, way in the back, understood what was happening. I had forgotten that these people could kill with their kiss.

Chen Po Chang's voice came from the far side of the universe, metallic and atonal. "The first one was just chemical. Call it truth serum. But the second one was a nanobandit."

I reached for my lap, and it wasn't where I had left it. Everything I found seemed to bend in the wrong directions; some of it felt wet and some of it was sticky to my questing fingers.

"Absorbed through the palm," he was saying, "one heartbeat to the brain, another second to crack the blood-brain barrier, then it starts secreting."

I had to find my lap—that was where I had left my gum! Gum? That wasn't right. Gub? I couldn't read my own goddamn handwriting. Where the hell was my fucking p-suit? Mist was closing in from all sides—

I beat at the mist, fought for control of my mind. I knew what I had to do. It was necessary to yell as loud and as clearly as possible, "Help me! I have been drugged and they're going to take me out of here and kill me." My old friend the waiter would then come and slap them both to death. My body was made of taffy, but I summoned all my will, directed all my desperate energy to making my mouth and tongue firm enough to function, obedient to my command.

"Productive marbles. Didn't to bite wonder-log with it, the palaces. Curt! Curt!"

The waiter was back. There were four of him. "I'm very sorry, sir," they all said slyly. "She had quite a few of those Irish coffees before you arrived. Maybe you'd better take her home. Can I call you a cab?"

"No, thank you," Kris Kringle said. "We have a car outside. We'll get her home."

"Both of you? My." Four eyebrows arched.

"Gunders," I said, smiling to show I was in mortal danger. "S'ab."

"She's been under a lot of stress lately," Robert/Po Chang said. His chest was closed up again now, but his face was melting. Never a dull moment with Chen Po Chang. It ran down his chest and formed an oily pool on the table. I tilted my head to see my reflection in it, and suddenly the local gravity changed. The spaceplane was taking evasive action. "Down" was *that* way. No, *that* way! No—

Lap dissolve.

△   △   △

Horrid dreams, that went on forever. My body was made of putty, which I twisted into the ugliest shapes I could devise. I butchered an infant, grew an enormous steel penis and raped a child, skinned and ate a living cat, burned a city, strangled a bird, poisoned a planet, masturbated with some-one's severed hand, stepped on a galaxy out of sheer malice, gutted God, gathered everything anywhere that had ever been good or beautiful and defecated on it. My laughter killed flowers, my gaze boiled steel, my touch made the Sun grow cold. I tortured my parents to death, brought them back to life and killed them again, and again, and again. I danced on Grandmother's face with razor feet for days on end. Throughout all this, horrid little things with leathery wings at the edges of my peripheral vision watched and chittered and cheered me on. A snail kept oozing past, leaving a greasy trail, offering arch aphorisms in a language I could almost understand. My old shrink Alma appeared once, in a hockey uniform, and told me that my trouble was I kept everyone at arm's length; I needed to open up and let someone love me. I vomited acid on her until she went away, and then cried carbonated tears.

Peace came at last, when the last star in the Universe burned out and the blessed darkness fell all around, like warm black snow in summer.

CHAPTER FOURTEEN

In pride, in reasoning pride, our error lies;
　　All quit their sphere, and rush into the skies.
Pride still is aiming at the blessed abodes,
　　Men would be Angels, Angels would be Gods . . .

　　　　　　　　　　　　　　—Pope, *Essay on Man*

A SWITCH WAS thrown and I was awake. My mind was clear, and my body was its normal shape and consistency. There was an insistent ringing in my ears, but otherwise reality seemed real again. The leather-winged things were gone. I was very glad of that.

I was sitting in a chair. I was naked. My bearded Chinese uncle was looking at me from half a meter away, clinical curiosity on his face. "Can you hear me all right?" he asked.

Lie. "Yes," I said. *Okay, you can't lie. More of that truth drug shit. Keep trying. Meanwhile, can you move?*

"The neuroscrambler should have largely dismantled itself by now. How do you feel?"

Yes, but without precision. So don't try any more now. "As if I were in free fall. Or wrapped in cotton." It was true. I felt light as a feather. I seemed to be sitting in a chair; involuntarily I gripped it to keep from drifting away.

"Do you have any questions?"

"Yes."

"You may ask them."

"Is there a bomb in me?"

"No. A single detonation was both necessary and sufficient."

"Why am I still alive?"

"I must know exactly what you know, and what you have done about it. You've already told me of the letter you left for your teacher, and I know your security code. But before I send

231

an erasure command after the letter, I want to know exactly
what it says."

I started to recite the letter verbatim; after a few sentences
he cut me off. "This will take forever. I have it: ask me any
questions you still have about our activities. The gaps in your
knowledge will define what you know. And you will have the
comfort of dying with no unanswered questions, a rare
blessing. It is safe enough: I know you are not wired in any
way. What would you like to know?"

I tried prioritizing my questions, but couldn't make them
hold still. All over my body and brain, switches were hanging
open, wires were cut. My mental thumb was mashed down on
the panic button, but somewhere between there and my
adrenal glands a line was down. In fact, the whole limbic
system seemed to be down; my emotions were nothing more
than opinions, with no power to command my body. My heart
wasn't even pounding particularly hard. I picked a question at
random, sent a yapping dog to cut it out of the herd, and
stampeded it toward Uncle Santa.

"Are you Chen Hsi-Feng?"

Why do they say, the corners of his mouth turned up? They
don't, you know; they just get farther apart and grow parentheses. "Ah, excellent: you are not certain. Yes, I am Chen
Hsi-Feng."

"Where are we?" Now there was a stupid, irrelevant
question. What the hell difference could it make? *Pick a better
one next time.*

"In one of my homes. Near Carmel, if it matters to you."

I had been in Carmel once, on my way somewhere else.
Down the coast from San Francisco. Upper-class stronghold;
high fences and killer dogs; Clint Eastwood had once been
Sheriff there or something. Estates big enough and private
enough to hold a massacre without disturbing the neighbors.

"How come you do your own hatchetwork? If I were you,
I'd be about eight layers of subordinates away, playing golf in
some public place."

He shook his head. "Your grasp of tactics is thirty years out
of date. Multilayer insulation was indeed useful in conspiracy
or fraud for centuries: before a fallible lazy human investigator

could work his way to the top of the chain he was likely to give up or be reassigned or retire or die. But then they started buying computers, and interconnecting them. Now every layer of intermediaries is merely another weak point, another thread the enemy may stumble across, and pull on to unravel the entire knot in a twinkling. I have many such chains of influence, whose sole purpose is to be found and keep investigators happy and harmlessly employed. Really important work I assign to the only person I know will not betray me. What else puzzles you?"

"Your ultimate aim. Do you plan to keep on blowing up Stardancers until they get annoyed and go away?"

"I plan to annihilate them, root and branch."

"But that's silly." Hunt down and kill more than forty thousand individuals in free space, who had low albedo, no waste heat, and nothing bigger than fillings in their teeth to show up on radar? Fat chance. With those huge variable light-sails attached to insignificant mass, they were more maneuverable than any vessel in space could ever be. What he proposed was not merely impossibly expensive, but impossible. "How could you hope to succeed?"

"By raising up an army against them," he said blandly. "And for that I need a technological edge, an unbeatable one. I need the Symbiote, tamed."

In my present state, I was incapable of shock. I was only mildly confused. I tightened my grip on the edges of my chair, so that I would not float away. " 'Tamed'?"

"You did not know. Good." He sat back and lit up a joint. No, a cigarette. My ex-husband had been a diehard smoker too. "By coincidence, it was a resident of Carmel, Sheldon Silverman, who first proposed the concept of a Symbiotic army—less than ten minutes after the existence and nature of the Symbiote was first revealed. It's in the Titan Transmission. But Charles Armstead pointed out the flaw in the idea. An immortal, telepathic soldier will mutiny the moment he joins the Starmind. He cannot be coerced anymore. I have tried placing spies in the Starmind; all ceased working at the instant of their Symbiosis. Fortunately I had anticipated this; none of them carried knowledge especially dangerous to me.

"But just suppose one could genetically modify the Symbiote, to produce a strain which does *not* convey telepathy, and has a limited life-span without regular reinfection."

He had not phrased it as a question, so I could not answer. I did as I was told, just supposed. The drug kept me physically calm, relaxed and at ease—but inside my head a tiny part of me was screaming, beating at the walls of my skull.

The toughest part of having an army is keeping it fed and supplied and in motion. If you had a Symbiotic army, all you'd have to do was issue them lasers and turn them loose. So long as they needed regular fresh doses of false Symbiote to keep breathing vacuum, they would follow orders.

"It would be useful," he went on, "to further modify the altered Symbiote so that it could survive terrestrial conditions. But I am told that is fundamentally impossible. No matter: who controls space controls the planet, in the final analysis. And the only military force in space that cannot be defended against is naked human beings who never hunger and thirst, an infantry who cannot be seen until it is too late. Do you see a flaw in the plan?"

"How can you genetically modify Symbiote? You can't get a *sample,* without giving yourself away."

Again his mouth grew tiny parentheses. "I have done so. That is precisely why your friends died."

The Symbiote Mass! Its mass and vector to several decimal places had been public information. Place an explosive of known force near it, trigger it by radio at a predetermined instant, apply a little chaos theory, and when the mass blows to smithereens . . . you'll know the projected new vector of the largest smithereens. There's no way anyone else can track shards of organic matter in open space—but you can happen to have a ship in the right place to intercept some.

I lacked the capacity to be horrified. I appraised the idea dispassionately, like the emotionless Vulcan Jerald in *Star Trek: the Third Generation* on 3V. The scheme was brilliant, without flaw that I could see. Not only did he have sample Symbiote for his geneticists to experiment on, no one even suspected that. His biggest problem would be making sure no human accidentally touched any of the Symbiote while work-

ing with it—but that's why they make remote-operated wal-
dos; it was nowhere near as complex a problem as coping with
dangerous nanoreplicators.

I'd been asked if I saw any flaws in the plan. "Stardancers
would still have tactical advantage in combat. Instant, perfect
communications."

He shrugged. "Telepathy is not *that* much more effective
than good radio, at close quarters. I will match my generalship
against any component of the Starmind. And they are utterly
unarmed."

"There are a lot of them."

"Do you have any idea how many men I can put in space in
a hurry, if I do not mind heavy losses in transit? At most, the
Stardancer population is one ten thousandth of that of the
People's Republic. The outcome is foreordained." He blew a
puff of smoke toward the ceiling. "Well, what do you think?"

"I think you are the biggest monster I ever heard of."

He nodded. "Thank you," he said.

A phone chimed beside him. He answered at once. "Yes?"

Maybe the drug enhanced my hearing. I could make out
Robert's voice. "Is she all right?"

Chen Hsi-Feng frowned slightly. "Did I not promise?"

"Let me speak to her."

"No."

"Then I'm coming in. I have to see her once more, before
you take her mind."

His frown deepened . . . then disappeared. "Of course.
Come."

He put down the phone, and took an object from an inner
pocket. My own Gyrojet, it looked like, or one like it. "There
is time for one last question," he said distractedly.

I nodded. "You're not going to let me live, are you? You
lied to him."

"Yes. I dare not simply wipe your memory. Organic
memory differs from electronic in that any erasure can be
undone, with enough time and effort. A pity: it will cost me a
son."

So I was going to die. And so was Robert, or Po Chang, or
whoever he was today. Interesting. Regrettable. At least I

would be forever safe from the things with the leather wings. Or perhaps not; perhaps they came from the land beyond life. No matter. An old traditional blues song went through my head.

> One more mile,
> Just one more mile to go.
> It's been a long distance journey:
> I won't have to cry no more.

"Sit there and be silent," he commanded me. He swiveled his chair away, faced the door with his back to me. The door opened and Robert came in. Not Chen Po Chang—my Robert Chen. The door closed behind him, and locked. He registered that at the same instant he saw the gun. His face did not change, but his shoulders hunched the least little bit, then relaxed again. "I have been stupid," he said.

His father nodded. "When you called *her* a romantic in the restaurant, I nearly laughed aloud. Do you remember what I told you on your thirteenth birthday?"

". . . 'Love is to be avoided, for it causes you to believe not what is so, but what you must believe.' You were right. You must kill her . . . and so you must kill me. Pray proceed."

No!

"I know you do not share my religious views," Chen Hsi-Feng said. "But I will summon a priest of any denomination you wish."

Robert grimaced. "No, thank you."

"You are sure? There is no hurry, and this much I can do for you. Of course, whoever shrives you must die also—but I have never understood why a good priest should fear death."

Robert shook his head without speaking.

"Is there anything else you want to do first?"

Robert thought about it. "Cut your throat," he suggested.

"So sorry," his father said, and lifted the gun.

I had spent the last seconds scurrying about inside my skull, recruiting every neuron I could. Now I threw everything I had into a massive last-ditch internal effort, trying desperately to throw off my chemical chains and regain control of my body. The counterrevolution was a qualified disaster. I could not invest the motor centers—or even, equally important to me, regain access to my emotional glandular system—but I managed to briefly retake the speech center. "He . . . is . . . your . . . son," I said in a slurring drawl.

I succeeded in surprising him. He stiffened slightly, and rolled his chair to one side so that he could watch me without taking his gaze off Robert. Then he answered. "He is my illegitimate son. True, he is worth two of my heirs. But that is exactly why I have not been able to afford him since the moment he stopped being ruled by self-interest. I can no longer predict his actions. Last words, Po Chang?"

"Fuck you," Robert said.

His father shot him in the face. The dart worked exactly as the demonstrator slug had worked on the rat. Robert stiffened momentarily, then began to tremble, then fell down and shivered himself to death. Blood ran from his eyes, ears, nose and mouth, then stopped. From the *huff* of the shot to the end of his death rattle took no more than five or ten seconds. I wished I could scream.

Chen Hsi-Feng spun his chair to me. "Last words?" he said again.

Even without emotions, and with nothing objective left to live for, I was not ready to die. "I would like to . . . I guess the word is, pray."

"Do you require a cleric of some kind? I'm afraid I will not go to as much trouble for you as I was prepared to for my son."

I shook my head. "I just want to sit zazen for a few minutes."

He nodded at once. "Ah—Zen! An excellent faith. You may have five minutes. Who knows? Perhaps you will attain enlightenment this time." He composed himself to wait.

I tried to get down from my chair and sit on the floor. But the persistent delusional feeling of being in low gravity threw me off; I fell to the floor with a crash. Distantly I heard the unmistakable sound of a bone cracking—every dancer's nightmare horror sound—but it didn't seem important at all. I didn't even bother identifying which bone it was. I established that I could still force my legs into lotus, with the ease of two months of training. I tried to straighten my spine, but could not get a strong fix on local vertical. "Antidote," I said. "Partial at least."

He shook his head. "No. It is not a drug that hinders you, but a team of nanoreplicators. They will completely disassemble themselves when your temperature falls below 20 Celsius, but until then nothing can counteract them. Do the best you can. You have five minutes."

All that is important is to sit, I had heard Reb say once. *And to breathe.* Last chance for both.

I closed my eyes and became my breath.

Time stopped, and so, for once, did I.

△   △   △

The state Buddhists call "enlightenment," or *satori,* is so elusive, so full of contradiction and paradox, that many outsiders throw up their hands and declare it a chimera, a verbal construct with no referent. You seek to attain thought that is no-thought, feeling that is no-feeling, being that is non-being, and the cosmic catch-22 is that if you try, you cannot succeed. You must free yourself of all attachments, including even your attachment to freeing yourself. This state seems, verbally at least, to be *so* synonymous with, so identical to, death, that some scholars go so far as to say that everyone becomes enlightened sooner or later in his or her own turn, and there is no problem in the universe. The literature is filled with cases of Buddhists who claimed to have found enlightenment in the moment that they looked certain death in the face. Uyesugi Kenshin once said, "Those who cling to life, die, and those who defy death live." Taisen Deshimaru said, "Human beings are afraid of dying. They are always running after something: money, honour, pleasure. But if you had to die now, what would you want?" And Reb Hawkins had once told Glenn and the rest of us in class, "Looked at from a certain angle, enlightenment is a kind of annihilation—a radical self-emptying."

Perhaps it was nearness to death, then. Perhaps the micro-

scopic nanoreplicators in my brain actually helped, by switching off emotions, making it impossible for me to feel thalamic
disturbance, insulating me from physical aches and restless-
ness and even boredom. Perhaps it was the brutal fact of my
despair—which is *not* an emotion, but a point of view.
Freedom's just another word for nothing left to lose.

Whatever the reason, all at once I attained *satori*.

I was one with all sentient beings, and there was nothing
that was not sentient in all the universe, not even space, not
even chance. Everything that was, was simply quantum
probability wavefronts collapsing into phenomena, dancing a
teleological dance that was choreographed and improvised at
the same time. "I" still existed, but I coexisted with and was
identical to everyone/everything else.

I had been here before, for brief instants in my life, up until
I gave my life to cynicism in my twenties—and then again, for
a scattered few seconds, in Top Step, during a long period of
kûkanzen. One of the things that had subconsciously held me
back from entering Symbiosis, I now saw, had been a desire to
experience it again for *more* than seconds, one last time the
"natural" way, before I gave up and ate it prepackaged. A kind
of spiritual pride.

It happened now, since I no longer yearned for it. Once
again I was little Rain M'Cloud dancing on a floating dock,
and was bobbing sea lions, and was the dance that connected
us, all at the same time. And then I was not even that.

Sentient beings are numberless, says the Great Vow. I
became one with that numberless number. And being one, we
perceived ourself, with great clarity.

First, the things called no-thing. Vacuum, space, time,
gravity, entropy, the void.

Next, the things called nonliving matter. Rock. Water.
Gases. Plasma. Endless reshuffled combinations of hydrogen
and the various ashes of its fusion.

Next, the things called living. The film of life that crawled
and swam and flew and ran through and ultimately sank back
into the surface of the Earth. I was all the viruses that swam in
the soup of the world, all the grasses that grew, insects and

reptiles and birds and fish and mammals, all striving to make ever-better copies of themselves. I seemed to be a part of all that lived, without being distinct from that which did not.

Then the things called sentient. I could *see* sentience as if it were a fire burning in the darkness. A tapestry of cool fires that was the dolphins and the orcas. Every dull selfish glow that was the consciousness of a cat. Every hot coal of fear and self-loathing that was a human being. I could pick out every Buddhist among them, tell the adepts from the students. There were all the Christians, and there the Muslims, those were the superstitious atheists and those all the lonely agnostics. I knew everyone on Earth who was happy, and everyone who was in agony. High overhead, and scattered about the Solar System from the orbit of Mercury to the fringes of the Oort Cloud, I saw/felt/was every Stardancer and all Stardancers, the Star-mind—for the first time I began to understand it, what it was and what it was trying to become. I knew that it was a Starseed, and that if/when it finally bore fruit, there would be joy among the stars, and on Earth.

And further out I sensed things that were as far beyond sentient as I was beyond an idiot. The Fireflies, who had grown all of this from Earthseed, and others greater even than them, beyond all describing or human understanding. Of all, they were furthest removed from my experience, and thus most interesting. I could know them, there was time, there was no-time—

But just as my awareness left Earth to expand and encompass them, began to pass through High Orbit . . . there was a change.

I became conscious of a level I had missed. It lay roughly halfway between human being and Stardancer, partaking of both. There were only a few of that nature, a tiny fraction of the sons and daughters of Eve—but a fraction that had stayed nearly constant for the last two million years. They were scattered here and there at apparent random, like salt particles in a bland soup, and they were all connected and interconnected by strands of something that has no name. Call them enlightened ones. Call them holy people. Call them the good and wise, or whatever you like. They had no collective name, only collective awareness. All their awareness was collective: none of them suffered from the delusion that they were anything more than neurons in a larger brain, cells in a body, atoms in a molecule. They were intimately connected with the Starmind, though separate from it.

In the same instant I became aware of their antithesis. Call them the destroyers. The truly evil, if you will. The ones who fear everything, and so seek to destroy everything they can reach. It did not surprise me that there were fewer of them by far. Their interconnections were fewer and much feebler. Each fought all the others, even when cooperation would further their aims. They were essentially stupid at their core, but so corrosively destructive in their childish rage that if they'd had numerical parity with their opposites, the human race would have ended long since.

Back in the reality I had left, frozen in the amber of now, one of them sat a few meters from me, waiting politely to kill me.

Ideas are like viruses. They transmit copies of themselves from host mind to host mind, changing themselves slightly in the process, and the ideas which are unfit soon perish, and the ones that survive grow strong. They compete for resources. Christianity competes with Islam for space in the brains of mankind; the idea of capitalism competes with the idea of Marxism, while theocratic monarchy nips at both their heels. The idea of freedom battles with the idea of responsibility, and so on.

On the highest level, the idea of Life competes with the idea of Death. Hope versus cynicism. Yes versus no. Joy versus despair. Enlightenment versus delusion. Conception versus suicide. This happens in all people . . . but some take sides.

I could see the human avatars of both sides, now. Call them the white magicians and the black, those who loved greatly and those who hated hugely, in awful stasis, terrible balance, like irresistible thrusters straining to move implacable mass. The black haters were far outnumbered, but they would not yield.

And they said nothing, put out nothing but a steady scream of rage and terror. While the others spoke, sang, reached out, reasoned, soothed. I could see them all, hear them all, almost touch them all.

One of them spoke to me from high over my head. **Morgan.**

Yes, Reb, I said, with my mind only.

Another sang, from a different direction. **Friend of my badundjari—**

Yes, Yarra.

Miz McLeod, said the widowed Harry Stein in a third location.

Harry.

Rain, said a fourth, from impossibly far away.

Hello, Shara.

I was connected to their kind by four strands, now. I could see the strands, like spacer's umbilicals, feel energy pulse along them in both directions.

Reb spoke for all. **Cusp approaches. Action is needful.**

I'm glad you know. Can you help me?

We shall.

What must I do?

Go within, deep within, and you will know.

I went within.

Deep within my own body, my own skull, my own bones. The knowledge of how to do so came from hundreds of minds, funneled through the four to whom I was connected. I went back past consciousness to preconsciousness. I was a fetus, swimming a warm saline sea, with a two-valved heart like a fish, parasitic on the mother-thing. I invested my limbs, kicked, dreamed. I was born, acquired a four-valved heart and eyes to match my ears, began my long battle with gravity. I was a growing youth, then a dying adult, and my awareness went further inward. I was a cell, absorbing nutrient and preparing to divide. I was a strand of DNA, scheming patiently to take over every speck of matter in the universe, measuring time in epochs.

Suddenly I was a corpuscle, racing through my own bloodstream like a cruise missile, singing at the top of my voice. I shrank down to an atom and roamed through tissue and bone and fluid. In moments I understood my whole body, better than any doctor ever could. I had the autonomic control of a yogi, a Zen master, a firewalker. Absentmindedly I destroyed the bacteria in my teeth, cured an incipient cold, strengthened my bad back and trick knee, began the repair of a lifetime of damage to my heart, lungs and other vital systems. I happened across the swarm of nanoreplicators deep in the vitals of my brain, huge slow clumsy things that moved at speeds measurable in great long picoseconds. I slipped inside one, studied its programming, and told it to become a factory for converting nanoreplicators like itself into norepinephrine, finishing with itself. Then I slipped out and down the medulla to the top of the spinal cord, checked all the skills I had spent a lifetime storing there, upgraded and enhanced them to their optimax. I located the bone I had cracked falling down, in my right ankle, saw that it would take at least half an hour to mend it, worked its limitation into my choreography, and ignored it thereafter. I devoted a huge portion of my body's emergency reserve energy to enhancing my strength and coordination.

I polished the choreography for an endless time, perhaps as much as a second, with a thousand minds looking over my figurative shoulder and doublechecking me, making suggestions for improvement. My four pipelines, Shara Drummond, Yarra, Harry Stein and Reb Hawkins took a personal interest, and there were a number of other dancers out there in the Starmind who had ideas to offer, in particular an Iranian Muslim named Ali Beheshti who had been a dervish before he accepted Symbiosis, and a former break-dancer from Harlem named Jumping Bean.

There was one last question to be decided. Was it necessary that Chen Hsi-Feng die? Opinion was divided, consensus oscillated.

Fat Humphrey spoke from near at hand. **Forget necessary or unnecessary. You know what he wants to drink. Serve him.**

The debate was ended.

△   △   △

I was out of full lotus and on my feet before he knew I was moving. The broken ankle made a horrid sound and hurt like blue fury, but I was expecting that, ignored it. I had not danced in a one-gee field for years, had not danced at all in weeks, but it didn't matter at all, I was now at least briefly capable of anything that any human could do, factory rebuilt from the inside out, in a controlled adrenalin frenzy. I became a dervish, spinning and whirling and leaping.

In my normal state of performance mania I am capable of moving faster than the eye can follow for brief periods. Now I was inspired, exalted. My feet had not kissed the stage in so long! I flashed to and fro before him, must have seemed to have multiple arms and legs, like the goddess Kali. I had no clothes to hinder me; my bare feet gripped the hardwood floor beautifully.

Instinctively he thrust his feet away from him so that he and his chair flew backwards away from me. He brought up his gun and gaped at me, thunderstruck.

I danced for him.

It was a true dance, a thing of art, a statement in movement. I knew he could sense that, even though he could not slow down his time-sense enough to grasp the statement. He stared, fascinated as a rabbit by a cobra, for nearly three seconds.

But he was no rabbit. He realized what my dance implied, and exactly when I had known he would, he shook off his shock and awe and pulled the trigger.

The first of the three remaining rocket-darts came floating toward me as slowly as a docking freighter in free fall. I could see the dot of wetness at its tip.

I made it part of the dance, teasing it as a matador teases a bull, eluded it with ludicrous ease.

The harsh flat sound of laser-rifle fire came from outside the room. Someone in the distance screamed. There was a *chuff* sound just outside the door. He sprang from the chair to a point where he could see both me and the door, the gun waving back and forth. I was waiting for that: I went into a spin, standing in one spot and whirling like a top, tempting him. Just after he passed out of my field of vision for the eighth time, he fired; the needle was halfway to me by the time I could see it. I had all the time in the world. It was heading for my heart; the easiest thing to do would have been to simply squat and let it pass overhead. Instead I *jumped,* impossibly high, and it passed under my feet. When I landed I broke out of the spin and resumed my dance, completing the second movement in two or three seconds. I reprised the final phrase, then did it again, and again, giving him a predictable pattern to extrapolate.

He had one rocket left, and just then something outside struck the door heavily. But he must have decided that whatever lay outside that door, it could only be human. Clearly I was not. Without any real hope—what could he know of real hope?—he sobbed and fired his last round at me.

The instant he did so his fight was over, one way or another. I could see him grasp that, and devote his last second to trying to comprehend the meaning of my dance.

I ran *toward* the dart, reached it halfway to him, before it had had a chance to build up to full speed, snatched it out of the air, let the force of it put me into a turn and then fling me at him again, and closed on him before he could lift a hand to defend himself.

And with an overhand looping right, I rammed his death dart down his throat.

As I was yanking my hand clear, he bit off the tip of my index finger in death-spasm. My ankle gave way beneath me at last and we went down together, side by side, facing in opposite directions. He kicked me sharply in the ribs, and died.

The door shattered. A man sprang into the room and landed in a crouch, beautifully. He wore black shirt and trousers, and was barefoot. His face and skull were clean-shaven. His expression was serene. There was a fresh laser burn through one of his outflung hands, but it didn't appear to bother him. He took in the scene in a glance and straightened up from his combat stance. Then he made deep *gassho.*

"I am Tenshin Norman Hunter," he said, with the mild voice of a teacher. "I am the Abbot of Tassajara, a Zen monastery in the mountains east of there."

I sat up, cupping my injured hand. I had already stopped the bleeding and sterilized the wound, was already beginning to regrow the missing fingertip, but it still hurt, and I could indulge things like that now. "I've heard of it," I said. "And I felt you coming. I am Rain M'Cloud, of Top Step. Thank you for coming."

"Reb called, when you were captured in San Francisco," he said. "I answered. It takes some time to come up over the mountain."

Thank you, Reb, for watching over me.

You're welcome, Rain.

I glanced at Robert's body. Whatever else he had done, he had died for love of me. I bade him goodbye, and looked away, forever. "Are there any hostiles left out there?"

The abbot shook his head. "All the guards sleep. The gas grenades we used are good for at least an hour. Three other monks are here: Katherine, and Yama, and Dôjô Sensei, who is badly wounded."

I got to my knees. "*Anmari-kuyokuyo-suru-na, kare-ga kitto umaku-yaru-sa,*" I rattled off.

He looked slightly discomfited. "I'm sorry, I don't really speak Japanese."

I smiled at him. "I don't either. Never mind, I just said 'don't worry, he'll make it.' "

"I think so. But it would be good to leave here quickly."

I managed to get my good leg under me and stand. The adrenalin was wearing off, and while I was cushioning it as much as I could, a crash was somewhere on my horizon. I had just used up about three days' worth of energy in less than a minute. "Let's go."

Tenshin Hunter had a large and rugged four-wheel drive ATV waiting. As soon as I was strapped into a seat, I relaxed a block in my brain, and human emotions returned to me for the first time since I'd blacked out in the restaurant. They didn't overwhelm me, didn't bring me back from my state of *satori*. I knew they were illusory, impermanent, transient. But I experienced them to the fullest. I had been storing up a backlog for a long ghastly time.

I cried and cried for the whole two hours it took us to crawl up over a mountain and crawl down to Tassajara, rocking with sobs, bawling like a child, while Katherine held my head to her shoulder and stroked my hair. I cried for Robert, and for Kirra and Ben, and Glenn, and Yumiko, and poor angry Sulke; for Grandmother and my parents; for my ex-husband David and the Chief Steward of my first shuttle flight to orbit; and for Morgan McLeod, who had suffered so bitterly for all her stubborn attachments.

When we finally reached Tassajara in the cool dark of evening, I was done with crying, done with a lifetime of suppressed crying. I never cried again, and I don't think I ever will.

△   △   △

Five days later I was in Top Step again, and eight hours after that—just long enough to conceive a child with Reb—I entered Symbiosis fully. Twelve hours ago, I came out of the Rapture of First Awakening. I have taken the time to tell this story, impressing it directly into the memory of Teena at the highest baud rate she can accept, because it is the consensus of the Starmind that the world must know what happened, and what nearly happened, and I am in the best position to tell it.

Now I am done, and now I will spread my blood-red wings and sail the photon currents beyond the orbit of Pluto, where something truly wonderful is happening. There I will physically touch, for the first time, Shara and Norrey Drummond and Charlie Armstead and Linda Parsons and Tom McGillicuddy, and a thousand more of my brothers and sisters. We will dance together.

We will always dance.

I am Rain M'Cloud, and my message to you is: the stars are at hand.

ABOUT THE AUTHORS

Spider and Jeanne Robinson met in Nova Scotia and now make their home in Vancouver, British Columbia.

Spider, born in New York, has been writing science fiction since 1972. He received the John W. Campbell Award for Best New Writer in 1974, and won the Hugo Award for his novella "By Any Other Name" in 1976 and for his short story "Melancholy Elephants" in 1983.

Jeanne, originally from Boston, is a former dancer/choreographer; she was founder and Artistic Director of Halifax's NOVA DANCE THEATRE, a professional modern dance company, from 1980 to 1987.

Together, Spider and Jeanne won both the Hugo and Nebula awards for "Stardance," a novella comprising the first third of the novel STARDANCE. (A radio play adapted from that novella by Ken Methold won the Australian Writers Guild award for best radio drama of 1980.)

They have a daughter, Terri Luanna.

SciFi Robinson S.   AF
Robinson, Spider.
Starseed /
WINTER PARK PUBLIC LIBRARY

3 9677 1107 3385 4

SCIENCE FICTION #   921-3876

Robinson, Spider.
     Starseed

DISCARD

YOU CAN RENEW
BY PHONE!
647-1638